"Captain—" Pike began. **"Regulations clearly state that a directive from Starfleet Command overrides—"**

"What directive?" Kamnach demanded. "That message is incomplete. Garbled by static. A day late and a dollar short. It may as well not be a message at all."

"Sir—"

"For all we know, the Vestians could have sent that message. For all we know, you did, Mr. Pike," Kamnach said incisively. "In any event, there isn't enough of it for us to be clear on Starfleet's intentions. We will proceed to exercise our own discretion in time of battle. Science Officer, resume your station. Mr. Pike, you're dismissed."

Pike rose to his feet.

"No, sir," he said quietly, hearing his voice echoing in his own head.

Was he out of his mind? He remembered Charlie's definition of heroism. Did the same concept apply to professional suicide?

"Captain Kamnach, refusing or ignoring a direct order from Starfleet Command is a violation of regulations. On that basis I am relieving you of command."

STAR TREK®
BURNING DREAMS

Margaret Wander Bonanno

**Based upon STAR TREK®
created by Gene Roddenberry**

POCKET BOOKS

New York London Toronto Sydney Elysium

An *Original* Publication of POCKET BOOKS

POCKET BOOKS, a division of Simon & Schuster, Inc.
1230 Avenue of the Americas, New York, NY 10020

This book is a work of fiction. Names, characters, places and incidents are products of the author's imagination or are used fictitiously. Any resemblance to actual events or locales or persons, living or dead, is entirely coincidental.

This book is published by Pocket Books, a division of Simon & Schuster, Inc., under exclusive license from CBS Studios Inc.

ISBN-13: 978-0-7434-9693-3
ISBN-10:   0-7434-9693-0

This Pocket Books paperback edition August 2006

10 9 8 7 6 5 4 3 2 1

POCKET and colophon are registered trademarks of Simon & Schuster, Inc.

Manufactured in the United States of America

For information regarding special discounts for bulk purchases, please contact Simon & Schuster Special Sales at 1-800-456-6798 or business@simonandschuster.com.

There is a gentleman named Rusty Van Reeves, who is by way of becoming a gifted novelist. (He can't help it. He was born and raised in Faulkner country, just down the road from where Eudora Welty lived and wrote. Whether it's something in the water or something in the blood, Rusty has it.)

Rusty understands Christopher Pike's dilemma. When he was fifteen years old, he broke his neck playing high school football, one vertebra below where Christopher Reeve sustained his now world-famous injury. What this means is that Rusty can breathe on his own and has some movement in his shoulders, but for more than a quarter of a century he has lived with a reality not unlike Christopher Pike's.

There is no Talos IV for Rusty.

That hasn't stopped him from running a business, writing a column for his local paper and a novel or three, drawing, painting, and generally being an interesting human being.

This novel is dedicated to Rusty, to the memory of Christopher Reeve, and to the too, too many others who share their plight, in the hope that, in the absence of Talosians, human medical research will transcend, and soon.

ACKNOWLEDGMENTS

I want to especially thank Marsha Valence, owner of Tribute Farm, who raises Morgan horses and names them after science fiction authors. It was Marsha who explained to this city kid the best way to train a good saddle horse, and the way in which young Chris Pike gentles, not breaks, Tango is told in her words.

Much gratitude to Marco Palmieri, for asking me, "How'd you like to write the definitive Pike novel?" and making it so, as well as for suggesting the title when I was clearly stumped. The environmental theme was entirely his idea, and a natural fit for the character of Pike.

Special thanks to Keith R. A. DeCandido for gentling the manuscript as Pike did Tango, and for finding a way to save a scene I was particularly fond of despite my talent for muddling linear time.

Lastly, my gratitude, always, to Jack . . . for being Jack. Nuff said, my love.

I have learned that if one advances confindently in the direction of his dreams and endeavors to live the life he has imagined, he will meet with a success unexpected in common hours.

—Henry David Thoreau

PROLOGUE

2320

The summons came as softly as the touch of a butterfly's wing, and yet with an urgency which, just as the first time, could not be left unanswered.

Spock considered what the summons had cost him that previous time. Could he seriously have believed it would never come again?

The average Vulcan performed the mind-meld seldom, and usually only with other Vulcans. In that way the individual mind remained sacrosanct, its blade-edged logic inviolate. But by no definition was Spock an average Vulcan. Even the most evolved of *Kolinahr* masters had not melded with the myriad minds he had encountered in his travels. They had been humanoid minds mostly—discordant, even inchoate, their wants and needs and emotions clashing against Spock's Vulcan mind (its integrity ever in question anyway because of the human genes composing one arm of the helix), like waves against rock, reshaping it.

Had they, over the decades he had treated with them, softened the corners of his sharp-honed discipline like water against stone, or rather polished it to a multifaceted jewel?

In essence, both.

Every mind-meld left trace evidence, a signature, a subtle

alteration of synapse and neural pathway. And more powerful even than these two-way interactions, these approximating equalities of mind, were the one-way transmissions from other telepaths.

Vulcans had a code. One did not initiate mind-meld without consent. And one never, ever entered the mind of another without permission.

Spock had violated that code, once, with Valeris, and paid a price for it. But the alternative would have been to allow a conspiracy by the war-hungry from two empires and his own Federation to flourish, and that was the greater evil. But now he was the recipient of a summons, like the one which had come to him unbidden decades before, from another species of telepath, far more advanced than Vulcans, and driven by a different ethic.

It was why General Order 7, forbidding any Federation citizen from visiting Talos IV, had been enacted in the first place.

Even then, Spock had wondered if the Federation Council truly understood that keeping humans physically removed from the Talosians was immaterial. If the Talosians wish to reach across a galaxy to invade a mind, any mind, they could do so.

It was how they had reached Christopher Pike, and Spock himself, more than half a century ago. And how they had reached him again, now.

Come to us, the summons said in the mind-voice of the Magistrate, the Talosian Christopher Pike had dubbed the Keeper. *For your captain. Come soon.*

Only that. All of that. Nothing more specific, yet specific enough. Christopher Pike, one of two humans who could command Spock's loyalty unto death, once again required Spock's presence on Talos IV, a presence which would once again put him at risk of the death penalty.

Spock calculated the years. Christopher Pike was now over one hundred years old, a somewhat elderly man, in human terms. Was he dying? Perhaps, given the constraints of the injuries that had brought him to Talos, already dead? Perhaps he had undergone a change of heart after so many decades on this world he had once alluded to as his "great ambivalence," his "captive freedom," and wished to leave, knowing only Spock could retrieve him? Had Vina died, leaving him alone?

Too many questions, Spock thought. No way of learning the answers while he lingered here. If the Talosians had wanted him to know more, they would have told him. *Procrastination,* Spock chided himself, *is a human trait. You must answer, then you must act. The rest is not important.*

The last journey to Talos IV had required considerable machinations. But Spock was no longer a mere lieutenant commander on a starship. As a Federation ambassador, he had a personal shuttle at his command at all times, could log a secret flight plan using a dozen different diplomatic reasons, all of them acceptable, and venture far off course before the aberration was detected. This didn't mean he would not be pursued, only that he would have more lead time before his absence was noted. The risk of being intercepted was not as great as it had been the first time.

But the risk once he arrived would be the same.

Since the moment Talos IV receded from view on *Enterprise*'s viewscreen for the second time fifty-two point seven-five-three years ago, Spock had known somehow that this day would come. Now that it was here, what was he to do?

Spock contemplated the means at his disposal, formed a plan, and answered the Magistrate's summons.

1

2267: TALOS IV

A man who cannot move can do little else but think.

Christopher Pike had always been an active man. This was not to say that he couldn't occasionally lose himself in a good book or a magnificent sunset or the eyes of a beautiful woman. It didn't mean he never thought deep thoughts or took a moment or ten or thirty to sit quietly and contemplate the meaning of life. It only meant that he did all of these things against the background of a need to move, to do, to participate, to make a difference.

As his ship's doctor once said, "A man either lives life as it happens to him, meets it head-on and licks it, or turns his back on it and starts to wither away."

Phil Boyce had been preaching to the choir when he said that. In the thirteen years since *Enterprise* had left Talos IV behind, Pike had been more active, more engaged, more "in the moment" than ever before in his always-active life. It was clear to anyone who knew him that he had been driving himself, though whether toward something or away from it only those who knew him well could truly say.

Not a few wondered if it had to do with whatever it was

that compelled Starfleet Command to enact General Order 7 following *Enterprise*'s mission to Talos.

Pike couldn't talk about it, of course. No one except those who had been to the surface and those who briefed them afterward had any idea what had transpired there, and even they did not know what Pike, as the last to beam up and the only one to see Vina as she truly was, knew about the Talosians and their power.

Not given to talking about himself at the best of times, Christopher Pike was especially reluctant to share the fact that he had spent those years away from Talos IV wondering if he would ever again be able to distinguish reality from dream.

All that had ended in a burst of light and noise and chaos and incredible, unbearable pain, on a cadet ship in a remote sector beyond Starbase 11 that Starfleet used for training exercises.

"Starfleet ought to decommission those Class-Js," Commodore Mendez grumbled when Fleet Captain Pike contacted him out of courtesy because they were passing through his space, and because Mendez had just been assigned to Starbase 11 to relieve Commodore Stone. Pike himself had put in a year at this particular base when he was first promoted to fleet captain. "But you didn't hear me say that, Chris."

Christopher Pike's handsome face had filled Mendez's viewscreen, his smile wry, those black eyebrows above the piercing blue eyes always frowning slightly no matter what the rest of his face was doing.

"Well, considering you've just broadcast it over an open frequency, José, you can't blame me if you end up with your ass in a sling."

Mendez was a less active man than Pike, a scholar in his spare time with degrees in heuristics and etymology, perfectly content to warm a desk on a starbase and vacation on

Earth once a year to see his grandkids. The irony of Pike's words (it was not Mendez, after all, who would end up quite literally in a sling) would haunt him for a long time after this conversation was wiped from the official records.

"Be careful, will you, Chris?" Mendez said sincerely, his deep voice made that much deeper by his concern. "Those ships had structural quirks when they were built, which was before you were born and damn near before I was. They're due to be decommissioned within the year, and I'm not thrilled about the fact you've been assigned to take a shipload of green kids out to the middle of nowhere in one of those rust buckets—"

"Yes, Mother," Pike had interrupted him, then softened his smile to assure Mendez he was taking him seriously. "José, I know the region. And I think after over twenty-five years on active duty, I just might know how to captain a ship under less than optimum conditions."

"Chris, I didn't mean—"

"This baby was okayed at Planitia before we left the Sol System. She'll fly us there, she'll challenge these soft-handed kids on maneuvers, and she'll fly us home."

"So you say," Mendez sighed, resigning himself. The two men had exchanged some small talk after that, and Pike promised to lay over at the starbase for a drink or two on the way back.

Neither man knew that the next time Pike arrived on Starbase 11, there would be no drinks, no celebration, but the return of a broken man.

Following Pike's "recovery," if such it could be called, Mendez had seen to it that he got the best suite in the medical wing, on the top floor of the administration building, where the view was best. One of the round-the-clock medical aides who saw to Pike's needs—which pretty much meant everything, considering his immobility—would position the motorized chair at one of the tall windows, at an angle which allowed him to overlook the distant hills and, since the planet's atmosphere was so thin, a realm of stars almost as glorious as one might see from the viewscreen of a starship at station-keeping.

This, Pike supposed, was meant to distract him, at least once in a while, from the fact that he was trapped inside his own body, unable to do more than communicate by sheer force of will, enough functioning motor neurons remaining to move the chair in an awkward chugging motion from time to time, affect a simple signal transducer to beep once or twice, and nothing more.

He could blink his eyes, sometimes move his head, but the machines did everything else. With careful concentration he could operate the transducer to blink once for yes, twice for no. Some of the medical experts who had examined him weren't sure he would even be capable of that much longer. The consensus was that his condition was degenerative. Off the machines for even a moment, he would begin to die.

What he could do, without restriction, was think. Remember the horrors he'd been through, acknowledge the time lost to unconsciousness and immobility, imagine the horrors that lay ahead, hope the doctors were wrong, hope against hope that it was all a dream and he would wake to find himself as he once was, sound of wind and limb, ready to take on the most mundane assignment, as long as he could buy back his freedom . . .

. . . only to wake to find that it was not a dream, and none of what he had once been able to do would ever be possible again.

One for yes, two for no.

Too bad, Christopher Pike thought, *that there is no signal for "Let me die."*

A man who cannot move can do little else but think. Until the day a few months later when he understood why Spock had come for him, all he could think of was death.

Had it really been only days ago? Spock had all but kidnapped him, against his protests.

(Not a protest against being taken. In truth he hadn't had time to decide if he wanted to go or not. His objection was to what he knew Spock would face if he were caught—would face in any event, unless he also chose to remain on Talos. Had he even thought it through? Or were the Talosians compelling him, as they so easily could? It was all of that roiling through Pike's mind that had him agitating himself, focusing his will on blinking "No, no, no!" Meaning "Don't do this to yourself. Not for me, not for anyone. The cost is too great and I will not be the cause of it!")

But Spock was adamant and, as he had said himself with characteristic understatement, he had it well planned. Well planned, that was, except that he'd miscalculated Jim Kirk's dogged determination that no one and nothing intervene between him and his ship. The shuttle with Kirk aboard had given chase until it ran out of fuel and, Spock being Spock, he was compelled to rescue the very officers who would put him on trial for his life.

The court-martial was the pièce de résistance, seeming so real that even Pike had believed Mendez was really there, and that Spock was doomed. Then Captain Kirk had asked the question, "Chris, is this what you want?"

What other answer could he have given them, after all of that? Before Spock came for him, death would have been welcome. Now he had been given a chance at life again. And more.

Now he had what he wanted. Didn't he? Why then did the thought of seeing Vina again, after all this time, after all he'd been through to get here, fill him with such trepidation?

How do you say hello to a woman you haven't seen in thirteen years—a woman you thought you'd never see again—when ever since that time you've kept her tucked safely away in your heart?

What was he afraid of? Was it the thought that, having almost been the cause of Spock's execution, having committed himself to spend the rest of his life as only one of two humans in this place, he had made a mistake? Was it the thought that Vina would not be as he remembered her? Would she appear as the "wild little animal" the Talosians had wanted him to see, still in her teens, vulnerable and innocent, yet possessed of a kittenish sex appeal enhanced by a wisdom that surpassed her years? Or would she appear as the woman she would have been had the *Columbia* never crashed, but returned to Earth, where he and she might have met at some Starfleet get-together, where his interest would have been polite but nothing more, because she was, after all, thirteen years his senior?

Would I really have been so shallow? he asked himself, and got no answer. His former life had been burned away by the trauma he had just survived. In the ordeal of the past few months, he had learned to disregard the trivial. Thus, he told himself, if their fates had been different and it had been Vina instead of someone else he had met at that diplomatic reception a little more than a year ago, he'd have found her just as attractive, if in an entirely different way, as he had when he thought she was a girl of eighteen and the only human on Talos.

There was a third possibility, Pike realized as he waited in the antechamber deep belowground where the Keeper—

No, he corrected himself: *the Magistrate. When they cap-*

*tured you that first time and kept you in a cage, "Keeper"
was appropriate. But hir proper title is Magistrate, and s/he
has offered you another chance at life. The least you can do
is set aside your old bitterness and begin anew.*

The Magistrate, then, had given Spock the coordinates to
beam Pike down to one of the hundreds of interconnected
chambers in one of several subterranean cities to which the
surviving Talosians had retreated after they had all but
destroyed the surface of their world. Following a brief
farewell, Spock had gone back to the ship, and the Magistrate—looking, Pike thought, more smug than ever—having
completed the necessary niceties that saw Spock on his way,
had merely observed Pike for a moment without speaking,
even in his mind, then floated ethereally into a nearby lift,
leaving him alone.

Now he heard the hum of the lift mechanism and surmised it was the Magistrate returning, bringing Vina to him.
His anticipation all but overcame him as he considered the
third possibility.

The Magistrate might have used the power of illusion to
vanish, instead of the mundane device of the lift. So too, the
Magistrate might have made Vina appear out of nowhere like
some magician's trick. Why the drawn-out process of leaving and returning, unless—?

Unless, Pike thought, *Vina and I are to be presented to
each other this time as what we "truly" are, she a "lump of
flesh," to use her cruel, self-deprecating words, a woman
whose body was as damaged as—*

As yours is? he chided himself. *Face it, Mister. It's not
how Vina will appear to you that worries you, but how you
will appear to her. When you left her here thirteen years
ago—abandoned her, some would say—what she saw was a
handsome, vital young man in his prime—strong, in command, exactly matching her image of perfection. What will*

she see now? Will they let her keep that idealized image of you she's been holding on to all this time, or will she see the ruined husk of you, your body insensate, useless, your mind still teeming with words and thoughts you can only communicate to other humans in binary, one light for yes, two for no?

Oh, yes, eventually the Talosians will give you each back the illusion you have of the other but, knowing what lies beneath, will that satisfy either of you?

It's not how she will seem to you that frightens you more than any enemy real or imagined, but how you will seem to her. What will you do if the sight of you is so repulsive to her that she turns away?

His thought process got no further than that. Suddenly, she was there.

"Vina . . ." someone said. Was that his voice? He no longer remembered what it sounded like. How were the Talosians doing that? In reality, he couldn't speak. But the Talosians were giving him the illusion that he could, just as they were convincing him that he was moving his arms, freeing them from the confines of the chair, his hands finding the mechanism that would detach all the sensors and tubes that connected him to the machines that breathed for him, forced his heart, his lungs, his digestive system, the entire complexity of his autonomic nervous system, to keep functioning.

He watched himself as if from a distance as he opened the front panel of the chair, only to discover that somehow all those mechanisms had vanished and he was free, free to move his legs, stand up as if he'd only been resting there, as if the chair was not the complex device it was, but merely a conveyance that he could discard at any time, walk away from, and move toward Vina and take her hands in his.

Her hands were cool, small and delicate, just as he

remembered them; when he held them, they fit neatly into his, as if they were meant to be there. *Don't think of it as illusion,* he warned himself, *or you'll go mad.*

"Christopher . . ." she said in return, her voice as sweet as he remembered, her small, heart-shaped face tilted up toward his, those feline eyes always a little sad, even when she smiled. "Chris . . ."

Had she called him that the first time? Had she called him anything at all? Or had she been so afraid of losing him, so desperate to convince him to stay, that she hadn't dared to even speak his name?

"It's good to see you," he said carefully, and a puzzled expression, for the briefest moment, crossed her face. Then he remembered that she'd been living with an image of him, another illusion created by her keepers, since he'd left.

"Then it is really you?" she asked, as if she wasn't sure. She slipped one hand out of his and touched his face, resting her hand on his cheek as if she'd done it a thousand times before, and Pike shook off the thought that she probably had. "They said you'd been ill, that this time you chose to come here. . . . I didn't dare hope . . . not that I wanted you to be ill, but . . ."

She stopped, as if she didn't know what she was saying even as she said it. He found himself taking her chin in his hand, something he'd wanted to do from the very first.

"I know they gave you the illusion that I'd never left," he heard that voice again, which must be his. He searched her face and it was just as he remembered it, and also not. She was no longer the lithe adolescent he'd wanted to cherish, keep safe, and yet she was, even as she was the mature woman she would have been if he'd met her in real life and her ship had never crashed on Talos IV. If he looked closely enough, he could see the devoted wife of several years' familiarity, and the Orion slave girl, and a thousand other incarnations, but only one Vina. As his thoughts raced, his voice seemed to have a mind of its own. "But I'm real this time, and I'm here with you. Here to stay."

Though even as he "said" this, he wondered if it was true. Because, in a sense, he'd never left her at all.

"Not your first love, then," she suggested knowingly, reaching her arms up to clasp her hands behind his neck, "but your last?"

"The only one that counts," he said, wondering if that was true as well.

She stood on tiptoe to kiss him, and for the first time illusion and reality overlapped and melded, because the kiss was exactly as he'd imagined it, if he'd only ever really imagined it, and he cupped her face in his hands and leaned into the kiss, no longer bothering to figure it out.

"I want you to tell me everything," she said, leaning back against his chest, his arms around her, the two of them contemplating the horizon as the sea breeze made ripples in the saw grass and wafted her silky hair against his chin, tickling pleasantly. "I want to know your whole life, from your earliest memories until the day before you first met me. Then everything that happened from the time you went back to your ship until Spock brought you here."

"Here" at the moment was a beach house belonging to an aunt, where she'd spent school holidays as a child. It was peaceful and private, and seemed a safe place to begin.

"Everything, hm?" he asked, settling into the illusion, trying not to search the edges to see where the scenery ended. *Pay no attention to that Talosian behind the curtain,* he thought grimly, forcing himself to relax.

Where should he begin? At the beginning? As the old saying went, "First you were born, and then what happened?" What was the first thing he remembered? Or would she find his recounting his entire childhood and adolescence tedious?

Should he start instead with the less emotionally fraught stuff, the swashbuckling adventures of the starship captain, youngest in the Fleet until James T. Kirk had taken *Enterprise* from him, to his great relief at the time? Should he tell her about the wonders he had seen—about the spacefaring Leviathans, living creatures transformed into interplanetary vessels? Or about a Vulcan gemstone so huge and fraught with history that even a Vulcan would kill to possess it? Should he tell her of the strange little watering hole in San Francisco where time seemed to stand still, and improbable tales were told? Or about a crewman named Dabisch who had a transparent skull? Or perhaps about a race called the Calligar, who lived on the other side of a time portal that opened only once every thirty-three years? Or of a sad and mysterious Trill woman named Audrid, who once upon a time, in a cavern deep inside a wayward comet—

No, he stopped himself. *Begin from the beginning. What's the first thing you remember?*

Pike closed his eyes and allowed himself to feel. Of all the faculties he had lost, that one was the most devastating. Following the accident he had lost all feeling, physical and emotional. At first his ruined nerves had screamed at him day and night as if they were on fire, and neither painkillers nor the auto-biofeedback monitors he'd been hooked up to could help him. In time the agony had eased and he'd gradually gone numb, and while at first he'd considered it a blessing, it had proved otherwise.

The emotional numbness was worse. All he'd wanted to do was to die. Until he overheard the doctors, making the mistake of thinking his hearing was as affected as his other senses (it was not; if anything, it had grown more acute since the accident), discussing his case in the hall outside, and he'd learned exactly what they expected the delta rays would ultimately do to him. Then, perversely, offered a slow and vegetating death, all he'd wanted to do was live.

Now here he was, as if all of that had been a dream and only this was reality—moving, speaking, feeling his own skin again, hearing his heartbeat rushing in his ears, aware of the scent of . . . something . . . it took him a moment to identify it as sea air and a touch of jasmine, and the scent of the bark of a particular tree he'd encountered on a world devoted to pleasure, and . . .

How did they do this? How did they know? He would ask them about that later. He had, after all, a life's worth of time.

He cradled Vina in his arms, rested his chin on the top of her head, thinking. Where should he begin? Ah, he had it now!

"Let me tell you about my first love . . ." he began.

2

2228: LEAVING EARTH

Her eyelashes were perfect. Thick as paintbrushes and the same bright reddish-brown as the cheek they lay against, they covered eyes Chris remembered as being as deep as pools, and such a dark, liquid brown they were almost black. Her name was Maia, and she was nine years old, the same age he was.

Chris knew Maia wouldn't open her eyes again until well after the ship docked at Elysium. He knew that not so much as an eyelash would flicker or a breath be drawn until the effects of the stasis had worn off, but he couldn't stop watching her through the thick plexisteel of the chamber, reassuring himself she was still alive.

"It's okay, son," he heard the deep rasp of his stepfather's voice behind him. "She'll go on looking just like that no matter whether you watch her for the entire trip or not. Kid your age ought to be looking at the stars on his first offworld voyage, or off playing with the other kids on board, not staring at a horse."

"She's not just any horse," Chris said with a nine-year-old's doggedness, still looking at Maia's slumbering face instead of at his stepfather. He was careful to avoid calling

the man anything; they'd had that discussion before they left
Earth. Just because Heston Prescott had married his mother
three months ago didn't mean Chris had to suddenly start
calling him "Dad." He touched his finger to the plexisteel, as
if counting the mare's eyelashes. "She's my favorite."

"She's no different than any of the rest of the stock we
brought along," Prescott said, apparently having forgotten
what it was like to be a child and find certain things special.
"And when we get to Elysium, she'll do her part in breeding
some of the finest horses on the planet."

You mean the only horses on the planet, Chris stopped
himself from saying, *because the teletutor told me there are
no large quadrupeds on Elysium.* Even at nine, he knew that
always telling the truth was a good way to get yourself into
trouble. Sometimes it was better to keep quiet.

"Go on now," Heston said, putting a hand on the boy's
shoulder. "You've got almost an hour before your next session with the teletutor. Go play with the other kids."

Chris knew the difference between a suggestion and an
order. Whining "But I don't *want* to play with the other
kids!" wasn't going to cut it. Besides, Chris wasn't a whiner.

"Okay," was all he said, heading for the corridor, leaving
Heston to check the gases in the stasis chambers holding the
six mares he hoped would be the start of herds of fine saddle
horses roaming free on the plains of Elysium.

There had been some controversy about letting Heston
Prescott be the first settler to bring horses to the colony
world. Prescott was a terraformer by profession, one of the
best in the business. He bred saddle horses as a hobby, which
mostly meant he invested in them and went out to the horse
farm on weekends to talk with the people who did the actual
work. Still, they were his horses, and they'd been given all
their inoculations and passed all the screenings, so Prescott
had permission to raise them on the property ceded to him

by the Elysium Council as one of the perqs for helping to make the planet self-supporting.

That was how Prescott, his new wife and stepson, six brood mares, and several dozen frozen horse embryos ready for implantation, happened to be on the slow intercolony ship bringing them to Elysium.

Elysium. When he first heard the word, Chris had asked his mother what it meant and, as always, Willa had sent him to the dictionary.

"If I tell you what it means it won't stick to your brain as well as if you look it up for yourself," she'd said, her smile making her words seem less like a lecture.

Mother and son had the same bright blue eyes, the same dark brown wavy hair (Willa's prematurely frosted with gray at the sides), the same dark eyebrows against the same pale, high brow, too often knit in a serious expression, no matter what the rest of the face was doing. It was as if son had been cloned from mother, Heston said, with no father required.

Willa's frown had deepened when he said that. "Hes, not in front of Chris, if you don't mind."

Chris didn't know who his birth father was. He'd been afraid he might not like the answer. Whoever he was had gone away and left Willa alone with a newborn son to raise.

Paradise, he thought once he'd looked up the word "Elysium." *The place where the Greek gods brought certain heroes after death. Pretty weird name for a Federation colony world.*

When Heston first announced that they were leaving Earth, Chris had gone to the computer to access a holo-program about the colony worlds—where they were, how they'd been discovered, how long they'd been settled. Elysium was one of the newest.

The holo showed a planet dominated by the blue of

oceans, wrapped in clouds like dabs of whipped cream, very much like Earth, right down to the Class-G sun and its position in the star system. As he manipulated the screen, the holo took Chris on a virtual landing through the cloud cover, skimming above mountains, polar caps, deserts. He knew enough about geography to recognize oceans and freshwater lakes and follow the course of rivers. A scrolling readout showed that climate and atmosphere were "within acceptable ranges" for human habitation.

"Will we be the only humans there?" Chris wanted to know, telling himself he wasn't scared at the thought.

"Not at all," Heston assured him. "There's a Starfleet base here . . ." He stopped the holo's movement and pinpointed the place, tucked into the curve of a bowl-shaped valley ringed about by snowcapped mountains. ". . . and colonists have begun settling further inland, mostly on small homesteads, near enough by hovercraft to get to the base in less than an hour. Your mother's part of the team that will be constructing the first real city. They're going to fill that entire valley with high-rises and parks and a transit system. Because there's an existing Starfleet footprint, everything else is already in place—the defense perimeter, a satellite grid . . ."

"A defense perimeter?" Willa had been busy cataloguing packing crates, but she'd heard that last part. "Is it necessary in that part of space?"

She bit her lip after she'd asked it, as if concerned that the question, not to mention the answer, might be something else Chris didn't need to hear. But the boy was more interested in how Starfleet could have "footprints." The way adults talked confused him sometimes.

Heston shook his head at the naiveté of Willa's question.

"The precaution's always necessary anywhere in deep space," he said. "In terms of its location, Elysium's probably

safer than Earth. Far enough away from either of the Evil
Empires . . ."

Klingons and Romulans, Chris supplied in his mind,
having heard his stepfather's speeches about both often
enough to know that was what he meant by "Evil Empires."
He wondered what it would be like to meet a Klingon. He'd
seen holos, and they looked pretty scary. No human had
ever seen a Romulan, though, and he wondered what they
looked like.

". . . and less of a target, in that we're not hosting Federation headquarters the way Earth is," Heston went on. "But
you never know what else might be lurking out there."

"What will you do when we get to Elysium?" Chris
wanted to know. He'd seen records of some of Heston's
work on barren worlds, asteroids and satellites mostly, as
well as stabilizing the tectonic plates beneath the underwater
environment where he and Willa had met, but couldn't imagine what his stepfather would be doing on a world that
seemed pretty much finished already.

"I'll be doing tectonics, just as I did on Earth," Heston
explained, pleased that the boy was interested. "Elysium's a
fairly young planet. There's still a lot of volcanic activity.
And in my spare time, I'm going to plant hardwood forests
and turn grasslands into croplands, the way humans have
done on Earth for hundreds of thousands of years. By the
time you're grown, Elysium won't need to wait for freighters
to bring her supplies; she'll be entirely self-sufficient.
There'll be millions of colonists in dozens of cities. Maybe
they'll even name one after your mother or me."

Willa had shaken her head in bemusement. She was a
quiet person, given to letting her work speak for her. Heston
was the one who'd insisted that the Elysium Council hire
him and Willa as a team, because one wouldn't leave Earth
without the other.

"We'll be the city mouse and the country mouse," was all she had to say about Heston's grandiose dreams.

"Oh," Heston added, "Did I mention I'm going to raise the finest herd of horses you've ever seen?"

It was on the tip of Chris's tongue to ask if he could have a horse of his own, but he didn't know Heston well enough yet to ask.

"He's a very smart man," Willa told Chris the night Heston proposed, her eyes shining almost as brightly as the engagement ring that had suddenly appeared on her finger. When they'd met on the deep-sea project over a year ago, what began as mutual professional admiration had gradually evolved into romance.

"Is that why you're going to marry him?" Chris had propped himself up on one elbow in bed, where he'd dashed at the last minute when he'd heard Willa keying the door code; he'd learned how to reprogram the timer on the child minder so it wouldn't give him away. "Do you love him?"

It wasn't as if he hadn't seen it coming. Even at his age he could recognize that misty look adults got when they were "in love," whatever that meant. At nine, he still considered girls to be some species of alien, scarier in their own way even than Klingons. Nice enough aliens, but as far as he was concerned there wasn't a universal translator made that could help him understand them, especially when they stood around in groups and giggled.

"The answer to both of those questions is 'yes,'" Willa said, kissing his forehead and tucking him in. "And I'm so happy right now I'm even willing to pretend I don't know that you've been up all night."

Chris had managed to look just guilty enough as she turned out the light. Lying there in the dark, he wondered what this was going to mean, his mother's marrying Heston

Prescott. For as long as he could remember, it had been just the two of them, mother and son, traveling from one site to the other all over Earth. They'd been to Antarctica and the Serengeti and most recently to South Sulawesi for the deep-sea project. In between they lived in the little town of Mojave, in a house based on one of Willa's earliest designs.

Moving around so much meant Chris usually took his lessons from the teletutor instead of attending a real school, and while he made friends easily and had gotten to know kids his own age all over Earth, it was hard to stay close to anyone. Still, he couldn't imagine what it was like to be stuck in one place your whole life.

But now there was a third person in the equation, and he wasn't sure how he felt about that.

Anytime he asked what had happened to his father, Willa had always answered, "when you're older," but apparently he still wasn't old enough. And now Heston Prescott was going to be a permanent part of their lives. Chris knew that meant some things would change; he only wondered how much.

He knew Heston traveled a lot, needing to be onsite for each new project, even though most of his work consisted of creating terrasims on a computer while others did the actual hands-on work. *Maybe he'll be gone most of the time,* Chris thought, *and Mom and I can just go on being Mom and me.*

So when, barely two months after they'd married, Heston came home all but bouncing on the soles of his feet with excitement to announce that they would be relocating on a colony world named Elysium, Chris was dumbfounded.

He had never been off Earth before. Well, unless school trips to the Moon and the various space stations counted. Never been out of the Sol system, at least, never traveled on anything bigger than an in-system ferry. Still, living on another planet couldn't be that much different from Antarctica or the Serengeti, could it?

He liked Heston, in a general sort of way. He was one of those adults who knew enough not to talk down to a kid or try to be a pal, a big, sandy man with a soft everyday voice that could go loud when he wanted it to, and a laugh as big as he was. Beside him even Willa, who was tall and active and athletic, seemed tiny, almost delicate. Until Heston came along, she'd been the strongest person Chris had ever known. He didn't like the idea of her suddenly seeming small, because it made him feel even smaller.

"I don't expect you to call me 'Dad,'" Heston said as if reading Chris's mind, once it was clear that he and Willa were serious. "Unless you want to. I figure a big guy like you who's managed just fine for nine whole years without such an appurtenance can decide for himself. My friends call me 'Hes.' That'll be fine."

Chris had wanted to ask what an "appurtenance" was. Instead he whispered the word to himself so he'd remember to ask the dictionary about it later.

"I haven't decided," he said when he realized Heston was still looking down at him expectantly. "Sir. I'll let you know when I do."

"Fair enough," the big man said, the corners of his mouth quirking in amusement.

But that had been nearly two months ago, and here they were aboard a space vessel leaving Earth, a family of three and a potential herd of horses off to set up a homestead, and Chris still hadn't decided. He went out of his way to avoid the possibility of ever having to call Heston anything, making sure he was right up close to him when they talked so there'd be no mistaking who he was talking to. It was awkward; it couldn't go on indefinitely. He'd have to make up his mind.

"Urbans!" was how Cotton Jonday, the head of the Neworlder congregation, had labeled them, not bothering with niceties, when they'd come aboard the intercolony ship and Captain Zameret had introduced them. Cotton was nearly as tall as Heston, and bulkier, his almost waist-length beard making him seem even bigger somehow. "Desk jockeys. Never worked with your hands. Soft, not like us. You won't last!"

Chris could tell Heston didn't care much for the man's arrogance. It was the Prescotts' first unpleasantness with the Neworlders, but it wouldn't be the last.

The Neworlders were agronomists, but of a rather old-fashioned kind. "Luddites," Heston called them, another word Chris planned to look up when he got a chance. They clung to what they considered "natural" ways which, to them, meant pre-Millennial. They shunned transporters and aircars, used devices called cell phones instead of comm units. Any technology created or even refined after the end of the twentieth century was anathema, sort of. They made exception, for example, for interplanetary travel, which baffled anyone outside the sect who tried to understand them. Insular and suspicious of strangers, the Neworlders liked it that way.

Heston Prescott had no patience for them. He wasn't hostile, he wasn't openly derogatory, but Chris could always tell when he was "having them on," as he put it. It was a secret they shared, and it raised Heston even further in his estimation.

They'd arrived aboard the big intercolony ship a full day before she was due for departure, and the shuttle bringing them to her was about as tame as the lunar ferry. Chris sat quietly in his assigned seat by one of the viewports, peering back a little wistfully toward Earth. In the seat beside him, Willa was rummaging in their carry-on luggage for something. She nudged Chris's shoulder gently and handed him a small box.

"What's this?" he asked, though the shape of the thing gave him an idea.

Willa didn't say anything. She settled back in her seat and closed her eyes, humming a tune she'd been humming for as long as Chris could remember.

Refusing to be cheered up, Chris opened the box and found his favorite lunch—a chicken-tuna sandwich with the crusts cut off the way he liked it, a crisp McIntosh apple and some carrot sticks, a container of chocolate milk, and two homemade brownies.

He looked at his mother, but she had her eyes closed. Still, the message was clear. The good things would remain the same.

The internal workings of the ship fascinated him. Captain Zameret had given her new passengers "the two-dollar tour," as she called it, and Chris found himself lingering in engineering, curious about all the conduits and gauges and doo-dads, wanting to know what everything was for. Captain Zameret had turned him over to her chief engineer, who took the boy under his wing for the next hour, showing him how everything worked while his parents got stowed away in their cabin.

"He's awful smart for a kid his age," was the engineer's comment. "Are you sure he's only nine?"

Chris knew there were families who lived their whole lives in space, kids who grew up on ships or space stations because their parents worked there. He wondered what it must be like.

When the big ship's engines powered up for departure, he could feel them through the deck plates, from the soles of his shoes almost to the top of his head. And the sight of Earth and the rest of the solar system moving away from them—or so it seemed—took his breath away. Once they were past the outer planets, though, he did find all that open space a little scary. He preferred to watch from a rear port as the star field sped away behind them.

"What do you think?" Willa asked when she'd gone looking for him and, with a mother's instinct, knew where he would be.

"It's better than a holo," Chris reported seriously.

"Better than taking the shuttle to Sulawesi?"

"Uh-huh," he said, unable to take his eyes from the star field, thinking of all the things he'd learned about distances in space and the properties of stars, nebulas, black holes, quarks, and so on. The facts seemed to slip away from him as quickly as the stars, leaving only beauty and a sense of wonder.

If no one else was around, he would close his eyes and hold out his arms like wings, imagining *he* was the ship, and he could soar through space all by himself.

He was doing that the first time he saw Silk.

She'd been watching him for a while before he saw her, and had had sense enough not to tease him. Still, once he opened his eyes and saw her watching him, he lowered his arms and scowled, feeling not a little silly at being caught, and by a girl at that.

Silk was as tan as Chris was pale, as blond as he was dark-haired. Even her eyelashes were blond, almost white, which made her dark brown eyes that much more startling. She was his age, but taller, as girls often were at nine. She might have been pretty, if her hair wasn't pulled back into two stark braids and she was wearing something other than those drab Neworlder clothes.

The intercolony ship had little room for passengers on this voyage. She was mostly loaded with supplies and equipment needed by those already on Elysium. The Prescott family and the Neworlders—several families interconnected into an extended clan, half of them children—were the only civilians aboard.

Willa had explained to Chris as much of the Neworlder philosophy as she understood and, knowing his tendency to blurt out whatever came to his mind, asked him to go easy on them.

"They're leaving Earth because they think it's too . . . tame," she began judiciously, "and because they object to a lot of the technology we've surrounded ourselves with. They want to make a fresh start in a true wilderness. Many people head for the colonies for that reason, Chris. It's not all that different from what we're doing."

"We don't make fun of people who don't think the way we do!" Chris had pointed out. Something in his tone told Willa there'd already been a confrontation in the ship's corridors or the many common areas where her son might have encountered members of the clan.

"They're a little . . . different, Chris," she explained patiently. "They have a different way of looking at the universe than we do."

Heston's assessment was a little harsher.

"It's like a religion for them," was his view. "No point arguing with them, son. Zealots are always right."

It had been Silk who first made the fuss about the horses.

"It's against Nature," she said, looking as if she was going to cry at the sight of the mares in their stasis chambers. Chris had brought her to the lab to share something special with her, and all she could do was find fault. "That's what my father says. Freezing them like that is against Nature."

"Hes—my stepfather—says horses are more sensitive to space travel than most animals," Chris said importantly. "It's for their own good. Besides, they'd need too much feed during the voyage. There wouldn't be enough room."

"Then you shouldn't have brought them. It's not Natural," Silk scolded.

From the day they'd first eyed each other at the aft port without speaking, Silk seemed to seek Chris out, getting too close to him, close enough for him to smell the scent of her, which was like new-mown grass, and feel the warmth of her breath against his face. It made him nervous.

"It's not Natural," she repeated in a singsong, turning her back on the horses as if she couldn't bear to look at them, and flouncing out into the corridor.

"Neither is space travel!" Chris called after her, following her in spite of himself. "Right now you're on a spaceship traveling thousands of miles an hour away from Earth to another planet. That's not natural, either."

Silk stopped and turned back toward him, her hands on her hips. "You're not very smart, are you, Chris-to-pher?" she said in that know-it-all voice most girls he knew seemed to have been born with. "The planets move through space all the time. We're doing the same thing they do. That's perfectly Natural."

"Planets don't have engines!" Chris shot back, but Silk was gone, skipping away from him, the closest thing she could do to running in these corridors, since Captain Zameret had very strict rules against running.

"I'm not listening to you!" she called over her shoulder, her braids bouncing against her back.

Girls! Chris thought. But Silk was only the beginning of his troubles.

"Christopher Prescott," the largest of the three Neworlder boys had said, looking him over as if he smelled bad. Behind him, the other two sniggered and elbowed each other knowingly. If they weren't twins, they could have been, and both were mouth-breathers. "What's a Christopher?"

"It's my name," Chris said warily, his hands in his pockets so the three wouldn't see that he was clenching his fists. He had good instincts about people usually, and something about this kid told him to be careful.

"But what does it mean?" the big kid persisted. "My name's Flax. That means something."

Chris knew Neworlders chose names related to agriculture. Only Willa's teaching him to accept people kept him from snickering the first few times he'd heard some of the names. But now this kid was implying that his name was somehow odd. He wasn't sure how to answer that.

He shrugged. "It's my name. That's what it means."

"What if I decided to call you Seepy?" Flax challenged him. "'Cos that's your initials . . . CP." The big kid nodded to himself, as if every time he had an original thought that was the only way he could remember it. Chris suppressed a chuckle. He'd seen Heston's horses do that, but never a human. This goofy kid was like a big dumb horse, he thought, but kept his mouth shut.

"Yep," the kid said. "That's what I'm gonna call you. Seepy."

The other two sniggered, watching Chris to see his reaction.

"Suit yourself," Chris shrugged, turning to walk away. The best way to avoid a fight was not to be there when it started. "Just don't expect me to answer to it!" he called over his shoulder.

The rest was sort of a blur while it was happening. It was only later that he'd remember it, and wish he could forget.

"You said they were different!" Chris muttered into his pillow, refusing to look at his mother. "You bet they are— different as in crazy!"

"You didn't fight with them, did you?" Willa wanted to know.

He rolled over and sat up, the dark eyebrows above those startlingly blue eyes all but meeting in the middle at the memory of it. "Yes, I did!" he said, sounding not at all contrite.

"Tell me exactly what happened," Willa said, determined not to pass judgment until she'd heard the whole story. Chris told her.

". . . then Flax ran up behind me and punched me in the back," he finished without rancor. "I heard him running, but I figured if I turned around or even flinched, that meant he'd win."

"Did he hurt you?"

"No!" he said grimly, just as she knew he would.

"And then what happened?"

The boy's jaw clenched and he swallowed hard. "You told me never to hit first. And I never do. But you also said—"

"—that if you had to defend yourself, you should do the best you can," his mother finished for him. She was almost afraid to ask the next question. She knew the Neworlder boy was older, nearly eleven, and big for his age. "What did you do?"

"I turned around and yelled at him first," Chris said, the defiant look replaced by something more ominous, an expression that said he'd figured out this early on that sometimes life was just plain unfair. "I told him he was a bully and that fists couldn't solve what words could."

Willa almost smiled. She'd taught him that, too.

"He had to think about that. He's not very smart—"

Willa bit back whatever response she might have had to that.

"But I figured he was going to hit me again, so I was going to duck and then clobber him if I had to, but then . . ."

The boy's eyes clouded over, and his lower lip trembled.

"Chris?" Willa resisted the urge to brush his hair back off his forehead. Instinctively she knew he wouldn't want to be touched right now. "It's all right. Whatever happened next, I won't criticize you, but I need to hear about it."

"His father was just there all of a sudden, and the other Neworlder men. I don't know where they came from, but it was like they planned it. They all started coming out into the corridor, the women and the kids, too. They just stood there staring at me.

"Then Flax's father started shouting at me. He said that he'd warned Silk's folks about me, and she wasn't allowed to go near me for the rest of the voyage because I—I had 'wrong ideas.' And all the time the other kids were staring at me, even Silk. I wanted to run, but I didn't."

Gently, hoping he wouldn't pull away—nine was such a tenuous age for a boy-child—Willa put her arm around his shoulder.

"What did you do then?" she asked, restraining herself from doing what she really wanted to do, which was to kiss the top of his head and rest her cheek against the dark hair and hold him the way she had when he was really small.

"I just stood there," he reported, as if he had failed somehow. "I didn't know what else to do. Then Captain Zameret came down from the bridge to say she'd heard shouting, and was everything okay? All the Neworlders just turned and walked away, first the grown-ups, then the kids. Even Silk."

His mother waited for him to finish.

"I didn't do anything wrong, Mom!" Chris said plaintively after a long moment. "So how come I feel like it's my fault?"

Willa had promised herself when he was a toddler that she would never talk down to him. "Sometimes . . ." she said, searching for the words, "any one of us can find ourselves in a situation where it seems like we could have done something differently, if only we knew what it was. We have to remember that we can only control our own actions, not someone else's. I know that's hard, but that's the way it is."

She wasn't sure if he accepted it, but she could tell he was thinking about it. There didn't seem to be anything else she could do right now, except leave him to his thoughts. Suppressing a last urge to kiss his brow, she tiptoed away.

The last time he saw her, the ranch house was engulfed in flames. He started to run toward her, but she called out to him.

"No, Chris, no! Don't come any closer—!"

A strong pair of arms wrapped around him then and lifted him bodily off the ground, flailing and screaming, clawing through the thick shirt at the iron grip that held him.

"Put me down! I have to save her! Let go of me!"

But the arms were implacable, and they dragged him away. Soon the horses' screams and the roar of the flames as they swallowed the house drowned out everything else.

3

2267: TALOS IV

"No!" he shouted, and sat up suddenly. Instead of fire there was only a soft breeze blowing sand onto the blanket and its occupants. Pike had leapt to his feet, brushing it off his arms and legs as if it burned him, before he remembered where he was.

"It's all right," Vina said, stroking his arm to comfort him. "You were dreaming. It's gone now."

"No!" Pike said again, suppressing a shudder. "It wasn't a dream. They've got the memories wrong. It didn't happen that way!"

Then again, how did he know he hadn't been dreaming? He'd dreamt about the fire ever since it happened. But this time . . . one minute he'd been telling Vina about Elysium, and then . . .

He didn't remember falling asleep, hadn't been aware of her leaving him to go for a swim, but apparently she had. The bright blue swimsuit that matched her eyes and not incidentally the color of the sky at zenith, was damp and clinging to her in all the right places, and her hair hung in wet tendrils against her neck. What was the difference between sleeping dream and waking dream in this place?

"Tell me what you were dreaming," Vina coaxed him as he looked around for the light robe he didn't remember bringing down to the beach, yet knew somehow would be rolled up in the duffel bag he didn't remember either. He slipped the robe on without tying it, but refused to sit beside her on the blanket again.

"I—I don't remember," he lied, wondering if she could tell it was a lie, or if the Talosians could. He and Vina didn't know each other well enough for that yet.

"It isn't working!" he said, angry and frustrated. "I can't give in to the illusion. Are either of us really here? How do I know I'm not just imagining you, and you're actually off somewhere else lost in an illusion of your own? What if one of us wants to do something, go somewhere, and the other doesn't?"

Only then did he notice that the sand was just a little too hot under his feet to be comfortable. Annoyed, he moved to stand on the blanket, then sat back down, defeated. The sheer joy of being able to feel anything again, even pain, should be sufficient to— *No!* he thought, more angry at himself than anyone else. *Don't get sidetracked! Focus! It wasn't about* this *illusion, this illusory here and now, but—*

Vina sighed, looking down at her hands. "I was afraid this would happen."

Before he could ask her what she meant, she also got to her feet, walking away a little, distancing herself from him the way she had all those years ago, as if only by avoiding proximity to him could she collect her thoughts; the hot sand didn't seem to bother her. *Or maybe,* Pike thought, *she's chosen herself a different illusion. She could be in another place entirely.*

"It might take them a while at first to adjust to the particular . . . patterns of your thoughts. Remember, they have to sustain the initial illusion—that we're both young, strong, healthy humans—all the time. That's hard enough for them at first. Whenever we summon a memory, an illusion inside the illusion—"

"—it's more of a challenge," Pike suggested not unkindly, wanting their minders, as much as Vina, to know he appreciated what they were trying to do for him.

"Exactly," she said. "There's also . . . the feeling that you're still fighting them, resisting. It . . . jangles things. That's the best way I can explain it."

"Are they telling you all this?" he wondered.

She nodded. "In a manner of speaking. It's hard to explain. You'll understand it better after you've . . . acclimated."

"All right." He held out a hand to her, inviting her to sit beside him again. "I have a reputation for occasionally being . . . impatient. At least that's one of the more polite words that's been applied to me over the years. So what should we do? Stay in the 'present' for now?"

Vina seemed to be listening to something. "Not necessarily. I think they have things under control. Yes, in fact . . ." she sat beside him, easing her body against his. "Everything's okay now. You can continue your memory, if you like." When he seemed reluctant to go back that far again, she laced her fingers through his and glanced up at him out of the corners of her eyes. "So, I see I had a rival. . . ."

"Here and here, Magistrate," the Archivist indicated, though the pattern of the readout was self-evident to all those gathered around to observe the monitor set into the cave wall, as well as to those accepting the transmission of thought from a distance. "These indicate the neural pathways in the forebrain where the subject's earliest memories are stored. . . ."

How long had it been since they had ceased to think of

each other as individuals with names, referring to each other instead by their function—Magistrate, Archivist, Physician, Technician, Provisioner and so on? Not that any of them had only one function; the necessity of living underground for hundreds of millennia required each of them to participate in a number of tasks. And there was more than one designee per category, though given the importance of the task of sustaining the humans in their illusion, each of those gathered here was the primary—Magistrate-1, Archivist-1, and so on—of their class. Each had been assigned or had assigned themselves—it had been so long ago no one could remember—a dominant task by which they were named, so that they had become one with their function.

Archivist-1, working with hir own staff as well as with Technician-1 and hirs, had begun with Vina's neural pathways and some of the ancient machinery, cobbling it together with components they had scavenged from the scattered bits of *Columbia,* and they were now able to track human neural pathways almost as readily as they could their own. Almost, because they had long since abandoned the practice among themselves, when the telepathy became paramount.

Centuries of exposure to the radiation from the war had altered their own neural pathways to such an extent that the weak psionic power with which most of them were born had been enhanced a hundredfold. There was no surviving Talosian who was not able to communicate purely via telepathy with every other.

Most humans were not so gifted. Perhaps the female Vina's intuition about certain things was as powerful as it got. As for the male, he gave off a different kind of energy.

The Magistrate studied the readout, and could see it.

"Will he need to relive these memories, Magistrate?" the Archivist wondered, hir temples pulsing, an expression—

subtle, as all Talosian facial expressions had become in the wake of their telepathy—which might have been concern touching the corners of hir eyes. "The memory of fire seems to particularly unsettle him."

"Are you suggesting he might find the memories damaging," the Magistrate wondered for all to hear, "or instructive?"

"Perhaps both, Magistrate," the Archivist admitted. "We are uncertain. Which is why I asked."

When, the Magistrate wondered, had they, all of them—because their minds were linked in such a way now that any thought affected all of them—ceased to think of the two human subjects as, well, subjects, as creatures, which was to say inferiors, and begun to think of them as co-equal? It was a puzzlement. Much of the Talosians' certainty about what they were doing and why had been challenged by the arrival of Christopher Pike thirteen years ago. Now that he was among them once again, the dynamic he brought to the equation would have to be considered very carefully.

They had had eighteen years to study the female. Would it take as long to learn the intricacies of Pike? Each of the humans individually was a challenge, but there was also a synergy between them which . . .

The Magistrate formed a decision s/he knew would be acceptable to the others. The intertwining of so many minds working separately, yet in cohesion, one might almost say collusion, after all this time, made certain thoughts unnecessary.

What the humans brought was randomness, which evoked uncertainty. Uncertainty, after all this time, might almost be welcome.

"His thought processes will be voluntary," the Magistrate announced. "We will merely facilitate. Should he need these memories, we will provide them. If he finds them painful, he can choose to abandon them. We will not commit the error we made the last time. This time, we will not interfere."

Let him talk, Vina told herself. *Just listen. There will be plenty of time for your story, if he's interested, and if not you can go to a place where you can imagine that he is.*

She had made her peace with the Talosians in the interregnum between Pike's departure and his return. She still, no matter how often she touched him, heard his voice, marveled at him, wasn't entirely sure he was really here. She would let him talk, until she herself was comfortable with this new dimension. So to keep the conversation light but challenging, she teased him.

"A rival? No, you didn't, not really," Chris said, noticing as she knelt beside him that her hair smelled of salt water and sea air. "I was only nine."

"But you know what they say about first loves," Vina reasoned, lacing her fingers through his. "They're the ones you never forget. She broke your heart." Her next words were flirtatious. "And apparently gave you a lifelong fascination with blondes."

"What blonde? Maia was a redhead. She was a chestnut; her coat was the color of an Irish setter's. When she'd just been curried, she gleamed."

"Not the horse!" Vina protested, digging her elbow into his ribs. She wanted to weep with joy. Talosians were always so serious; she missed human playfulness most of all. She was a natural tease, and hadn't had a worthy sparring partner since Theo. *Don't think about Theo!* she cautioned herself. *That's dangerous territory, even now!*

"Oh, you mean the *girl*—!" Chris said, as if he'd only just figured it out. He wondered if Vina was ticklish, deciding to find out.

She was, and so was he, and they ended up chasing each other along the beach like a couple of kids, running into the surprisingly warm surf and splashing each other until they were both out of breath and they could almost hear the music swell as he took her face in his hands and they sank to their knees at the tide line as if they had been choreographed and . . .

And for the first time since he'd arrived, Christopher Pike forgot that everything he and Vina did was being watched.

It was too grandiose to be called a beach house; it was more of a villa, with half a dozen bedrooms, each with its own balcony and private bath, overlooking half an acre of landscaped gardens planted with native flora resistant to the salt air. Vina led him barefoot up the deeply carpeted staircase against his protests.

"We're soaking wet! And we're getting sand all over everything!"

"It's all right!" she giggled. "I'll program the servitor to clean the carpets while we shower."

"Shower?" he echoed her, finding himself tugged into a marble-lined, glass-enclosed real-water shower unit big enough for two people, with multiple spray heads at several levels. His senses awash in luxury (What *was* that aromatic bubbly stuff she was rubbing all over him?), he remembered that the one thing he liked least about space travel was the sonic showers. This was more like it.

As they toweled each other off afterward, Pike realized it could be this way forever if he wanted it to be, just the two of them alone in this place. Or they could people it with a few dozen of their friends and throw a party every night. Or they could go someplace different every night, together or separately. Who was to say whether Vina was really here, or whether she'd gotten bored—the beach house, after all, had belonged to her aunt in real life—and perhaps gone off on some newer, less mundane adventure?

The thought that they could both be here, yet lost in separate illusions instead of with each other, or not, or sometimes, and that through all of this their thoughts remained separate so that when the other spoke it was always a surprise, and wrapped around all of these realities was the reality of their true damaged bodies, and the Talosians, outside them, watching them, yet inside the illusions they created, all at the same time, made his brain hurt.

Stop overthinking it! he warned himself, following Vina down the stairs, which had in fact by now been vacuumed free of sand, though he hadn't heard a sound, and into the kitchen, where she ordered hot soup from the food dispenser, which was exactly what he suddenly realized he wanted. Out of the corner of his eye he could see that the long table in the dining room had been set for two, and vague but delectable aromas told him the soup was only the beginning, but he would savor all of this one increment at a time.

"Tell me more," she coaxed him. They did not repair to the dining room, but stood leaning against the kitchen counter smiling at each other over the edges of their soup mugs like mischievous children. "I'm listening."

Is there anything more appealing, he wondered, finding the soup too hot to taste just yet, *than a woman who hangs on your every word?*

2228: ELYSIUM

At first glance, Elysium City was little more than a cluster of glorified Quonset huts, dwarfed by the landscape surrounding it. As the shuttle ferry brought the Prescotts downplanet from the ship, Chris had his face pressed against the port, looking for landmarks.

Oceans and rivers and lakes began to take shape once they'd passed through the spun-sugar clouds. Long stretches of grassy plain and forests of stunted, scrubby trees alternated with lava fields where nothing grew. And there were volcanoes, lots of them.

They were everywhere, some linked together like beads on a string, some sprung up alone in the middle of otherwise flat plains. Most were inactive, their cinder cones softened by trees and brush; some of the taller ones were even snow-capped. But here and there one smoked fitfully, others steamed softly like cooling teakettles, and Chris's eyes widened as he watched one spewing a slow trickle of incredibly hot orange-red lava into a nearby lake, where it set up a roiling cloud of steam and twisted and hardened almost instantly into dense, grotesquely shaped black rock. Though the shuttle ferry was a good kilometer above the pyrotechnic display and her thick clearsteel ports shut out any ambient noise, Chris swore he could hear the bubbling hiss of liquid turned to stone.

The ferry pilot had deliberately taken the long way around to give the newcomers a bird's-eye view of their world. Now he banked and headed for the planet's only city. After what they'd just seen, the sight of human-built creation seemed almost anticlimactic.

Begun in a bowl-shaped valley ringed about by rolling hills, some of them with the distinctive cinder cones of still more inactive volcanoes, Elysium City was planned to expand into those hills, then be connected to the outlying homesteads by paved roads and pneumo-tubes as well as aircar routes.

Over the ensuing months, clearsteel-and-transparent-aluminum high-rises would spire upward like growing crystals even as the urban infrastructure spiderwebbed outward toward the horizon in all directions. Buildings would grow overnight like mushrooms, fitted together like gigantic children's construction sets out of prefab units brought down-planet from where they'd been stored in orbit. No matter how many times he watched the process, Chris never got tired of it.

One minute he'd be looking up at an empty Elysian sky, tinged a slightly greener blue than the sky of Earth, dotted with small puffy clouds. Then a tiny dot would appear just where his mother, coordinating the effort from a small Starfleet-issue comm unit in her palm, had promised him it would.

As he tilted his head back, squinting against the sun, the dot grew larger and larger, taking shape as a shuttlecraft carrying a modular construction unit under its belly, which it would maneuver into position for the waiting robots to snap into place in whatever configuration was designated for that site—a shopping mall, an office building, school or apartment complex.

There were no schools on Elysium yet; in fact the Council hadn't decided, given how far-flung the inhabitants were, whether children would be required to attend school in an actual classroom, or could conduct all their lessons through the teletutor. As long as his lessons got done somehow, Chris was free to scramble about the building sites, following Willa up a lift or down a tunnel to see close-up how things took shape.

Best of all, there were no Neworlders here; they'd all gone off to the remoter regions to live far away from a city that they, not surprisingly, condemned as not Natural. Chris only ran into them occasionally when one or two stopped by the ranch to express their disapproval of what Heston was doing there.

Heston had chosen a homestead far enough from where the city was expected to ultimately expand, but close enough to commute by aircar. A house and barn had been built of prefab units similar to the ones forming the city. Heston had chosen the spot especially because of the thermal vents.

"See those?" he'd asked Chris the day they arrived, as if anyone could miss the bizarre-looking lava formations, like dozens of petrified gopher runs, striating the landscape every few meters. Where they differed from gopher runs, aside from being harder than basalt, was that some of them steamed slightly.

"Uh-huh," Chris answered, as the two crouched in the low-growing grasses that covered the ground as far as he could see. He laid his palm against one of the lava tubes and found it a little warmer to the touch than was strictly comfortable.

"Thermal vents from a volcano five kilometers from here," Heston explained. "Elysium has several sources of energy already—solar, wind power, fuel cells, but I'm going to try something different, something they've been using in Iceland for centuries . . . volcano power. It's a natural for this world. Did you know you could set up a greenhouse on top of a thermal vent and grow pineapples and bananas during the coldest winter?"

Chris shook his head, fascinated.

"Well, I'm going to do much more than that. I've designed a gizmo that will provide all our energy, read the weather, measure the water table, even warn of earthquakes, all from the power of a single volcano."

"Don't they have all that stuff in the city?" Chris wanted to know.

"Most of it," Heston conceded. "But I'm working on designs for the individual homesteader, so we won't have to be dependent on the city for anything." He stood up and turned slowly in a circle, surveying the open land around them. "Someday this homestead will be its own little universe. We'll grow all our own food, create all our own energy, and there'll be herds of horses running wild in the hills, living on the native grasses, as far as the eye can see. Oh, and the hot tub—did I mention we'll have a hot tub?"

He said it with a nudge and wink, which made Chris chuckle.

"Can we have a pool, too?" he wanted to know.

"You want a swimming pool? You've got one," Heston said, waving his hand as if he could make it appear in an instant. "We'll make it look like a natural formation—oh, say, over there by that tumble of rocks, with its own waterfall. . . ."

"What if the volcano erupts?" Chris asked. The valley the ranch was set in was ringed around with low hills, but they looked older than the ones around the city, and none of them were smoking. The volcano must be behind them, he figured, but was that far away enough?

"It won't," Heston said confidently. "Starfleet engineers have been monitoring it for over a decade. They can work backward and forward and project when it might erupt again. Long before it does, I'll be able to harness it."

"Harness it?" Chris echoed him, thinking of horses.

"You'll see," was all Heston would tell him, going off to tinker with the generator that, if he was to be believed, would do just about anything.

Chris spent a lot of time hanging on the split-rail fence watching Maia and the other mares exploring their new paddock beside the barn. They'd been brought here and awakened from stasis and seemed none the worse for wear. They would be happier, he hoped, once Heston turned them loose in the hills, though he knew he would miss Maia. For now the barn was open to the mild air, but once Heston got his invention running, it would be as comfortable as the ranch house—cooled in summer, heated in winter, bright with natural light from skylights built into the roof.

Chris stroked Maia's neck as she nuzzled him, her sweet breath blowing in his hair. He wished his stepfather would teach him to ride, but Heston was possessive of his horses.

"They're not pets," he'd pointed out. "They need to get acclimated to their new surroundings, and I don't want them overexcited," he'd said, but Chris wondered if that was the real reason. Heston himself rode one of them out sometimes to survey the property. Chris had overheard him telling Willa, "Yeah, I know he's a rugged kid, but he's only nine. Maybe after the first run of foals, but not now."

That would be more than a year from now, Chris realized, wishing he had the nerve to just grab hold of Maia's mane and swing himself over the top rail and onto her back. But he sensed that would really tick Heston off. And he wasn't sure he could do it without falling off. *Maybe,* he thought, *after the foals are born, he might let me have one.*

The thought would have to sustain him for now. He gave Maia a final pat, climbed down from the fence and went off to run wild through the tall grass, waiting quietly for the native critters—birds and lizards and some sort of small furry hopping quadruped whose name he didn't know that looked like a kangaroo rat with a platypus bill—or skipping stones across the small creek in back of the house where Heston had joked about a swimming pool, or hiking halfway up the nearest inactive cinder cone until Willa caught sight of him and called him down. He figured it would take him all summer to explore every corner of his new world.

"It'll never fly!" Cotton Jonday announced, watching Heston tinker with the interface for what he'd informed their Neworlder neighbors would be the state of the art in thermodynamic environmental control systems. He and his son seemed to have come all the way over to the Prescott homestead just to criticize Heston's latest creation.

"If I'd wanted it to fly, neighbor, I'd have given it a propulsion system," Heston retorted, just to annoy Cotton, which he'd discovered was surprisingly easy to do.

The Gizmo, as Heston had dubbed it, stood in a clearing halfway between the house and the barn. While Heston tinkered, Cotton and his son Flax stood around with their hands deep in the pockets of their bib overalls, barely contained sneers on their faces. Chris and Silk watched from the porch, barely stifling their laughter.

Silk, Chris had learned, was Cotton's niece. She'd been allowed to tag along, apparently no longer forbidden to associate with the Prescotts, as long as her uncle was curious about what Heston was up to, and she'd decided she and Chris were friends again.

While they watched the interplay between Heston and the Jondays, Chris had opened the back of Silk's cell phone to see if he could get it to interface with his comm unit.

"Settling your family in so close to active thermal vents isn't safe," Cotton went on doggedly, kicking at the dirt with the toe of his boot. "There's gases coming out of those clefts that can kill you and your livestock with you."

"That's largely misinformation, neighbor. And on the odd chance that this particular beast turns out to be flatulent . . ." Chris and Silk both snorted and poked each other with glee. ". . . that's what this is for." Heston tapped the face of one of the banks of gauges on the device and it presented him with a series of readouts. "Measures everything. Temperature, pressure, exact composition of escaping gases—which are captured by the array over here . . ." He bobbed and wove amid the maze of conduits with practiced ease. ". . . and broken down to the molecular level here . . ." Ducking under and around. ". . . and converted into energy here."

"Reducing Nature to its molecular components isn't Natural. . . ." Cotton began.

"My friend, every time you sit down to the dinner table, that's exactly what you're doing!" Heston cut him off, squinting against the sun, a socket wrench in one hand and an oily rag in the other. "If you didn't, you'd have starved to death at your mother's breast and wouldn't be here annoying me today."

Chris and Silk couldn't hold it in any longer. They laughed until they were weak, noticing too late that Cotton had heard them and turned on his heel, heading for the porch, his sullen overgrown son in tow. The two of them suddenly grew very serious.

"I've designed thermal capture systems for entire cities!" Heston called after Cotton, trying to distract him before there was an incident. "I think I can manage to do the same for my own household."

But Cotton was not to be diverted. He loomed over the two on the porch. "You find this amusing, do you?" he demanded of Silk, not even looking at Chris.

"No, sir . . ." Silk began, but Chris intervened.

"She wasn't laughing, sir. It was me. She sort of . . . caught it from me. You know, contagious, like yawning."

Cotton jerked his thumb toward their car, an old-fashioned contraption with an internal combustion engine. Where he found the gasoline to run it was anyone's guess, though Heston had been heard muttering something about "chicken heads."

"We're leaving now," he said, and Silk, not daring to look Chris in the eye, reluctantly jumped off the porch, braids bouncing.

"You forgot your . . . um . . . cell phone!" Chris called after her, dropping it into her palm with a wink that said he'd rigged it so that from now on she could use it to talk to him.

"Good-bye, Christopher!" she called out over her shoulder. Chris could see Heston watching them, a slow grin spreading over his face, whether at Silk, who hadn't yet been entirely corrupted by the Neworlder philosophy, or at Chris's standing up to Cotton, Chris wasn't sure.

"Designing something on a computer's one thing!" Cotton repeated his recurring theme as he slammed the door of the antiquated vehicle. "You softhands try to do anything in real life, you invariably make a mess of it. And the climate's wrong for them horses!"

"We'll see about that!" Heston called after him as the car sputtered off in a hydrocarbon haze.

"Silkie and Seepy sittin' in a tree, K-I-S-S-I-N-G . . ."

Children's singsong rhymes, especially the mocking ones, endure down the centuries, and were just as stinging in Chris's time as they might have been for his great-great grandfather. The first time Silk called him on her cell phone, he could hear Flax teasing her in the background. He felt his fists clenching.

"Has he been singing that since the day you were here?" Chris asked. His commscreen showed only static, since Silk's phone didn't have visual, but her voice came through loud and clear. So, unfortunately, did Flax's.

"He'll get bored soon," Silk said, not exactly answering the question. "His brain's too small to hold more than one thought at a time."

But Chris didn't laugh as Silk had hoped he would.

"I bet if I was there, I could make him stop!"

Lately he had decided he liked Silk. He was ten now, after all, and finally taller than she, and not as squeamish as he had been when he was only nine. He wished he could finish the fight Flax had started on the ship almost a year ago.

"Did your father get the Gizmo running?" Silk wanted to know.

Heston's my stepfather, Chris wanted to say, but let it go. "Uh-huh."

"Uncle Cotton says he knows why your mares won't conceive. . . ."

Chris wondered if he should pursue that, but decided against it. For one thing, getting the mares to breed was Heston's problem, not his, especially if Heston wouldn't let him have a foal. For another, he hadn't noticed Cotton Jonday being right about much of anything so far. And third, Heston was hardly ever around, and when he was, he was preoccupied and barely listening.

As Chris had hoped, most of the time Heston was somewhere else on the planet, planting trees, changing the course of rivers, setting off controlled magma releases from some of the volcanoes in order to take the pressure off earthquake faults. Willa either worked from home or took Chris with her into the city, so he had his mom back, but he wished the homestead wasn't out in the middle of nowhere, or that more settlers would move close by. The Neworlders' farm lay on the other side of the foothills, but there was no one else for kilometers. The other kids he'd been in touch with on Earth were out of reach to anyone who didn't have a subspace communicator, and even that would take weeks. Except for his illicit conversations with Silk, Chris spent an awful lot of time in his own company.

The novelty of his new home had worn off, and he kept wishing for something exciting to happen.

That was when the earthquakes began.

4

ELYSIUM

It was a Sunday morning and, as he usually did, Chris leapt out of bed and bolted for the barn where the brood mares were. He was halfway there, running across the grass in his bare feet no matter how many times Willa told him not to, when a distant rumble turned into movement beneath his feet, as if the grass was a rug someone was trying to yank out from under him. He staggered and almost fell, stumbling to a halt. But the ground kept moving. One of the mares whinnied nervously.

He knew as much as any curious kid did about earthquakes, but he'd never experienced one, not even in Mojave which, like most of California, had been stabilized by people like Heston ages ago. Something told him to sit down before he fell down, and wait it out. Hunkered down on the grass hugging his knees, he watched the one-year saplings they'd planted as soon as they got here start to sway, their leaves shimmering as if in a strong breeze, except that the air was still, as if it was holding its breath. A cloud of dust rose from the mountainside where he'd been hiking only yesterday, and hovered in the air without settling.

The tremor probably lasted all of fifteen seconds, but it

wasn't until a lone bird somewhere took up its usual cry that Chris trusted the ground to stay still, and clambered to his feet. Only then did he realize how unnaturally quiet it had been before the quake. He would remember that from now on, in case there were more.

There were. In the city, a series of tremors over the ensuing weeks were a sound more than a feeling, and might have been mistaken for the rumble of some of the heavy machinery setting another high-rise in place. But out on the homesteads, the quakes did some damage, and set everybody's nerves on edge. Chris got into the habit of just hunkering down wherever he was, checking in with his mother on his personal comm unit to tell her he was all right, and riding it out.

He came home from the grasslands after a particularly bad quake when Willa's voice didn't sound right. He found her in the kitchen amid a mess of broken glass and crockery.

"Everything fell out of the cabinets," she said distractedly. She held what was left of a favorite serving platter in both hands. She saw the concern on Chris's face and smiled. "Never liked those dishes, anyway. It knocked the Gizmo off-line for a bit, but Heston fixed it. He's a little puzzled why it didn't predict this last quake, but he says he can modify it. We'll be okay."

"Sure, Mom," Chris said, more to reassure her than himself.

But Heston's modifications had to wait. He was needed in the city.

"Some hoo-ha about whether the monorail pylons are stable enough," he said, packing an overnight bag. "I told the Council their best bet was a free-floating gimbal system; even gave them the specs for one, but bureaucrats always have to fiddle with things. Every ship brings more Neworlders; the Council's full of them. I'll need a few days to wade through the red tape, do some on-site inspections . . ."

"We'll be fine here," Willa said, kissing him on the cheek. "Chris and I will earthquake-proof the place while you're gone."

Neither of the adults said *We should have done that when we first settled here,* but it hung unspoken between them.

Heston was gone more than a few days. Every comm message from him was full of complaints about bureaucrats and armchair quarterbacks, and Willa made soothing noises. Chris took over Heston's work with the horses, feeding and watering them, letting them out into the paddock to run while he mucked out the stalls. It was a lot of work, but he didn't mind it.

None of the mares had gotten pregnant yet. Chris figured he'd have to be grown and on his own, maybe away at college, before he'd ever learn to ride.

Then Charlie came, and everything changed.

Chris had been in the city with his mother all day. As she put the aircar on hover and let it float into the yard, Chris saw Heston, who'd finally solved the problems with the monorail system and had been home from the city for a few days ("at least until the next crisis," was how he put it), leaning on the paddock fence, talking to a stranger.

". . . thought I'd be able to manage it myself," Heston was saying. Both men had their backs to the yard, studying the mares grazing quietly in the paddock. "But now I think I may have bitten off more than I can chew. None of them will implant, and I have to be back and forth to the city so much I can't devote the time to figuring out why."

"Lot of reasons why a mare can't stay in foal," the stranger said. He'd glanced over at the occupants of the aircar as they got out, tipping his slouch hat to Willa, who stood very still for a moment, then hurried into the house.

Chris thought that was odd. They so seldom had visitors that his mother always went out of her way to make them welcome. But his curiosity about the stranger was overpowering. He moved just close enough to listen to the two men, and just quietly enough not to attract attention.

"Could be the travel. Could be the stasis itself. Transporting horses in space is still a fairly new thing," the stranger was saying. "Could be the turnaround in the seasons when you all arrived, or something in the feed, even a little imbalance in the atmosphere, or those quakes you had a while back. Any of those things could have thrown their rhythm off. . . ."

The stranger was not as tall as Heston, and seemed to Chris to be slightly older, though he wasn't good at guessing adults' ages. Maybe it was that the thick, brushy hair revealed when he took off his slouch hat to run his fingers through it was almost completely gray, or the fact that even when he wasn't smiling the crinkles around his dark brown eyes remained, as if he spent a lot of time either laughing or squinting into the sun, or maybe both.

There was something familiar about him, Chris thought, maybe only the fact that he dressed and spoke like some of the men and women, descendants of the original settlers, who lived in and around Mojave, where he and his mother had lived whenever they weren't traveling, before she met Heston. In any event, Chris was mightily intrigued by both the man and what he was saying.

". . . could be they just need someone to be with them every day to settle them. Horses are sensitive. Some people think they're stupid, but they aren't, on the whole. It's just a different kind of intelligence. But if you'll consider my offer . . ."

"I'll want to check your credentials first," Heston said. "I'm not suspicious by nature, but a man shows up off a passing starship claiming to know all about horse breeding, it's just a bit too convenient, if you don't mind my saying so."

"Don't mind at all," the stranger said. He seemed to sense rather than see Chris standing practically at his elbow. "Is this your son?" he asked.

"This is Christopher," Heston said, resting a hand on the boy's shoulder.

"How do you do, sir?" Chris said as his mother had taught him.

"Christopher," the man said, offering a hand to shake. His smile widened. "My name's Charlie."

"Are you going to be taking care of the horses?" Chris would never know what made him blurt that out just then. He was too young to realize it was putting Heston on the spot. In retrospect, he was glad it did.

Charlie didn't answer. He took off his hat and ran his fingers through his hair again and looked at Heston as if to say: *It's up to you.*

Heston looked as if he was about to say something, but then Chris heard his mother calling him from the porch. By the time he ran to the house, she was holding the door open for him, Heston and the stranger were disappearing into the stables, and Willa was looking after them, her face unreadable.

Chris would always wonder how things might have been different if he hadn't asked that question.

From that day on, Chris found himself following Charlie around the way he'd once followed Heston. It wasn't as if he was being disloyal to his stepfather, he told himself, just that Charlie was around more.

Because that was how things were. Willa still divided her time between home and the city, and Heston was spending more and more time out in the field. Charlie, meanwhile, settled into the barn loft and made it home.

"We could build you a guesthouse," Willa offered when his gear had been beamed down from the ship he'd arrived on. "It would take less than a day."

"The ladies and I need to get to know each other," Charlie told her, his eyes crinkling. Chris figured out by now that he meant the mares. He also called them his "harem," another word Chris would have to look up. "If we all live in the same house, they'll accept me as one of them, and that'll make my job easier."

"Hero worship!" Heston muttered, watching the boy following the new hired hand everywhere.

"Do I hear a tinge of jealousy?" Willa teased him.

"Just a little concern about Charlie as a role model. You saw his record. The guy's had more jobs than most people have eyelashes. If you don't mind your son getting the idea that it's okay to just drift through life . . ."

"I want my son to know as much about all kinds of people as he can learn," Willa interrupted him gently but firmly. "That's how he'll come to know their value."

"Pennyroyal," Charlie said, getting up from a crouch and dusting his hands on his jeans. He held an unprepossessing little weed with small white flowers that he'd uprooted from one corner of the paddock. "*Monardella exilis,* or a kissing cousin native to this world. A mare eats enough of it, it'll prevent her from conceiving, or if she does conceive, she'll likely miscarry."

"Well, I'll be damned," Heston said. "Why didn't the tricorders pick it up?"

"They did. But since you didn't calibrate them to look for abortifacient factors in the native flora, they weren't looking for it. Machine's only as smart as you program it to be. I've worked around horses all my life. I know what they should and shouldn't eat."

Hanging on the rail fence, Chris listened. Charlie had just gone up another notch in his estimation. Heston was a bit more skeptical.

"So you're telling me all we have to do is clear this weed out of the paddock and the mares will carry?"

"No," Charlie said. "I'm saying clear the weed out of the paddock and you've eliminated one reason why they won't."

Before the winter was over, Charlie's words proved prophetic. He'd successfully implanted two of the mares from the stock of frozen embryos. Heston set aside his skepticism and ordered him to continue with the remaining four.

"All in good time," Charlie said. "You really don't want to have to deliver six foals simultaneously. Trust me on that."

Again, watching and listening, Chris could tell from the expression on Heston's face that he'd never even thought of that. In some subtle way the boy could see but not yet understand, the balance of power on the homestead had shifted. Heston might be calling the shots, but it was Charlie who made things happen.

Heston's preliminary survey of the Neworlder lands showed they'd chosen a floodplain too near a river. Refusing to accept his "unNatural" findings, they'd built there anyway. The following spring the rains were heavier than usual, and the river rose above its banks, sweeping everything in its path. Boulders the size of houses rolled along the river bottom, traveling inexorably downstream, smashing through logjams formed by uprooted trees, taking houses and barns with them.

Starfleet diverted one of its newer starships to monitor from orbit and, over their vociferous protests, the Neworlders were evacuated to higher ground. Even more infuriating to them was the fact that Heston Prescott was assigned to redivert the river and move the floodplain, actions they deemed particularly unNatural. If they refused, they were told, they would have to move to higher ground. Grudgingly, they let Heston do his job.

There was some erosion of the hillsides surrounding the Prescott homestead, but Heston had a solution for that, too.

"Hybrid grasses," he announced as all four of them trudged about in their waterproof boots surveying the deep-etched runnels that hadn't been there only a few days before. "Crossbred from perennial prairie grasses and annual crops like corn and wheat. Stuff's got roots that go down four times deeper than the tops grow up. Helped repopulate the Dust Bowl a century after overcultivation nearly destroyed it."

"Might want to check your oxygen mix first," Charlie said thoughtfully.

"How's that?"

Chris wasn't sure when or how the two men had begun competing with each other. He figured it had something to do with Charlie's being smarter than Heston about the horses eating the pennyroyal. All he knew for sure was that Heston was usually short-tempered when Charlie was around.

"Oxygen concentration's a little higher here. Not everything that grows on Earth can safely be transplanted elsewhere—" Charlie began.

"So now you're a botanist as well?" Heston cut him off. Before Charlie could answer, Willa spoke.

"Hes? What about my truck farm? It's experimental," she explained to Charlie, a pleading look in her eyes, as if she was begging him not to pursue with Heston what could only become an argument. "We were going to grow specialty vegetables, maybe even start a fish farm. So far the only people willing to try conventional farming here are the Neworlders. If we can show them a better way—"

"Waste of time!" Heston snorted, his boots squishing in the muck as he turned back toward the house. "Pretty soon they'll own the damn planet!"

The upshot of the argument was that Willa's experiment would have to wait. Heston planted the hillsides and a good portion of the flat plain in hybrid grasses and forbade Chris the run of the land until they took root.

"You can go play somewhere else!" he announced. Chris got a stubborn look, as if he was about to argue that now there weren't many places close to the house left where he could play. But arguing with Heston, he'd discovered, was about as productive as arguing with either of the Jondays. Heston was too busy gloating about how he'd been right and the Neworlders wrong about the floodplain.

Heston's satisfaction was short-lived. The engineers aboard the starship had done their own independent survey of his land as well.

"We're sorry to contact you at this late hour, Dr. Prescott, but it's oh-nine-hundred where we are, and we're leaving orbit at twelve-hundred hours. We'd have come out to the homestead to discuss this with you personally, but there wasn't time . . ."

"Go ahead. I'm listening," Heston said gruffly, coincidentally leaning back in his chair so that Chris could see the two official-looking men in Starfleet uniforms on the comm-screen.

"Sir, the revised survey indicates several new fault lines under your property . . ."

Chris was supposed to be in bed, but he'd overheard Heston talking to someone on the comm and crept to the top of the stairs to listen.

"The revised survey's wrong!" he heard Heston say, his voice sharper than Chris had ever heard it before. "Try to remember who you're talking to here, gentlemen. I'm not some Neworlder rube who can't read a seismic map. I've rearranged whole continents on a dozen worlds, including this one, and I've been over these hills with my own equipment dozens of times."

Peering through the stair rails, Chris couldn't see Heston's face, but he could see the inspector's face filling the commscreen. A muscle worked in the man's jaw, as if he was trying to control his temper.

"Dr. Prescott . . ." he began. "I can show you what the orbital survey indicates after those last tremors—"

"Look, excuse me—" Heston was on his feet, one finger hovering over the Terminate toggle. "—but I've got a full day ahead of me. I thank you for your concern, and I assure you I'll be out in the hills this weekend going over my readings one more time."

"That's all well and good, sir," the inspector said tightly. "But you're to be informed that Starfleet has made arrangements with the Elysium Planetary Council to stabilize those fault lines. We've got some supplies to deliver to the Omicron Ceti system. We expect to be back this way in another six months or so. We wanted to give you sufficient advance warning that you and your family will need to be evacuated while we do the stabilization. If we're not successful—"

"Hold on a second," Heston interrupted. "Are you making the Neworlders evacuate?"

"The Neworlder homesteads are far enough away from the fault lines to—"

"That's what I thought! I'll tell you this much for free— by the time you people come back around here, I'll have those fault lines stabilized myself!"

Chris waited just long enough to make sure he saw Heston's finger come down on the Terminate before he scrambled back to his room. As he heard Heston's tread on the stairs, he risked a glance out the window toward the stables. The light in the loft was on, which told him Charlie couldn't sleep either. Chris pulled the covers up to his chin and closed his eyes just as he heard Heston's footsteps stop at his doorway.

After his stepfather had checked up on him and continued down the hall to the room he shared with Willa, Chris crept out of bed once more and, aware that the stair treads creaked, sat down and slid down them on his butt one by one. He was out the door and halfway across the yard, skipping over the thermal vents from memory in the dark, before it occurred to him it might be rude to bother Charlie in the middle of the night.

Charlie, however, was not up in the loft. He was checking the rheostat on the embryo chamber, and talking soothingly to Petula, the bay mare who was due to foal first. Seeing Chris in the doorway, he didn't seem at all surprised.

"Ground's kind of cold for bare feet this time of year," he observed.

"That's what my mom says," Chris grimaced, wondering if all adults had to lecture.

But Charlie wasn't given to lectures. "Your mom's a smart woman. I just made some cocoa. Want some?"

"No, thank you."

"But you do want to unload whatever's on your mind."

Charlie gave Petula a final pat, gestured for Chris to make himself comfortable on one of the hay bales against the side wall near the embryo chamber, and settled himself and his own mug of cocoa beside him. Chris told him what he'd just overheard.

"So what's your worry?" Charlie asked when he'd finished.

"I don't want anything bad to happen," the boy said. "But I'm just a kid. I'm not supposed to know what's going on. I wish I could do something to help."

Charlie weighed that before he answered. "Well, what you could do is let me know what's bothering you, just like you're doing now."

"How's that going to help?" Chris wanted to know.

"Gets it off your chest, for one thing. Gives you an ally among the grown-ups in case things get out of hand."

"You think they will?"

Charlie finished his cocoa and put the empty mug on one of the steps leading up to the loft. "I think your mother's sensible enough to talk Heston out of being so stubborn." Chris barely heard him add under his breath: "At least I hope so . . ." Charlie said, a little louder, ". . . and you'd better get back to bed before you're missed."

Sliding up the stairs the same way he'd gone down them, Chris stopped halfway up when he heard voices. Heston and Willa were arguing in whispers in the dark.

". . . so once those grasses take root, I suppose I can kiss my truck farm good-bye," he heard Willa say.

"It wasn't practical anyway," was Heston's reply. "We didn't come here to be farmers."

"That's easy for you to say. What if I said the same about the horses?"

"They're more important."

"More important how? Just because they were your idea?"

"They're a legacy, Willa. This planet has no large indigenous quadrupeds, and no predators to hunt them. The goal is to fill the plains with herds of the best horses."

"Ah, so now your hobby is more important than mine."

"I didn't say that. . . ."

"Because they are just hobbies, you know. Our 'legacy' is the city. Your infrastructure, my buildings. The rest is extra. And I wonder if the Neworlders aren't right about our tampering with nature. Maybe there are reasons why there are no large quadrupeds on this world."

Heston snorted. "Neworlders! These are people who run their vehicles on chicken guts. I'm beginning to worry about you. . . ."

Chris had heard enough. More than enough, enough to make him worry more than ever. For the first time since they'd come here, he wished they'd never left Earth. He could handle earthquakes, floods, even the fact that he might never have a horse of his own. What he wasn't sure he could handle was his mother and Heston starting to fight.

Because then he'd have to hate Heston, and he didn't want to do that.

"Maybe we ought to hold off on implanting the other four mares," Charlie suggested when Willa told him about the Starfleet directive. Heston had gone off into the hills early that morning to run his readings, and refused to talk about it. "They'd be much more difficult to move if they were pregnant during the evacuation."

"You'll have to take that up with Heston," Willa said, avoiding his eyes. "The horses are his department."

Coming back after dark, his skimmer covered with volcanic dust, Heston was having none of this.

"There isn't going to be any evacuation!" he announced. "I know what this is about. There was another Neworlder elected to the Elysium Council in the last vote. They're coming here by the boatload, and they're lobbying against any kind of progress, and against me in particular. If they had their way they'd convert this entire colony to their Luddite mentality.

I'll show them *and* Starfleet. By the time that starship comes back, I'll have this solved. The volcano is the key . . ."

He refused to elaborate. Once again Chris caught Charlie and Willa exchanging warning glances. Something had shifted, and it wasn't just the ground beneath them.

Then Charlie went into town for a few days and came back with a box full of mysterious plants which he went about—with Willa's permission; the horses might be Heston's territory, but the flora were hers—planting around the foundations of the house and the barn.

"What're those?" Chris wanted to know, seeing them change color when the sunlight struck them, and again as Charlie patted the soil around their roots, and a third time when he watered them.

"Jellyplants," Charlie explained. "A long time ago, when humans hadn't gotten any farther away from Earth than their own moon, the ancestors of these creatures were developed by NASA. You know what NASA was, don't you?"

Chris nodded. "National Aeronautics and Space Administration. One of a whole bunch of different space agencies that formed Earth's Starfleet in the twenty-second century. But you called them 'creatures.'"

"Not much gets by you, does it?" Charlie marveled. "In a sense, they are creatures as much as plants. NASA scientists combined the genetic codes of certain algae with those of certain species of luminescent jellyfish. What you get is plants that change color under certain chemical conditions. They can tell you if there isn't enough oxygen in the air you're breathing, or if there's too much of another gas that might harm you. In the past two hundred years, scientists have used those same jellyfish codes to create many different kinds of plants that can do many different things."

"What do these guys do?" Chris wondered. Except for the color changes, this particular species of jellyplant looked like asparagus ferns, soft and feathery and inviting to the touch. He wondered if they'd feel anything if he petted them.

"These guys," Charlie said, "can not only read atmospheric gases, but they can predict earthquakes as well."

The information eased Chris's mind somewhat after recent events.

"Just like the Gizmo?" he asked.

"Maybe even better than the Gizmo. Of course, if Heston found out, it might hurt his feelings . . ."

Chris had been reading spy stories lately, and he grinned. "This tape will self-destruct in ten seconds."

Now every morning, even before he ran to the barn to visit Maia, he stopped to check the jellyplants.

Petula went into foal just before dawn on a Monday morning. Chris heard Heston answer what must have been a comm call from Charlie, then rush down the stairs still clambering into his jeans. He saw the lights on in the barn and, still in his pajamas, tore across the yard. Willa was the last to arrive, tying the belt on her robe, twisting her hair up out of the way. She fished in the pockets of the robe and handed Chris his slippers without a word.

The mare leaned against the side of the box stall, panting. Charlie stood beside her, his touch calming her. Heston was attaching various devices that would monitor her blood pressure and heart rate, as well as the foal's. The other horses had their heads over the sides of their stalls, watching silently.

"Can I stay, Mom?" Chris whispered after a few moments. But before Willa could speak, Heston did.

"Too many humans around will make her skittish . . ."

"Hes . . ." Willa started to say, but Charlie intervened.

"Could take all day, Chris," he said, looking at the boy under his eyebrows with an expression that said: *Don't fight this one.* "We'll keep the comm open. You can watch from the house if you keep the sound off at your end."

That advice seemed to satisfy everyone. Chris and his mother went back to the house. By midafternoon Jenna, the second mare, had also started to labor. By nightfall Petula had delivered a sturdy bay colt, and somewhere around dawn Jenna's chestnut filly arrived.

For once Heston had enough to do to keep him from obsessing about the Gizmo, the fault lines, even the Neworlders, though the last were never far from his mind.

"Wrong climate for horses, eh?" were his final words as he wiped his brow, clapped Charlie on the back, and watched the filly stagger to her feet and start to nurse. "We'll see about that!"

Sometime the next afternoon, after both men had caught up on much-needed sleep, Heston ordered Charlie to implant the remaining mares, Starfleet evacuation plans be damned.

5

TALOS IV

"I sense something ominous about to happen," Vina said quietly beside him.

"Are you reading my mind?" Pike asked, bemused. He'd wondered if she could from the beginning.

She shook her head. "I saw it in your eyes the first time you looked at me."

"Then you're very perceptive," he said. "But why am I not surprised?"

They stood side by side on one of the balconies, watching the sun go down over the sea. Surreptitiously he studied the planes of her face in the setting sun. He still wasn't sure if she was exactly as he remembered her. There were times when she seemed as familiar as if they'd been together for years, and times like this when he was reminded that their relationship was still in its nascent phase.

"You're right," he said grimly, deciding to trust her. "The earthquakes and the floods were only the beginning . . ."

ELYSIUM

The Gizmo grew bigger. It now occupied most of the space between the house and the barn and threatened to spread into the front yard until Willa protested and Heston began expanding it away from the house into the fields beyond. Added to the power station were deep-core probes to read seismic activity, and a high-atmosphere weather drone. Chris was fascinated by the weather station, its old-fashioned anemometer whirling in the morning breeze, the ambient temperature and humidity altering by the second. Mischievous, he liked to breathe on the humidity index just before Heston came around to check it every morning.

"Funny . . ." Heston would mutter to himself, rubbing the back of his neck and gazing up at a cloudless sky. "It doesn't seem that damp . . ."

Every time Heston went into the city, he came back with more bits and pieces which he spent the next day or so, well into the night, fitting into place.

"Pretty soon that thing's going to be able to predict the future," Charlie remarked dryly, trying to cheer Willa up. It only made her frown deepen.

"It's becoming his whole life," she said, shaking her head. "And if it doesn't do what he says it'll do, it's not just about our having to abandon the homestead. He'll take it to mean that he failed somehow. A man who can move continents, but can't manage his own land . . ."

Whatever dire predictions the Starfleet engineers might have made about new fault lines, everything was quiet for now. Summer came and went, and the winter rains returned, but less violently this time. The new colt and filly flourished, and soon it was evident that Maia and another mare were carrying as well.

Chris grew like a weed. By his eleventh birthday, he was

nearly as tall as Willa. Working with the horses, running and climbing, had made him wiry and strong. Charlie made note of him watching the foals longingly from the rail fence, and made a decision.

"Too young?" Charlie repeated what Heston had just said. Charlie usually steered away from the Gizmo unless Heston specifically asked him to help, but he'd risked it today. "Heston, I sat a horse before I could walk. He can start on Petula as soon as her colt's weaned."

The day was overcast, and it would probably rain. Chris was up in his room doing math problems, but the windows were open and the damp air made the men's voices carry farther than usual. Leaning cautiously out the window, he held his breath, not daring to hope.

"Maybe," he heard Heston say. "You don't have enough else to do? You'd have time to teach him to ride?"

"It'd be a privilege," Charlie said.

"All right, you've worn me down," Heston grumped.

Chris didn't dare breathe. He went to the window and stuck his head out, hoping neither man would look up and notice him eavesdropping.

"What?" he heard Heston say. "Is that it?"

"If Maia has a colt . . ." Charlie began.

"Oh, no, you don't! These horses aren't pets; they're an investment."

"You want me to break 'em for you," was all Charlie said.

There was a long silence.

"This is beginning to sound like blackmail," Heston said, only half joking.

"Maia's got the best bloodlines of the six," Charlie said evenly, unperturbed by the accusation. "If she has a filly, you'll want her as part of the next generation of breeders. But if it's a colt . . ."

"Fifty-fifty odds," Heston said. "You drive a hard bargain. All right. If it's a colt, Chris can raise it. But I'll decide down the road whether or not he gets to keep it."

Chris nearly cracked his head on the window frame in his haste. With a whoop that startled both men, he came tearing down the stairs and out into the yard.

"Thanks . . . Dad!" he blurted, throwing himself at Heston in a wild bear hug that nearly knocked them both over.

It was the first time he'd called Heston that, and the big man actually flushed with pride. Only then did Chris remember the real reason he was getting his wish. He turned to Charlie. "And thank you, Charlie."

Charlie's eyes crinkled. "Maybe you won't thank me when you find out how much work it's going to be . . ."

Charlie led Petula over to the rail fence. Chris swung up onto the mare's back the way Charlie had shown him, a little awkwardly, but Charlie seemed not to notice. He adjusted the stirrups for the boy's long legs, showed him how to hold the reins and said, "Give her her head. She'll know what to do."

It took Chris a moment to realize just how high off the ground he was. He wondered if horses, like dogs and big cats, could smell fear. Consciously he relaxed the muscles in his legs until he was "holding" Petula just the way Charlie had shown him. Feeling him settle, the mare responded by walking quietly around the paddock for a few turns.

"Now give her a nudge," Charlie instructed quietly, and he did.

The mare eased into a gentle loping trot. Suddenly confident, Chris nudged her again and clucked to her the way he'd heard Charlie do, and she began to gallop.

At once terrified and exhilarated, Chris held on as Petula made the circuit of the paddock three times, four times before he reined her in, exactly the way Charlie had shown him. By the time he slid down to the ground, his cheeks were flushed and his eyes were glowing, and he was grinning from ear to ear. Only then did he notice Heston, leaning on the rail fence beside Charlie, scowling.

Chris looked from Heston to Charlie, wondering if it was something he'd done wrong. But Heston just made a noise in the back of his throat and went back to tinkering with the Gizmo.

"He's determined to harness that volcano even without Starfleet's help . . ." Willa muttered grimly, watching him from the porch. Chris noticed she'd developed a tendency to talk to herself as if no one else was around. But it was the word "harness" that caught his attention.

"Heston said something about that when we first came here. What does it mean?"

"It means . . ." Willa sighed. She was holding the small of her back as if it ached her. ". . . he's going to scavenge parts from the Gizmo and move them in sections up to a weak spot in the magma core and channel some of the flow underground into the water table. It'll harden almost instantly, raise the groundwater levels, and stabilize those faults."

"It sounds dangerous."

Willa shook her head. "It's part of what he does, but usually with much more sophisticated equipment. The Council has refused to give him the permits or the equipment to do it on his own land, but he's determined to go ahead on his own anyway . . ."

So, apparently, was the volcano.

The rumble under Chris's feet was different this time. He saw it before he heard or felt it.

Heston had gone off in one of the 'cars that morning to, as he put it, "talk to the volcano," bringing a section of the Gizmo with him. Willa was in the city overseeing a new shipment of building modules. Chris and Charlie were getting ready to drive the horses upland to graze on some of the new grass when the wind suddenly dropped and the birds went silent.

Charlie had been tightening the saddle cinch under Jenna's belly. His head came up, listening, even before hers did.

"Uh-oh," he said, looking over to where Chris was. "Hang on."

Chris instinctively looked up to make sure nothing would fall on his head if it was a bad one, then braced himself against a support beam. Through the open barn door, he witnessed the most amazing thing. The open ground between the barn and the house began to ripple like a series of waves incoming on a beach, moving toward and past them.

The yearlings, who were out in the paddock and less acclimated than the mares, began rearing and running in frenzied circles. Chris held on as the waves reached the barn and the ground bucked beneath him. He heard things smashing in the house, watched as Willa's hanging planters on the porch swung like lanterns on a ship in a storm. The jellyplants around the foundation had gone fluorescent, warning of danger. There hadn't been any quakes in so long, he'd gotten out of the habit of checking them.

Mesmerized despite the racket the horses were making, not to mention the rolling thunder of the ground beneath them, Chris found himself counting the "waves." When they reached thirteen, they stopped. Not sure if it was safe to move yet, he did anyway, hurrying outside to survey the yard, amazed that there was so little damage. The grass was torn up in places, and cracks had formed in some of the drier dirt, like crazes in glass when a rock hits it. One of the thermal vents was steaming a little more energetically than usual.

Distant rumbles suggested the waves were still continuing, moving away, and he wondered if they'd reach the Neworlders' farm. Beyond that, it was unnaturally quiet.

Then the Gizmo fell.

There was no warning. The central core simply started to lean, then with a creaking, groaning sound that escalated into a high-pitched shriek, it tore away from the maze of interwoven jointed pipes and conduits and probes and circuits and toppled over with a great thundering, shaking the ground more than the worst of the quakes had, sending the horses rearing again. Instinctively Chris clamped his hands over his ears, then tentatively took them away, listening for something else to fall and break.

But the damage was done. The Gizmo lay on its side like some gigantic beached squid, all functions off-line, and with them everything on the homestead that ran through it.

"Aux power," Charlie said quietly. The main connector was adjacent to the embryo chamber.

"Heston took it off-line!" Chris said, slamming the side of the chamber in frustration. "He's been scavenging it to grow the Gizmo. He did this, you know!" He turned on Charlie. "It's him fooling with that volcano that did this! I hope it kills him!"

Charlie didn't say anything. He was outside seeing what he could reclaim from the Gizmo when Chris came running after him.

"I didn't mean that," he said.

"Yes, you did," Charlie said, not looking at him. "Contrary to popular opinion, it's when we're angriest that we say what we really mean. You said it, and you got it out of your system, and no one heard it but the horses and me, and I'm not talking. You might have to give Maia a little extra sugar to keep her quiet, though."

That made Chris laugh and broke the mood. He was helping Charlie pull pieces out of the fallen Gizmo when Heston's aircar came sailing into the yard.

"Leave that alone!" he shouted, sliding the windscreen aside while the 'car was still powering down. He strode across the yard and stood between Charlie and the Gizmo, hands on his hips, scowling.

"Looks like you poured your thermocrete over a weak spot in the bedrock," Charlie pointed out calmly, unperturbed by the bluster. "Your little 'talk' with the volcano set the wave motion going, cracked it right in half."

"It's not irreparable!" Heston barked. "We'll have it up and running in less than a day."

"You'll need aux power before that," Charlie pointed out. "Everything from your lights to your comm to the embryo chamber is out."

"The embryos—!" If they started to thaw, he would lose them. Heston stormed toward the barn. Charlie calmly went back to what he'd been doing. He and Chris had the aux power up again within the hour.

Two days later, the volcano erupted, for the first time since Starfleet had surveyed the planet over two decades earlier. And Heston ended up seriously hurt.

"Spawned a little fumarole on the east flank, threw off a lot of steam and enough ash to make flyspecks on the Neworlders' windowsills," Heston dismissed it, climbing over a knot of twisted piping to assess the damage to the Gizmo from a different angle. "Had absolutely nothing to do with the experiments I was running, no matter what Cotton Jonday says. Matter of fact, I was on my way back to tell you my readings indicated the beast was due for an eruption when the wave motion started. Anyway, we got the power back without losing a single embryo. And as soon as I get the Gizmo back online, I'm going to try a different approach."

He made it sound as if he'd planned the whole thing, and no one had the energy to contradict him. He'd drafted Chris and Charlie to help him get the Gizmo repaired. Willa had started to pitch in, too, but he stopped her.

"Not until the doctor okays it," he said gruffly.

"Doctor?" Chris repeated, turning to look at Willa in alarm. He saw his mother and stepfather exchange one of those looks then that made him wish he were older, or maybe younger, too young to constantly be caught between them.

In an extraordinary display of temper, Willa flung the spanner she'd been holding into the shrubbery.

"Thank you so much!" she spat at Heston. "I wanted to tell Chris myself!"

She stormed toward the house. Chris expected Heston to go after her, but Heston just picked up where he'd left off. Charlie took the conduit Chris had been holding in place and jerked his chin in Willa's direction, and the boy ran after his mother.

"We still need your help with this!" Heston called after him, but Chris ignored him.

He and Willa sat on the porch while she told him her news.

"In a week or so we'll know if it's a boy or a girl," she said when it was clear he didn't know what to say. "Or we can decide to be surprised. What do you think?"

"I think I wish you'd told me before . . . before Heston said what he did."

"I'm sorry. I should have told you as soon as I knew. I was trying to find the right moment. Are you disappointed?"

"About having a little brother or sister? No. I think it's great. I just wish Heston didn't have to try to run everything!"

"He'll be all right once he gets the Gizmo going again," Willa said, staring off into the distance, refusing to look in the direction of the two men and the sound of hammering.

"I wouldn't bet on it!" Chris muttered grimly. Then he saw the crestfallen look on his mother's face. Somehow it had become his job to cheer her up, instead of the other way around. Impulsively, he hugged her. "I'm happy, Mom. I really am."

Heston's voice summoned him back to work, and the moment was shattered. But the thought of being a big brother made him grin for the rest of the day. Even Heston's mood couldn't spoil that.

Only the Neworlders could. Flax Jonday had grown larger over the years, but no smarter. Silk confided in Chris that he'd smashed his computer and refused to bother with school, running wild with his cousins Sorrel and Sorghum, the two mouth-breathers Chris remembered from the voyage here. The sputter of a badly tuned internal combustion engine off in the hills meant they were joyriding, falling afoul of Council law for setting small brushfires, generally causing mayhem.

"I'd tell my stepfather to put some security around that Gizmo if I were you," Silk said knowingly, her voice the only thing, still, that reached him from her cell phone.

"What do you mean, 'security'?" Chris had been woolgathering, thinking how much better it would be if he could see Silk's face when they talked, and hadn't been paying attention.

But the signal from her cell phone faded, and he lost the connection.

The following night around dinnertime something in the yard exploded, and Heston was right in the middle of it.

Heston's eyebrows were singed, and from the chest up he looked as if he had a bad sunburn. He also had three broken ribs and a broken left femur. Willa shot him full of antibiotics, painkillers, and a tranquilizer from the emergency kit, and he was out cold before he could see Charlie come back in shaking his head. The explosive had been crude, probably homemade, but it had done considerable damage.

"How bad is it?" Willa whispered, watching Heston's face to make sure he was really out of it.

"The weather station still works," Charlie reported wryly.

The next day the doctor from the city clinic paid them a visit, put a regen patch on the leg and told Heston to stay off it for at least a week. Heston was hobbling around on the crutches she'd left before her 'car was out of sight.

He was too weak to work on the Gizmo. That didn't stop him from keeping watch over it every night.

"Mom?" Chris could see Heston sitting in the yard, his back to the house, from his bedroom window. "Where did he get the laser rifle?"

"He usually only carries it when he's traveling," she said, not exactly answering his question. "Some of the places he's worked have been a little . . . rough. Don't worry—he's got it locked on stun."

"How long is this going to go on?" What he meant was, *Why don't you stand up to him? What's going to happen when the starship comes back?*

"Until he succeeds, or until Starfleet moves us," Willa said, also looking down at the big man, diminished by the distance, ensconced in a rocking chair below the window, his crutches propped up against the upended Gizmo, the laser rifle across his lap. "He filed a complaint with the Council about what happened last night. Their response was that whoever sabotaged the Gizmo had probably heard the rumors that he was tampering with the volcano, which he had no authorization to do without a permit, and they weren't going to issue a permit."

"So in other words, they're not going to do anything."

"That's about right."

"And neither are we until the starship returns."

Willa gave him a concerned look. Impulsively she hugged him and stroked his hair. He was old enough now to tolerate that again. "Has it really been so bad for you?"

Chris shrugged. "Not as long as Charlie's here, and I can ride the horses."

It wasn't long before even that changed.

Worn out from his nightly vigils, Heston slept away the days now. Nobody seemed to mind. So one morning early, Chris was surprised to hear the deep resonance of a male voice, and Willa answering, coming from the kitchen. Did they have a visitor? He hadn't heard a 'car approach. He didn't mean to eavesdrop, but couldn't help himself.

". . . I'd leave in a heartbeat if I thought it would help, Willa. I know how he feels about me. But with the two mares in foal, I can't. And I'm concerned about the effect this is having on Chris."

"And you think I'm not?" Willa's voice was shaky, as if she was near tears. "I've noticed the change in him. He's a man obsessed. The minute his leg heals, he's going to be back tickling that volcano, and it's one thing to do it from space with state-of-the-art equipment, but that damn Gizmo's held together with spit and good wishes."

There was a silence while she tried to control her voice,

which had gotten shrill. "I've thought about leaving, at least until the starship returns, but I'm afraid he'll get even more reckless without me around. But if I stay, he interprets it as encouraging him. Charlie, for the first time in my life, I don't know what to do."

"I'll help you any way I can, Willa. You know that."

Silent and unmoving, Chris tried to process what he was hearing. Young as he was, he sensed an intimacy in Charlie's tone and his mother's response that he didn't understand, perhaps didn't want to understand. He wanted to run away, to block out the words, but he couldn't move.

"You and the boy could leave," Charlie began. "Maybe take an apartment in the city, at least for a little while. Tell Heston the commute is too much for you, with the pregnancy. I have to stay for the horses, but I can ride herd on Heston, too."

Chris could picture his mother shaking her head. "I can't ask you to do that. And anyway, Chris won't want to leave Maia . . ."

"He will if you tell him why. I'm concerned about your safety, Willa."

"Oh, don't be ridiculous! It's not as extreme as all that."

"I'm not saying he'd mean to hurt you, but he's got tunnel vision. He's an accident waiting to happen."

Chris heard his mother sigh. He imagined her twisting the hair at the nape of her neck around her fingers, something she did when she was preoccupied or stressed.

"The starship's due back at the end of this month," she said finally.

"You think that's going to solve anything, or only postpone it?"

"I don't know!" Willa said sharply, slamming the palms of her hands on something—the table, the countertop—from where he was lurking, Chris couldn't see. "I'm sorry, I . . ."

When she spoke again, her voice was muffled. "Charlie? If anything does happen . . ."

Chris couldn't listen anymore. Somehow he found his legs and bolted for the barn, where he buried his face in Maia's neck and wept as he hadn't since he was a very small boy.

TALOS IV

"You thought they were having an affair," Vina said knowingly. "Were they?"

"I don't want to talk about that right now!"

"Ah, I see. Volcanoes and earthquakes and paranoid stepfathers and reactionary neighbors are minor annoyances. But when a boy finds out his mother isn't perfect . . ."

"I said I didn't want to talk about it!" Pike said roughly. He'd been here, what? Less than a day, and already they were quarreling? He changed the subject. "Why don't we talk about you?"

"We can if you want," she offered.

"I have a confession to make," he said suddenly. "After I left the last time, I . . . looked you up."

"Looked me up?"

"In the library computer. Number One had researched *Columbia*'s crew after I was captured—"

"—so she could point out to you how old I was," Vina said incisively.

"Procedure," Chris corrected her. "To determine whether you were real or entirely illusion."

"I see."

"Anyway, I know you were born in Paris, that you trained to be a dancer. I found out everything I could about you from the official records—"

"Procedure?" Vina suggested.

"Well, yes, but . . ." Chris stopped. This wasn't going very well. "I wanted to know more, then and now. What were you doing when I was on Elysium?"

"You mean when I was almost twelve, or when you were?" she countered a little too quickly. She was not looking at him, but staring out to sea as the sun slipped below the horizon, as if this was the first sunset she'd ever seen, or the last. "You have to remember I'm that much older than you."

"It's only a few years," he said, perhaps too honestly—she managed to look hurt for a moment—then stopped himself. He was picking on her to avoid talking about himself. He changed his tone. "Besides, what is time here? It's meaningless. You can start your narrative at the same age as me, or even make yourself younger."

She shook her head. "No. That wouldn't be fair, don't you see? I have to tell it just as it happened, match you year for year." She eyed him curiously. "You were trying to discover if I'm vain. It was a test, wasn't it?"

"And not a very worthy one," he admitted. "I'm being defensive. And I still can't wrap my mind around . . . All right, then. What were you doing when I was almost twelve?"

He watched her calculate the numbers in her head. "Let's see . . . that was the year I signed on for my first deep-space voyage. But I'll need to give you a little background first . . ."

As a child, Vina never realized what an advantage growing up in Paris was. The city was as much a center of culture as it had been since the twelfth century, and would continue to be well into the twenty-third, but to her it was simply home. She took it for granted that everyone spent their days in art museums and antique shops and bookstores and charming little cafés, their nights at the theater or the opera.

Her father was a dancer. Born in Brussels, he first danced with and later became choreographer for the Ballet Russe, and married one of the most famous pastry chefs in Paris. Her mother was what one of her patrons called *"une petite dynamo,"* a small blond bundle of energy who rose with the dawn every morning to supervise a patisserie that catered to some of the most important people in the City of Light, not least of whom were the many species who comprised the United Federation of Planets, whose diplomats lived and worked in and around the city-within-a-city that was the Palais de la Concorde. That large high-rise on the Champs-Elysées, the flow of aircars going to and fro, and the exotic looking creatures in their various coutures stepping in and out of it, was as mundane to the little elf-child with the winsome personality as the rest of the city surrounding it.

Following her mother from the time she could walk, Vina knew the grounds and corridors of those edifices well. One Federation President, struck by the fragile beauty and bright wit of the little girl with the spun-sugar hair and her father's grace (she'd begun ballet classes at the age of three), had promised Vina a castle of her very own if she ever visited her homeworld, and even the very serious young Vulcan attaché could not hide the twinkle in his eye at the sight of her, solemn as a judge, carrying one of her mother's special confections, all whipped cream and chocolate curls, into one of the reception halls.

Hers was a dream childhood marred only by schoolwork, which she did in between dance classes, growing up in a house where the most delectable smells floated up from the ground floor where the patisserie was, safe in the embrace of a loving family. It wasn't that she wasn't bright in school—

in fact, the work came easily to her—there just wasn't any particular thing she was interested in.

She had almost enough talent to be a professional dancer, her teachers told her father when she was twelve, but she lacked a certain discipline that would have taken her to the next level and, more important, she lacked fire. Her battements were technically perfect, but almost absentminded, and the tug between live performance and its replacement with CGI, which had begun before she was born, made her wonder if this was any kind of career. When, at seventeen, her teachers told her she didn't have to continue, she was actually relieved. Though what she was going to do with the rest of her life suddenly loomed too large to think about, so she didn't.

Instead, she fell in love with Theo.

TALOS IV

"I'd been involved with boys my age," Vina explained. She'd gotten bored with the beach house scenario, and Pike had agreed to her suggestion that they take one of the hovercars out of the garage and go for a drive up the coast. "But they were just that . . . boys, all testosterone and desperation. Theo was older than I, stable, centered, and so very brilliant—a full professor before he was twenty-five. He knew who he was and what he wanted. I was impressed. It's hard to impress a girl who grew up in Paris."

"An egghead," Chris Pike guessed, taking the 'car around a hairpin curve, enjoying its responsiveness beneath his hands too much to put it on cruise control. The 'car was an antique, of the kind that responded to road surfaces and hovered on a cushion of air less than a foot above the tarmac, requiring real hands-on skill which, in this reality, came naturally to him. "Somehow I can't see you falling for an egghead. Or maybe I can. By the way, where are we? This looks like Earth, but I never thought to ask you where your aunt had her beach house. Or are we someplace else entirely?"

"It's Earth," she told him. She was wearing a long silk scarf that fluttered out behind her in the back draft from the open moon roof. "We're in Lebanon, on the coast just north of Beirut. Do you smell the cedars?"

Chris Pike's knowledge of Earth history beyond a certain point was eclectic at best. He remembered something about this part of the world being reduced to rubble in a series of wars some three hundred years ago, or was it two hundred? In any event, from what he could see around him—to their right a dark, stately evergreen forest dotted with white-columned houses built into the cliffsides and gleaming in the moonlight, to the left a sheer drop to the foaming Mediterranean below—the scars had long since healed over.

"I'm sorry," he said, "I interrupted you. You were telling me about Theo."

Vina nodded. At first, immediately after the crash, she'd thought of him constantly—the Talosians had used her memories of him to gain access to her mind—but she hadn't thought of him in years. She told herself she would not cry, not after all this time.

"I spent a few years after high school flitting around, unsure what I wanted. Learned languages, dabbled in theater, became a licensed pilot, would you believe it? Daddy offered to stake me to my own little charter company, but oh, no, that was too much responsibility for me! I didn't want to be tied down to anyone or anything.

"So I flew other people's ships, mostly on tourist runs to Luna. Most of my 'customers' were visiting diplomats from all over the Federation. For a while the junior Centaurian ambassador hired me as his personal pilot. We . . . became involved, briefly. When the affair crashed and burned, so did my flying career. I needed a change.

"So, being a creature of extremes, I registered at the university and became a bookworm. Took courses in *everything,* with no focus toward a career. The only reason I ended up in Theo's geology class was because I registered too late and was shut out of something else. I couldn't even tell you what that other course was . . ."

"And you fell for one of your professors," Chris said, filling in the gaps. "Geology, though. That can be a very dry subject. Particularly for a cultured little prima ballerina who could have gone to live in a castle on a faraway world."

Vina didn't speak. She was watching the scenery flow by.

"I'm guessing the relationship went south a long time before you met me," Pike said, then remembered she'd been alone on Talos for eighteen years before his arrival. He winced at his own stupidity, but Vina didn't seem to notice. Maybe there was someplace she went inside her own head whenever something painful happened that she didn't want to deal with. "I'm sorry. That was crass."

"It was a long time ago." Vina smiled weakly, which told him she'd registered, and felt, everything he'd just said.

Pike watched the moonlit ribbon of road for a long moment, wondering what he could possibly say next that wouldn't sound cruel.

"Ask you something?" he said finally, trying to make it sound light.

"Anything," Vina answered.

"What the hell did you see in a rube like me? Really, what was the attraction?"

Vina laughed then, and he realized he'd never heard her laugh before. It was a sound like bells, but genuine, and it suited her.

"Someone who tried to hide his own intellect under the

guise of being a rube," she said. "A starship captain, a leader of men, at home on worlds all over known space. You were anything but a rube."

"Then I'd suggest you don't know my kind very well," Pike said. "Some starship captains—"

"I didn't fall for 'some starship captains,' just you," Vina interrupted him. "Remember what you said about me so long ago? That I was exactly the kind of woman you'd be attracted to? The reverse was also true. You were exactly the kind of man I'd find irresistible."

A troubled look crossed her face then. Even in the moonlight he could see it, or maybe only sense it.

"We can change the subject, if you want," Pike suggested.

"No, let me finish," Vina said, and the frown faded, replaced by a look of determination. "Once I've told the whole story . . . to another human . . . perhaps it will finally make sense . . ."

Objectively, geology might seem like a dry subject, but the gangly young professor with the wavy dark hair and a voice like velvet made it fascinating. Or maybe it was her fascination with him that made it interesting. Vina would never know for sure. After that one course with him, though, she transferred to other professors' classes. She didn't want either of them to run afoul of the ethics against faculty dating students. Because he was as interested in her as she was in him.

"He was boyish," she told Chris now. "More than a decade older than I was, but something about his enthusiasm made me want to mother him. I admired his mind, and I felt safe in his arms. It wasn't some great passionate affair, but it was comfortable.

"Can we stop here?" she asked suddenly, indicating a turnoff overlooking the sea. They never seemed to be too far from the sea. "I want to look at the stars."

Pike obliged, bringing the car to a gentle stop and sliding the convertible top back. They were far enough away from any city lights and, as if on cue, the moon began to slip down the sky, leaving them to the stars. Vina leaned back against the headrest, her head tilted upward, talking as much to the stars as to her companion.

"We traveled together, Theo and I. I became his archivist and assistant. There were expeditions leaving all the time, stretching the limits of explored space." She began pointing out specific lights in the sky, ticking off their names as she did. "I've been to that one, and that one and . . . oh, the other one's only visible in the southern sky . . . Where is Elysium?" She was looking at Pike now. "I don't think you told me the name of its primary."

"It only had a number then," Chris said tightly. He'd hoped they could stay away from his memories for a while. Something else he'd noticed was that when either of them was reliving their own memory, the other couldn't participate. He'd tried to see Paris through Vina's eyes, tried to see her as a little girl, but couldn't; he'd had to rely exclusively on her words. He wondered if it was his reluctance to show her everything about his past that excluded him from seeing hers. "After I . . . left . . . they gave it a name, but I don't know if I ever found out what it was."

"You mean after you were accepted at the Academy?" Vina guessed. She doubted very much that a Starfleet officer would not know the name of Elysium's star, but if he chose not to tell her, that didn't matter. Chris's hands tightened on the steering wheel until his knuckles went white. He was trying mightily not to go back into that particular memory just yet. Vina seemed not to notice.

"I was just thinking, when you were talking about the earthquakes, that it's too bad Heston never met Theo," she went on. "He might have been able to offer him a second opinion he'd accept. Theo could be very persuasive, you might remember."

Her words brought Chris out of his reverie.

"How would I remember that?"

Vina wasn't looking at him, but rather at the silk scarf, which she'd taken off and was twisting nervously in her hands. Her voice trembled slightly.

"Of course, the man you met was just a projection of what he would have been like if he'd lived, but they did an uncannily good job . . ."

"Theo," Chris repeated the name, and finally the penny dropped. "Not Dr. Theodore Haskins—?"

"—of the American Continent Institute . . ." they said together.

Pike remembered his "encounter" with Haskins at the survivors' camp—the illusion of a survivors' camp—before the Talosians drugged him and secreted him beneath the surface.

"He seemed like a nice old guy," he said before he realized what he was saying.

Vina wore a bemused expression. "That 'nice old guy' wasn't quite so old when I knew him . . ."

Suddenly everything he'd said a moment ago about being a rube seemed hopelessly true. Chris hadn't felt this flummoxed in the presence of a female since Silk. He all but leapt out of the aircar, and strode to the edge of the fieldstone wall at the cliff's edge and back before he trusted himself to speak.

"Vina, I'm sorry. I don't know where to put myself. Everything I say must seem designed to hurt you, but that's the last thing I want to do. This whole time distortion of here and now and then and your being younger than me and older than me and . . ."

". . . and you struggling mightily to keep me from intruding into your memories," she said.

"Was it that obvious?"

She nodded without speaking, patted the seat he'd leapt out of, and he stopped acting like a fool and came to sit beside her.

"I'll make you a deal," she said. "I won't pester you to tell me what terrible thing happened in your childhood—because there was some terrible thing; the way you reacted to the Talosians' first attempts to control you made that clear—but you'll tell me in your own good time. Now, we can be quiet and just drive back to the villa, or we can wish ourselves there in an instant, or go anywhere or do whatever you want."

"Or we can finish telling our stories."

"Or that. In my case, there isn't much else to tell." Her voice took on a dreamy quality. She lolled her head back and was once more studying the stars. "Part of Theo's appeal was that, like my diplomats, he'd been everywhere. But in his case it was about exploring uninhabited worlds, worlds that might be suitable for colonies, just like Elysium. For all I know, Elysium might have been one of the worlds he mapped for the institute. He was a visiting professor at the university until the institute could get another expedition together. I was still finishing my degree when he hired me as his assistant. On most voyages, I was the youngest member of the team . . ."

The teams might be composed of a dozen or more—geologists, astronomers, biologists and entomologists, paleontologists and zoologists and speleologists, oh my—under the aegis of groups like the American Continent Institute, the Olduvai Society, the Aldebaran Rock Hounds, and any one of a score of others, all under contract to the Federation to explore one uncharted planet after another, categorizing rocks and minerals, flora and fauna.

A group would form at a starbase, bunk on a starship

patrolling a region, visit a previously unexplored world, hitch a ride back to the starbase when the starship came by again, then go their separate ways, only to regroup—losing some members, adding others—the next time there was a potential colony, or source of mineral wealth, that needed cataloging.

It was a gypsy life under the stars of worlds where no human had trod before, with tales told around campfires nightly to the tune of many human musics and the imbibing of various human beverages.

"People think scientists are dull," Vina said. "Nothing could be further from the truth. We worked hard by day, and partied hard at night. The stories I heard, the people I got to know . . . they were my extended family."

"Some of them were 'there' when my crew and I first beamed down," Pike guessed.

Vina nodded. "They kept me company during the early months, when I was too damaged to move. The Talosians saw to that. They exactly captured each of the scientists who was aboard *Columbia*, replicating them from the data they salvaged from the library computer, and from what I knew about each of them."

Her eyes glistened with tears in the starlight.

"We were heading home. Theo and I had asked the captain to marry us on the return voyage. We were passing the Talos Star Group . . ."

There was a long silence.

"There's something about ships named *Columbia* . . ." Pike said softly, not knowing what else to say.

"Sometimes the biggest mistake we make when we're young," Vina said, her face turned away from him so he couldn't read her expression, though her voice told him she was weeping, "is in thinking we have our whole lives ahead of us. If I'd known . . ."

She turned toward him then. "You don't know how painful it was to act out the illusion they created when you beamed down that first time. To see Theo as the mature man he'd never have a chance to be, while I had to pretend to be someone he thought of as a child . . ."

Chris could picture the old man now, hear his voice, see him chucking Vina under the chin as if she were a favorite child: "This is Vina. Her parents are dead. She was born almost as we crashed."

"Your parents . . ." Chris said now, but couldn't finish.

"It was a lie, obviously. My parents never left Earth. For all I know, *Maman* is still delivering fresh croissants to the Federation commissary every morning, and Daddy is planning yet another production of *Coppelia*. They'd be quite elderly now. The shock of seeing me, if I decided to return from the dead . . ."

She shook her head, unable to finish the thought.

"I told you the Talosians made mistakes that first time. They were so frantic to capture you, to win you over, the whole thing had an air of improvisation . . ."

Chris really didn't know what to say to that, so he said nothing. The road among the cedars was becoming oppressive. "Would you mind if we ended this and did something else?" he asked finally.

Vina shook her head. "Not at all."

The aircar dissolved around them; so did her silk scarf.

He thought of the homestead on Elysium and immediately it took shape around him. He could see from the expression on Vina's face that she saw it, too. He wondered how her presence would affect his memory of the place and what had transpired there. He searched his mind for an image of a petite blond woman—an adult when he was a child—and couldn't remember her.

As if he were walking through a gradually clearing mist, Pike saw the familiar half-timbered two-story ranch house take shape, though it seemed smaller than he remembered it. There were the flowering shrubs Willa had persuaded to grow around the foundation, and Charlie's jellyplants. There were the outbuildings, the barn and the storage silos which, ultimately, were never used to store anything, the paddock for the horses, and of course the infernal Gizmo. What he saw next startled him.

He was standing outside the scene with Vina, watching himself as a boy. It was like looking at a family video, though he couldn't remember anyone taking images of him at this time, and even if they had, they'd have been lost in what happened later.

"It's the next phase," he heard her say beside him. He didn't remember how long they'd been holding hands. "The Magistrate and the others . . . they're getting used to you. The first time you were here, you spent so much time fighting them, they never got a chance to really learn you . . ."

As they watched, young Chris emerged from the house, the screen door slamming behind him as he raced across the yard to the paddock, where he climbed the fence and whistled to Maia, who was not yet sleek and fat with pregnancy. His glance moved inevitably toward the Gizmo, and he could see it was only a fraction of the size it ultimately became.

So the tape has been rewound, he thought. This was before the bad things happened, maybe even before Charlie came.

"Oh, look at you!" Vina said softly, a smile in her voice. "You're adorable!"

"Adorable—?" he snorted. "People said I was a good-looking kid, but—"

"Adorable," she repeated. "I want to just grab you and hug you and ruffle that gorgeous wavy hair!"

"At that age I'd have hated it, but now . . ."

"Shh," Vina said. "Don't spoil the moment."

Pike studied his younger self and saw a sturdy, cheerful small boy, exuberant and running free, not the anguished preteen whose nights were spent awake and watchful (hearing Heston shift in his chair just below his window, scowling at things unseen in the dark, the laser rifle across his lap), and whose days were spent overhearing things he couldn't do anything about.

The Talosians' purpose, he supposed, was to have him relive this portion with Vina seeing it through his eyes, up until where he'd left off, and what happened next.

"I don't know," he said, taking Vina's arm and wanting to lead her—where? They could turn their backs on the homestead, but could they step out of the illusion? "I don't know if it's a good idea for you to see this part."

"Why not?" she asked with a sudden intensity. "It's what joins us, isn't it? What we saw in each other's eyes from the beginning . . . we've each had a baptism of fire . . ."

Toward the final months of her pregnancy, Charlie put Maia entirely in Chris's care. He fed her, groomed her, exercised her. His grades started to fall off, and Willa almost intervened, but watching him commune with the big chestnut mare over the eleven months of her pregnancy, she realized this was his greatest joy in what had become a fairly bleak existence for all of them, and she let him be. Even when, at Charlie's suggestion, he began sleeping on a cot outside Maia's stall during the last month, his mother had the wisdom to leave him alone.

He wasn't as lucky with Heston.

"We're going to solve this thing before the starship gets

back," the big man announced one morning barely a day after the doctor told Heston his leg was healed enough to walk on. Chris was alone in the barn, mucking out Maia's stall. "You can finish that later. Come with me."

Chris opened his mouth to argue, but saw the dangerous look in his stepfather's eye. He gave Maia a pat and the last lump of sugar in his pocket and followed Heston to the 'car. As they passed Charlie in the yard, Chris wanted to say something, but he wasn't sure what. He was aware of Charlie's eyes on them as the 'car lifted off and skimmed just above the low hills surrounding the homestead.

The 'car seemed to be flying low, lumbering as if it were carrying more than the recommended weight. A glance back at the cargo compartment told Chris it was packed full of strange equipment whose function he couldn't begin to guess. But he wasn't at all surprised when Heston settled the 'car on a natural ledge near the rim of the still-steaming volcano and began off-loading various contraptions.

Peering over the rim, Chris could see what Heston had been tinkering with all these weeks. He had no idea what it was supposed to do, but he couldn't help noticing how far down inside the cone it was, and that parts of it projected into the side, and down beyond where he could see.

"We're not going down there, are we?" he said, forcibly keeping the fear out of his voice.

"You bet we are," Heston said, handing him a rock climber's harness like the one he'd snapped on himself while the boy was peering over the rim. "Let's not waste any time. We've got a lot of work to do."

Heston showed him how to rappel down the treacherously sheer sides of the cone, bringing various pieces of equipment with them each time. Getting back up was harder, even empty-handed. The cone was the consistency of glass in some places, crumbling and scattering cinders in others. His stepfather had been doing this long enough to make it look easy, but Chris was struggling, trying not to notice the impatient way Heston scowled at him when he'd once again beaten him to the top.

For the rest of the morning and well into the afternoon, he and Heston transported the contents of the cargo bay down to the construction point midway down inside the cinder cone. The ambient temperature grew hotter the farther down they went, and no matter how much he drank, Chris couldn't replenish his sweat fast enough. He no longer wondered if he was imagining the volcano suddenly erupting, spewing lava toward them and swallowing them whole, or if it was really happening.

Heston worked like a madman, stopping neither to rest, eat or drink. Every time Chris stopped for water or an energy bar to keep from shaking with hunger, Heston would glower at him, wiping sweat and black volcanic ash off his face, not saying anything, but implying that he thought Chris was weak for having to stop.

"Mind telling me what we're doing?" the boy asked sullenly after Heston had assigned him to bring the rest of the stuff down while he went to work, hammering and soldering, and the silence, punctuated only by banging and sawing and grunts of "hand me that" and "bring the red container down next," had gone on for several hours.

"Making a pact with Nature," Heston said tightly, fitting an angled bit of pipe into place. "The Neworlders treat her like a jealous god, always tiptoeing around her. Me, I treat her as an equal. We understand each other, we work together, we both benefit."

"What's the benefit to Nature if we harness the volcano?" Chris wanted to know, but Heston didn't answer. He jerked his chin in the direction of the 'car.

"You're slacking. There are three more containers up there."

"How about I just secure them and lower them in a sling instead of having to bring them down by hand?" Chris asked.

Heston scowled. "If your rig starts to sway and strikes the side, you can damage the container. Maybe rip it open and lose everything. Lazy as well as slacking. Get up there and get busy!"

It was half in Chris's mind to pull himself up to the rim, his arms and shoulders aching from the labor, find an accessible slope to get down to the base of the mountain, and keep walking, back to the homestead, which he'd estimated was only a couple of miles away, though working his way through the foothills would make it almost twice the distance. He wasn't supposed to know how to drive the aircar, though he could in a pinch. But as if anticipating rebellion, Heston had removed the starter and sealed it up in a pocket of his shirt.

Still, as he stood there for a long moment holding a case full of small parts and looking down at the now doll-sized figure of his stepfather scurrying and tinkering like some ancient caveman designing a trap for some unspecified prey, Chris was tempted.

"What a bully!" he heard Vina say beside him. "I'd have told him to stuff it and gone home."

"Remember what you told me about how the Talosians kept at you and at you until they wore you down?" Chris said a little testily.

"I'm sorry," she said. "It's your memory. I'll be quiet."

Three more containers, he told himself, *and then I'm gone. He can't keep me here!* He realized his stepfather intended to drill straight into the core of the volcano.

"Special alloy . . ." he was muttering when Chris arrived on the ledge. ". . . can withstand temperatures that would melt most metals. Had to go through all manner of maneuvering to get it here, bribes to have it brought down in a shuttle instead of beamed in. Here, hold this."

"How many times have you done this?" Chris asked, choosing his words carefully.

"Several dozen," Heston muttered. "You're wasting time. There are still two more containers."

"I don't mean by remote, or from space," Chris continued doggedly, not moving. "I mean by hand, like we're doing now."

Heston wasn't looking at him, but at the contraption he was working on. "This technique has been employed for over three hundred years," he said between clenched teeth. "I'm not about to let some kid tell me—"

"But you've never done it this way yourself," Chris persisted.

There was an ominous silence. The heat was getting to him. He wiped his brow uselessly, trying not to look down at the seething cauldron that seemed to be beckoning to him. When he looked at Heston again, the big man had his high beams on him.

"If Starfleet and those damn Neworlders hadn't balked me, I wouldn't need to—dammit, why am I wasting my time trying to explain this? If you were smarter, if you paid attention, you wouldn't need to ask all these questions," Heston said narrowly, twisting something into place and wiping his brow again. His face and hair and clothes were completely covered in black ash now; only his eyes and teeth gleamed through, giving him a maniacal look. "Stop stalling and bring down the next load!"

Chris absorbed the insults, his mind as numb to them by now as his arms and shoulders were to the climber's harness. Up on the rim again, he scanned his surroundings. From this elevation there was nothing but rolling hills, covered with virgin forest, as far as the eye could see. He'd been careful to watch what direction they'd come from this morning and, watching the sun slide down the sky, thought he could find his way home.

But what if that was the wrong thing to do? Maybe if he stayed, he could talk some sense into Heston or, barring that, drop something or break something so Heston couldn't finish his infernal device. His stepfather had already called him incompetent; he could absorb whatever other abuse he might aim at him, if it prevented something dangerous from happening.

But as if reading his mind, Heston was watching him very closely this time.

"Explain it to me," Chris suggested, suddenly reaching a decision. "Tell me what you're doing and why, and maybe I can understand it."

"Or try to sabotage it," Heston said knowingly. "Just do as you're told!"

Was he letting his hurt feelings cloud his vision? Chris wondered. He reminded himself that Heston had terraformed entire planets before they came here. If he didn't know what he was doing, who would? Besides, his mother believed in him. But his mother was blinded by love, Chris reminded himself. Or was she? After that conversation he'd overheard between her and Charlie—

Thinking of Charlie reminded him of another conversation he'd overheard, this one between Charlie and Heston, about "breaking" the yearlings.

"No need to break 'em," Charlie was arguing. "If you gentle 'em, you end up with a much better horse."

"Yeah, after five years!" Heston grumped. "You can break a horse to saddle in an afternoon. Don't tell me my business!"

It was the difference, Chris realized, between what Heston was doing right now, trying to force Nature to his will too quickly and haphazardly, and waiting for the Starfleet engineers to do it right. Setting down the second to last container where Heston could reach it, Chris hauled himself back to the rim, as if to get the last one, turned on his heel and quietly started to walk away. It would be dark soon, and Heston hadn't eaten or rested all day. He'd have to quit and come home, and then Willa could talk some sense into him.

If she would even bother. Remembering the scene in the kitchen, Chris wondered if Willa would leave Heston for Charlie. As much as he loathed Heston right now, it somehow didn't seem right. Weary and confused, he wondered if any of the adults in his world could be trusted.

His thoughts were shattered by Heston's voice. With a madman's instinct, he had guessed what Chris was planning, pulled himself back up to the rim, and was bearing down on the boy, his look murderous. "Where do you think you're going?"

"I was just catching my breath," Chris said, trying to sound offended, but he didn't know how to lie; he'd never had to before. It was half in his mind to tell Heston what he knew about his mother and Charlie, but what *did* he know, really? And how could he betray his mother to a crazy man?

"You don't fool me!" Heston growled, looming over him. "You were going to walk away!"

"Yes, I am!" Chris clenched his fists. His anger flared, and he couldn't stop himself. "This is crazy, and I'm not helping you anymore!"

"Who are you calling crazy?" Heston grabbed his shirt, spittle flying. "Don't you dare disobey me, you little bastard! I can make your life a living hell!"

"You already have!"

Where he got the strength from, Chris would never know. He shoved Heston as hard as he could. The big man's heels slipped on the cinders and he fell backward, tearing Chris's shirt and losing his grip, landing on his butt, his boot heels scrabbling. Without looking back, Chris half-ran, half-slid down the treacherous slope, then set off in what he hoped was the direction of home, running until he couldn't run anymore.

About an hour later, staggering from exhaustion, barely able to see his hand in front of him—he'd tried raising the homestead on his personal comm, but metals in the volcanic core seemed to be interfering with it, and he'd used its ambient light for guidance until the battery ran down—he thought he heard the careful plod of hooves. Was he only imagining that light up ahead?

"Christopher?" Charlie emerged through the woods, riding Jenna, with Petula on a lead.

"Heston . . ." the boy managed hoarsely, leaning against Petula's welcoming side for a moment before pulling himself up, putting aside the fact, in his desperation, that he couldn't trust Charlie either. He thought of all the times he'd gone to the barn looking for him to confide in whenever Heston was being particularly oppressive. He hadn't done that since the morning in the kitchen; if Charlie noticed, he hadn't mentioned it. Chris shook the thoughts out of his head. No time for that now. ". . . the volcano . . ."

"We'll worry about Heston later," Charlie said and, young as he was, Chris couldn't help wondering if there wasn't more than one meaning to those words. "Maia's in labor. She's fine," he said seeing the boy's head come up in spite of his exhaustion. "But we need to get back. Just hold on to the pommel; I'll lead her.

"Don't fall asleep on me now . . ." Charlie's voice was steady, reassuring. "I don't need to be picking you up off the trail if you can't hold on. There's coffee and sandwiches in the saddlebag. Your mom says you're too young to drink coffee, but we'll worry about that later, too . . ."

Somehow Chris found his second wind by the time they reached the homestead. He would worry about the adults and their complicated world some other time. Here, at least, there was a problem he could do something about.

After so long in the dark woods, the light in the barn seemed unnaturally bright. Chris rubbed his eyes, leaning against the wall of the big box stall Charlie used for birthing, talking soothingly to Maia, who was still on her feet, but breathing with a deep rasping sound, listening to the life process transpiring inside her.

"Charlie?" The moment seemed sacred; Chris was afraid to raise his voice. "Let me stay, please? I promise I won't get in the way."

And I'll try to forget, at least for now, what I heard you and my mother talking about . . .

"Get in the way?" Charlie echoed him. He was washing his hands up to the elbows in the utility sink. "I expect you to give me a hand."

Even years later, the details of that night and part of the next morning would never arrange themselves in chronological order in Chris's mind. He remembered at one point that Willa brought him and Charlie food and blankets in case either of them had time to eat or sleep, but he didn't remember doing either.

All he remembered really was holding Maia's head in his lap after she'd gone ponderously to her knees and then rolled to one side, laboring in earnest—he'd learned from Charlie how vulnerable a horse was on the rare occasion it was off its feet—and Charlie moving about like a shadow, unspeaking except to murmur occasionally to Maia, animated and seemingly tireless, doing whatever it was he needed to do.

Finally, after nearly twelve hours, Maia presented the world with a spindly little bay colt with a black mane and tail and a white blaze from his forehead down over his nose, who immediately wobbled upright on his matchstick legs and staggered a few steps before toppling over beside his weary mother, who pulled herself to her feet, inspected him thoroughly, and began to clean him vigorously. And Chris, beside himself with amazement, was still whispering.

"Charlie? He's okay, isn't he?"

"Better than okay," Charlie said, as the little guy began to nurse. "I'd say perfect."

"It's a colt. Heston said if it was a colt . . ."

It was the first time he'd thought of Heston since he'd left him. He realized he had no idea where his stepfather was, whether he'd succeeded in his lunatic mission or given up and come home, or whether the volcano had opened its maw like a comic book character and swallowed him whole. He also realized he didn't care.

"I know," Charlie said. "Come here now and give me a hand."

Maia was still cleaning the little colt, who occasionally squeaked in protest when her tongue got too rough. Charlie showed Chris how to check the afterbirth for tears before disposing of it. He'd also wanted the boy out of the stall until the colt had finished nursing, then he motioned him back inside the enclosure.

Moving very slowly, Chris followed the instructions Charlie had given him weeks ago in preparation for this moment. He talked softly to Maia, just as he always did, praising her for the wonderful job she'd done. Warily, she seemed to be keeping one eye on the colt even as she nudged Chris with her nose in the old familiar way, then began nibbling at his jeans pockets looking for sugar.

Still soothing her, Chris gave her the sugar and a couple of carrots, then, hardly daring to breathe, he moved toward the colt, running his hands over the little guy, touching him everywhere. Still watchful, Maia seemed to approve. When

Chris looked up at Charlie, his eyes were twinkling, and he too nodded his approval.

"Okay, now," he said. "Come on out and let mother and son have some quiet time. You can come back in an hour and repeat what you've just done. You'll do that every day. Maia already considers you family. Soon the colt will, too."

Reluctant to let the moment end, Chris did as he was told. In a rare moment of affection, Charlie put his arm around his shoulder as they walked back to the house.

"I don't know about you, but I'm thinking of hotcakes and sausage and fresh orange juice and maybe a side of home fries . . ." he said.

Chris ate as if he hadn't eaten in days. He felt as if he were floating. For the first time in a long time, something had gone right.

7

ELYSIUM

For the next few days, Chris's world devolved down to Maia and the colt. Every hour he visited them, repeating the ritual Charlie had shown him immediately after the colt was born.

Sometimes he would run a soft brush over the colt's back. Other times he would pick up his feet, all the time talking reassuringly to the colt and to Maia. The next time he would repeat these motions, then set a towel or a small blanket on the colt's back so that when the time came he would accept a saddle. Charlie had made a special baby halter, and he would put the colt's head in that for a few minutes, waiting a little longer each time before removing it, until the colt accepted it.

"What you're doing is known as imprinting," Charlie explained. "You're allowing mother and son to bond, but you're making sure you and the colt bond, too. You're family now. Any idea what you'll name him?"

Focused on the colt, Chris shook his head.

"Didn't think so," Charlie said, moving off to leave the two of them alone. He had one more foal to deliver in the coming weeks; Chris was on his own now. "When he's ready, he'll tell you."

A less perceptive kid might have wondered what that meant. Chris accepted it. He'd also decided to accept, or at least not think about, whatever dynamic was taking place among the adults. He'd been trying to find a way to talk to his mother, but didn't have the words for it. Maybe, as she'd told Charlie, she'd take some action once the starship returned.

Or maybe, Chris thought, it wouldn't even be necessary. Maybe Heston would starve to death poking at that volcano. Or maybe the volcano would finally have enough and poke back. He almost wished it would.

At this point in his young life, however, he'd decided he preferred horses to humans. Horses didn't keep secrets, or boss you around. They were what they appeared to be.

The next day he led Maia out to the paddock for the first time since the birth, the colt following her. The little guy's reaction to the sunlight and all that wide open space was something wondrous to behold.

At first he balked in the doorway, his long legs stiff, head thrown back, as if there were some actual physical barrier preventing him from moving. But seeing his mother make the transition into this alien environment, he started forward. A splash of sunlight fell across the white blaze on his forehead, and he startled, bunching his hooves together suddenly and leaping like a goat. Turning back to look at him, Chris laughed out loud.

The noise startled the colt a second time, and he bolted, and was soon tearing around the paddock like a wild thing. The two yearlings looked down their noses at the new arrival, forgetting they had once been as amazed at everything as he was.

"I showed them!" The sound of Heston's voice was little more than background noise to Chris now. He had no idea when his stepfather had returned, and didn't care. "Wait until those Starfleet engineers see the new readings. Evacuate us, give us another parcel of land as far away from the city as the Neworlders would have us? I don't think so!"

A few days later, when the starship returned and scanned the homestead from orbit, the engineers did indeed find that the water table had risen and the fault lines they had discovered on their last visit had apparently disappeared. The captain sent a landing party with tricorders to survey the entire sector, including the volcano, which showed some recent activity, but no sign of human intervention. Heston had done what he had said he would do, then dismantled his work so that no one could prove it. There was nothing Starfleet or the Elysium Council could do but let him be.

Chris avoided his stepfather for as long as he could, knowing a confrontation was inevitable. It wasn't easy. Possessed of a strange manic energy, Heston seemed to be everywhere except the barn, which was where Chris took refuge, working with the colt, grooming him, helping Charlie with the others. He would sneak into the kitchen when no one else was around, grab something from the food dispenser, and hurry out again. His schoolwork was forgotten. He went back to sleeping beside Maia's stall. Preoccupied with work, worry about Heston, and her growing pregnancy, his mother seemed not to notice. But Heston did, and went looking for him.

"You should have had more faith in me," the big man began, not bothering with pleasantries. Chris was grooming the colt, and didn't even look up. "Maybe I was a little harsh with you, but I knew what I was doing. It took me twice as long to dismantle what I'd done without you around."

"What you did was dangerous," Chris said evenly, currying the colt in long, steady strokes. "And against the law. The Council said—"

"To hell with the Council!" Heston growled, forcibly controlling his voice in case Charlie was around; he was still loud enough to make several of the horses lay their ears back. "Sometimes regulations are wrong. Did I solve the problem or didn't I?"

"You did," Chris answered reluctantly.

"Then I'll tell you this much, Goody Two-Shoes . . ." Heston abandoned any attempt at civility; his voice took on that all-too-familiar threatening tone again. "You show me up one more time, it's going to cost you. You're only raising that colt; I haven't said you can keep him. You keep up this defiant attitude, that's the least it's going to cost you!"

If Heston felt any embarrassment at bullying a twelve-year-old, it wasn't apparent. He strode away without giving Chris a chance to respond. It was the last meaningful conversation they would ever have.

The little colt with the white blaze grew and flourished. The challenge was finding a name for him.

"We could call him Blaze," Chris suggested to Charlie one late afternoon as they watched him try out his long legs in the paddock, the rays of the setting sun giving him a shadow several times his size. Whatever the dynamic among the adults, he decided, they could solve it for themselves. He needed Charlie's wisdom to raise the colt right; he would concentrate on that.

"Maybe," Charlie said quietly. Unlike most adults, Charlie could spend long periods of time just being quiet, not needing to fill the time with talk. "There's no hurry, though. Take your time."

As they watched, the colt startled at something—a shadow, a sound only he could hear—leapt into the air and raced around like a mad thing, then skidded to a stop and cocked his head to one side, ears and tail flicking, as if he was trying to remember something. He shook his head, and then did something Chris had never seen a horse do before.

"Well, I'll be . . ." Charlie said. "This little guy is a natural dancer!"

"How about Dancer?" Chris suggested, but Charlie put a hand on his arm to silence him.

"Just watch," he said.

They did. The little horse made moves, however inexpertly, that most horses had to be trained to for years. He waltzed, he sidestepped, he glided, then changed direction and began to strut, picking up his hooves and placing them down again delicately, all with a look of utter concentration on his face, as if it was the only way he could get those four long legs to work in coordination.

"Looks like he can do everything but tango," Charlie said appreciatively.

Chris felt a big grin spread across his face.

"Tango," he said quietly, and the name stuck.

In retrospect and with the benefit of hindsight, what happened next seemed self-evident, but at the time no one saw it coming.

It would be years before the true cause of the conflagration was known. Was it arson, as some suggested? Or simply nature, helped by shortsightedness, taking its course?

"Excessive oxygen enrichment," the official report would read. "Unforeseen interaction of transplanted Terran hybrid grass with climatological variances in a nonnative environment causing spontaneous combustion under dry conditions. Duplication of the event under laboratory conditions indicates . . ."

And so on. Dry bureaucratese to describe a conflagration that nearly destroyed a colony before it was contained.

Several of the evacuees, notably an adolescent girl named Silk, reported seeing a group of boys from the Neworlder settlement setting fires the day before in the brush on the border where Neworlder land abutted the Prescott holding. But the pattern of the main conflagration indicated it had actually spread away in an entirely different direction, and eyewitness reports were deemed inconclusive.

Sifting through the evidence provided by the charred and ruined land once the embers had cooled, investigators found several new steam vents spawned by the volcano at the southernmost edge of the Prescott holding. While they found no new magma flows, this did not indicate conclusively that there had not been, and did confirm that a few sparks or embers, or even the intense heat of a bubbling magma pool, might have been all that was needed to start the grasses on fire.

In summary, they concluded, the grass might have ignited spontaneously, as the result of human intervention, or sparked by a new outgrowth of the volcano, or any combination thereof. Two things only could be deduced. One, that these particular varieties of grasses ought not in future to be transplanted from Earth without careful testing under all possible planetary conditions and, two, that if the grass had not been growing on Elysium, either humans or the volcano might have produced a small conflagration or two, but not the maelstrom that resulted.

Sheets of flame roared up one hillside, crested, then flowed down the other side, destroying everything in their path. They devoured the acres of new trees that several homesteaders, following Heston's lead, had planted around their holdings, leapt over creeks and streams, slowed a bit at the well-irrigated fields of the Neworlders, but eventually gobbled them up as well, then headed for the houses. Traveling with the prevailing wind, the fire was difficult to battle. No sooner had fleets of shuttles from the city and volunteers on the ground contained it in one place than it sprang up in another.

Fighting brushfires was an antique art, not needed on Earth since the early part of the twenty-first century, and not prepared for on most colony worlds. With the growing number of settlements on Elysium, however, a requisition for fire containment technology had been submitted to the Federation Colonial Division for Environmental Safety only the week before. The subspace message had no doubt reached Earth by now, but the necessary equipment would be months in coming.

The sky was dark with smoke, the air hot and almost tangible. The sun shone a demonic red-orange, and the sky glowed eerily at night. Outdoors it was difficult to breathe.

Standing at the edge of the yard, too restless to stay indoors in spite of the smoke, Chris was startled by the sudden violent movement of the tall grass as far as the eye could see, and wondered if it meant more earthquakes, along with everything else. Instead, he watched in amazement as tens of thousands of the small native rodents, birds, and lizards, abandoning their primeval rivalry over food supply, leapt and scurried past him, around him, even over his feet in their haste to flee the destruction. He covered his face with his arms until they had passed, then stared off the way they'd come, curious to see how close the fire was.

"Don't go far!" Willa pleaded with him. "As soon as we find a way to move the horses, we're evacuating."

"All of us?" Chris asked pointedly, picking off a couple of stunned lizards still clinging to his shirt and jeans and watching them scuttle away.

"I don't know yet, Chris," his mother said.

She assembled them all, even Charlie, in the living room, and keyed in a map of the homestead on a flat screen in the center of the coffee table. The comm was on in the background, issuing up-to-the-minute reports on the status and location of the fire.

"I've modified the irrigation system to provide a continuous soaking on the entire perimeter," Willa said. Her voice was calm, but she couldn't help biting her lip occasionally. "The buildings are fireproofed; I saw to that. If it were just smoke we had to worry about, we could seal the barn and the house and keep the environmental controls cranking. But if the fire breaks through the irrigation system . . ."

"It shouldn't," Heston interrupted. "Not if you built it right."

Willa ignored the comment. "One way or the other, tomorrow Chris and I are evacuating. Charlie? What can be done about the horses?"

"If you tell me it's safe to seal that barn, I'd leave enough forage down for them for three or four days. But what concerns me is whether we'd be allowed back in, and whether or not the power supply can sustain uninterrupted. I've heard some of the outer homesteads lost power when the fire came through. Horses might be better off let loose to fend for themselves. Better than being locked up to suffocate or starve."

"You're awfully free with my property!" Heston said.

"I'm trying to save your property!" Charlie shot back.

"You keep them in that barn until I tell you otherwise!"

The shrill of the comm unit interrupted them.

". . . Evacuation to begin immediately. Each person permitted to bring whatever can be carried . . . Livestock to be secured and, if possible, retrieved after all human inhabitants have been safely removed . . . personal vehicles to remain grounded so as not to get in the way of official evacuation vehicles . . ."

There was a crackle of static, followed by a long silence. Charlie got to his feet.

"Let's go," he said to Chris.

Heston left the house with them, and Chris wondered if he was going to help them for once. No one was prepared for him to run toward one of the aircars and take off without a word of explanation to anyone.

Within minutes, they heard the explosion. Wherever he was going, whatever he had intended to do, Heston must have flown too close to one of the runnels of flame, and the 'car had gone up like a rocket.

The sound brought Willa out to the porch, and she stood stock-still, the knuckles of one hand pressed against her mouth, her other hand resting on the slight bulge of her pregnancy. She swayed for a moment, but did not cry out.

It all happened rather quickly after that.

Very large fires create their own wind, a searing sirocco that drives the flames before it, and feeds off them, whirling in circles, impossible to contain. By now what had been distant smoke was accompanied by ominous crackling sounds, and the wind.

Rescue shuttles were battling that wind. Chris watched as a formation of three soared by overhead, not stopping. Were there others in greater danger than they? The wind spun dust devils where the ground wasn't wet enough, flung ash and stinging cinders into their eyes.

Suddenly all the power went out.

Sources would later insist that it was to cut off excess oxygen supply from the environmental controls that was feeding the fire, but by now it didn't matter. The irrigation system stopped; the plashing water fell to a trickle. The flames raced beyond the perimeter, and headed for the last ring of hills protecting the homestead. The wind seemed to be sucking all the oxygen out of the air, and even with breather masks every breath was an effort.

Inside the barn, there was turmoil. Panicked, the horses reared and screamed, kicking out at the walls of their stalls, eyes rolled back in terror. Charlie heard the environmental controls click off and shook his head.

"Too little too late!"

As Chris watched him, it was clear Charlie had anticipated the worst and prepared for it. He began with the last stall at the rear and, using a soft piece of sacking as a blindfold, took Petula by the halter, calmed her, and led her toward the open door. He seemed to be listening to the air.

"Fire's currently traveling west to east," he told Chris. "They may be able to run out ahead of it."

He slid the towel off Petula's eyes, slapped her on the rump, and she was off.

"But we can't just—!" Chris stood between Maia and Tango, unable to bear the thought of letting them go.

Charlie didn't answer. He handed Chris a piece of sack-cloth for Maia, and went to open the hasp on the next stall.

His eyes stinging from more than the smoke, Chris was leading Maia out, Tango jostling beside her, when they heard the scream.

". . . the house . . ." he told Vina, his voice tight, as if even now, a lifetime later, it was hard to breathe. ". . . my mother was right, the house itself was fireproof, but the vegetation around it, and some of the contents . . . there were investigations and reports, reams of red tape after the fact . . . they're filed away somewhere . . . I've blocked the details out of my mind. But the house went up like it was made of paper, and my mother was inside . . ."

"Run, Chris, *run!*" Willa screamed, the wall of flame moving rapidly behind her, around her, the great wind it created whipping her clothes, embers catching in her hair as she screamed for him to flee, to get away.

Run he did, not away from her and the danger, which was what she wanted, but toward her, to save her, pull her out of the roofless wreckage of the house, save her, must save her . . .

He got as far as the burning porch, eyes swollen shut from the smoke. Blinded, he managed to grab the door handle, oblivious to the fact that it was so hot that the flesh of his hands would melt into it. The house imploded then, throwing him backward into the yard, his hands burned, his sleeves on fire. Somehow he staggered to his feet, slapping out the flames engulfing his arms, taking flesh with them, and would have tried again, though there was no sound from within now except the rush of flames—

—but a pair of powerful arms wrapped themselves around him, lifting his gangly twelve-year-old self bodily off the ground, dragging him not toward, but away.

"No, you don't!" the voice said gruffly, harshly. "You can't save her, son. It's too late . . ."

Chris fought then, kicking and clawing, howling like an animal, the screams of the panicked horses as the fire engulfed the barn drowning out the sounds that after a while it seemed only he could hear. The house was gone, his mother was gone, and the world was a wall of flame . . .

He couldn't breathe, except to cough. Something the size of an elephant was apparently sitting on his chest, and he couldn't get his eyes or hands to work at all. When he tried to sit up, something held him back. All he could do was hear.

". . . triox taking effect . . . vital signs stable . . . moving him now . . . Sir, you'll have to come now; we won't be coming back this way."

"You're forgetting something . . ." Was that Charlie's voice?

"Sir, I'm sorry . . . there's no more room. The shuttle's barely able to lift off as it is."

"She can handle the extra weight if you balance her right." There was a sound of large objects being moved across a metal surface. "You take the three of us, or just the boy. It's important."

Three of us?! Chris wondered. Had his mother survived somehow? Maybe by some miracle she'd been thrown clear of the house. He wished it wasn't so dark in here. He had to see.

"Charlie?" he tried to say, but his throat was closed from the smoke and it emerged as a croak, lost in the engine hum. The next thing he heard was the sounds of a life-signs monitor.

"Mom—!" He sat bolt upright, and was overcome with a wave of dizziness. He would have fallen off the diagnostic bed if Charlie hadn't been there.

"Easy," he said, easing him back down.

His eyes focused finally. "Where are we?"

"Starship sickbay."

"My hands—"

"Sterile dressings. Medical officer tells me the tissue has to rest overnight, then they'll treat you with regen tomorrow. And you have to rest, too. They'll only let me stay with you if you promise to stay put."

Chris looked Charlie over. He must have stayed with him

throughout. He'd sustained a few scrapes; his shirt was torn and covered with soot. His eyes were red-rimmed, and he wiped them frequently. *From the smoke,* Chris thought.

"You okay?" he asked.

"I've been worse," Charlie answered.

Chris swallowed hard. He knew the answer to the question he was about to ask, but he had to ask it anyway.

"Charlie? Where is she? You said 'three.' When we were rescued, you told them to take the three of us—"

The look in Charlie's eyes made him stop. For the first time since he'd appeared out of nowhere to change Chris's life, there was no mirth in them.

"I'm sorry, Christopher. I'm truly, truly sorry . . ."

The whole weight of it crashed down on him, and he sobbed like a baby, his tears soaking into Charlie's shirt.

His hands would heal in a day or two. But nothing would heal the pain in his heart.

TALOS IV

"Now I see why they failed with you the first time," Vina whispered, stroking his hair in the dark. "They should never have tried to terrorize you with fire. They couldn't know it would only make you stronger . . ."

That first time, his keepers had changed his surroundings so often and so abruptly that, even after he had figured out that everything except Vina and the four walls was an illusion (and he still wasn't entirely sure about Vina), it took him some time to adjust.

He found himself crouched on all fours, struggling to get to his feet, but the pain was too great. It distracted him, weakened him, made it impossible for him to do anything but try to fight it, though he knew it was useless, and that this time there would be no one to save him, and he was going to die.

He saw flames ripple through the fabric of his tunic, devour it like paper, begin to attack the flesh underneath; he could smell the all-too-familiar stink of burning flesh. Helplessly he beat his hands against the ground, trying to extinguish the flames, but that only seemed to make things worse. He told himself he would not cry out, he would not, even as the hoarse, agonal howl tore from his throat, a sound he hadn't made since—

Since I tried to save her. I tried, but I couldn't, I couldn't . . .

"If you continue to disobey," came the inexorable voice, with its prim superiority, its need to dominate, to scold, "from deeper in your mind there are things even more unpleasant."

The pain receded then, the illusion that he was trapped in an unquenchable fire—oh, he'd read the myths about a place called Hell, but descriptions on a page were pallid compared to the actual experience—his clothing and his very flesh burning, skin already burned away, sera leaching away in a process that could only lead to death (if he let himself believe even for a moment that they'd actually kill him, and of that he wasn't sure), ended as abruptly as it had begun. Christopher Pike gathered his thoughts, defiant. The Keeper had made a critical mistake.

More unpleasant? he wondered, in fact, from deeper in his mind, a place the Keeper hadn't yet been able to access, because the labyrinthine neural pathways of each human mind were unique. He pulled himself to his feet, murder in his eye. *No, now there you'd be wrong. Nothing can be more "unpleasant" to me than fire.*

"Why not put irresistible hunger in my mind?" he'd challenged them. "Is it because you can't?"

He had maintained the defiance for as long as he could,

not allowing them to get near the truth, which was that the way to reach him had always been fire. They hadn't learned that secret the first time. In sharing his deepest memories with Vina, had he given them too much this time?

"We sometimes make the mistake with aliens of thinking that just because they're superior to us in certain things, they are in everything." Vina was only a voice in the darkness, the tender touch of a hand against his brow. "They aren't, you know. They're just as fallible as we, only in different ways."

They lay in bed as if they were an old married couple talking over the events of the day, not two strangers caught in an eerie déjà vu telling each other their innermost thoughts. Had he really wept in her arms the way he had in Charlie's all those years ago? What must she think of him? Had the listening exhausted her as much as the telling had him? In any event, it was enough, for now. He propped himself up on one elbow, seeking out the shape of her in the dark, cradling her face in his free hand.

"You mean like when they 'repaired' you?"

"Yes. But not only that. Also in interpreting us, what we mean. When you first arrived, for example, they weren't used to you, to all that raw, male energy. All they had to go on about humans was *Columbia*'s memory banks, and me."

She sat up, cross-legged like a child, and took his hand between her own. "What a terrible thing, to lose your mother when you were so very young—! Did you ever find your father?"

"Well, yes, but that was much later."

"And you never went back to Elysium?"

"No. Years later I heard there was some kind of inquiry. Allegations that the Council had been negligent about evacuation procedures. I'm told that to cover up their own mistakes they made Heston Prescott some kind of hero. Named their second city after him. My mother had a street named after her in Elysium City; that was the best they could do for her. No, I never went back . . ."

LEAVING ELYSIUM

The fires ultimately consumed hundreds of thousands of acres, killed countless wild creatures, and displaced several settlements before it was contained, though mercifully there were only two human casualties. As the starship left orbit, the path of the conflagration was visible even from space. Chris insisted on seeing it.

The ship's surgeon released him from sickbay as soon as his hands were healed. Charlie came to pick him up. He was wearing a Starfleet uniform, and carrying another.

"I guessed at your size," he said, holding the unadorned gold shirt up against the boy's chest. Charlie's shirt, Chris saw, was red. "Captain has invited us up to the bridge once we've left orbit."

Chris shook his head vaguely. "Do we have to?"

"I told him you were grieving. Maybe in a day or two."

Too numb to question anything, he followed Charlie down the half-deserted corridors, where passing crew members murmured, "I'm sorry for your loss," and he thanked them. His mother would have wanted it that way. He wondered if any of the other colonists had been evacuated and whether they were on the ship, or if he and Charlie were the only ones. He had a thousand questions, but was too tired to ask them. When Charlie keyed in the combination to open the door into a two-man crew member's quarters, Chris took the bunk farthest from the door and jerked his chin toward the comm unit.

"Can I—*May* I watch us leave orbit?"

Charlie knew what the real question was. "Are you sure you want to?"

Chris nodded. "I want to see how bad it is."

He watched the planet recede with a kind of leaden resignation. The destruction was visible even from this distance, a vast charred scar across a once-pristine landscape. Chris stared until the ship shot into warp, his mind's eye filled with fire and his last glimpse of his mother's face. He wished he had died with her.

Seeing the look on the boy's face, Charlie wondered if he'd done the right thing. But he told himself it was better for Chris to see the reality, fix it in his mind, than to have it hidden from him so that for the rest of his life he would imagine it far worse than it actually was.

As if anything could be worse than losing your mother at such a tender age, Charlie thought grimly. He would keep his own loss to himself for now.

When there was nothing but the warp effect to see, Chris flicked off the commscreen, rolled over with his back to Charlie, and tumbled into a sleep like death.

8

2231: SOMEWHERE IN SPACE

He had no idea how long he slept curled in a fetal position with his face turned toward the bulkhead. When he woke, he found that Charlie had left him a note on the comm saying he'd be back at eighteen hundred hours, but Chris was to feel free to roam about the common areas of the ship, or ask a crew member for directions. The idea held no appeal for him, and he went back to his bunk, where he sat with his knees drawn up for a very long time, staring at nothing.

When Charlie did return, carrying a tray full of covered dishes, Chris barely glanced at him. Something smelled wonderful, but he didn't feel like eating. Charlie sat at the desk that doubled as a table for meals and broke the silence.

"How you feeling?" he ventured, trying to make it sound casual.

"How do you think I feel?" Chris's voice was raw and surly.

Charlie was doling out something Chris would later learn was called Engine Room Stew, its ingredients a never-ending mystery as each shift added new ingredients from the food dispensers, or from planets they had visited. "My guess is you're afraid to feel. Got it all sealed up inside, telling yourself you'll get to it later, hoping later never comes."

"That's not true!" the boy said too quickly.

"I had a word with the ship's surgeon," Charlie said, keeping his voice casual. "She says if you'd like to talk to somebody . . ."

"You mean a shrink? So I can feel better about what happened? I don't want to feel better!"

Charlie let that go. "There's something you need to know about your mother . . ."

"Don't you dare talk about my mother!" Chris snapped. "You don't know anything about her!"

Or maybe you know too much about her, and I don't want to know how much you know! was his next thought. What did it matter, if his mother was dead?

He turned away again, but Charlie could hear him crying. When the sound devolved down into a kind of soft hiccuping, he ventured into the room and sat on the edge of his bunk. The boy felt the weight and shrank away from him. Charlie touched his shoulder lightly and he shrugged him off.

"I'm sorry, Chris . . ." Charlie began, but got no further.

"You had no right to drag me out of there!" Chris's voice was muffled by the pillow. "I hate you!"

"Do you still think you could have saved her?"

Chris sat up abruptly, fury in his face. "Yes! No . . . I don't know . . . but it was my choice to make, not yours!"

"And because it would have been easier for you to die trying to rescue her than live knowing you couldn't," Charlie said quietly.

"Somebody should have done something!"

"You're right!" Charlie agreed, an edge to his voice. "Your stepfather should have acted like a responsible adult, and when it was clear he wouldn't, someone should have intervened. Maybe I should have reported him to the Council. Or your mother should have left him and taken you with her. Heston would be just as dead, but she'd still be alive."

"Don't you dare try to blame this on my mother—!"

"I'm not!" Charlie said, loudly enough to make the boy twitch, then lowered his voice to its usual soft-spoken level. "Adults make mistakes, Christopher. All of us should have done things differently. I thought of leaving as soon as the first foals were born. I stayed because I thought I could do something. We all failed you, Chris. There's no way around that."

Chris had no answer for that.

"One thing's for certain, though," Charlie went on, "and it's that none of what happened is your fault."

Chris started to say something, then forgot what it was. What sense did it make for him to blame Charlie for saving his life?

He thought about those last moments before the house caught fire, remembered the trembling weight of Tango leaning against him, his eyes rolled back with fear, his nostrils flaring against the smoke. He'd been just about to release him, send him and Maia out ahead of the fire . . .

Too little too late. Maia was gone, Tango was gone, the homestead destroyed, and his mother dead. All he had left was Charlie.

Leaving him alone to sort things out, Charlie had gone back to dishing out the stew. Suddenly Chris realized how hungry he was. When had he eaten last, and what? Everything had tasted like ash in those last few days. His legs as wobbly as a newborn colt's, he staggered over to sit on the other side of the desk from Charlie, and began to eat, cleaned his plate, and helped himself to seconds. The fog he'd been under since he woke in sickbay began to clear, and he realized he needed the answers to an awful lot of questions.

"How many of the other colonists are heading back to Earth?"

"Just a few," Charlie said. "Most just took temporary shelter in the city. They'll be going home as soon as it's safe. The Neworlders decided to stay."

Silk was safe, then, if growing up a Neworlder could be considered safe. Chris realized they'd never be able to communicate again.

"So Heston was right. They're going to take over the whole planet."

Charlie shrugged. "Maybe. That's not our concern."

"Is that why we're going back to Earth?"

"Not exactly," Charlie said, watching with approval as Chris finished his second plateful. If he could eat, he could heal, and the wonderful thing about youth was that, nurtured properly, it could heal quickly. "I started to tell you about your mother . . . during the last month or so, after Heston was acting so smug about taming the volcano . . . she and I had a little conversation about you."

That's not the only thing you had a conversation about! Chris thought, but tried mightily not to let it show on his face.

"She asked me . . . if anything was to happen to her—and by that she meant her and Heston—if I would see that you got back to Earth. She even had a legal document drawn up . . . you can read it if you want to . . ." Charlie dug into his personal kit and produced a computer disk.

Chris shook his head. He doubted he could make sense of some long-winded official document.

"I'll take your word for it," he said. "What happens when we get back to Earth?"

"I understand you've got an aunt and uncle in Argentina . . ."

Chris had met them a few times, found his aunt clingy and neurotic, his uncle domineering and disapproving of his mother's lifestyle. Their visits hadn't been pleasant ones.

Charlie watched the despair return to the boy's face. "It's not a decision you have to make right now. Your mother named me as your guardian. When we reach Earth, you can stay with me while you think it over."

A few minutes ago, Chris had been running from a horrific past, into an unknown future. Suddenly the future seemed to have some sort of definition, though he couldn't entirely see what it was. Still, he had choices, which was more than he'd had an hour ago.

"In the meantime," Charlie broke into his thoughts, "after you've showered and dressed and we maybe track down the ship's barber to do something with that hair, there's someone I'd like you to talk to."

"Not a shrink!"

"No, not a shrink."

"The ship's captain?" Chris guessed. "Guess it's been pretty rude of me to avoid him all this time."

"We'll meet with the captain eventually," Charlie assured him. "As my commanding officer, he's been rather insistent on it."

Chris's eyes widened. Suddenly the gold uniform made sense.

"This is your ship?"

"Was, is. Sometimes. Starfleet occasionally offers a dispensation for idle types like me who have a particular skill."

Chris was about to object to that—on the homestead, Charlie had done as much work as any two men. *Idle* was not a word he'd have applied to him. Maybe what he meant was that he wasn't one of those spit-and-polish types who signed on for long missions and devoted their entire lives to Starfleet, but—

Charlie broke into his thoughts again.

"You asked about other colonists. There is another young-ster aboard. Lost his mother in the fire, too. He's a lot younger than you, and it's hard for him to understand what happened. I thought maybe you could . . ."

He left his thought unfinished. Chris got to his feet immediately. His mother had taught him many things, valu-able things he would carry with him all his life. One of the most important was to lend a hand whenever he could. A trace of the carefree kid with the lopsided smile peeked through his overburdening sorrow. "I can get a haircut any old time. Let's go!"

He couldn't believe his eyes. "Tango!"

The little colt had been housed in a hastily constructed straw-lined pen in the ship's arboretum. Unharmed by the fire, he nevertheless looked bedraggled—his coat dull, his eyes without luster, his head hanging forlornly, and he looked as if he'd lost weight. When he heard Chris say his name, he raised his head and nickered softly. Chris knelt in the straw beside him and put his arms around him, and the colt nuzzled him gratefully. The warmth of him, the smell of him, the sheer normalcy of the moment anchored him to the here and now, and the assurance that tomorrow would somehow take care of itself.

TALOS IV

"I see now why Tango was so important to you," Vina said. "And why the Talosians made another mistake in thinking they could just pull him out of your memory and make you respond positively."

Pike nodded, lost in thought. "We'd bonded from the moment he was born, but the fire forged it. He hadn't been weaned yet, and he refused to nurse unless I held the bottle. I became his surrogate mother, his whole world, and he and Charlie were mine."

"So you didn't go to live with your aunt and uncle?"

Pike shook his head. "Charlie adopted me. He and his wife had a ranch not far from where my mother and I had lived in Mojave. I thought he'd seemed familiar the first time I saw him . . ."

At his request, they'd forgone one level of illusion, the one he thought of as the outermost one—the one in which they could be in a villa on the Lebanese coast, or on Rigel VII, or in an intergalactic trader's harem—the one which the Talosians in their haste thirteen years ago had tried to wrap around his healthy, robust self without understanding who that self really was. Absent the outer illusion, he and Vina faced the reality of Talos's underground metropolis, its miles and miles of corridors crudely hewn out of the native stone, interconnecting like the tunnels of some vast anthill, yet not uncomfortable overall, somehow heated and cooled and provided with breathable air and ambient light. It was his curiosity about how this subterranean world functioned—a curiosity he hadn't had the luxury for the last time—that had brought them here.

For reasons of practicality, though, he and Vina retained the core illusion that both were still young, healthy, attractive and, in his case, ambulatory. But those idealized selves, which Pike thought of as the innermost level of illusion, were extant in the here and now, in the subterranean corridors of Talos IV, where its people had lived for thousands of centuries following their near self-destruction.

Penned in a cage the first time, Pike had seen only a minuscule portion of that underground world. This time he had asked Vina to be his guide in seeing the real world where he had chosen to spend the remainder of his days.

"So you went to live with Charlie," Vina said as they studied the zoo specimens—the animals and plants and, in some cases, creatures that, like Charlie's jellyplants, were both and neither—that were housed in preparation for someday being reintroduced to the surface. "And you and Tango rode out every morning. By the time you were, oh, about fifteen, there was probably a different girl every week . . ."

"Don't get ahead of the story," Pike teased her, studying the ostrich-sized bird with the parrot-like head in the cage in front of them. "What's this one called?"

"It's a moabird," she said, indulging him. "Native to the southern hemisphere. There are several hundred unhatched eggs in another chamber. Radiation levels in some spots have gone down almost enough to reintroduce them, but there's still some concern about radiation drift weakening the integrity of the shell structure. In another hundred years, maybe . . ."

"Don't they know about molecular scrubbers?" Pike wondered. "For such an advanced civilization . . ."

"For which so much data was lost in the holocaust," Vina reminded him, tugging his hand to lead him to the next cage. "I'm just realizing a common theme. Fire, again. For you, your mother's death. For me, *Columbia*'s destruction. For the Talosians, their entire world."

"That's too poetic for me!" Pike said, moving on. In reality, he supposed she was pushing his wheelchair. The illusion was much nicer.

"Yes, of course!" Vina demurred, not half believing him. "You're a rube, not an egghead. I keep forgetting."

"Tell me more about the Talosians themselves," Pike prompted her. There was a sense of déjà vu to his questions; they were not too different from the questions he'd asked the first time. "Were they always androgynous?"

"They only seem that way," Vina explained. "Their . . . sexuality . . . is less rigidly defined than ours. Each is a balance of male and female traits, but most lean slightly to one side of the spectrum or another. When you get to know them better, you'll be able to classify each individual as 'male' or 'female.' If you want to. After a while, those distinctions seem less important."

"I hope that doesn't mean those distinctions will seem less important to you and me."

"Never!" she assured him.

He wanted to ask if there were children. Had they reproduced at all since the holocaust, or had it frightened them into keeping their population static until the last of them died out? And that was another question: How long did they live? Had their life span been affected by the ambient radiation? Had these same Talosians been alive all those thousands of centuries ago?

He wouldn't pester her with those things, but would ask the Magistrate, or one of the others. And, come to think of it, it was time he got to know some of the others.

While all of this was spinning in his head, they'd arrived at the next habitat, where several members of a species of three-eyed lizard the size of a house cat had made their home amid a number of the singing blue-leaved plants Pike remembered from the surface. The lizards remained motionless, all but blending in with the foliage, but their eyes followed Pike in a kind of sequential synchrony that made him want to laugh out loud. A Talosian he didn't recognize was tending the plants, and nodded to them as they passed. Pike nodded back.

"Kerinithis," Vina named the lizards. "Much more adaptable than the birds. Some have already been reintroduced in the equatorial regions, and they seem to be thriving . . ."

2231: MOJAVE

"Collared lizards," Charlie whispered, indicating with his chin rather than pointing, his voice just loud enough to carry over the desert wind. He and Chris had been camping, and the early morning desert was full of surprises. Lying on their bellies peering over a small grassy hummock, they were watching life pass them by. "Three of them in the shade of that piñon, see? Now, over there's the sidewinder. See how he camouflages himself? He can stay that way without moving for hours, breathing only once or twice a minute, because if the lizard sees him, he's gone. What else do you see?"

Behind them, well-trained enough to stay without being tethered, two of Charlie's saddle horses grazed peacefully. When one of them, possibly sensing the presence of the rattler, shifted its feet on the hard soil, the snake, deaf as all snakes were, but feeling the vibration, raised its head slightly and slithered off. The movement caused the lizards to scatter in all directions, and Chris tried hard not to laugh. Whoever had called this place a desert hadn't known what they were talking about; it was anything but deserted.

"Tracks," he answered Charlie's question, indicating with a jerk of his chin, emulating Charlie. What a month ago would have looked like merely heat cracks in the caliche he could now clearly see was the path the snake had made in its traverse of the desert floor. "The sidewinder's, the lizards', maybe a roadrunner, and some kind of rodent."

"Species?"

"Mouse, but I don't know what type."

Charlie nodded, satisfied. "You will." He glanced up at

the sun, stretched out his lower back, and went to where the horses waited. "Time to head for home. Hobelia said something about signing you up for a real school. She wants to take you around to see some of them today so you can choose."

"I'd rather stay out here with you!" Chris followed reluctantly, swinging up into the saddle with practiced ease now.

"There'll be plenty of time for that." Charlie turned his horse with a simple voice command. "Race you to the Joshua trees!" he shouted, and they were off.

That was how it had been since Chris arrived, and how he wished it could stay forever. Coming back to Mojave, where he'd been born, had in a sense been like coming home, but he'd never really known anything about the desert beyond.

From a dusty little nineteenth-century mining town and insignificant spur of the railroads pushing inexorably West, to a forgotten twentieth-century stopover of burger joints and auto repair shops, Mojave, California, had benefited from the nascent environmentalism of that early era and become one of the models for integrated human habitation into the following centuries.

From the wind turbines providing power to nearby Palm Springs as early as the 1990s to the weather screens of the late twenty-first century, what began as desert had been transformed into a virtual Garden of Eden, patterned on the Vulcan model, which surrounded desert cities with parklands to keep the heat and sand at bay, mitigating the climate for those in town without upsetting the ecology of the flora and fauna in the desert beyond.

Forests of native trees—pines and junipers, redwoods and live oaks and scarlet-leaved liquidambar—alternated with rolling meadows lush with grasses and wildflowers, all of it crisscrossed with walking and riding paths, forming rings around small individual communities of pretty little houses built into cliffsides or nestled on sprawling properties that blended into the ecosystem, linked together into the Greater Mojave Area.

In its natural state, the Mojave Desert could only have sustained a fraction of the population living there not quite three centuries after the adaptation began. The key was the weather screens.

Constructed of a special alloy that could float at stratospheric levels and "tethered" by navigational beacons so that they remained in synchronous orbit above the cities they were designed for, examined close-up they really did look like screens, or perhaps fishnets—an open mesh that interacted with atmospheric conditions and made hot days cooler and cold nights warmer.

Over northern cities, they raised the ambient temperature slightly and mitigated the wind chill but still allowed the snow to fall. Above Mojave, there was seldom a need to mitigate the cold. True, desert nights were chilly, and often winter mornings found patches of frost lingering in the shady places, but it was the desert heat that most needed management. Before the weather screens, days of hundred-degree temperatures were not uncommon. Once the screens were in place to moderate temperatures over the city itself and, to a lesser degree (so as not to disturb the natural growth and dormant cycles of the greenery), over the parks and forests, an interesting side effect was discovered.

The contrast between desert temperatures and city temperatures created excess moisture, which could be collected and allowed to fall in the parklands as rain, and which, guided into reservoirs, raised the water table and, consequently, increased the number of inhabitants per square mile the desert could sustain.

Christopher vaguely knew some of this. He would become more conversant with it as he grew older. For now, he knew not to be in the parks between five and seven a.m.

unless he didn't mind getting soaked. It was the least of his concerns; he had more important things on his mind.

For one thing, he discovered that Charlie had a wife, for another, that Charlie was something of a hero. The two factors changed how Chris saw Charlie—no longer as a loner who drifted from job to job ("an underachiever" Heston had styled him once, during a particularly bad mood), but in whom he still found much to admire—but as a different man entirely.

"You mean he didn't tell you?" Hobelia marveled, watching Chris examine the medals and commendations in their case on the mantel. "That's our Charlie! Doesn't talk, just does. Some of those he got just for everyday things. You know, stopping a warp-core breach, transporting a landing party during a red alert—"

"Hobe . . ." Charlie began, knowing it was useless.

"But that big one there? That's for saving his captain's life. And almost losing his own in the process."

"Hobelia, that's enough!"

She'd wrapped one arm around his waist and beamed at Chris, who was taking all this in. "He doesn't believe he's a hero!"

"'Hero'!" Charlie snorted. "Never knew what that word meant. I just do what I need to do to be able to sleep at night, that's all . . ."

"He took a laser blast that was meant for his captain," Hobelia translated. "Shoved him out of the way, knowing he'd probably die."

"Just my dumb luck I lived through it," Charlie remarked. "Reflexes got in the way of common sense. Still don't see what all the fuss is about."

Hobelia shook her head, as if they'd had this conversation a thousand times before. "Man believes no good deed goes unpunished!"

Chris soon learned that Hobelia was a force to be reckoned with. Solidly built, with jet-black eyes and strong cheekbones and hands that were always busy—chopping vegetables, gentling horses, cuddling the neighbors' babies—she barely came up to Charlie's shoulder. Her long black hair hung in a single plait down her back, except when she was riding, in which case she coiled it up on top of her head, or for important occasions when she brushed it out and let it hang loose, dense and shimmering as silk, almost to her knees. Whenever he heard the term *Earth mother,* he would always think of Hobelia.

"Her people have been here almost as long as the land," Charlie explained after he'd taken her in his arms without a word and they simply held each other for a long moment, their eyes closed, his chin resting on the top of her head. "She's mostly Mojave, with a little bit of Navajo. One of her grandfathers ventured out of Dineteh and came here."

"Wow," Chris said, not knowing what else to say.

"Guess he didn't tell you he's part Native, too, did he?" Hobelia asked Chris, who didn't know what to say to that, either. "Only he's an outlander. Cherokee came from Oklahoma originally, spread all through the South and Midwest until the Trail of Tears."

"Plenty of time for history lessons," Charlie said, sensing Chris was more than a little overwhelmed with all this information. "Thought you might want to meet Tango."

Hobelia clapped one hand over her mouth, surprised at her forgetfulness. "Of course! Poor little guy—let's see what we can do for him."

The colt had made some progress on the voyage home. Charlie and one of the other engineers had programmed the food dispenser for a formula that closely resembled the chemical composition of mare's milk and designed a bottle for him to drink from, and after some balking and a lot of spluttering he'd finally gotten the hang of it. But he missed his mother and, even reunited with Chris, he still seemed inconsolable.

"You leave him to me!" Hobelia said, stroking him and speaking to him in a language Chris didn't understand. A little hesitantly, Tango let her lead him out of the trailer.

Unlike Heston's horses, Charlie's horses were allowed to roam free. A few were grazing in an open field beside the house, and watched the arrival of the young stranger curiously. Hobelia led Tango near a mare with an almost-weaned yearling. Mare and colt touched noses and investigated each other. By the end of the day, Tango had a foster mother and a vast extended family.

Tango was six months old when he arrived on Earth. As he grew, Chris worked with him daily, teaching him to walk on a lead, to stand in cross ties for grooming, to permit his feet to be trimmed, to load and unload from the trailer without balking. Most times when he rode out with Charlie or Hobelia or both, he would ride the mare who had adopted Tango and "pony" him, letting him run alongside the mare while Chris rode her on the trails. In time he would show the colt in halter at local fairs and the annual rodeo.

By the time Tango was a yearling, his serious training would begin. Chris exposed him to all sorts of stimuli—leading him over tarps, puddles, the natural land bridges on the mountain trails—conditioning him so he'd be less likely to spook under unfamiliar circumstances.

When Tango was two, Chris would begin "long-lining" him, having him obey commands while being led in a circle on a long lead. Next came double-lining, having him walk while Chris walked behind him holding two leads attached to either side of his halter. In true Western fashion, he would start working him in a hackamore, a bridle that looped over

Tango's nose, rather than a bit, and accustom him to wearing a saddle.

By the time Tango was three, Chris would start leaning heavily against him to accustom him to his weight. When he finally swung himself into the saddle, Tango would be so used to him he wouldn't buck. He would accept a snaffle bit and eventually a curb bit, and by the time he was five, he'd have herded cattle, ridden many kinds of trails; he'd have learned to jump and even barrel race. He would be a perfect working saddle horse, and he and Chris would move and think as one. Leaving him behind to attend the Academy would be one of the most difficult things Chris ever had to do; only knowing that Tango would recognize him and take up where they had left off every time he came home on leave made it possible.

But all that was yet to come, and most humans could not foresee the future. Some, though, had a way of reading into events in the present that made it seem so.

"I don't know, Hobe," Charlie said quietly, watching boy and horse together, he and Hobelia resting their chins on their arms atop the split-rail fence the way he and Chris sometimes did. "He's remembered how to smile again. The nightmares seem to have eased, and God knows there's nothing wrong with his appetite—if he doesn't stop growing we'll have to raise the doorways—but part of me thinks he may never heal completely."

"It's early yet," Hobelia soothed him, rubbing his back idly. "Boy only has but one mother. One thing, though. I think it's past time you told him about his father."

Charlie gave her a sideways look. "I don't have to tell you his father's a tough case. Plenty of time to ease him into the idea."

"Says you!" Hobelia snorted. She stopped rubbing his back to clap her hands and cheer at some clever thing Tango had just done. "The longer you wait, the less he's apt to forgive you for keeping it from him."

"I'd still be happier if he got some counseling," Charlie said to change the subject.

Hobelia indicated boy and horse working as one. "That's all the counseling he needs."

"Says you."

Hobelia punched him lightly on the arm. "Yeah, Charlie Pike, says me! That boy there is *sumach a'hot*. Gifted."

Charlie raised his eyebrows. "Be careful with that."

"I only say it when I mean it," Hobelia said with a look Charlie had learned meant she would not be contradicted. "Christopher has a gift that will take him far. But it will be a bittersweet gift . . ."

EARTH

There was a dreamlike quality to Christopher Pike's adolescence. Could life really be this easy? Or had he earned this somehow, because of his past?

The possibility of living with his aunt and uncle in Argentina somehow never came up again after that first time. On his thirteenth birthday, along with a hand-tooled saddle and his first real cowboy boots, Charlie handed him an old-fashioned printed document rolled up with a ribbon in the form of a scroll. It was an offer of adoption. Chris couldn't think of any reasons not to accept.

The following day he, Charlie, and Hobelia visited a lawyer in town and signed the document, and Chris kept his copy among his treasures. At first the name *Christopher Pike* struck him as odd but, trying it out in his mind and on his tongue, he found it suited him.

He did well in school. Because of the way Willa had taught him to investigate things from the time he was a little boy, learning came easily to him, and he was very popular in his new school. He was absorbed by the knowledge itself and didn't care about the grades.

Nor did his learning limit itself to the classroom. Charlie

taught him to live off the land, to acknowledge every creature who lived on it, to find water in the desert and food in seeming barren places, to sleep beneath the stars and know their names. Hobelia taught him to recognize that past, present, and future were not always distinct things, and that a wise man never dismissed his dreams.

His boundless energy found outlet in riding and showing Tango at as many local shows as he could manage, and somehow he found time to captain the school football team, and allow the local girls to worship him. The sight of the handsome young man with the lopsided grin riding up to school on the striking bay gelding who was true to his name, strutting and waltzing and sidestepping in place—as much a clown and a show-off as his master was quiet and thoughtful—was enough to turn any girl's head.

He never got too deeply involved with any one girl; Charlie joked that he'd have needed a flyswatter to shoo the extra ones away if he had. And if once in a while a shadow fell across his face, and those dark eyebrows drew down in a frown and his gaze seemed very far away, if he was a little more serious than most young men his age—not quite standoffish, but reluctant to engage in the clowning and roughhousing of his peers—the story of how his mother had died before his eyes when he was very young would make the rounds, and those who knew him would cut him some slack.

Every so often when he thought about Willa—and he thought about her a lot—he recalled that overheard conversation in the kitchen and he wondered. Wondered if it had meant what he thought it meant at the time, wondered if he should mention it to Charlie.

What if Charlie and his mother had been having an affair? What if they hadn't? It occurred to Chris a thousand times to ask, lead up to it in some subtle or not-so-subtle way, but he never did. What did it matter now, anyway?

During his growing up years, Charlie left on two more one-year voyages, and Chris and Hobelia ran the ranch. When Charlie came home, Chris pestered him for stories, filling in the blanks in his own mind around Charlie's laconic version. The Starfleet uniform Chris had been given to wear when his own clothes were destroyed in the fire still hung in his closet, though it had been made for a smaller person, and he'd long since outgrown it. Like the adoption scroll, it was a talisman, a piece of the past that might give him a clue to the future.

Life was as close as any real thing could be to idyllic. How could he possibly give it up for what he needed to do next?

"What do you want, Chris?" Charlie asked him on the cusp of his senior year. The two men—Chris was taller than Charlie by now and nearly as broad in the shoulders, no longer a child by any definition—stood as they always did, chins resting on their folded arms, leaning on the top rail of the split-rail fence, savoring the evening with one eye on the horses.

"Want?" Chris pretended to be puzzled by the question. "I don't want anything, Hoss. I've got everything right here."

Charlie gave him a sideways look. "Say that again and convince me you mean it. You know what I'm talking about. College, travel, something else? I've never heard you talk with any enthusiasm about anything other than horses and girls, not necessarily in that order. It didn't seem to be my business to press you on it, but there are some decisions to be made soon."

"I know."

"I've also seen you looking at the stars, wondering."

Chris looked chagrined. "Okay, Hoss, you caught me. I've been thinking about joining Starfleet."

"Have you, now?" Charlie feigned surprise. He'd noticed

the application hovering on Chris's computer screen for months now.

Chris nodded. "I want to see what's out there. Can't put it in any fancier words than that."

Charlie suppressed a small smile. "Don't know that you need to."

Chris settled back down on the top rail with his chin on his folded arms, comfortable with the silence. Charlie squinted at the horizon, guessing what time it was. A finger to the wind told him tomorrow's weather.

"Academy deadline's not far away," he offered finally.

"Starfleet Academy? I was thinking of enlisting. Don't know that I'd qualify for the Academy."

Charlie took off his slouch hat and whapped him playfully upside the head with it. "Now I know you're fishing! Why wouldn't you qualify? You've got excellent grades, natural leadership qualities, you're in top physical condition. A few little things like that. Plus you did look damn good in the uniform, even as a kid."

"Yeah, I did, didn't I?" Chris said with his lopsided grin. "So—?"

"So I don't think there's much use for a wrangler on a starship. I don't have the engineering skills you have, and I'm okay at the sciences, but there's no great passion for it. I don't see that I have anything unique to offer."

Charlie scratched one ear thoughtfully. "Then by process of elimination, there's nothing left but the command track."

"Oh, is that how it works?" Chris knew half of Charlie's reasons for not staying in Starfleet had had to do with his resistance to authority.

"Well, don't take my word for it," Charlie demurred. "But they didn't make you captain of the football team or student class president solely on the basis of your charm and good looks. You're a leader, Chris. No avoiding it."

"Maybe."

"And—?"

"And that's what scares me. I guess I could handle running a department or something. Even leading a landing party under dangerous conditions is something I'd have to think hard about. But captaining a ship? A hundred or more people's lives in my hands, out there in the middle of the unknown?" Chris frowned. "I don't want that kind of responsibility."

Charlie let that statement hang in the air unaddressed for a long moment. Finally he said, "It's not your fault she died, Chris."

Chris started as if he'd been slapped. "I know that! Where the hell did that come from?"

"Do you?" Charlie asked, unperturbed. "Do you really know that? Or do you still have some little shred of doubt that's holding you back?"

"That's got nothing to do with—"

"—with why you push yourself to be the best at everything you do, then duck out of the awards ceremonies and skip the homecoming parade? With why you've got everything going for you, but you'd rather enlist in Starfleet as a grunt and work your way up the hard way or not at all than apply for the Academy, knowing you'd get in in a heartbeat? Yeah, I think it has everything to do with it."

A dozen angry retorts roiled through Chris's mind, but he left them there. "It's like you say, I do what I have to do to be able to sleep at night," he said finally.

"Will you be able to sleep at night if you don't fill out that application you've had up on your computer screen for a month or more?" Charlie asked quietly.

Chris's cheeks flushed. "I'm just not sure I've got the right stuff."

"Only one way to find out," Charlie suggested.

"I guess so," Chris acknowledged. "One thing, though . . . I don't want you pulling any strings for me. Putting in a good word with Admiral Straczeskie or anything. You do know he's an admiral now?"

"Seems to me I heard that," Charlie acknowledged.

"Promise me you won't say anything to him about me?"

"It's not as if a rear admiral is going to be influenced by anything a transporter chief has to say . . ."

". . . unless of course that transporter chief took a laser blast for him."

Charlie sighed. "Okay, if that's what you want. I promise I won't say another word."

It took Chris a moment to register what he'd just said.

"You didn't—!" Chris started to sputter. "Damn it, Charlie . . ."

"*If* you apply, *if* you pass all the testing, Admiral Straczeskie will be the one to conduct your admission interview, that's all. The rest is up to you."

"As if he'd turn me down once I got that far!" Chris snorted.

Charlie rounded on him, a little annoyed. "He'd be out of his mind to turn you down, Christopher. If it's what you want, you have every right to strive for it. And you'll make it. I know you will, even without my help." Charlie turned on his heel and headed back toward the house, his shadow long in the setting sun. "Now, I don't know about you, but I'm finished talking about this."

Christopher Pike applied for Starfleet Academy and, not surprisingly, aced most of the entrance exams. He went on to excel in all his classes. Math, sciences, languages, leadership, and first-contact skills came naturally to him, and the endurance tests and survival skills were a breeze for someone with his stamina and experience.

He did have one flaw, and that was an almost obsessive need to be perfect. He brooded over mistakes, went back and retested himself until he got as close to the highest score as possible. While it looked good on his academic record, it also made him his own worst enemy, and more than one of his examiners hesitated. Still, they gave him the benefit of the doubt, and ultimately he would graduate at the top of his class. More than one of his instructors remarked that if Earth could produce the ideal young Starfleet officer, Christopher Pike would be that officer.

10

2320: EN ROUTE TO TALOS IV

A Vulcan lute has many voices. All are beautiful, but some are more plaintive than others. Spock stilled the strings with one long hand and rested the neck of the instrument against his shoulder. His mood was contemplative.

The journey is simpler this time, he thought as he set the lute aside and scanned the vicinity yet again, listening for comm chatter at the full range of the shuttle's receivers and hearing only static, running scanners to satisfy himself that no vessel was in pursuit, and that there was nothing up ahead he need concern himself about, yet. *But simplicity is no guarantee of outcome.*

The first such journey had been predicated on a lie. The Talosians had duped him into believing he was receiving a personal comm message from Fleet Captain Pike requesting that *Enterprise* divert to Starbase 11. Only after Kirk had complied with this ostensible request and changed course did the Magistrate communicate to Spock precisely what hir people were doing and why; by then he was caught up in their agenda and, truly, as he told Pike, "had no choice."

He had wondered ever since if the humans involved truly understood the implications of the Talosians' ability to contact a single individual by power of mind from across parsecs of space, and manipulate him to their will.

"What about Vina?" Number One asked once Pike appeared on the transporter platform. "Isn't she coming with us?"

"No," Pike answered, "and I agreed with her reasons."

With that the landing party had returned to the bridge, Pike gave the order to leave orbit, and they were finally able to set course for the Vega colony. It was not until they were there and Pike was downplanet overseeing the care of the sick and wounded that Number One assembled everyone else in the landing party to give a report, from their own perspective, on what they had witnessed on Talos.

Spock corroborated what everyone else had seen—the barren landscape, the deceptively frail aliens with their incredible power of mind, the illusions they had created—but when he began to talk about that power and those illusions, Number One had cut him off abruptly.

"Yes, yes, that's all very well, Mr. Spock, but we're concerned with measurable effects here, not soft science. If telepathy can even be considered a science."

Young and still outspoken, Spock had been perturbed at her dismissing telepathy as "soft science," and attempted to say so.

"On the contrary, Number One, I don't think you realize the very real, quantifiable effect an encounter with a telepathic species of the Talosians' superiority can have."

"I said that's enough, Mr. Spock!" she'd snapped, and it didn't need telepathy for him to read in her face and voice a message which said, loud and clear, *Don't talk about this now, because the captain for one is still in a precarious state of mind, and Yeoman Colt's not the most stable personality at the best of times. If either of them starts to think too deeply about this, we're all in trouble. Stow it for now, possibly for-*

ever, or as your superior officer I guarantee I will make your life exceedingly difficult!

Impervious to the threat, Spock did finally see the reasoning behind it, and while he might disagree with Number One's not entirely objective response, he had been constrained to silence.

He'd wondered ever since if he was the only one at that briefing to consider the fact that once a Talosian mind entered a human's, it could do so again with that particular human at any time, and that, by implication, the Talosians could follow the course of "their" humans' lives from any distance, across any number of years or even decades, for as long as that human or, as he had realized on Starbase 11, Vulcan might live.

It was how they had known about Pike's accident aboard the cadet ship. It was how they had known to use Spock to bring Pike back to Talos. And it was how they had found Spock, and summoned him, once again, more than half a century later.

The escape from Starbase 11 had been a logistical nightmare, however well planned: smuggling Pike out of the medical suite and onto *Enterprise,* altering standing orders, commandeering the ship and locking her on course, evading pursuit—by Captain Kirk and, Spock believed until midway into his court-martial, Commodore Mendez in the shuttle—and, for all he knew, by every other ship in the 'fleet, all on the supposition that he would eventually either be caught, extradited and condemned to death, or exiled forever with Pike on Talos. The odds against his success, even with the complicity of the Talosians, had been less than optimal.

And yet, he had succeeded.

When the trial was over, with Kirk's permission, he had beamed down to Talos IV with Pike, expecting perhaps a flutter of the eyelids from the wounded man, a single flash of light that signified "Yes . . . thank you . . . good-bye."

But the Magistrate met them at the beam-down point, and Spock had felt compelled to ask a question.

"Captain Pike," he had begun. "I must return to the *Enterprise*. Are you certain you wish to remain here?"

The Magistrate had, as Spock had come to expect, worn that small, enigmatic smile, having read Spock's thought before he voiced it. Was there a hint of genuine humor in hir eyes as s/he "listened" to Pike's voice in hir mind?

"He says to tell you, 'You're asking me this now, *after* you've risked your life to get me here? Not very logical, Mr. Spock.'"

The Magistrate, Spock realized, could very well be misleading him. But the words had the tone and tenor of the Christopher Pike he knew, and they rang true.

He said his farewells and left Pike there, and as it is not a Vulcan's wont to brood or second-guess himself, he had returned to *Enterprise* without succumbing to the slightest doubt that he had done the right thing.

That first time had demanded a complex and arduous journey leading to the optimal conclusion. This time, the journey had been simplicity itself. Spock had merely notified his staff that he would be taking some of his considerable unused leave time, logged a flight plan with Starfleet Command, and flown his personal shuttle in a leisurely arc away from Vestios Prime, where he had been attending an economic summit celebrating the tenth anniversary of the Vestians' admission to the Federation, as if he were bound for Vulcan.

He never actually said he was going to Vulcan, but the flight plan was consistent with that destination, and he simply allowed the curious to assume that it was where he was going. Given the increasing numbers of Vulcans in Starfleet and the diplomatic corps, enough was known, and far more conjectured, about Vulcan mating rituals so that humans at last knew better than to ask.

There was in fact little to draw him to Vulcan these days. His mother was dead, his relationship with his father strained yet again. His property was overseen by able administrators; he had no wife or offspring to welcome his arrival. For a Vulcan, he was remarkably free of extended family; for a Starfleet officer, he was remarkably free of the interpersonal entanglements that made people wonder where you'd disappeared to if they didn't hear from you after a few days. Since Jim Kirk's death, he had buried himself in work and solitude. No one had questioned his departure and, to this point several days into his journey, apparently no one was looking for him. So far, so good.

Less than a day away from Vestios, he had abandoned the flight plan and set course through a little-traveled, minimally charted sector he hoped would bring him to Talos before the shuttle's fuel cells gave out. After that . . .

There might not be an "after that." He would cross that bridge when he came to it.

For now, all that mattered was to stay out of scanner range of Starfleet vessels in the area and not give anyone any reason to think he had gone walkabout. He had recorded several subspace messages which he would "bounce" off uninhabited moons or larger asteroids along his path so as to redirect them along a trajectory where they would reach the requisite starbases and suggest that he had adhered to his original course.

He was, this time as last time, the Talosians had seen, the perfect choice—his past loyalty to Pike unquestionable, his life expendable by their standards. Fortuitous that even the festivities on Vestios had concluded the night before he was summoned. Or was it fortuitous? Had the Talosians known, in such exact detail, that he would not be missed? Were they watching him, even now?

He and Christopher Pike had discussed that very possibility a long, long time ago. Because what Number One had feared was true: Christopher Pike understood the dangers of Talosian telepathy all too well.

". . . because once they're inside your head, they never leave. Don't tell me that thought's never occurred to you, Mr. Spock."

It was night, a night made that much darker by the fact that the planet where they were stranded had no moon. Pike and Spock had, for reasons of expediency, taken shelter in the canopy of a very tall tree. Below them, a search party composed of a species of intelligent predator with an unpleasant habit of killing and eating whole whatever it hunted, was stalking them.

They had discovered that the predators, like Earth's snakes, were also congenitally deaf, so Pike and Spock could talk in low voices even with several of the hunters in proximity. There were other things they couldn't safely do, which they'd found out the hard way when the rest of their landing party had been killed, but at the moment the two survivors were as safe as they could be between now and the time *Enterprise* came back to look for them, if it did. The only way to keep the "heebie-jeebies" away, as Pike called them, was to keep talking.

"Indeed, Captain," Spock had offered tersely, still not certain that they were entirely safe. His eyes were more adapted to the dark, and he could see movement slithering among the shadows perhaps fifty meters below them. Eventually the temperature would drop and the cold-blooded hunters would have to seek shelter, and he and Pike could climb down from their perch and move on, but for now . . . "I have considered the likelihood that the Talosians may be listening to us even now."

"You said 'listening to us,' " Pike remarked. "Can they see us, do you think?"

"Uncertain, Captain. Theirs is a complex form of tele-pathic communication quite unlike a Vulcan's. I regret we could not remain on Talos IV long enough for me to study it."

"Maybe they'd have been better off keeping you as a specimen instead of me!" Pike said, only half-joking. "Sorry, I didn't mean . . . the whole episode makes me jumpy, even now. Sometimes I find myself wondering whether they ever really did let me go, or if everything that's happened since has been a dream . . ."

The conversation had been brief, and never repeated. Spock might have wished there had been other occasions to continue the discussion, particularly since the more he thought about it, the more he became convinced that the rea-son he had been summoned to Talos this time was that Christopher Pike was either dying or already dead. He had no way of knowing this for certain, but it was the premise he had been operating under since he had received the summons.

Perhaps, he thought, *it is only a matter of his wanting to see Earth once more before he dies. Or some last wish to have his remains returned to the planet of his birth. Even so, would he put me at risk of the death penalty for such a wish? Not the Christopher Pike I once knew. There is something more here. Nevertheless . . .*

Methodically, Spock scanned the vicinity once again. The day before he had found it necessary to take shelter behind a nickel-cored moon in order to elude a convoy of Ferengi scavengers looting an untethered satellite floating loose in the system, but other than that he had had this sector of space largely to himself. He'd taken the liberty of using his diplomatic access to ascertain the locations of any Starfleet vessels deployed in the vicinity, and hoped to avoid them.

That hope had been realized thus far. But a telltale bleeped and he checked his scanners. He was no longer alone. A vessel was on approach at one-ninety-four mark five, as yet too distant to identify. Spock scanned for a comm signature. There was none, not even random chatter. Apparently, whoever she was, she was on silent running. This was not good. Warily, Spock weighed whether evasive maneuvers would help him elude notice, or rather serve to give his position away. There was nothing nearby to hide behind this time. He chose to remain on his present course. He had a fair idea who was out there.

Within moments, scanners confirmed ship's configuration: Federation starship, *Excelsior* class. Spock suppressed the ghost of a smile. If there had been no last-minute changes since his last briefing with Starfleet Command, all would be well.

He did not have long to wait.

"My, my, my . . ." a familiar voice came through on discrete—someone knew the DiploCorps' coded frequencies. "Ambassador Spock, I presume?"

"Correct, Captain Sulu."

"How long has it been?"

"Entirely too long, Captain. I trust you are well?"

"Flourishing, Ambassador. And you?"

"Quite well, thank you."

The familiar face materialized on the forward screen. In these his later years, Hikaru Sulu had grown leaner and more striking than ever. The planes of his face may have become more angular, and the jet-black hair gone iron-gray, but he still moved with the panther-like grace of a much younger man, and his voice, always deep and resonant, had acquired a richness and a calm that evidenced the serenity of his inner self.

Even after all these years, Sulu was still given to collecting rare plants and expanding his collection of exotic antique weaponry from cultures all over the quadrant. As his image solidified on the shuttle's forward screen, Spock could see a few of his prize specimens mounted on the bulkhead behind him, and a many-tendrilled *liana beauregardis,* draped over one shoulder, purred as he caressed it.

Spock noted with some satisfaction that Sulu was speaking to him from his quarters, not from the bridge. It was very possible he would delete the message trail once this conversation terminated.

"Imagine running into you out here . . ." Sulu mused, trying hard to keep a straight face. "Here we are in the middle of nowhere, field-testing some modifications to *Excelsior*'s warp drive, and what do our scanners show ping-ponging about among the asteroids, but a diplomat's shuttle that, however indirect its route, seems to be eventually headed for one particular star system. Very difficult to explain."

"Indeed," was all Spock said.

"You're going to have to stop wasting energy on evasive maneuvers if you want your 'cells to hold out until you get there," Sulu said, dropping the light tone and going deadly serious. "And you have no contingency for getting back."

Spock thought carefully before he answered. "Speculation, Captain. You have no way of knowing where I am going."

Nor will I tell you, and implicate you in my crime, he was about to say, but Sulu cut him off.

"You're on course for Talos IV," Sulu said flatly. "It's Pike, isn't it?"

Spock said nothing.

"Come on, Spock, you can't fool an old helmsman. I know where you're going, no matter how much fancy maneuvering you do. There's nothing else in that sector except the Talos star group."

"If you say so, Captain."

"You know there's been talk of revising General Order 7. Essentially pretending the Talos group doesn't exist. It's remote enough so you'd have to go out of your way to get there. The Powers That Be can't decide whether to delete it from the starmaps or put a security perimeter around it, the way we did with the Guardian of Forever, and removing the capital offense from the books. You couldn't wait another few months for them to sort that out?"

"Unfortunately not."

"So if it were to be known that you were defying General Order 7, you'd be screwed."

"Indeed."

"But you'd expect me to cover for you, just like old times. All for one and one for all, right?"

"I would rather we had not encountered each other at this juncture at all."

"Then why—?"

"However, were my vessel to be seen returning from the Talos star group at some point in the near future—hypothetically, of course—"

"Of course."

"—it would be to my advantage to encounter *Excelsior* during that part of my journey."

"I don't see how," Sulu said, frowning.

Nor, entirely, do I, Spock thought but didn't say.

"But if that's what you want . . ." Sulu said carefully. "We'll be in this sector for the next three weeks." He weighed what he was going to say next. "In the meantime, I can have the sensors recalibrated. Obviously whatever we thought was bouncing around out here was just space dust. Or maybe just a ghost in the machine."

Spock inclined his head slightly in gratitude. "Captain, I would be most appreciative."

His finger hovered over the comm toggle, but Sulu wasn't about to let him go just yet.

"You know, Ambassador," he said dryly, undraping the *beauregardis* from around his neck and trying very hard not to smile. "Seems to me this isn't the first time I've had to cover for one or more of my old crewmates from *Enterprise*. There are only so many times I can do that without buying some very bad karma."

Spock allowed himself the hint of a smile. *We who are about to die salute you.*

"Captain," he said, "I respectfully submit that the concept of a 'karma' or fate which predestines human lives to a particular course or outcome is at worst a fiction, at best an unsubstantiated hypothesis."

Sulu pinched the bridge of his nose between his thumb and forefinger and sighed. "I suppose there's no way of knowing how long you'd be on Talos . . . if you were going to Talos. Hypothetically."

Spock considered. "I would surmise not long. Perhaps a matter of days."

"So if *Excelsior* happened to be heading back this way, and you happened to send out a signal, and we happened to meet again, that would be kismet."

Spock raised an eyebrow. "First karma, now kismet? Captain . . ."

"All right, all right!" Sulu waved him off. "Get the hell out of here before I remember I saw you. Sulu out."

Speaking to Sulu had a strange effect on Spock. Watching *Excelsior*'s signature move off scanners into oblivion, he was conscious of his own solitude for the first time. This was illogical, since he had been just as alone before speaking to

Sulu as he was after. Was it Sulu's incredulity at the sheer folly of this escapade that caused him to reflect on it, as he perhaps should have done before he agreed to it?

Others, many others, have commented on your loyalty to Christopher Pike, Spock mused. *For what reasons are you so loyal to this man?*

Spock knew Christopher Pike's service record almost as well as he knew his own. Having graduated from the Academy in the ninety-eighth percentile, his rise through the ranks had been, if not meteoric—

The cliché gave Spock pause. Humans and their metaphors—! Did they not understand that a meteor did not rise, but in fact tumbled aimlessly through space until seized by some larger body's gravity, whence it plummeted inexorably to its death, either burning up in atmosphere or being driven into the ground? To describe someone's career as "meteoric" was, in actuality, to wish them destruction.

The closeness of the metaphor to what had actually happened to Christopher Pike disturbed him. What might have become of Pike had he not been stricken in his prime? Speculation was pointless.

A career not meteoric, then, but steady and impressive, as the handsome young man rose from ensign to lieutenant and, while still in his twenties, by a synergistic mix of talent, energy, proximity, and another man's misfortune, found himself first officer aboard the space cutter *U.S.S. Aldrin* . . .

Spock was sixteen the first time he heard the name Christopher Pike. Traveling with his parents on a diplomatic junket, he was as yet uncertain of how he would fit into this world, following in his father's considerable footsteps as was expected of him. Diplomatic channels were abuzz with the story of the near-disastrous events aboard the *Aldrin* and Lieutenant Commander Pike's impending court-martial. Naturally it was the main topic around the table at a formal dinner at the Antarean embassy where even Sarek, ordinarily immune to gossip, was asked to contribute his thoughts.

"Mutiny aboard a Federation starship is sufficiently rare as to be almost without precedent," the senior Vulcan offered thoughtfully. "Whatever else the outcome, Starfleet regulations will have to be rewritten to prevent such an unfortunate cascade of circumstances from occurring again."

There had been murmurs of assent and dissent, and someone changed the subject. Afterward, in the 'car on the way back to their apartments, Amanda offered her opinion in private.

"If they have any sense, they'll acquit that young man," she said with not a little fire. "He was following regulations to the letter. And ultimately he not only saved the ship, but prevented an interplanetary incident."

"Nevertheless, my wife, he could not have foreseen that outcome when he defied his superior officer and commandeered the ship," Sarek countered. "The inherent weakness of the structure of any military command is that it does not allow for such circumstances as this officer faced."

"Well, then, as you say, they'll have to rewrite the regulations," Amanda said pragmatically. "And instead of a court-martial, they should give that young man a commendation!"

"A not-atypically emotional response . . ." Sarek said mildly. Amanda responded as she often did to his teasing when no one but family was around—she stuck her tongue out at him. Lest he respond to that, Sarek turned his attention to Spock.

"You are pensive, my son. Have you any thoughts to share with us on the *Aldrin* affair?"

Spock had many thoughts indeed. The event fascinated him for a number of reasons, not least of which was his curiosity about what he would have done in Commander Pike's place.

"I believe both the captain and his first officer were right, and both were wrong," he blurted, remembering too late that whenever he offered so absolute an opinion, Sarek would invariably spend the next hour pulling it to shreds.

"Do you, indeed?" Sarek replied with a gleam in his eye. "Explain."

11

2246: *U.S.S. ALDRIN*

San Francisco's city fathers, caught between those inhabitants who loved the region's characteristic fog and those who didn't, had promised that someday the city would have its own weather shield, but for now it was pouring rain on the grounds of Starfleet HQ as the command crew of the cutter *Aldrin* gathered in the main shuttlebay. *Aldrin*'s captain was already aboard, and regular crew had been beamed up in groups over the past day, but the command crew was by tradition to be brought up to the ship by shuttle so that they could appreciate her sleek beauty from space. The smell of damp uniforms was distinct as the senior officers packed themselves into the shuttle faster than the atmospherics could keep pace.

The weather contributed to an already dark collective mood. All but one of the officers crammed into the shuttle had been aboard *Aldrin* on her recently completed one-year mission. She had been due for a refit, and they for R&R, when a crisis in a habitually troubled sector of space required her presence as backup for ships already in the area. Less than a week after they'd returned to Earth, they were going back out again. There was not a little grumbling.

Seated in the last row of the shuttle, keeping his own counsel, Christopher Pike was the only one not complaining.

Less than forty-eight hours ago, he'd been kicking around Luna waiting to catch a transport for Earth, looking forward to a few days of desert trekking with Tango before his next assignment, wondering if he could persuade the cute young thing he'd met in the officers' lounge (Hana, he reminded himself, Lieutenant Hana Flowers; like most comm officers, she had a particularly delightful voice, so delightful it had almost made him forget her name, but at least he'd gotten her comm code) to accompany him. He hadn't expected to have his leave cut short and his next commission in place so soon.

Nor had he expected to see Lieutenant Flowers seated in the shuttle beside *Aldrin*'s science officer when he arrived.

In the five years since he'd graduated with honors from the Academy, he had managed to acquit himself ably wherever he was assigned, working his way up from ensign to lieutenant, rotating among assignments from comm to helm to navigator to science officer's relief. Fate and an exceptionally strong pool of other officer candidates had conspired with him to keep him in the command loop without any danger of his actually being called upon to command anything larger than the occasional landing party until two days ago, when he'd found himself transferred from navigator on a science vessel to first officer on a front-line cutter, assigned to a deep-space mission on combat alert, in a move that made his head spin. He wasn't sure if he should be honored or scared out of his wits, and tried to settle his thoughts somewhere in between.

Rumor had been rampant for days. The Vestios system was in turmoil, the latest civil war between two of its worlds threatening to spill over into Federation space. Federation ships had engaged Vestian ships before, and not to their advantage. *Aldrin* was being sent in to keep an eye on the situation, and provide backup if necessary.

As bait, some suggested, daring the Vestians to cross the line. As a stalking horse, Chris Pike preferred to think of it. To think otherwise was to break out in a sweat at the mission they'd been assigned.

Still, he told himself as he leaned back in his seat, hoping to be alone with his thoughts as the others joked with each other out of long familiarity in close quarters and he tried unsuccessfully to catch Flowers's eye, he would enjoy the challenge of working with one of the fleet's mavericks.

He knew Captain Kamnach by reputation. Charlie had served under him several times, including this last mission aboard *Aldrin*.

"He's a character, Chris," Charlie said. "There aren't many Denebians in command positions and, like most colonials, they're a prickly lot. Kamnach's one of the last to work his way up the hard way. Never got into the Academy. So he's got his quirks, and he loves ragging new officers, but he's a good commander when it counts. Never guesses wrong in a combat situation. Still, mind your words around him. You say something he takes wrong, and he'll never let you forget it . . ."

There were two levels of irony here, Pike thought. One was that Charlie had promised Hobelia he'd settle down after this, and had actually been breaking in a replacement, looking forward to stepping down, when the Vestios situation had flared up and he was heading back out there again, duration unknown.

The other was that he and Charlie would be serving on the same ship for the first time. It was a big fleet, and the odds were against it, but here it was. *Aldrin* was on comm lockdown until she left spacedock. Chris wondered if Charlie knew yet that he had kin aboard.

Captain Kamnach had noticed immediately.

Pike had stood at ease in front of the captain's desk while *Aldrin*'s second officer, a portly Centaurian named Hanley about the captain's age, stood off to one side to observe the interview. For a fleeting moment Pike wondered why the second hadn't been promoted to first; he would figure that out on the voyage, he supposed. Still, the thought that he might have been promoted ahead of a more senior officer on his own ship was not an easy one.

"My former first officer had a death in the family," Kamnach began, looking not at Pike but at his service jacket. He was a big, loose-limbed man gone soft in the middle, with thinning ginger hair and bushy eyebrows that seemed skeptical even when the rest of his face wasn't. "Got home leave on one of those godsforsaken remote colony worlds before this crisis hit. Won't get back on time, so they assigned you." He sat back in his chair with his hands folded over his stomach and looked Pike over for the first time. "Admiral Straczeskie seems to think you can do the job. Thought I'd get an idea what you're like before you show up on my bridge."

He laughed then, a short, unpleasant sound, and Pike wondered what was funny.

"Buddy of mine on another ship—both of which shall remain nameless—just lost his first, too," Kamnach started to explain, with a wink in the direction of his second. "His first is a Vulcan. Evoked some obscure regulation, said he was going home to get married. Didn't look too happy about it. Not that Vulcans ever look happy about anything, but this one was particularly glum. Somehow I don't picture shotguns being involved, but it had that sense of urgency, if you know what I mean. You like opera, Mr. Pike?"

His rhythm was wrong, Pike realized. He got you thinking about how to answer him without sharing his obvious prejudice against Vulcans, then threw you something completely different, with a twinkle in his eye and a little smirk that made you wonder what was so funny. It might be just his way of training his officers to think on their feet, but it was unnerving.

"Opera? No, sir, I don't," Pike answered after what he hoped didn't sound like hesitation. He'd discovered long ago that the truth was far easier to keep track of than a lie, and he doubted he could be transferred off the ship because of his taste in music.

Kamnach's little smirk widened. "Neither do I. Glad to see you weren't trying to suck up to me because you thought I did. Crew list tells me I've got another Pike on board," he said, changing course abruptly again, looking down at the report on his desk and then back up at Pike. "Any connection?"

"Yes, sir. Charlie Pike is my father."

It had always been that way. From the moment they'd concurred on the adoption, it had never occurred to him to say "adoptive father." Charlie was what had been missing from that part of his life.

"Mr. Pike is my transporter chief," Kamnach said as if he were correcting him. "Strange career path. Guy doesn't seem to know whether he wants in or out. Your record, on the other hand, tells me you're serious about your career. So like father, not like son. And I guess I don't need to tell you I don't care to see my senior officers fraternizing with crew."

"No, sir."

Kamnach leaned back in his chair again, swinging it from side to side. "Well, let me just emphasize that, Commander

Pike, so there's no misunderstanding. You're not to communicate with my transporter chief unless and until you're required to as a matter of duty. Not in person, not in private. Not only no 'Meet you in the crew lounge after hours,' but no 'Stop by my cabin for a brandy,' either. No comm chat, no passing notes in the hall. Am I clear?"

Clear that you're being a hard-ass for no particular reason, Pike thought, wondering where this was going and why.

"Clear, sir."

"As you were, then, Number One. I'll expect you on the bridge with everybody else at oh-eight-hundred tomorrow."

Pike felt a slight tightening in his gut as he stepped out of the shuttle after the others, feeling a little out of place, though Flowers's turning to smile at him was encouraging, and faced Captain Kamnach for the first time aboard his ship.

The bosun's whistle sounded, and the officers lined up in rank order. Out of the corner of his eye, Pike caught sight of Charlie standing at attention with some of the other engineering crew, but did not turn so much as an eyelash in his direction. He could tell without even looking at him that Kamnach was watching him narrowly. He wondered if Charlie had been given the same orders he had.

As Kamnach started at the end of the line, each officer in turn stood to attention and said: "Permission to come aboard, Captain."

To which Kamnach responded to each with a little personalization—a smile, a nod, a clap on the shoulder, a wink to Hanley that said the two had gotten into some mischief together on at least one shore leave, an exceptionally warm smile for Flowers. He offered Pike an enigmatic smile and a brief handshake.

"Permission granted, Mr. Pike. Welcome aboard."

Kamnach's voice was noncommital, but Pike thought he saw a flicker of disappointment in his eyes. He'd wanted him to at least nod in Charlie's direction, wanted Charlie to react. To Pike it seemed petty, but if that was the way it was going to be . . .

The turbolift on the bridge had barely shut behind the last of the arriving officers, and Pike was still finding his place by the science station, when Kamnach opened the intercraft.

"All hands, this is the captain. I want to cut down on the chatter and give you the straight scoop from the horse's mouth, so to speak. After you've been briefed, I'll appreciate your keeping speculative chatter to a minimum. You'll know what you need to know when you need to know it. In the interim, you'll keep your opinions to yourselves.

"We are headed, as you know, for the Vestios sector. Federation ships have tangled with the Vestians in the past but, for the last several years, we had a treaty which more or less kept them off our asses.

"Now, however, two of their planets are engaged in open hostilities, and anyone not smart enough to avoid their ships has gotten caught in the cross fire. No Federation vessel has as yet been fired upon, but we will not stand passively by waiting for that to happen.

"Our mission—and we are operating under sealed orders, so any whisper of this beyond the hull of this ship will visit you with a court-martial; make no mistake about my seriousness here—is to patrol the border set by the aforementioned treaty to make certain none of the Vestians' little internecine battles spill over into Federation space or interfere with friendly trade routes.

"A Vestian vessel encountered on our side of the treaty border is a Vestian vessel challenged. A challenge ignored earns a shot across the bow. Any aggression is returned in kind. Scanner and sensor techs, look sharp. These people have ships and weaponry at least equivalent to ours. Effective now, oh-eight-hundred hours, we are on yellow alert. Stations."

With that he flicked off the intercraft and spoke over his shoulder.

"Mr. Pike, secure all bridge stations. Helm, warp factor three . . ."

Maybe he's a different man once he's on his ship, Pike thought after that first day. Kamnach wasn't exactly Santa Claus on the bridge, but there was little evidence of the hard-ass act he'd put on during Pike's interview. Out here he was all business—a little crude, overplaying the tough guy routine—but essentially a good commander. So far.

On their third day out, Pike showed up for breakfast after an early morning run through the lesser-used corridors and a session with the heavy bag in the ship's minuscule gym, ready to perform the usual morning dance around the food dispenser. Room on a fully crewed cutter was at a premium, and the officers' mess was a tight fit. With the long dining table in the middle, two average-sized humans trying to serve themselves at the food dispenser more often than not ended up bumping elbows.

As usual, the chief engineer was there ahead of Pike. Chee Wee Chua was a compact, smiling man with a wicked sense of humor; his crew called him Chewy. Most mornings he and Pike performed an elaborate choreography around the coffeepot to keep from spilling anything.

"After you, my dear Alphonse!" Chewy joked this morning. Softly so that only Pike could hear, he said: "Your dad says hello. First time you two served together?"

Pike nodded, wondering if he could trust Chewy with a message back to Charlie. The damnable thing about Kamnach's divide-and-conquer policy was it made you wary of trusting your crewmates.

"*Shiok!*" Chewy said. "Awesome! You guys need to talk, you let me know."

"Appreciate that," was all Pike said, and Chewy took his place at the table as the others began to arrive.

"Twenty credits says he'll have us running drills 'round the clock as soon as we're within a day of the border," the helmsman, a prematurely gray guy named Wesley who'd been a few years ahead of Pike at the Academy, was saying as he strolled in. "Run us so ragged that if we are under attack, we won't be able to tell the real thing from a drill."

"No one's taking your money, Wesley," the science officer—Renkova, Pike remembered—laughed as she joined Pike at the food dispenser. "We all know the captain too well!"

"New mission, same old conversation." Hanley was usually the last to arrive. "Captain Kamnach never went to charm school, but he's got the highest kill-to-casualty rate in the 'fleet."

"That's not necessarily something to brag about, Hanley," Wesley remarked. "Losing the fewest of your own crew, yes, that's commendable. But there's talk that some of those engagements might have been prevented by a captain with less temper and more diplomacy."

Hanley snorted. "Diplomacy!"

"Well, we're still within subspace range, remember," Chewy remarked. "How soon before we hit the dead zones, Wesley?"

"On our present heading? Just about where we might expect to bump into a rogue Vestian vessel, if there happened to be one out there."

Chewy saw Pike's bemused expression and was only too happy to elaborate. "We're coming up on a debris field just before the no-man's-land between us and Vestios. Mostly dust and small particles, with the occasional big chunk of rock. Also a lot of junked vessels from the Vestians' last war. Kamnach's famous for hiding in debris fields and confusing the other guy's sensors."

"Which is good and bad," Wesley elaborated, "because all that tinfoil sometimes confuses our sensors, too, not to mention comm. Next to impossible to send or receive subspace as long as we're in there."

"Which is exactly what he wants," Renkova suggested.

"I don't understand," Pike said, playing the innocent. He had a fair idea what they were driving at, but he wanted to hear it said before he passed judgment.

"You'll find out," Renkova said knowingly, with a nervous glance at Hanley, who looked as if he were going to argue, "as soon as the captain gives the Three Most Powerful speech."

"Which should be right before he assigns 'round-the-clock drills," Chewy added.

Before Pike could ask what the Three Most Powerful speech was, the intercraft sounded. "Captain to Number One. Mr. Pike, if you would, report to the bridge a few minutes early, please."

Pike gulped his coffee—Kamnach frowned on food or drink on his bridge unless he specifically allowed it—grabbed a piece of toast to eat in the 'lift, and was just stepping out onto the bridge wiping the last of the crumbs off his mouth when Kamnach addressed the entire ship.

"All hands, this is the captain. Our ETA at the Vestian border is approximately twenty-two point five hours. In that time, I want all watch commanders to run emergency drills every hour on the hour. At the end of each drill, log your crew's times into ship's main computers for my perusal. Mr. Pike will oversee all departments. I expect everyone's times to improve at each subsequent drill."

It's not how I would have done it, Pike thought, hoping it didn't show on his face. *You don't get a better crew that way, just a more tired one.*

Alpha shift was still trickling in and gamma shift was making the handoff, and Pike was making the rounds to secure all stations when he became aware that Kamnach had swung the captain's chair around as far as it would go and was watching him.

"Number One?"

Pike straightened up a little too quickly. "Sir?"

"In your considered opinion, who are the three most powerful people in the quadrant?"

Pike avoided looking at Renkova. So this was what she'd been talking about. Too many options ran through his mind. He sensed that this was more important even than the opera question, and that a considerable part of his comfort level, or lack of same, on this voyage would depend on his answer. He was also very glad Chewy was down in engineering, because he'd have had a hard time avoiding his eyes. *You were wrong about the sequence, my friend, but not about Kamnach's predictability.* Trying to keep his voice light, he said: "I'll trust you to tell me, Captain."

Kamnach ticked them off on his fingers. "The President of the Federation, CinC Starfleet, and the captain of a starship. And out where the ships move faster than the subspace communications, Mr. Pike, which of those would you say is the most powerful?"

Pike felt like the new kid at school who didn't know the rules yet. He didn't like the feeling.

"I think the answer's self-evident, Captain," he said after a moment's hesitation.

Kamnach gave him a narrow look. "You always think your answers through so carefully, Mr. Pike?"

For some reason Pike found himself remembering the Neworlders and a scene in a freighter's corridor many, many years ago. He couldn't exactly stick his hands in his pockets and shrug as if he didn't care this time.

He tried his lopsided grin instead. "Only when they're important, Captain. And never during a red alert," he added.

He saw Kamnach's eyes narrow, but the captain let it go.

The red alert wasn't long in coming.

"Message from Starbase 3, Captain," Lieutenant Flowers reported. "Relayed from Starfleet Command on Scramble."

Kamnach did not look up from the report Pike had just handed him, which contained each department's times from the last of three emergency drills. The times had not improved, and the numbers did not please him. Everyone was sleep-deprived and on edge, except for Kamnach, who seemed to thrive on stress.

"On speakers," he said finally, after he'd allowed the tension to build for a long moment. "I think we all have a fair idea what the message is, but I want everybody to hear it. Keep rumor to a minimum."

"Aye, sir."

A few moments later, Admiral Straczeskie's voice filtered through the static.

". . . reports indicating the government of Vestios II has been toppled by insurgents from Vestios V, who have announced they will disregard treaty and attack any Federation vessel within three parsecs of the treaty border between our space and theirs . . . Tellarite freighter and science vessel *Colwell* have not responded to our hails and are presumed missing . . . *Aldrin* is to proceed with Sequence 142-alpha. Straczeskie out . . ."

"Acknowledge that, Comm," Kamnach said tersely, "and open intercraft."

"Aye, sir."

"Well, people, this is it," he announced. "We're not playing anymore. Navigator, lay in course alpha-tango-zulu. All stations, set your scanners for debris trails. Report anything that looks as if it might be a piece of a freighter or a science vessel. Number One," he added without pausing for breath. "You'll continue the emergency drills belowdecks."

"Sir?"

Kamnach swung his chair around. "No better time to practice for an emergency than in an emergency. You'll instruct the department heads I want five minutes shaved off the last drill time, or I'll know the reason why."

Kamnach was taking a nap when the first sighting occurred. He'd been on the bridge for three shifts straight, and gave the conn to Pike with a yawn.

"Twenty minutes is all I need. You watch out for bogeys in the meantime."

"Aye, sir."

Ten minutes into Kamnach's twenty-minute nap, Pike and Wesley simultaneously spotted a distinct scatter pattern running through the background debris.

"Helm, slow to impulse," Pike said, leaning forward in the captain's chair, still an uneasy fit. He waited until Wesley had done so. "Analysis, Renkova?"

"Scanning, sir," she replied. "Predominantly manufactured, with some organic scree."

Before Pike could open a discrete to order the transporter room to beam some of the debris aboard, Kamnach strode out of the turbolift. The change from warp to impulse had been enough to tumble him out of a deep sleep and catapult him onto the bridge.

"I have the conn," he announced abruptly, impatient for Pike to get out of his chair. "What have we got?"

Renkova's initial assessment was correct. The debris was metallic, manufactured, but their initial sweep hadn't scooped up enough of it to make an identification.

"Definitely a vessel hull, Captain," Pike reported, indicating the readout in the center of the briefing room table. "Consistent with materials the Tellarites use, but also historically used by several other species in their ship manufacture, not all of them members of the Federation."

Kamnach made an impatient gesture. "I'm not interested in 'historical' data, Mr. Pike, just the here and now. That debris is from a destroyed space vessel, yes? I want to know what destroyed it."

"We're not certain of that yet, either, Captain," Renkova chimed in. "If we had more debris, or more time—"

"Or an opportunity to scan for a vector backwards to a possible attack vessel—" Pike interjected.

"We don't have any of that!" Kamnach said. "No time, no luxury to pussyfoot around playing detective. Destroying a Federation vessel is an act of war. And given our proximity to Vestian space, there's no question in my mind who's responsible. Any Vestian vessel caught on *either* side of the border is, in my estimation, fair game. Mr. Pike? You have anything to add?"

"Only that unless we get official clearance from Starfleet Command we shouldn't—"

"Lieutenant Flowers? On our current heading, how soon before we lose subspace comm with Starbase 3?"

Flowers hesitated, fiddled with something on the table in front of her. Pike caught Chewy's glance from across the table.

"Approximately one hour from now, sir," Flowers said at last. "Debris from the region in Sector 47B will obscure our signal. I can't guarantee you incoming or outgoing until we clear the field, sir."

"Good enough," Kamnach said, cutting her off. He leaned forward so that he was eye to eye with Pike. "That means once we enter that debris field, we're on our own, Number One. You check your regulations for standard procedure under those conditions."

"No need, Captain," Pike said evenly, holding Kamnach's gaze. "I'm aware of the regulations. Once out of subspace comm range, all combat decisions are at captain's discretion."

"Best you remember that, Mr. Pike." Kamnach pulled himself to his feet. "Keep your eyes peeled, gentlemen. A hundred credits out of my personal account to the first one who spots a Vestian vessel. Dismissed."

". . . perfectly legitimate tactical maneuver," Hanley the weapons officer was arguing in the rec room late that night. Kamnach had finally relaxed the 'round-the-clock drills, and most of the bridge officers at last had a chance to decompress.

"Not the way I'd have done it necessarily, but well within bounds," Wesley conceded, pouring himself another beer from the communal pitcher in the center of the table.

He and Hanley were discussing a previous mission with Kamnach in command. In that instance the "target of opportunity," as Hanley called it, had been a Klingon vessel.

Pike had researched Kamnach's record; he knew which battle they were talking about.

"Slightly different situation there, wouldn't you say, Hanley?" he chimed in, taking an empty chair and reaching for the pitcher when Wesley was through. "The Klingons were in clear violation of the border in the Jeris II incident. And Kamnach's was the only ship in the sector. Out here, we've got backup."

"Intention is half the law, Pike," Hanley said stonily. "We're at war."

"Are we?" Pike arranged his chair so that Lieutenant Flowers, at another table with a couple of female crew members, was within his line of vision. "I don't recall any official declaration. Unless that occurred after we left Earth and Admiral Straczeskie just forgot to notify us."

Hanley muttered something about people who had regulation books in place of their spines and pushed off, taking his beer mug with him. Pike got up as if to follow him and ask him to come back and finish the debate, then thought the better of it, using Hanley's abrupt departure as an excuse to stroll past Flowers's table.

"Buy you ladies a drink?" he asked. The other two shook their heads, but Flowers beamed at him.

"That would be nice, Commander. I'll have a Tarkalian tea, please."

". . . never been on a combat vessel before," Hana was saying. Hana and Chris . . . they were on a first-name basis by now. Her two girlfriends had wisely moved off, and the rec room was mostly empty. She looked down at her teacup, too shy this close to meet his eyes. "I've only ever been on in-system vessels before, off Vega mostly. That's where I'm from."

"So you're as much a newbie on *Aldrin* as I am."

She nodded.

Pike waited for her to go on. When she didn't, he said, "You know what? I've never been in combat, either."

"Really?" Her eyes were even more beautiful close-up, a surprising pale gray against her coffee-colored skin. Pike remembered women who looked like her in Sulawesi when he was a boy. "But you seemed so calm and in control."

"Running drills? Sure. Anybody can do that. But nobody

knows how they'll react in a real combat situation until they get there." He changed the subject. "Will you walk in the arboretum with me?"

"I'd like that," she said, getting up first. "As long as you don't make any jokes about flowers."

He didn't understand her at first. "I'm sorry?"

"Because of my name," she explained. "Every man I've ever known has made a joke about it. 'Flowers for a flower . . . a rose by any other name . . .' Even my father used to joke that he should have named me 'Rose.'"

"No jokes," Pike promised, falling into step beside her.

The arboretum, like all spaces on a cutter, was small, really not much more than a roomful of potted plants— some of them knocked over during evasive maneuvers in the drills, and he helped Hana set them upright, their hands touching as they scooped the soil off the deck and patted it around the roots—but cool and inviting, a universe away from the chronic tension on Kamnach's bridge.

Pike had already decided that as soon as this mission was over, he'd request a transfer. Assuming, given Kamnach's eagerness to find and engage a Vestian ship, that this mission would be over, and safely, anytime soon.

For the moment, though, he focused on the burbling of an invisible stream, the cries of the nightbirds—piped in, he knew, and they'd gotten the mockingbird wrong—but the scent of Hana's hair was real, and so was the warmth of her skin, the touch of her hands on his face.

What were her plans, her dreams? he wondered. Starfleet never discouraged shipboard romances, but didn't encourage them, either. Pike knew of a couple of officers and even more enlisted personnel who had formed permanent relationships, even married, but they were uncommon. The kind of relationship Charlie and Hobelia had was even more unusual. He'd tried long distance relationships a few times and failed. Rare was the woman who would wait for him to show up between missions.

Concentrate on the here and now, he thought as he kissed Hana good night at the door to her quarters and returned to his own. *There may not be a tomorrow.*

12

U.S.S. ALDRIN

Pike crawled through the smoke to the vicinity of the captain's chair, grabbed an armrest and pulled himself upright, fumbling for the intercraft. "Engineering . . . damage report!" he shouted past the whooping of the red alert. "Comm, turn off that klaxon! I don't think anyone needs to be reminded we're on red alert."

From engineering came the sounds of voices overlapping, orders being shouted and confirmed, a feedback echo from the red alert klaxon sounding belowdecks as well. Comm was abandoned; Flowers had been injured by a small explosion at her station during the initial attack. Pike pulled himself toward the comm station against the wonky gravity, and quashed the klaxon.

"Engineering?" he repeated, deciding he was better off staying at comm. Even in Kamnach's absence, it didn't feel right for him to be sitting in the captain's chair. "Pike to engineering . . . what's going on down there?"

Finally a hoarse voice he didn't recognize managed to stop coughing long enough to say, "Warp engines off-line, life support compromised, sir. Shields down to thirty-five percent. We've had to seal off decks twelve and thirteen to contain the fire."

Pike started to speak, coughed, started again. "Casualties?"

"Three dead, eight injured, four in the vicinity of the hull breach still unaccounted for."

Charlie! he thought, but suppressed the thought immediately. Nothing he could do from where he was, anyway.

"Chewy? How soon before . . ."

"Sir . . . Lieutenant Chua's dead."

Pike sat back in the chair, momentarily stunned. The chief engineer's cheerful face flashed through his mind. Chua and the others had died on his watch. The others, possibly including Charlie, and if Flowers's injuries were severe . . . This was the burden of command, the thing he'd dreaded most. No time for dread now; he had to get the ship back online and away from the border before more Vestian vessels found them and finished the job.

Around him the skeleton of a bridge crew had contained the circuitry fires at the bridge stations. Wesley made the rounds with a fire extinguisher, but the smoke lingered in the air, a dirty yellow haze. With life support laboring on backup controls, the smoke refused to dissipate.

"Wesley, belay that and get back to your station. Plot us a course out of here," Pike said sharply.

Wesley, still not sure if he should be obeying the first officer or starting a counter-mutiny, did as he was told.

Pike assumed as much, and went on talking to engineering. "Shields and life support first, weapons later. We need to breathe before we can fight. Pike out."

Tell me I'm dreaming! he thought with the tiny little corner of his brain that wasn't ticking with procedures, regulations, and the sinking feeling that if they got out of this alive and returned home, he and those who had sided with him were facing court-martial. *Tell me I'll wake up and none of this will be happening!*

But it was no dream. They'd met and fought one Vestian vessel, destroying it. A second battle had nearly destroyed them, though not before Pike had relieved Captain Kamnach of command and confined him to his quarters, effectively staging a mutiny, but within the letter of the law of Starfleet regulations as he understood them.

He'd done everything he knew how to avoid a confrontation, and now there was no way out.

They'd spotted the first vessel early that morning. Vestian ships were top-heavy with weaponry, but their sensors had blind spots, and they hadn't spotted *Aldrin*.

"Half impulse," Kamnach said quietly. "Arm lasers."

"Armed and ready, sir," Hanley reported just as quietly.

"Warning shot across her bow on my mark . . ."

"Aye, sir." Hanley's finger hovered over the button.

From the science station, where he'd relieved Renkova, who was still analyzing the debris from the presumed Tellarite vessel, Pike cleared his throat. "Captain?"

"What is it, Mr. Pike?"

"She's still on her side of the border, sir. Regulations—"

"—specify that we should hail her first, and if there's no response to our challenge, then we fire across her bow. You familiar with the weapons array on a Vestian *Aloku*-class battleship, Mr. Pike? Ever try to pick up a sea urchin?"

Prior to this mission he hadn't been, but Pike had done his research. The visual on the forward screen confirmed what he'd learned. The Vestian ship bristled with weapons ports in all directions. Depending upon the situation, it could fire those weapons in sequence, transforming itself into a spacefaring Gatling gun, or all at once, spewing plasma fire like darts in all directions.

"No, sir. But I've accidentally brushed up against a saguaro and not been able to sit down for the rest of the day," Pike answered, keeping his voice light. "Which is why—"

"Which is why, in spite of your folksy little tale, we are not going to hail that ship and risk getting spiked," Kamnach finished for him. "Weapons, fire when ready."

Pike winced as the laser released, holding his breath until he saw it lance through empty space well ahead of the Vestian ship, which abruptly turned toward them, searching for the source of the fire. Pike could see Flowers scanning for any comm from the Vestian ship. Catching his eye, she shook her head: *Nothing*. They were not even attempting to communicate with *Aldrin*. Maybe Kamnach's decision was the right one.

Simultaneously, Kamnach was barking orders, maneuvering *Aldrin* into position behind a particularly large chunk of rock—not big enough to hide them completely, but big enough to confuse the *Aloku*'s sensors.

Whoever was captaining the *Aloku* didn't seem to care. The ship's forward weapons ports began to glow, and then she fired.

By the book, *Aldrin* should not have even fired a warning shot unless the *Aloku* violated the border. Strictly speaking, the *Aloku* was well within her rights to fire back. It all happened rather quickly after that.

"Target her aft shields, there!" Kamnach ordered, jabbing a blunt finger at the schematic on the screen between the helm and nav stations. "Short burst ought to get her to pay attention and back off. Even a Vestian won't fight with no shields."

Weapons fired. A short burst should have just knocked out the shields. Instead, the entire ship went up in a fireball.

The forward viewscreen damped some of it, but for several moments the bridge crew was virtually blinded. The shock wave came next.

"Hang on!" Kamnach said unnecessarily as they braced for impact.

Did Pike only imagine he saw the captain and his weapons officer exchanging triumphant glances?

As the shock wave dissipated, Kamnach slouched back in his chair, hands tented over his stomach. "Oops!" he said with a small, smug smile. "Guess we put a little too much punch into that. All hands, stand down from red alert. Helm, return to original course and speed. Comm, notify Starbase 3 we have met and dispatched one Vestian *Aloku* fighter-class vessel found in violation of treaty border, blah-blah-blah. Give them the current time and coordinates."

"Aye, sir," Flowers responded.

The current coordinates, Pike realized, checking, were well over on the Federation side. Whatever remained of the *Aloku* would drift in all directions. Nothing but the captain's say-so as to which side of the border she'd been on when the exchange began, and that was that. Or was it?

"You could get us both in very big trouble, Mr. Pike," Renkova said grimly. "I was going to transfer off this ship of fools before we got drafted for this mission. I don't fancy spending any part of it in the brig."

"I understand," Pike said, equally grim. "If there were any other way to do this . . . but I don't have the science skills; you do."

Renkova sighed. A handsome woman, her long, curly hair just a tad over regulation length framing a high-cheekboned face with mournful brown Ukrainian eyes, she'd watched the slow dance between Hana Flowers and the handsome first officer wistfully. Time was she'd have gone after Pike herself, but no more.

"Should be easy enough to correlate the coordinates in ship's logs with . . . hello!" she said.

"What is it?" Pike leaned over her shoulder to see what she was looking at.

"According to the log entry, we never violated the Vestian border."

"Renkova, I was there. I saw what happened," Pike objected, scowling.

She shrugged. "Logs can be altered," she suggested carefully.

Pike weighed the import of what she was saying. Before he'd come down here, he'd checked the engineering logs and found that the settings on Hanley's lasers had been recalibrated slightly higher than they should have been. He was willing to bet that if he double-checked now, they'd have been reset to normal.

"Would you be able to tell if the logs were altered?" he asked Renkova carefully.

"Depends on the skill of the person who altered them," she said, equally carefully. Neither was sure they could trust the other; Kamnach's divide-and-conquer command mode saw to that. Renkova hesitated. "However, a really skilled science tech could probably find artifacts suggesting tampering, without leaving any traces of her own."

Pike took her meaning. "It sure would help if we had someone that skilled aboard . . ."

Later, alone in his cabin, he weighed the evidence. He had in fact double-checked the laser settings, and this time they were normal. He cursed himself for not logging the previous settings when he found them, but he'd only checked on a hunch, and hadn't wanted to believe what he saw.

Kamnach and Hanley were using the tensions between the Federation and the Vestians as a hunting expedition, a personal vendetta, a chance to rack up points for some sort of blaze of glory—call it what you would, they were skirting regulations for their own ends.

Why?

Pike's research on Kamnach had revealed a loner, a commanding officer who spent his off-hours alone in his cabin playing computer chess, his leave time cruising the watering holes in whatever port he was in, drinking hard, but never causing problems. If he'd ever had a wife or children, they weren't in his profile.

His weapons officer Hanley was much the same. Both men were at an age where, traditionally, they ought to have been kicked upstairs to desk jobs, or taken early retirement to do other things with their lives. The fact that both were still locked into their seats on a Starfleet vessel's bridge said that it was all they had.

Looking to go out in a blaze of glory, and take as many people with them as they could. That might work for Vikings or Klingons or Egyptian pharaohs, but Pike had no intention of joining anyone's funeral pyre, or letting his commanding officer's juggernaut take Charlie and Hana and the rest of the crew with him.

By this time tomorrow they would be out of range of even Starbase 3 comm. No need to hide in the debris field to avoid messages from Starfleet Command updating them on the Vestian situation—which might easily have resolved itself, if past rumblings between Vestios II and V were any indication—or to tell them to return to base.

Does he think he'll get away with this? Pike wondered. *Does he realize hunting Vestian ships against orders could turn a little border skirmish into a full-blown war? Does he care?*

Kamnach's "Three Most Powerful" speech rang in his head. Yes, Kamnach did think he could get away with it. And unless Pike monitored him very carefully, he probably would.

"Captain?" Wesley's voice wavered nervously. The situation was all but identical to yesterday's—a Vestian fighter, bristling with weapons ports, patrolling her side of the border, as yet unaware of the *Aldrin*.

"I see her," Kamnach replied, leaning forward in his chair, a feral look on his face. "Weapons—"

"Armed and ready, sir," Hanley replied a little too eagerly.

"Captain—" Pike made sure his own voice was steady before he spoke. "She's on her side of the border. Just like the ship we engaged yesterday."

He shouldn't have added that last part, but he had to. All eyes on the bridge turned toward him. He knew without looking at any of them who was with him and who wasn't.

"I know, I know," Chewy had said when he and Pike had met at the food dispenser that morning before the others arrived in the officers' mess. "I'm not in a position to do anything on my own, but if you challenge him, I'm with you, Pike."

Renkova had made her feelings clear the night before in the Sciences lab.

Pike steered clear of Hanley. He didn't need him anyway. But helm and comm were important.

"You're talking mutiny," were Wesley's first words after he'd heard Pike out.

"It's not mutiny to refuse an order that goes against your

principles," Pike argued. "C'mon, Wesley, I'm the one with the reg book up my spine. You're supposed to be more flexible. What they're doing is—"

"—is within captain's discretion when out of subspace range in time of war," Wesley cut him off.

"'Time of war'—!" Pike snorted. "Where's the declaration of war, Wesley? Where are our orders from Starfleet Command telling us to engage Vestian vessels on their side of the border, recalibrate the laser settings, then doctor the logs afterward?"

Wesley's gaze faltered. "Don't push me, Chris. I'm just a helmsman. I leave policy to the policy makers." He swallowed hard, reaching a decision. "I won't stand in your way, but don't ask me to stand with you."

"So that's the way it is!" Pike said, more than a little annoyed.

"Hey, you follow your conscience, I follow mine!" Wesley called after him, a little too loudly.

Hana Flowers was even more conflicted.

"I can't, Chris! Please don't ask me to disobey orders!" There were tears in her eyes when she said it. "I told you, I've never been in combat before. I couldn't sleep last night, thinking about the people on that Vestian ship. I know they're aliens, but they had lives . . ."

"Don't you see I'm trying to prevent unnecessary loss of life?" Pike reasoned with her. "Including ours. What Kamnach's doing is wrong. It's a court-martial offense. And it could get us all killed."

Hana pulled away from him, hands over her ears to block out his words.

"I'm not listening to you! I don't know anything about tactics or politics or any of that stuff. I'm just a comm officer. It's hard enough for me to do my job without thinking too hard about the messages I'm relaying. Please, Chris, leave me out of this!"

It wasn't the answer he'd been hoping for, but at least he

was reasonably certain she wouldn't turn against him if and when the time came. Wasn't he?

They were all on the bridge, except for Chewy, and they were all looking his way, each of them committed to their own belief in what was right. If he needed to defy Kamnach, could he make it stick with only the chief engineer and the science officer backing him up? And Charlie, of course, for whatever use a transporter chief might be, particularly when he couldn't talk to him directly.

"Eyes on your stations!" Kamnach barked, breaking Pike's reverie. When everyone else had complied, his gimlet eyes bored into Pike's.

"I'm aware of the position of the Vestian vessel, Mr. Pike. I'm also aware of your reluctance to do your job in helping us repel an enemy from its path of destruction. I should have reprimanded you after yesterday's little performance, but I didn't. Guess I'm getting soft in my old age. But I'll tell you this: You feel uncomfortable with the current situation, Mr. Pike, you feel free to transfer off my ship, effective immediately. Otherwise, mind your own damn business and do your job!"

Without pausing for breath, he rotated his chair so that Pike was no longer even in his peripheral vision and opened the intercraft. "All hands, this is the captain. Go to red alert. Prepare for battle."

It might have been a repeat of yesterday's event, but two things happened. First was Lieutenant Flowers's voice cutting through the red alert klaxon.

"Captain? The Vestian vessel is hailing us, sir. And I'm receiving a delayed transmission from Starbase 3."

Kamnach did not so much as acknowledge that she had spoken. With his back to her, he made a chopping motion with his hand that said *Not now!*

The second thing that happened was that Pike motioned Renkova out of her chair and said: "Flowers, relay both messages to the science station."

Kamnach swung his chair around. "What the hell do you think you're doing?"

Pike didn't answer. Methodically he unscrambled the message from Starbase 3 and put it on speakers.

". . . terminate all activity and . . ." A burst of static. ". . . Vestian Council has . . ." Another. ". . . repeat, *Aldrin,* you are to return to . . ."

The message ended there.

The red alert was the only sound on the bridge. For a long moment everything seemed to move in slow motion as Pike and Kamnach eyeballed each other, as much at odds as *Aldrin* and the Vestian vessel.

"Comm . . ." Kamnach said slowly, never taking his eyes off Pike. "Terminate all incoming."

"A-aye, sir," Flowers stammered.

"Interesting timing on that message," Kamnach said deliberately, taking his time, oblivious to the red alert and the fact that everyone else on the ship was scrambling to comply with it.

"Captain—" Pike began. "Regulations clearly state that a directive from Starfleet Command overrides—"

"What directive?" Kamnach demanded. "That message is incomplete. Garbled by static. A day late and a dollar short. It may as well not be a message at all."

"Sir—"

"For all we know, the Vestians could have sent that message, Mr. Pike," Kamnach said incisively. "In any event, there isn't enough of it for us to be clear on Starfleet's intentions. We will proceed to exercise our own discretion in time of battle. Science Officer, resume your station. Mr. Pike, you're dismissed."

Pike rose to his feet.

"No, sir," he said quietly, hearing his voice echoing in his own head.

Was he out of his mind? He remembered Charlie's definition of heroism. Did the same concept apply to professional suicide?

"Captain Kamnach, refusing or ignoring a direct order from Starfleet Command is a violation of regulations. On that basis I am relieving you of command."

"You're *what*?!" Kamnach was also on his feet, his hands fisted, eyes blazing.

Pike was peripherally aware that Wesley and Flowers were sitting with their hands in their laps. Behind him, he could sense Renkova poised for action, though what that action might be, neither of them knew. He motioned to the ubiquitous security guard by the turbolift. *Banarjee,* he remembered. *Hope he knows the regulations as well as I do.*

"Mr. Banarjee," he said carefully. "You'll escort Captain Kamnach to his quarters, please."

Banarjee was moving forward as the ship shuddered with the release of a laser blast, aimed at the Vestian vessel.

Hanley! Pike thought, too late. He'd expected the big man to wait for Kamnach's order, but he'd taken the law into his own hands.

The rest was a blur.

The laser blast had been hasty and badly aimed. It caught the Vestian vessel amidships, damaging two of her weapons ports. What Hanley should have realized was that, given the unusual configuration of Vestian ships, this would automatically trigger the ports on either side of the damaged area to release their weapons, sending fire in all directions.

Aldrin reeled from two plasma weapon blasts. Bridge

stations sparked with explosions as she absorbed the impact. One of those injured was Hanley. With a surprisingly high-pitched scream, he flung himself backward in his chair, hands burned and uniform smoking, lost his balance as the ship careened out of control, struck his head on his console and was out cold.

Beside him, Wesley took control without waiting for orders and tried to steer the ship. As he'd told Pike, his priority was doing his job.

Flowers had been knocked out of her chair; she lay on the deck unmoving as Renkova hailed sickbay. The security guard, Banarjee, managed to stay on his feet and, taking advantage of the confusion, helped Kamnach to his and, hand on the laser at his belt, said, "Sorry, sir," and escorted the furious captain into the 'lift as the medical team arrived. When they went to tend to Hanley, Pike ordered the weapons officer held in confinement.

As the doors to the turbolift closed, Kamnach, nursing a head wound where he'd struck the arm of the command chair, shouted: "You'll regret this, Pike! You'll regret this for the rest of your life!"

Pike wasn't listening. He had to prepare himself for a battle he'd tried to prevent.

It didn't last long. The Vestian vessel fired one more salvo aimed at *Aldrin*'s engine room, then retreated, well within its own borders, as if defying them to violate the treaty and come closer.

Under Kamnach, they might have. If they hadn't been so seriously damaged.

Aldrin was yawing again, sending people flying. That last barrage must have damaged the artificial gravity. Fighting nausea, Pike picked himself up from the deck and crawled through the smoke to the captain's chair, flinging himself into the last place he wanted to be for the second time.

"Engineering . . . damage report . . ."

When they told him Chewy and two others were dead, and they'd had to seal off two decks to contain the damage, leaving four more of the crew unaccounted for, it was all he could do to stop himself from asking about Charlie.

So this is what command is like outside of Academy scenarios, he thought grimly, then ordered his thoughts. The turbolift seemed to be working all right; Flowers's relief arrived to survey the damage to the station. And the Vestian vessel did not renew hostilities. Perhaps it was just waiting to see how much damage *Aldrin* had sustained before it fired again.

But from what Pike knew of Vestians, that was when they usually closed for the kill. Had the message from Starfleet meant that the rebellion had been put down, and the Federation and the Vestians had returned to *status quo ante bellum*? It was how he'd interpreted the message, and how Kamnach should have as well, if he hadn't been blinded by his desire to take out one more ship.

"What's your status, Comm?" Pike asked as the new man surveyed the damage to the station.

"Nominal, Cap—uh, Number One."

"As you were. Send to commander Vestian vessel. 'Our apologies for unwarranted attack. We have called off all hostilities and await your decision.' Then do your damnedest to punch through to Starbase 3. Apprise them of the current situation, including the fact that I've relieved Captain Kamnach of command."

"Aye, sir," the comm officer said, trying not to sound flustered. "Uh, discrete from engineering, sir."

"Let's hear it."

The news was not good. Aux power could maintain life support for less than two hours, and so far even the most creative bypassing and jury-rigging hadn't gotten the main controls back online. Barring a miracle this far out, if they couldn't get main power restored . . .

". . . we have a choice between freezing to death or running out of air," Pike told the crew. "Neither is a choice I'd like to have to make. Let's get on it. Reduce all unnecessary power use . . ." The bridge lights dimmed even as he said it; they were way ahead of him. "And keep me informed."

He terminated the intercraft and waited, watching the Vestian ship on the forward screen. It hadn't moved. There was no response to their transmission. And it could be hours before they got a reply from Starbase 3.

So this is command! Pike thought grimly. He wanted to be down in engineering helping them with life support. Or with the sick bay team tending to the wounded. Or off-duty, free to roam the corridors and make sure Charlie was okay. In short, he wanted to be anywhere but here.

"Number One?" It was the replacement comm officer; Pike didn't know his name. "Reply from the Vestian vessel, sir."

"Go ahead."

"Running it through the translator now, sir . . ." He listened, reporting as the translation program fed him data. "They say the war's over, sir. Rebels repelled from Vestios II, shipping lanes are open again. The vessel we destroyed yesterday belonged to the rebels, but this one . . . they'll accept our apology since they've sustained only minor damage . . ." He took the earpiece out of his ear. "They're leaving, sir."

Motion on the forward screen confirmed this. The Vestian vessel executed a one-hundred-twenty-degree turn, then winked into warp.

"No harm, no foul, if we can believe them!" Pike muttered, scowling. "Except we've lost three good men, possibly more. Finalize that translation and make sure the entire crew hears it. Especially Captain Kamnach. We're still not moving until we hear from Starbase 3. Somebody get me a communicator."

He couldn't sit still any longer. He got out of the center seat, hooked the communicator onto his belt and headed for the turbolift.

"Mr. Wesley, you have the conn. Continue scanning for Vestian vessels, on the odd chance some of the rebels haven't been informed the war is over. Comm, relay any message from Starbase 3 to me immediately."

"Aye, sir," both men said simultaneously.

It wasn't until the 'lift doors closed and he slumped against the wall in exhaustion that Pike realized how lucky he'd been. No one but Hanley had defied him or resisted his attempt to relieve Kamnach of command.

So far.

Lucky? he thought as the 'lift decanted him near the transporter room. *Commanding a crippled ship with less than two hours of oxygen left and facing a court-martial when you get home, if you get home. Some luck!*

But the next two hours denied him the luxury of even thinking about such things.

The team repairing the hull breach on decks twelve and thirteen was almost done. The four unaccounted for when the hull ruptured were confirmed dead. Three had been sucked out into vacuum, and the fourth had simply not been able to get out in time. Seven dead, Pike noted grimly. He'd get the names for the log entry later, inform the next of kin as soon as possible, captain's duty. Satisfied that the repairs were proceeding as quickly as possible, he ordered those corridors resealed until life support was restored. Then he headed for engineering.

He literally bumped into Charlie backing out of a Jefferies tube.

"Rumors are generating enough hot air to offset anything we're doing down here," the older man said, wasting no time on pleasantries. "What happened up there?"

Pike filled Charlie in as they got to the engine room, where he could survey the damage and observe the crew members scrambling to repair it.

"Who's in charge here?" he demanded. *Now that Chewy's dead,* he thought but didn't say.

"Chief Pike is, sir," a flustered ensign reported, looking from one man with the same name to the other.

"As you were, Ensign," Pike said and, for the first time in days, he found himself laughing.

"Looks like I've got nothing to worry about, Hoss," he started to say as his communicator beeped. "Pike here."

"Disturbance near the captain's quarters, Number One. Captain Kamnach's unaccounted for."

"On my way."

13

U.S.S. ALDRIN

He should have ordered Kamnach to the brig, but he'd wanted to leave the man some dignity. He would find out later that Kamnach had taken advantage of his generosity to jury-rig a comm device and stage a counter-mutiny, contacting key personnel loyal to him, including two security guards who had rather forcibly relieved the two guarding his quarters. Kamnach was loose somewhere on the ship, no doubt intent on resuming command.

"Charlie . . ."

"Chewy's crew won't let him do any harm down here," was Charlie's opinion.

Cursing himself for leaving the bridge, Pike ordered security to check the weapons lockers and report anything missing. Then he ordered Wesley to secure the turbolift.

"Nobody enters or leaves the bridge until I give the order. Wesley? Answer me!" There was no reply. He could hear shouting and scuffling, then a long silence punctuated by console noises. "Bridge? What's going on up there?"

"Renkova," she reported, a little breathlessly. "Mr. Wesley is . . . indisposed. Turbolift's secured."

Pike could guess what had happened. "I assume you have the conn. Hope you didn't hurt him."

Renkova's voice was diffident. "Little trick I learned from an Andorian martial artist. Love to teach it to you sometime."

Pike found himself grinning. "Carry on."

Okay, now what? Open the intercraft and tell the entire ship that their former captain was on the loose and possibly dangerous? Or try to contain this with as little uproar as possible? If he were Kamnach, where would he try to go first?

The bridge, obviously. That was secure. The engine room, ditto. Frustrated in both places, would Kamnach try to commandeer the transporter and risk an intraship beam-out?

Charlie was reading his mind. "He'd have to get past me first. Tell you what we can do—you find him, I'll grab him and whoever's with him and beam 'em anywhere you want."

"Can you do that?" Pike asked.

"Can Tango dance?"

Speechless, Pike just clapped him on the shoulder and checked in with security. Three phasers were missing from the main weapons locker, and wherever Kamnach was, they hadn't found him yet.

Beyond exhausted, Pike stationed himself at the auxiliary engineer's station, trying not to notice Chewy's family photos in the holocube stuck on the console. In an ideal world, word from Starfleet Command would come through just as life support systems came back on, Captain Kamnach and whoever was with him would hear the transmission, realize it had all been a mistake, everyone would go back to their stations, and *Aldrin* could return home. And no one would have died and no one been injured. With a sigh, Pike hailed sickbay.

"Minor burns and a concussion," was the report on Hanley. "Confined as ordered."

"And Lieutenant Flowers?"

"A little shocky, but nothing twenty-four hours' rest won't cure."

"Thanks. Number One out."

Around him, the lights in engineering flickered, and some of the toggles went off-line for an instant. The temperature was cooler than was strictly comfortable, but at least the smoke had been cleared and the air was still breathable.

Too many of us running around the corridors using it up too fast! Pike thought. Beside him on the console, his communicator bleeped, interrupting his reverie.

"Number One? I think we've got him, sir. Three unauthorized personnel making their way through Jefferies tube six-B."

That tube, Pike knew, led indirectly to the bridge.

"Secure that tube. No one gets in or out. Pike to transporter chief . . ."

"Standing by," came Charlie's voice.

"No need for your services this time, Hoss, but thanks." Pike made his way to where Jefferies tube six-B opened out into the corridor near the officers' mess.

Ultimately, it didn't happen quite the way Pike had envisioned it, and the dead were still dead and the injured still injured. But he'd no sooner arrived to see a red-faced, sweating Kamnach easing himself out of the Jefferies tube onto the deck under the watchful eyes of two security guards, his cohorts following, than Flowers's relief broadcast the incoming message from Starfleet Command on the intercraft.

". . . repeat . . . Vestian Council has reported the rebellion put down, and all rebel-controlled vessels surrendered to Vestios II authority. *Aldrin* is to return to base effective immediately."

It confirmed what the captain of the Vestian vessel had told them before moving off. Motionless in the corridor outside the Jefferies tube, they could all hear Renkova's voice responding.

"Affirmative, Admiral. *Aldrin* has sustained some damage in a recent skirmish. Captain Kamnach and our Number One are . . . overseeing repairs. As soon as we have full power restored, we're coming in, sir."

Bless you, Renkova! Pike thought as Straczeskie said, "As you were, *Aldrin*. Starbase 3 out."

Did Pike only imagine he heard cheering echoing throughout the ship? They still didn't have life support restored. They weren't out of the woods yet. He nodded to Banarjee.

"Secure Captain Kamnach and the others in the officers' mess and disable the comm system in there. Then get the rest of your men down to engineering and—"

"Makes more sense to put us all in the brig," Kamnach interrupted, having wiped the sweat off his face and recovered his dignity. "Including Hanley. No need to disable comm, and you'll only need one guard to monitor the force-field."

It made a certain sense, but—

"Captain—" Pike started to say.

"We'll haggle at the court-martial, Number One," Kamnach said tightly. "Because we both know there'll be a court-martial. I hope you're satisfied. My career's pretty much winding down, but I think you may find yours is over before it began."

Unrepentant, he turned on his heel and headed in the direction of the brig.

TALOS IV

"Christopher?" It was the Magistrate's voice in his mind. Pike no longer considered it odd or intrusive. "So many choices . . . to relive your past, or reinvent it. Why this one?"

"Milestones, I guess," he thought back. "Catharsis. Getting rid of the bad stuff."

"'Bad stuff'?" the Magistrate repeated curiously. "Some would call what you did heroic."

Pike dismissed it. "I'm like Charlie. I don't know what that word means. I was thinking more about the path we humans have carved through space. What do we leave in our wake but debris?"

"As do we all," the Magistrate reminded him, and Pike saw in his mind the ruined surface of Talos, heard the echo of Vina's words ("war . . . thousands of centuries ago . . ."), and wondered how a species so seemingly advanced could have fallen so far.

"A thought we have had millennia to ponder ourselves," the Magistrate added. "Without having arrived at a satisfactory conclusion . . ."

2246: STARFLEET HQ, EARTH

Ultimately *Aldrin* limped home on aux power, the hull breach sealed, but too tetchy to risk warp drive for more than an hour at a time. The extra power was transferred to maintain life support, and no one who didn't know any better would have noticed anything wrong with the gravity, the air or the temperature.

Given the extra time, both Pike and Kamnach filed their log entries and sent them on ahead to Starfleet Command. The sooner the matter was dealt with, the better.

Their slow return gave Command plenty of time to arrange for a court-martial as soon as they reached Earth.

With rare exception, Starfleet courts-martial are kept in the family and not shared with the outside world, but this one got the media's attention, and it was soon being talked about all over the quadrant. Doubtless the rumors were still making their way out to the remoter worlds by the time it was over, because once all the testimony was gathered and compared with the log entries and navigational charts, a verdict was returned in less than a day.

Strangely unperturbed, Christopher Pike sat in the hearing room throughout the trial, even when his presence was not required. He listened to the testimony about Captain Kamnach's actions and his own as if they were about two people he didn't know.

In view of his nearly half a century of service, Captain Kamnach was granted the courtesy of testifying in closed court, which disturbed Pike not a little. He'd gotten a glimpse of Kamnach on his way into chambers, and saw a spit-and-polish senior officer presenting a perfect facade. There was no sign of the obsessive near-madman he'd removed under guard from the bridge. Which side of Kamnach's personality would his testimony reflect?

The only part of the open-court testimony that made Pike smile was Renkova's, particularly when she talked about "persuading" Wesley to surrender the helm. Seeing Hana Flowers on the stand made him more than a little sad. He knew whatever might have become of their relationship was probably lost forever. Flowers confirmed that for him in the corridor during a recess.

"I know you'll never forgive me, Chris . . ." she began.

"That's not true at all. You did what you thought was right."

"But I was wrong! If we'd destroyed that second ship, there might have been a war."

"You didn't know that at the time." He found himself trying to comfort her. "None of us did," he added, not entirely truthfully.

"I should have trusted you!" she said plaintively.

He'd taken her hands in his then. "Hana, it's over. Whatever happens shouldn't affect what you and I—"

"Even if they drum you out of the service?" She shook her head. "No, Chris. If they do, I'm at least partly responsible. I can't—"

"And if they don't?" he asked, not quite daring to hope for it. What did it matter, really? There were other things he could do with his life. He didn't know what they were just now, or how being dishonorably discharged from Starfleet at the ripe old age of twenty-seven would affect his chances, but he couldn't think about that unless it happened. "I'd still like to see you again."

"I'm sorry, Chris!" was all she said, pulling her hands free and all but running down the corridor, as if that could help her escape her feelings.

When it was time for the verdict to be announced, and Pike and Kamnach stood before the three-admiral panel to hear the charges read, they might as well have been about someone else.

"I don't know which of you I want to yell at first," the admiral in the center, a crusty old veteran named Oberon who'd spent more time in the judicial system than he ever had in space, grumbled, eyeballing both of them balefully. "The fact that this situation could have turned out quite differently, with us at war with the Vestians, would be enough to keep me up at night if I weren't already an insomniac.

"In a way, you're both guilty of taking the law into your own hands, and in a way you're both good officers following regulations as you understand them. That's what makes this such a thorny problem. It's the regulations that are at fault, and we who establish them are guilty of not seeing the kind of loophole that causes situations like the *Aldrin*'s to happen. So you've embarrassed us. And we don't like being embarrassed.

"Commander Hanley's actions were simple to adjudicate.

Testimony and the logs show that he fired a laser weapon without authorization, and he'll be tried on that basis. But you two . . ."

Admiral Oberon paused, poured himself a glass of water, still glaring from one to the other, sweating them. Strangely, neither man was sweating. Captain Kamnach was unreadable. He seemed remarkably serene, more serene perhaps than Pike had ever seen him aboard his ship. As for Pike, it was all he could do to keep his mind on the here and now and not on the departed Flowers. Compared to what he'd dealt with on the Vestian border, the events in this room seemed strangely unimportant.

Admiral Oberon cleared his throat, consulted the documents on the table before him, and continued. "Lieutenant Commander Pike, based on the testimony of all personnel involved, given both here and in ship's logs, and particularly that of Captain Kamnach, this panel is prepared to give its verdict as follows . . ."

Oberon paused, took a sip of water, and glanced up at Pike under his eyebrows. Whatever reaction he was expecting, he got none. Christopher Pike returned his gaze evenly. He would wait as long as it took. Oberon cleared his throat again and consulted his notes.

"Given his decades of distinguished service to the 'fleet, we have accepted Captain Kamnach's request for early retirement, with honors, the record to state that he comported himself in a manner consistent with Starfleet Regulations in the instance of the confrontation with a Vestian vessel in Sector 114 on Stardate . . ."

Pike couldn't believe what he was hearing. This sounded like a whitewash. It was all he could do to keep from shouting his outrage, but discipline held him back.

". . . where, given garbled communications, he acted as he saw fit in a crisis situation," Admiral Oberon concluded, the look in his eye indicating he knew exactly what Pike was thinking, and at the least respected him for not saying it, given that his career seemed to be hanging in the balance.

"As for you, Mr. Pike," Oberon said, not to be hurried. "It is Captain Kamnach's recommendation that all charges pursuant to this court-martial be dropped, and that you be promoted to the rank of commander and transferred to the next ship available with all due alacrity. Do you wish to contest that verdict, Mr. Pike?"

Pike's knees felt weak. He struggled to find his voice. "N-no sir."

Did he only imagine that Oberon's eyebrows twitched in wry amusement? "Very well. We're adjourned."

The buzz in the corridors was confirmed. With the exception of Second Officer Hanley, all crew of the *Aldrin*, regardless of which side they'd taken during the Vestian event, were exonerated of all charges for following their respective consciences pursuant to orders.

Science Officer Renkova was given a commendation for "expedient thinking in time of crisis," as fancy a way as there was to describe knocking Wesley out and commandeering the helm. Pike made his way through the throng of well-wishers and curiosity seekers to congratulate her.

"Congratulations yourself, Pike!" she beamed at him. "Want to hear something funny? Wesley's asked me out to dinner!"

Pike smiled back. "Hope you're going to take him up on it."

"I haven't decided yet . . ." she started to say, when they were descended upon by the media.

Scattering "No comments" interspersed with "Excuse mes," Pike eased his way through the crowd and out onto the grounds. He needed to walk. He needed to think.

Why was the victory so bittersweet? Hana Flowers aside, why did he still not feel justified? Did he so strongly need Kamnach to be brought to justice that he couldn't let it go? Kamnach was essentially being forced into retirement—probably a fate worse than death for a commander who'd done nothing else for nearly half a century. Still, he was out of harm's way, and could never take the law into his own hands again. And Hanley would at the least be demoted to a position where he wasn't allowed to fire on anyone ever again. Wasn't that enough?

Pike thought of Kamnach leaving the hearing room by a side door to avoid the media, walking away alone. No one had been waiting to congratulate him. With a bizarre twinge of something—guilt, second thoughts, or just that obsessive need for perfection—Pike almost envied him. He almost wished he could be that alone.

It was not to be. Halfway across the quadrangle, he saw the formidable figure of Admiral Straczeskie bearing down on him.

"Got a minute, son?" Straczeskie was nearly a hundred, and the brisk walk had made him wheeze a little. "We need to talk."

"Admiral, I appreciate your congratulations, but—"

"I didn't track you halfway across the grounds to congratulate you," Straczeskie said gruffly, as if annoyed that anyone with Pike's intelligence would even suggest such a thing. "And that was not a request."

Following the outcome of the trial, Pike thought he was beyond surprise. What Straczeskie told him behind closed doors proved him wrong.

". . . bottom line, we'd had our eye on Kamnach for quite some time," Straczeskie finished. "There was evidence he was taking the law into his own hands out there on the frontier, but we needed something conclusive. But most of his crew had been with him for years and didn't want to risk their own necks and, frankly, we didn't want to hang them out to dry, either. So we needed to bring someone in from the outside. His first officer's needing leave time was the perfect opportunity."

Pike said nothing. Whatever he hadn't allowed himself to feel during the hearing, he was feeling now. The predominant urge was to put his fist through a wall. He tightened his jaw and kept that thought from showing on his face.

"I'm sorry it had to be you, Chris," Straczeskie said not unkindly. "But in a way you were the perfect choice. You're nothing if not honest, and a perfectionist to boot. If anyone could be counted on to be aware of what Kamnach was up to and call him on it, it was you."

"So I was the stalking horse," was all Pike trusted himself to say.

Straczeskie eyed him carefully, assessing his mood. "That would be a fair characterization of your role in the affair, yes. I'm only telling you now because I thought you deserved to know. And because I know this conversation will never leave this room."

Pike thought about that. "Permission to speak candidly, sir?" Straczeskie nodded. "Captain Kamnach destroyed that Vestian ship on the wrong side of the border. That alone should have been sufficient grounds for disciplinary action."

Straczeskie sat down heavily, passed a hand over his eyes. "I know that," he said, and his voice was suddenly that of an old, and tired, man. "And if it were anyone but Kamnach, it might have been. But it turns out it was a rebel ship, and it did in fact destroy the Tellarite vessel whose debris trail *Aldrin* intercepted.

"An eye for an eye. As part of our new treaty, the Vestians

have accepted that. So the destruction of the *Aloku* wasn't enough to hang Kamnach on. But ignoring a direct order from Command was—if, and only if, a senior officer was willing to call him on it. And because you put yourself at risk to do that, regulations will be reviewed, and most likely changed, to prevent a commander in the field from taking that kind of liberty in the future."

Straczeskie looked up at Pike, standing at ease but not easy, and his look was almost pleading. "You comported yourself well, Commander. I know you're not one to gloat, but this was a win-win scenario for the service, and for you personally. The least you can do is say 'Thank you, sir' and savor it."

Pike unclenched his jaw, stood a little straighter and said, "Thank you, sir."

Straczeskie gave a short bark of a laugh, and shook his head. "You'll thank me, but you won't enjoy it. You are your father's son! Are all Pikes this stubborn?"

Pike realized he was being a tight-ass, and forced himself to relax a little. "Afraid so, sir."

"So am I, Mr. Pike. So am I." Straczeskie waved him off. "Get out of here. I understand your family's waiting to celebrate your promotion."

Something occurred to Pike as he was halfway out the door. "Sir? Does Charlie know?"

"About what you and I didn't just talk about?" Straczeskie nodded. "I owe Charlie Pike my life. And I ran into him before I found you. He knows."

Christopher Pike's anger didn't end there. He brought it with him back to the ranch in Mojave, and even three days' ride through the arroyos with Charlie didn't dissipate it. Tango, picking up some of Chris's mood, was unusually

skittish, and startled at a sidewinder on the trail, stumbling
and coming up near lame.

Checking Tango's feet for stones and walking him a
while to ease him, Chris finally let go of everything he'd
been keeping inside.

"It isn't right, Charlie! I wasn't thinking about my career
out there on the border. I was thinking about avoiding a war,
and getting the crew home safely. Command had no right to
use me that way!"

Charlie had dismounted and was walking his own horse
as well to keep Chris company. "Guess you forgot the second half of the oath, then," he said diffidently. "You got the
'protect' part down, but you forgot about the 'serve.'"

Chris snorted in disgust. "Or maybe I'm just not cut out
for command!"

"Or maybe that's exactly why you are cut out for command," Charlie suggested quietly, stopping to watch a pair of
hummingbirds cavorting around each other in midair. "Because you think of the larger picture and not your personal
agenda."

"Ah . . ." Chris shook that off irritably, then blurted out
what was really on his mind. "I'm thinking of quitting, Charlie. Resigning my commission. I don't like being used!"

Charlie did not react the way another man might. He let
the words dissipate on the clear desert air for several minutes without answering them. The two men came to a
riverbed, dry most of the year, but recently replenished by
the winter rains, and stopped to let the horses drink, making
themselves comfortable under an overhang in the rock wall
enclosing the trail, carved by a million years of blowing
sand.

"Well?" Chris demanded as the silence, punctuated by the
sounds of the horses snorting and blowing, the cry of a raptor

too high up in the blue to be visible, went on too long for his comfort. "Aren't you going to talk me out of it?"

"You'd like that, wouldn't you?" Charlie mused. "Make it easier for you to decide."

Chris looked chagrined, busied himself picking up a small, rounded stone from the ground at his feet and studying it intently.

"Chris, why do you think I've spent my whole life turning down promotions?" Charlie asked, studying his son's handsome bowed head, his defeated posture. "Why do you think I never stayed in but for one mission at a time? It's because I don't have the courage to make those decisions. You do."

Chris scowled at him. "Dammit, Charlie, don't twist it around!"

"I may not know what heroism is, but I recognize fear when I see it," Charlie challenged him.

"You're right!" Chris snapped, springing to his feet and flinging the stone hard enough to carry it across the riverbed. "I am afraid. Afraid they'll use me again, turn my strengths into weaknesses, play games behind my back, games that involve my crewmates' lives. That's not what I signed on for!"

Charlie tugged at one ear. "Then I guess you're right. You ought to quit."

"Now you're twisting it the other way!" Chris said angrily, heading down to the water's edge to bathe his face and calm himself.

"If you say so." Charlie inhaled sharply, sighed, studied the horizon, chose his next words carefully. "Your father took the coward's way out. I thought you'd be stronger."

Chris stood up so fast his head swam. From where he was standing, Charlie's face was in shadow and he couldn't read his expression. He tried to process what he'd just heard.

"Wait a minute. Are you saying you knew my father?"

Charlie nodded. He was studying his slouch hat, turning it slowly in his hands as if he'd never seen it before. "Know him still. Inasmuch as a man ever really knows himself."

Above them the raptor cried again, a high ascending scream broken abruptly as it plummeted after prey. Tango had finished drinking and was nosing at Chris's pockets, searching for sugar. Chris seemed to have grown roots. He didn't know what to say, was almost afraid to move, afraid somehow to believe what he was hearing. Finally he recovered enough to push the big bay's head aside and went to crouch beside Charlie under the overhang, out of the sun.

"Why didn't you tell me?" His voice wavered, first with incredible sorrow, transforming slowly into rage. "*You son-ofabitch, why didn't you tell me?!*"

The memory did not fade this time, but broke off abruptly, and all the layers of illusion surrounding it split away, leaving only a man trapped in his own body, trapped in a motorized chair, enclosed in a subterranean chamber carved out of raw rock, on a world not his own.

"That is the crux of it, then," the Magistrate suggested.

Pike had not heard hir approach, but knew somehow that s/he was truly "there," and not illusion, even as he knew Vina was not there, for the first time since he'd arrived. He hadn't realized until now how much she'd become his muse, his reason for wanting to tell the story of who he was and why.

"I don't understand," he said. Spoke? Thought? They were one and the same now, though he accompanied his thought by tilting his head back, looking the Magistrate in the eye, despite the effort it cost him.

"I think you do. You spoke of 'debris.' Is it not the emotional debris you and Charlie created that concerns you more than long-ago starship battles?"

"Are you a psychiatrist as well?" Pike asked dryly. "Yes,

it's all debris, all so unnecessary. The Vestian ship, the dead aboard our own, the wreck of Kamnach's career, Charlie's telling me something he should have told me from the very beginning. Or maybe it was my fault for not asking. Maybe he thought I didn't want to know."

"Maybe?" the Magistrate echoed. "Did you never talk about it again?"

S/he had taken hold of Pike's chair and was pushing it, slowly but purposefully, out of the featureless chamber where Pike had ended the memory, along a well-traveled path between the rock walls that, it seemed to Pike, slanted gradually upward.

"We did. But not for a long time after that day. He saw how angry I was, and didn't make excuses. Once again it was Hobelia who told me the whole story. Charlie and my mother were together for about a year before she realized his restlessness would never allow him to stay with her. Being Willa, she set him free, didn't bother telling him she was pregnant. He came back after another year-long voyage and there I was.

"He offered to stay, offered to marry her. She sent him packing, and he didn't fight her. Kept an eye on me from a distance after that, until we moved to Elysium. He sized Heston up and knew he was a recipe for disaster, so for the first time in his life he committed to something, and stuck around."

The chair continued to move forward. He hadn't imagined it—the path beneath them did slope gradually upward through a number of labyrinthine twists and turns, occasionally branching off in other directions, though they stayed on the main path, the walls marked at intervals with glyphs Pike took to be numbers, directions—to where? Why not take the 'lift? Why not create the illusion that they were going somewhere instead of actually making this arduous journey? He sensed this was important, and didn't question it.

"Go on," the Magistrate urged him.

"That old affair, the affair that created me, was the subtext that I overheard that day when Charlie and Willa were talking in the kitchen. But without knowing the background, I was too young to understand it."

He could sense, rather than see, the Magistrate nodding in comprehension. "Human relationships are quite complex, and very different from ours."

"I'd like to know more about yours," Pike said suddenly. "It seems to me I ought to learn as much about you as you are about me."

"So you shall," the Magistrate assured him, still pushing the chair, perhaps a little faster than before. Was that daylight up ahead? Were they headed for the surface? "Presently. But please continue with your thoughts."

"What else is there to say?" Pike wondered. "I wasn't angry with Charlie for leaving. He saw it as an act of cowardice, but I didn't. No, I was angry with him for not telling me sooner—oh, maybe not while Heston was still around, but after. After the fire, on the way back to Earth, once I'd agreed to stay with him and Hobelia—at any time along there, he could have said something."

"Did he give a reason why he did not?" the Magistrate asked.

"He said he believed events should just take their course without his interference. The only reason he spoke that day at the river was because he'd realized either one or both of us could have died aboard the *Aldrin*, and he wanted to set things right."

"So you blamed him for being human?" the Magistrate observed.

Inwardly, Pike was scowling. "What would you know about that?" he said a little crossly. "I'll give you points for irony, though. Yes, I was judging him, and not kindly. And when my commission on the *York* came through, I grabbed it. Cut my leave time short with the excuse that I was headed out on a long mission and I wanted to get to know the ship and her crew better than I'd had time to on the *Aldrin*."

"So you left matters unfinished?"

"Another debris trail," Pike admitted.

The light up ahead proved to be natural daylight, the mouth of a large tunnel that had perhaps at one time been the entrance to a mine or an underground rail system. Pike thought he could discern the faint impression of a rail bed. It led at an angle toward what might once have been the bank of a river, long since silted over with natural and manufactured debris. On the other side of the river was a sight that caught his attention and held it so that he could not look away.

14

2267: TALOS IV

The first time the *Enterprise* landing party had gone in search of survivors of *Columbia,* they'd beamed down in a valley surrounded by mountains, mountains that hid the devastated city beyond. Had they had time to look further, they might have noticed from a certain perspective a ruined spire or two thrust skeletally into the sky, but they had been in haste and quickly overwhelmed by the Talosian illusions, and in as much haste to depart once the mission was over. Here, now, Pike could see in this one city a microcosm of what the ancient war had wrought worldwide.

He had been to many worlds, encountered many species, marveled at their technology and the sometimes improbability of their architecture, yet one thing had always impressed him—a certain familiarity about the way sentient bipedal oxygen breathers built their cities. From the evolution of city-states into nations, continental unions, and finally to the Earth which met the first alien visitors a century and a half before Pike was born, the patterns were similar and, to the son of an architect, easily identifiable. Was he surprised to find that this Talosian city was not dissimilar?

Did it have a name? Had it, like human cities, been built around a central fortification, expanded outward from a water source, or spread in a grid to the length and breadth of the land allotted it, either by natural boundary or by legislative mandate? From where Pike contemplated it, it seemed to do all three, yet it was his thought that if he could have walked those streets—climbing over rubble in places, avoiding twisted metal or shards of shattered glass in others, the way he'd clambered over the beginnings of the works-in-progress Willa had made on Earth and elsewhere—he would know somehow which places were the centers of power, and which were the homes people made for themselves, simply by the shape of things.

"How bad are the radiation levels?" he asked for want of something to say. The emptiness of the place disturbed him. A wind he hadn't noticed on his first visit here howled across the open space between the city and the tunnel entrance where he and the Magistrate sheltered, and in the city he could see things moving. A blind or curtain flapping in a paneless window? A door half off its hinges swaying crazily, ceaselessly, for hundreds of thousands of years? Or only his imagination suggesting things that couldn't possibly be? From this distance, he couldn't be sure.

"The structures have been assessed as safe," the Magistrate replied. "It is only the organic aspects—the soil, the water, what flora have been able to survive or mutate—that remain toxic."

"That's easy enough to fix, you know," Pike said. "I'd like to go closer, see it from the inside if possible."

"We have preserved thought records of what once was," the Magistrate suggested gently. Was it possible even s/he was saddened by what s/he saw? "But as we have not ventured extensively within except to take radiation readings, there is nothing more current."

Mentally, Pike shrugged that off. "I can view the records later. I'd like to see the reality now. Isn't that what you brought me up here to see?"

"What was the war about?" he asked after a small eternity, standing within a small illusion—the illusion that he could still stand and walk and move—within the larger reality. He and the Magistrate stood in what was left of a vast plaza that had once been ringed about with tall buildings. He'd have been content to remain in the reality of the imprisoning chair, but the Magistrate wished him to stand beside hir, so he had acquiesced to that much.

"What are all wars about?" the Magistrate mused. "Territory, resources, ideologies? In the end, are they not all about fear? 'You have and I want' or 'I believe and you must accept.' In truth, it was so long ago, we no longer remember, or care."

"Well, that's a beginning, I suppose," Pike suggested, not entirely believing hir. There would be plenty of time to talk about it later. "When you realize none of those things are worth fighting over, maybe that's one reason to stop fighting."

His boots were dusty with walking through the inch or two of fine grit covering the cut and dressed flagstones of the plaza (some sort of highly polished stone, he saw, crouching and brushing some of the gray-white grit away—marble or granite or something else fine-grained and attractive). Lumpish shapes—sculptures, he supposed—of wrought metal and carved stone were scattered here and there and also covered with that layer of whitish grit. Beyond the sculptures, devastation.

Turning slowly a full circle around, Pike counted what was left of seven structures, or was it eight, arranged around this central plaza. Some looked as if they had simply sighed and crumbled into rubble, resigned to death. Two in particular appeared to have died screaming, tons of structural steel and the thousands of lives they'd contained twisting and burning and howling in protest as they went.

And as far as the eye could see, the rest of the city was the same.

"There are tunnels," the Magistrate said, reading his thoughts. "Once they comprised our transportation system, a rather elaborate system of pneumatic tubes of which we were quite proud, extending from city to city all over our world. After the wars, they became our subterranean world, the world you are familiar with. When you spoke of humans leaving debris in your wake . . ."

"You've made your point," Pike acknowledged grimly. "We're all fallible, and we all make mistakes."

He stood up and tried to brush the dust from his hands. Some of it scattered in the fretful breeze, but the rest still clung to him, and he found himself trying to brush it off his trousers, anxious to get rid of it, illusory though it was.

"Its composition is interesting," the Magistrate said, hir head tilted to one side, studying him. "The bulk of it is manufactured—the components of the buildings that were destroyed. The rest is . . . organic in nature."

Pike understood. A course on early weaponry at the Academy had taught him about the nuclear shadows of Hiroshima—a human life reduced to shadow on a flight of steps—the instantaneity of death, witnessed worldwide, at a place known as Ground Zero, the fallout of the Third World War. The dust on his hands, even in illusion, was all that remained of countless Talosians.

No consolation in knowing they had been born and died millennia before he was born. They should not have died like this.

What was it the Magistrate had said? Resources, territory,

ideologies, indeed. He couldn't imagine so advanced a species fighting over resources or territory.

"Ideology, then," he said.

"Indeed."

Did he only imagine he heard the Magistrate sigh? The familiar shimmer in the air which indicated an illusion was ending blurred Pike's vision for a moment, and he was back in his chair, the Magistrate pushing it—not easily—through the accumulated grit, out of the plaza and back toward the cave. The air shimmered again, and Pike found himself in the Talosian city as it once had been.

Some sort of conference was taking place. A room perhaps the size of the Federation Council chamber, round as all conference rooms seemed to be (to eliminate shadows and corners assassins could hide in?), held perhaps a thousand Talosians, all in the same silver robes as those Pike had met in reality, all seated at long curved tables arranged in rising tiers around a central nexus where seven of their fellows sat facing outward toward them. On the curvilinear walls around them, hundreds of screens showed more Talosians observing and participating in the conference on a video feed.

The conspicuous difference between this and any humanoid conference Pike had ever witnessed was the silence.

The Talosians communed entirely by thought. If Pike looked closely he could see the veins in their huge crania throbbing, some placidly, others almost frenetically. He took this to mean they were arguing, though their faces remained serene.

"You are correct," he heard the Magistrate's voice somewhere, like that of a narrator in an interactive video. "The war was a war of thought. Dream had already become more important to us than reality—an addiction, if you will. Our society was already showing the negative effects of it—structures falling into ruin, machines into disrepair. There was no incentive for anyone to fix anything, when all one had to do was shrug it off and slip back into Dream.

"Yet some were disturbed by the disintegration. It was they who suggested we needed new blood, so to speak. Slaves, not to put too fine a point on it, from lesser species who could not share our power of mind unless passively, whom we would train to do our work for us."

"Just like your original plan for Vina and me," Pike said incisively.

The Magistrate did not answer.

"So this 'war of ideas' turned into a war of weapons," Pike guessed, still watching the superficially serene conference in the illusion, realizing now how much violence seethed under its surface. "How did that happen?"

"Not simply, and not all at once," the Magistrate said. The conference scene faded, and Pike found himself . . . nowhere.

When he "returned," to find himself back in his chair, the Magistrate was pushing it over what remained of a paved road leading away from the city, back toward the tunnel. He felt as if several volumes of Talosian history had been force-fed directly into his memory. In effect, they had. He suddenly had a violent headache.

"Our Physician will teach you techniques for the headache," the Magistrate assured him. "The amount of data you have been given is small, but we did not want to overtax you on the first attempt."

"Very thoughtful of you!" Pike said wryly. What the "small" amount of history data told him was that for all their superior mental powers, the Talosians who had begun the war had been just as hidebound and fanatical as humans had been in their ancient past.

"None of us starts out intending to do harm," he said, finding himself in the odd position of trying to console a

Talosian. "Most of us just put one foot in front of the other until the day we die. Some few have a vision, a desire to leave a legacy."

"As you did?" the Magistrate suggested.

"Maybe." Pike thought of a conversation he'd had with an unattainable woman just weeks before the accident that had brought him here. "It's like Vina said—we should never take our days for granted, assume we have an unlimited number of them. Being as long-lived as you are, I don't imagine that's easy for you to understand."

"Not entirely," the Magistrate said, bringing the chair to a halt at the mouth of the tunnel. Was it possible s/he was winded from the effort? "Do not assume we have no understanding of mortality. You cannot know what it is like to lose all but a remnant of your people."

"Hadn't thought of it quite that way," Pike said.

"However, your life is not over, Christopher," the Magistrate reminded him after a thoughtful silence. "Here it can be whatever you wish."

"Yes, it can, can't it?" he mused.

"There is, we have observed, a tendency in the human toward regret, toward reliving those parts of the past that are painful. This we have discovered in the literature stored in your *Enterprise*'s logs, and in you and the female as well. You will only allow yourselves the escape of the pleasurable after you have relived the pain. But once you have finished with your early memories, found your catharsis, perhaps you will expand your repertoire as the female has.

"In this reality, you can save your mother from the fire. You can see to it that she is never even in danger. Even that she never marries Heston Prescott, but remains on Earth with you . . ."

"And we all live happily ever after?" Pike mused. In spite of himself, he could see it—a patchwork of memories of

Willa he'd clung to all these years, stitched together with
if-only and might-have-been. What would Willa look like
now, seasoned to a handsome eighty-something, still active,
perhaps still designing cities on some far-flung world?

Was it coincidence that the Magistrate had angled the
chair so that he could still see the ruined city? What would
Willa have done with it? Probably rolled up her sleeves and
gone to work. If he let his mind go there, he could almost see
her, standing in that ruined plaza surrounded by a gaggle of
Talosians, blueprints in one hand, the other waving gracefully as she sketched in the air her visions of what they
would build here and here and here, where the fountain
would go, and the gardens, and perhaps a memorial to the
dead and—

The thought grieved Pike, and he dismissed it.

"Uh-uh. No thanks. I've seen what that kind of wishful
thinking can do . . . I can see it here, all around me. Instead
of dreaming, you might have taken your city back."

"We had to wait for the radiation to dissipate. Surely you
can see that."

"Or you could have devised methods to get rid of it and
been out here a thousand years sooner, if you'd had a little
initiative."

He wondered if his words were too harsh, but since the
Magistrate could read them in his mind regardless—

"It is that initiative which we lack," s/he admitted, apparently unperturbed by Pike's vehemence. "It was what we
found so admirable in your species from the first."

"You sure had a bizarre way of showing your admiration!"

*Wrong thinking is punishable, right thinking will be as
quickly rewarded. You will find the combination an effective
one.*

"The last vestiges of the mind-set which led to the wars," the Magistrate acknowledged wryly. "And the arrogant assumption that because your brain had evolved differently than ours, it was perforce inferior. In your absence, we have rethought that. We should not have attempted to coerce you the first time. For that we apologize. We had not hoped to have a second chance . . ."

"You've given me a second chance as well," Pike reminded hir. He couldn't help thinking of his own primitive reactions, from attempting to strangle the Magistrate, to allowing Number One to set her phaser on self-destruct. To this day he didn't know if she meant it as a bluff or not. "Neither side acquitted themselves all that well the first time around."

The Magistrate's smile was benevolent. "Then perhaps at last we can work together."

Work? Pike hadn't even considered that. Enured to the idea of immobility, his dynamic spirit tamed, he'd expected to squander the rest of his years in dream—far preferable to what would have been his fate on Starbase 11, but an end, not a beginning.

He looked at the ruined city and saw it as it once was, as it could be again. He thought of what Willa would have done. Could that kind of energy be found in two ruined humans and a handful of Talosians? What would it hurt to try?

15

2254: *U.S.S. ENTERPRISE*

". . . and in conclusion," Pike said wearily, ". . . this Command Report will state that Talos contains absolutely no benefits to humanity. It is my recommendation that any and all Federation vessels be restricted from the region, and that no Starfleet vessel shall hereafter visit Talos IV . . ."

The door buzzer sounded, and he finished quickly.

"Captain's log, stardate . . . oh, whatever the hell . . . Computer, enter appropriate stardate. End log. Come!" he said, raising his voice slightly, shutting off the log more than a little irritably.

He'd had a hunch it would be Boyce, checking up on him, and his hunch was correct. The white-haired ship's surgeon, bouncing on his heels like a much younger man, little black bag in hand, quickly made himself at home.

"Skip the martini this time around, Phil," Pike said shortly. "I don't know if it's wise for me to be drinking right now."

Boyce looked disappointed.

"Well, I hate to drink alone," he sighed, leaving the little black bag on the desk and settling into the cabin's only chair. "You put up a brave front for the crew when we were leaving

Talos, but you're coming apart at the seams now. Want to talk about it?"

"No," Pike said testily. "Yes. Maybe. I don't know. But if that's the only reason you're here . . ."

Boyce handed him a report.

"Assessments on your yeoman and your first officer since returning from the surface of Talos. Disturbed sleep, restlessness, irritability, some anxiety in Yeoman Colt's case. Classic symptoms of post-traumatic stress disorder.

"Not unlike their captain," he finished dryly, rummaging in the black bag and retrieving, not the fixings for a couple of martinis this time, but a half-size bottle of Saurian brandy. It was exactly the shape of a full-size bottle, but small enough to fit in a medical bag, the curved neck and the tethered stopper and the markings on the label attesting to its authenticity. Pike found himself smiling in spite of himself as Boyce poured two shots and handed him one.

Boyce finished his first and got down to business. "I've read the official report, but I want to know what the hell really happened down there to turn two hardened veterans—and a flighty young thing—into basket cases."

"In absolute confidence?"

"Of course."

Studying the amber liquid at the bottom of his half-empty glass, Pike told him. When he'd finished, Boyce whistled softly and poured them both another drink, which they finished in silence.

"So when Mr. Spock briefed us on just how dangerous pure telepaths could be, he wasn't kidding," Boyce said finally, pouring a third shot for each of them. Pike left his untouched.

"Is that the mistake we make, Doctor?" he asked, as if he'd thought something through in his head and was only now voicing it aloud. "Do we always assume that every new species we encounter will be superior to us?"

"I'm not sure I follow you," Boyce said, though he did in fact, quite well. But he was a staunch believer in the talking cure.

Pike got up and began to pace. "What I mean is, is it just because, as likely as not, we discover they do have something we lack—superior strength, let's say, or the ability to see colors we can't—that we inevitably feel inferior? Or is it the fact that the first species we encountered were Vulcans, and we couldn't help getting the feeling they were at best humoring us, at worst viewing us as impetuous children?"

"Is your second officer still making you that uncomfortable?" Boyce remarked, eyeing what was left in the bottle suspiciously, as if wondering where the rest had gone so quickly.

"You know that's not what I mean!" Pike sat on the edge of his bunk and scowled at him. Boyce had a fine range of tones from dry to sardonic; sometimes it was hard to tell one from the other. This one could be classified as Wry, with a touch of Sarcasm, Pike decided. It was like trying to describe a vintage wine. "I'm talking about the Talosians."

"In other words, *Enterprise* may have left Talos IV, but Talos IV hasn't left you."

"All that intellect . . . telepathy, even, and they didn't have the memory or the energy to tinker with an environmental control unit or clean up the nuclear sites on their planet's surface," Pike was musing. "What's the point of being that smart if you don't do anything with it?"

"Maybe that's where they cease to be superior to us and the tables are turned," Boyce suggested. "And maybe a thousand years from now, when humans have learned to shield against their mental powers, we can develop some sort of trade agreement with them."

Which won't do you any good, he thought, studying the captain over the rim of his glass as he decided to hell with niceties and knocked his fourth drink back in one gulp. If he was going to have a hangover—and there were plenty of remedies in sickbay if he did—he might as well enjoy the process of getting there.

"It's not really about the Talosians, is it, Chris?" he asked when Pike had gone silent too long.

"What? No, you're right, it isn't. I keep thinking there must have been some way we—I—could have persuaded Vina to come with us. But there wasn't enough time. My concern was with the ship, with my crew, in case the Talosians weren't really giving up that easily. If they'd tried their power of illusion again before we could leave—"

"You did the right thing, Chris," Boyce said emphatically, putting his empty glass down on the table a bit too forcefully. There were still two shots left in the bottle, but he wasn't going to have another. "Vina made a choice. The right one, as far as she was concerned. Stop trying to second-guess yourself . . . as usual."

"She could have come back with us," Pike said half to himself. "There are advanced techniques that could have . . . no, you're right." Though he'd drunk almost as much as Boyce, he didn't seem at all affected. "I've almost learned to distance myself from most of the missions where things went wrong, instead of spending weeks afterward thinking of what I could have done differently . . ."

Boyce bit his tongue to keep from reminding Pike about a conversation they'd had about the Kaylar on Rigel VII in this very room only moments before they'd beamed down to Talos.

". . . but Vina . . ." Pike didn't finish. He put his glass down too, rubbed the back of his neck. The captain's quarters suddenly seemed claustrophobic, like a cage.

"Something about its being better to have loved and lost than never to have loved at all springs to mind here," Boyce suggested.

Pike gave him a skeptical look. "You're drunk, Doctor. And I'm going to send you packing in a few minutes, because I want to make sure you get back to your quarters without my having to carry you there."

Boyce tried to look indignant, but it wasn't working. He closed the medical bag and retrieved the report from where Pike had tossed it aside after he'd signed it.

"I'm recommending some short-term trauma therapy for Number One and Yeoman Colt," he said, back in his official capacity. "Colt will go for it; Number One will balk unless you make it official."

"All right then, it's official," Pike said dismissively. He was frankly tired of the entire conversation, tired of all conversation. He wanted to be left alone to brood a while longer.

"And when she asks why you're not undergoing therapy?" Boyce asked.

"You remind her who's the captain of this ship!" Pike was angry. "Nice try, Doctor, but I've had enough others poking around inside my head recently. I'll thank you to stay out!"

He realized then what had brought Boyce to his cabin, when the doctor might as easily have sent his medical assessments to Pike's computer instead of delivering them in person. He'd lost his temper on the bridge, something he couldn't remember ever doing before.

What had set him off was the two women bickering. They'd begun the minute Colt had been assigned to him. Number One would deny it, but she saw the "flighty young thing," as Boyce described her, as a threat, and not just to the safety of the ship. And Colt herself could be . . . distracting. Their sniping had been nothing more than background noise—no more annoying than the whir and bleep of the consoles, the hum of the engines beneath the deck plates—until he'd returned from Talos.

Maybe it was the layover at the Vega Colony, the endless meetings and debriefings that had him on edge, Pike told himself at first, though he knew he was lying. The real reason was the fact that he couldn't get Vina—or something Number One had said about her—out of his head.

"'An adult crewman'?" He'd asked to see her in his quarters and repeated her words back to her.

"Sir?"

"When we were in the cage . . . you said something about Vina's being an adult crewman on *Columbia*."

"That's correct."

"Meaning you did some research on the *Columbia* while I was . . . being held down there."

He had tried to keep his voice as neutral as possible. *Just want to know what steps you took—officially—to effect my release. Any little bit of information you could glean from the record tapes—officially, of course—would have helped, and you're to be commended for it. Nothing more behind my question than that.*

"It's in my report, sir." Number One was watching him carefully. No one knew, likely no one would ever know, what took place between Pike and Vina during those days he was held prisoner, much less what finally transpired between them to make him so certain she would want to stay behind. "I accessed everything in the library computer about *Columbia*, her crew, last known coordinates, date of disappearance . . ."

"Of course." Pike closed his eyes wearily for a moment. "I haven't had a chance to . . . so many reports. I should have realized you'd have been . . . thorough."

"Of course, sir."

And eager to point out the difference in age between the "real" Vina and the illusion of a woman the Talosians presented us with. Purely officially, of course.

"Thank you, Number One. That will be all."

It wasn't, though. The door had barely whooshed closed behind his first officer when Pike accessed the library computer. He told himself he would just read the crew manifests and the log entries. Yet the first thing he did was bring up her image. Then he found he couldn't turn away.

Soon *Columbia*'s records weren't enough. Armed with a last name, date and place of birth, he'd had to search further, back as far as the records would allow him. By the time he knew everything there was to know about her—education, where she'd lived, what she'd done with her life before she boarded *Columbia* for its last fateful mission, even her parents' names and professions, Pike found he was only hungry for more.

Why had he embarked on this fool's errand? What was he trying to prove? In trying to put Vina out of his mind— codify her, put her in a little box with a label that said "unattainable," he'd only allowed her further in.

Would Number One know he'd been poking around searching for more information? Was it any of her business if he had? Pike wasn't unaware of his first officer's feelings for him, how ever well she tried to disguise them. He'd never know if her remark about Vina's age had been made purely to convince him of the illusion, or if she'd had an ulterior motive.

Well, what was he supposed to do about it, anyway?

What he ended up doing was losing his temper.

"I wonder how they reproduce?" The question had been Yeoman Colt's, obviously. The woman seemed to live in a constant hormonal haze. "The Talosians, I mean."

"Judging from their median age and the absence of any offspring, I'd say they haven't, at least not for a very long time," Number One shot back. "None of our business anyway."

"But imagine their thinking they could keep the captain prisoner in their little zoo, and he'd just naturally want to mate with . . . with that woman," Colt finished with a giggle. She didn't realize her voice was carrying.

Number One might have been on the verge of silencing her, but Pike beat her to it.

"I'll thank you both to belay the chatter!" he snapped, loudly enough to make Colt jump. "Save it for the ladies' sewing circle!"

The first statement was a clear order, and well within bounds. The second raised a few eyebrows, not least of which Number One's. Pike compounded the bad judgment call by storming off the bridge for no stated reason. He returned a few moments later, after he'd cooled down, but by then there was an unnatural quiet on the bridge, which lingered until the end of shift.

The fact was that, in his current state, he found the presence of any woman oppressive. Usually gregarious, dropping by the various lounges whenever he was off shift, he now retreated to his cabin on deck five instead. He hadn't even gone to the gym—a favorite haunt—since they'd left Talos.

Alone in the dark of his cabin he thought of Vina, alone for eighteen years before his arrival. He couldn't imagine that kind of solitude, wasn't sure he'd have been able to survive it. Yet she had. And the first thing he'd done was attack her for the compromises she'd made in order to do so.

". . . they can't read through primitive emotions," she'd told him. "But you can't keep it up for long enough. I've tried! They keep at you and at you, year after year, tricking and punishing, and they won. They own me . . . I know you must hate me for that."

"Oh, no!" he'd responded, with the first genuine feeling he'd had for her. "I don't hate you. I can guess what it was like . . ."

Tossing and turning, mindful of the sound and feel of the ship's engines in a way he hadn't been since he was a cadet still getting his space legs, he wondered where he'd found the gall to say that. How could he possibly have guessed what it was like? No one who hadn't experienced it possibly could . . .

"You see now why I can't go with you?" she'd said quietly, with as much dignity as she could muster in the face of the barely concealed horror on his face. "They found me, a lump of flesh in the wreckage . . . dying. They 'repaired' me. Everything works. But they had never seen a human before."

She had not been exaggerating. It was pure fluke that helped her survive the crash—pure fluke and the love of Theo Haskins—and an incredible fortuity of time and place that brought the hurtling piece of fuselage to ground under the only circumstances under which the Talosians could have saved her life.

One minute the scientists were gathered in the rec room, laughing, celebrating, the sample bags in their quarters bulging with specimens, eager to head back into known space and publish their research, in the interim enjoying the fact that the head of the expedition and his favorite assistant were about to enter a partnership of a different sort. The captain was off duty and had broken out a case of champagne from his private store when the ship suddenly jolted and the red alert snapped on.

Vina would never know exactly what caused the malfunction. The captain conferred with his first officer on the bridge and then quickly rushed away, ordering the expedition members to stay where they were until the crisis was over, too hurried to offer any further explanation. The scientists did as instructed and remained in the rec room, the safest part of the ship, lashing themselves and their equipment to chairs, tables, anything secure. The captain had accidentally left the intercraft open and they could hear reports and orders and confirmations flying back and forth. There was nothing for them to do but listen helplessly.

Theo tried to calm them, his voice soothing, his manner tranquil, as if he knew somehow that all would be well. At one point he saw the terror in Vina's eyes and reached one hand out across the distance between their chairs. She clung to his hand as if it were a lifeline that would pull the ship back on course.

From what they could glean from intercraft chatter, one of the engines had apparently failed, though because it had been struck by something or simply malfunctioned, they would never know. The ship was unable to right herself, and she began to yaw, then to pitch forward at a steep angle, taxing the artificial gravity, inertial dampers straining. A forgotten champagne bottle tumbled past, spraying them all with vintage wine before crashing against a bulkhead, glass spattering in all directions. The voices on the intercraft became more and more frantic.

There were escape pods, but *Columbia* was the only ship out this far, and they were too far from a known system to risk simply scattering them like dandelion seeds into the void. Seeking refuge in the pods would most likely only prolong death. When it was clear that the ship could not be saved, the helmsman simply yanked her around toward the nearest star system, where there was one planet with an oxygen atmosphere, and they all held on and prayed.

As *Columbia* plummeted toward the planet's surface, streaking across the sky like some erratic meteor, g-forces increased incrementally, so that simply turning one's head became difficult. At the same time, thought processes seemed to speed up, so that even as Vina found it almost impossible to move her arm, her mind was free to toy with the dilemma of whether it would be preferable to burn to death or be crushed to death, since both seemed to be the only current options.

What gave Theo the strength to free himself and her from their chairs, and all but carry her across the rec room to the built-in refrigeration unit under the wet bar from which the captain had produced the champagne? Love is not scientifically quantifiable, which is not to say it is not one of the most powerful forces in the universe.

"What are you doing?!" she remembered screaming, or trying to; it was as difficult to speak now as it was to move or breathe.

Theo didn't answer. He somehow forced the door of the unit open and shoved her inside.

Vina was tiny, and Theo had calculated that with her legs folded under her she would just fit into the space. The power had gone off, so it wasn't unbearably cold, and with the ship's outer hull now reaching incendiary temperatures, it would remain comfortable—solidly built, insulated—longer than the room outside. The rec room was situated in the very center of the ship. If any part of *Columbia* survived atmosphere and impact, it would be the rec room. And if any part of the rec room survived intact or nearly intact, it would be this small space.

"No!" Vina thought she screamed. Even thinking was becoming difficult now. She held out her hands to Theo to say, *Take me out of here! Don't leave me! If you're going to die, I want to die with you!*

With the last of his strength, he pushed her hands away, and slammed the door. There was an emergency release on the inside, but Vina couldn't find it in the dark, and she wouldn't have had the strength to release it in this gravity if she had. She would live or die in this small space, Theo's kindly, loving face etched into her memory for as long as she lived. Curling herself up in a fetal position, arms wrapped around her knees, sobbing bitterly, she waited.

There was no way to calculate the odds against *Columbia*'s wobbly trajectory actually getting her close enough to Talos IV to attempt a landing, but she made it that far. Attempts to brake and bring her down slowly were less successful, and she began to break up at about sixty kilometers above the surface, low enough for chunks of fuselage and interior components to survive, scattering a debris field more than eight hundred kilometers long. Incredibly, two sections of the interior survived with only minor damage— the main library computer, and a refrigeration unit.

It splashed down and tumbled over itself into a long-neglected marsh, whose waters cooled its overheated surface with a great hissing rush of steam. A few meters farther or a slightly faster entry speed would have plunged it into the deeper waters of the river that fed the marsh, and the burned and broken Vina would have drowned. Instead, unconscious, damaged beyond the knowledge of most human medical technology, she lay unmoving within, still breathing, barely. The impact had warped the frame of the unit, bursting the door open, which provided her with needed oxygen, saving her life a second time.

The Talosians saved it a third.

They had watched the ship's progress across the sky, surmised what it was, and noted where the debris would come to land. A scan of the debris field revealed the charred remains of numerous carbon-based life-forms, and one that showed faint life signs. A hover-sled brought several Talosians to the marsh where Vina lay. They would not locate the library computer or determine what it was until some days later.

Gentle hands of surprising strength eased Vina's broken body out of its enclosure, wrapped her burns in cooling cloths, carried her in a sling to the waiting sled. A medical scanner revealed internal organs whose functions were similar to their own. But they were differently juxtaposed within the thoracic cavity, and the blood and tissue type were totally incompatible. Their subject could be rehydrated, sedated, and kept on life support, bones could be set, charred flesh peeled away, the ruptured organ they would later identify as a spleen could be removed, but there was no possibility of transplant or scar regeneration or even a blood transfusion.

The internal organs were salvaged and replaced in an arrangement compatible with Talosian physiology, stitched together in a way that made sense in terms of function, if not esthetics. The broken bones and the horrible burns would have to heal themselves, or not.

What the subject needed most was quiet, and mental techniques to bypass her pain. The conditioning began.

Eighteen years later, the Magistrate entered the room where Vina lay dreaming.

Pity, s/he thought, studying the humped spine, the spindly, uneven legs, the once-beautiful face crisscrossed with scars, *that we had to work so quickly to repair her lest she die. Had we had more time, we might have gotten it right, tapped into her mind, if not her ship's computers, to see what she should look like and effect it. Now the organs have healed in the places where we set them, the scar tissue solidified. There is nothing more we can do, except what I am about to propose to her now.*

For eighteen years the human's fantasies and dreams had entertained the entire remnant of the Talosian race, even as they sustained and succored Vina. But there were limits to what a lone human could provide them. The desire to rebuild, to reproduce more than the handful of grim off-spring necessary to sustain their society, to return to the surface and return the Dream to its proper place in their ethos—as a supplement to, not a substitute for, life—required more. After eighteen years of sending *Columbia*'s distress call into the void, the opportunity had at last presented itself. It must not be allowed to slip away, and Vina's involvement was key.

Vina, the Magistrate thought softly, and the human floated up from the depths of what she had been dreaming— an alternate timeline in which she had stayed on Earth, parted amicably from Theo, joined her father in his dance troupe, and was touring the Federation's inner worlds to universal acclaim (that night's performance was, ironically, *Sleeping Beauty*)—turned her face toward the deceptively frail, large-browed creature in the doorway, and spoke aloud.

"What is it?"

There is something we would like you to see . . .

The Magistrate showed her the "survivors' encampment" that would lure the *Enterprise* to their world. Over the years Vina had entertained a thousand and one scenarios in which her crewmates had survived, and some looked not unlike this, though she would have afforded them more luxuries than these shabby makeshift huts, the ragged clothes. Most times she endowed them with a little city of their own, in a place where the radiation wasn't so deadly, where they could coexist with the Talosians without losing who they were.

In some respects, it was what the Talosians might have

wished for as well. Christopher Pike's characterization of "a race of slaves" was made in haste and anger and without sufficient information. The Talosians' goal, had more than a single human survived, would have been a captivity not quite so harsh as the one he envisioned.

But as Vina saw what her keepers had created on their own this time without her input, she questioned it.

"Why this? Why now?" she asked the Magistrate. "I'm past all this. I've finally gotten over what happened to me, and the others. Why bring them back, and like this?"

"There is something you must do for us . . ." the Magistrate explained.

Thus as the landing party beamed down into the clearing and looked about, orienting themselves, discovering that the mournful singing sound carried on the breeze was caused by the vibrating blue leaves of the *hrigee* plant—waiting in the wings like an ingenue worried about missing her cue, was Vina.

She looked them over from her vantage point, five humans and a Vulcan, wearing uniforms not unlike those the crew of *Columbia* had worn (did she dare hope they'd come from Earth?), wanting to study them all equally, learn everything she could about them, since they would determine her fate. But her eye traveled quickly over the Vulcan-looking one, the wry-looking white-haired human, the three interchangeable (in her eyes) youngsters with their equipment packs and their weapons at the ready, and focused on *him*.

Oh, yes! she thought. *Yes, you. Please be real, and not an illusion within the illusion, yet another test of my abilities by my however-benevolent captors, but a flesh-and-blood man to wake the sleeping princess with a kiss!*

She hated herself for what she was about to do. But the images of her lost crewmates had startled her. How had the

Talosians known to age them to exactly the way they'd look now had they lived? It was cruel. Crueler still that her captors could do such things with their minds but hadn't been able to help her tormented body when they found her. Eighteen years ago, she told herself. She had kept track, once she was conscious, ambulatory, able to take the first tentative steps, leaning on a Talosian's arm, through the tunnels to daylight, to see the sky. Why she had insisted on seeing the sky she didn't know, since she was doomed to never leave this place.

Focus on the here and now, she told herself, all her attention on Christopher Pike, once the Magistrate had briefed her. *You mustn't lose him. Everything depends on his seeing you as the woman of his dreams—nubile, vulnerable, quintessentially feminine. It is he or no one, because the chance of another Earth ship ever venturing this far is . . . well, no chance at all.*

Terrified lest she fail, she found her voice. "You appear to be healthy and intelligent, Captain. A prime specimen."

Oh, good beginning! she chided herself even as the words were barely out of her mouth. *You've been among the Talosians too long and have forgotten the nuances of ordinary human discourse. What now?*

But the Magistrate had compensated by giving "Theo" the next line ("You'll have to forgive her, Captain. She's spent her entire life among a group of aging scientists"), and Pike was put off only for a moment.

And later, with his hand in hers (yes, real. The touch of a human hand after all these years! She wanted to weep with joy, but she had a job to do), she had led him toward the lift, light-footed, winsome, diverting him:

"Can you feel it?" she had asked him, alluring, gesturing toward something that wasn't there, hoping the Magistrate or one of the others would supply some vision so irresistible that even if he didn't find her attractive—though his eyes told her he did—it would be sufficient to stay him long enough, just long enough. "Here, and here . . ."

Is he really here? some corner of her mind still nagged at her even as the warmth of his hand reassured her, *or have they conjured him out of my dreams? Because he is so exactly right, I cannot believe that in all the galaxy, at least the human parts—*

No, wait, they couldn't have—! Had they searched among the ships passing parsecs distant and chosen him especially because they knew he would please her?

They had come to know her at her most vulnerable. In the early months she had literally been reborn under their tutelage, lying in a darkened and especially warm room, formless as an egg in an incubator, her mind that of an infant struggling to learn a new language. They had learned all her secrets, focusing especially on the romantic entanglements of her past, seeking a common theme, a role model for her to choose from in order to best encourage her to propagate her species.

That her damaged and displaced internal organs might not be capable of such propagation had not occurred to them. Or did they, despite their amnesia about so much of their technology, have the capability to foster human offspring as they did their own, *in vitro,* floating in rows upon rows of little liquid chambers awaiting a need—a librarian or archivist or technician or even a magistrate who was dying and had to be replaced in order for the species to nominally continue—before their growth was accelerated and they were "born"?

How many offspring had they hoped to produce from a single human pair? Did they understand that there could have been but one generation, which could not interbreed? Had they even thought it through that far? Or had they scanned surrounding space for passing vessels until they found one captained by a human male who fit her ideal and, hoping she would lead the way, planned to lure the entire crew down one by one or in groups, to form a human colony?

The thought that they had chosen Christopher Pike expressly because she would find him irresistible filled her with horror, and she almost stumbled as she led him up the incline, hearing the lift approaching. Then the Archivist and the Librarian with their sleeping potion emerged and downed him and— *No!* she wanted to cry. *It's too soon; I'm not prepared for this!* Too late. They had him now, the lift closing, moving downward even as the rest of his crewmates realized what had happened, too late. Too late.

And if he refused to cooperate? She tortured herself with this one last question. They would not let him go, in any event; of that she was certain. But if he refused her, what was gained? Instead of one desolately lonely human on this world, there would be two.

"You can begin with the obvious," the Magistrate schooled her while they waited for the sleeping potion to wear off and for Pike to awaken in his cage. "Try to lure him with your sexuality. That, as we have read in the records, is usually the best approach in attracting a human male."

"Oh, don't believe everything you read!" she'd tried. Amazingly, she hadn't lost her sense of humor in all this time, though she'd had little opportunity to keep it sharp.

"If that is inadequate, the appeal to pity is usually effective," the Magistrate went on. "Or helplessness. The Damsel in Distress, I believe it is called."

"I never was very good at improv," she tried one last feeble joke. The Magistrate was impervious and, beyond hir, though she could not see them, Vina knew that the minds of other Talosians were watching, listening, waiting. It was all on her fragile, damaged shoulders. She forced herself to

calm. "If he doesn't want me . . . if I fail . . ." She was almost
afraid to ask the question. ". . . what will become of him?"

"I would suggest," the Magistrate said solemnly, turning
on hir heel to walk away, "that you do not fail."

They'd stacked the deck, skewed the outcome, by setting her down at first within his memory of the battle with
the Kaylar on Rigel VII. Call it the Actor's Nightmare in
real time—she did not know the script, though at the sight
of the huge, fanged creature with the deadly battle-ax
searching for them, drawing ever closer, she learned it
quickly enough. The voluminous skirts and silly soft
boots hampered her; she'd have rather had hiking shorts
and a decent pair of trainers, but the Talosians were not
obliging.

Very well then, play the Damsel in Distress, barely able to
run in such ridiculous clothes, though she did make some
use of the oversized broadsword and a nasty spiked mace she
found littering the floor of the castle once they reached it.
But *he* kept rationalizing it, questioning her, looking for
explanations instead of playing along.

She'd had to force the illusion, clumsily (she was a
dancer; she was never clumsy) knocking something over to
attract the Kaylar's attention so the human would fight and
stop talking at her, feel the illusion as he was meant to. After
that, nothing to do but play her role, frail little female fighting off the twice-her-size Kaylar as best she could and, failing that, letting loose the obligatory scream.

She had always hated movie heroines who screamed. But
more was riding on this than a part in the director's next film,
so scream she did. It spurred him to greater action, and he
killed the Kaylar and the illusion ended.

That had been the easy part. But back in the cage, she'd
fumbled her lines ("Why are you here?" "To please you"),

come dangerously close to revealing too much, and she'd been recalled.

"No, don't punish me!" she shrieked, then vanished. Appeal to pity, indeed.

Because that was another lie. The Talosians had never tortured her. At first, recovering from her injuries, she'd suffered horrible neuropathic pain, so that anytime she stopped dreaming her nerve endings would scream at her, and the pain in her head, a kind of psychic rebound syndrome, became unbearable. The only cure had been to re-immerse herself in dream, for years, until the pain at last subsided.

It was the memory of that pain she was trading on when she heard the Magistrate's voice in her thoughts (*Enough! Answer no more of his questions! The first illusion has failed to convince him. Retreat, now, and we will instruct you further!*) and, just to assure authenticity, one of the Talosians had reminded her of past pain and she began to writhe and scream: "No, don't punish me—!"

. . . and found herself back in her own chamber with the Magistrate looking on.

"There!" she said, more than a little out of breath. "Did I do a good job? Was I convincing? After all this time away from other humans, I wasn't sure . . ."

The Magistrate was observing Pike on the screen following Vina's disappearance, the dress she'd worn clutched in his hands. The human seemed distraught.

"You were excellent," the Magistrate assured her. "He was completely taken in by you, if not by the memory of the battle. His desire to protect you has been enhanced. You have done well, for now."

"God, I wish I felt better about it!" Vina cried. "I feel dirty, disgusted. No," she said off the Magistrate's mildly puzzled look. "I don't expect you to understand."

"Vina . . . if the experiment is to succeed, it is essential for our specimens to be happy."

She had shouted then, fists clenched, wishing she could hit something.

"*I'm not a 'specimen'!* Don't you *ever* call me that again! I am human—as real, as *important,* as any one of you. More important in some respects, because you need me now as much as I needed you in the beginning."

The Magistrate frowned slightly. "Without us, you would have died."

Vina made an almost animal noise of frustration then. "And I can't tell you how many times I wish I had!"

The Magistrate's frown deepened. "Do you still feel that way now?"

She had to think about that. "Since I've seen . . . him? No. For the first time in a long time, I have something to live for." She shook her head grimly. "But don't make me regret it!"

A day later, she would have died for it, too. When Number One set her phaser for a forced-chamber explosion, and Pike ordered Vina back underground, she had refused.

"I suppose if they have one human, they might try again," she'd said without hesitation, willing to sacrifice herself . . . for them, for him, for anything except a return to solitude.

Christopher Pike had seen many kinds of courage in his lifetime, but Vina's moved him in a way no one else's had, and he couldn't get her out of his mind. Nor could he avoid the echo of another Talosian's words:

"Your unsuitability has condemned the Talosian race to eventual death. Is this not sufficient?"

At the time, still angry ("And that's it? No apology?"), he'd shrugged it off as not his problem. His obligation was first and foremost to his crew. He'd proven that when he'd ignored the first automated distress call. Without proof of survivors, his crew's well-being took precedence. Only when the Talosians upped the ante by creating the illusion of the survivors' camp had he relented.

The deck had been stacked from the beginning. He'd done the best he could. Why wasn't it enough? Why did the Talos incident still feel like unfinished business? Tossing and turning, unable to sleep as his ship, his life, moved ever farther and farther away from Talos IV and Vina, he fought against the urge to go back and claim her, plead with her to reconsider. Was it his own impulse, or were the Talosians still manipulating him? Pike could not know.

But he had to assure that no other human would ever have to endure what he had. And though he knew it not only condemned the Talosians to eventual extinction, but Vina to lifelong solitude (Would she be content very long with the illusion of him? He doubted it. But she had made her choice), Pike did the only thing he knew how.

His command report was incorporated into General Order 7, recommending that no human ever again visit Talos IV.

16

2262: SOMEWHERE IN THE KANES SYSTEM

It was a waking nightmare. But everything about this mission, Christopher Pike thought grimly, had felt wrong from the beginning.

He thought he had seen everything in his first five years as captain of the *Enterprise*. He was wrong. In the fading light, he glanced once more at the clearing where four of his crew had met their deaths. No trace remained of his comrades, but their killers were everywhere. There was nothing he and his science officer could do but wait for nightfall, and hope to escape.

During the yearlong layover while his ship was undergoing a refit, he'd decided he needed a refit of his own, and toyed with the idea of asking for a desk assignment, something close enough to Earth where he could visit the ranch more often. Charlie and Hobelia were still in their prime, still "fit and flourishing" as Hobelia liked to put it. If he'd seen them every day, Chris might not have noticed the subtle signs of aging, but after five years away they were undeniable. Added to the number of crew he'd lost over five years in space, they made him all too aware of his own mortality.

And then there was Tango.

With advances in veterinary science over the centuries, it wasn't unusual for a horse to live past fifty, so at twenty-seven Tango was really just on the cusp of middle age. He still lived up to his name, nodding his head and dancing sideways whenever Chris approached the paddock, but the burnished bay coat was flecked with white, and his gait had slowed a bit, especially on steep trails. He was no longer a mischievous youngster, and Chris wondered how much more time he'd have with the old devil if he accepted another five-year mission.

So he was surprised, as the refit neared completion, to find himself restless, bored with the routine of paper-pushing and staff meetings, feeling as if his brain was rusting, eager to get back into space. Charlie found it amusing.

"Bit more of the old man in you than you'd maybe like to admit," he suggested, the brown eyes twinkling.

"You think so?" Chris wondered, his smile bemused and more than half frown.

"Wouldn't have anything to do with the young lady you brought by for dinner the other week, would it?"

"It might," Chris said, his face clouding. "That was a mistake."

"What? Bringing her to meet your parents, or getting involved with her in the first place?" Charlie wanted to know.

Chris didn't answer.

He hadn't wanted to get involved with the young woman he'd met at the officers' club, on the arm of her father, who just happened to be his commanding officer while he was planetside. But she'd more or less attached herself to him, and it had taken not a little diplomacy to persuade her they really weren't meant for each other without jeopardizing his career prospects.

There had been an uncomfortable few moments in his CO's office one morning a week or so later when the commodore had asked Pike rather pointedly what his "intentions" were, and Pike had responded, "Effective now, sir? None." But he'd braved the older man's glare without blinking, until the commodore remembered aloud that his subordinates' private lives were just that—private—and they'd gone on to talk about repair estimates and how soon *Enterprise* could be expected to be back in space, and the commodore's daughter was not mentioned again.

Extricated from what could have been a very unpleasant situation, Pike thought he'd be relieved. But when he found himself getting in the way of the repair crews at Planitia and underfoot at the ranch, he decided to spend some off-duty time exploring the planet of his birth. But wherever he went, he kept seeing Vina's face in crowds.

Too many forces kept pushing him in directions he hadn't meant to go in. He found himself assigned as part of the Starfleet presence at the yearly Federation Council Plenary Meeting in Paris. He'd tried to respectfully decline, request they send someone else. The last place on Earth he wanted to be was Paris.

Paris was where Vina had been born, where her parents probably still lived, if they were still alive. ("This is Vina. Her parents are dead"—an illusion, not a real man, had told him that.) He remembered the impact that merely finding her image in the library computer had had on him. He really did not want to go to Paris.

But his CO insisted on it and, in view of his recent history with his CO's daughter, Pike decided it was probably wise to comply.

Much of his time in Paris was spent cooling his heels between meetings and receptions. Unable to stay cooped up in a hotel suite with the city at his feet, he found himself walking at all hours of the day and night. There he seemed to encounter Vina at every turn.

She haunted him, her petite, graceful figure, the feline blue eyes and spun-sugar hair appearing through the distortion of storefront windows, sipping café au lait or cognac alone at the tables of sidewalk cafés as if waiting for him, slipstreaming through the crowds along the Champs-Elysées, an apparition in a short skirt and striped sailor blouse, a dark beret perched at an improbable angle on her pale hair, glancing at him over her shoulder in one of the many narrow cobbled streets in the older *arrondissements* of the city. When he blinked, these apparitions became other women entirely, strangers on whose face and form his mind (or the Talosians'?) had momentarily superimposed those of the woman he had left behind.

Was it by his own will or the trace of that Talosian mind within his own that he found himself standing on the cobbles outside a traditional patisserie in the heart of the city, exactly where the city directory had indicated it would be, looking exactly as he had imagined it would?

A small bell tinkled as he closed the door behind him. To his relief a young, slightly plump, dark-haired woman behind the counter smiled and wished him *"Bonjour"* and asked could she perhaps help *Monsieur* with something?

Maybe the shop has changed hands, he thought, almost hoping it had.

He returned the young woman's smile and said he would like to look around, and might have done just that, then thanked her and escaped unscathed. But his eye was caught by a set of holograms suspended in midair off to the side of the long counter, above a few small tables where a handful of locals congregated to savor their dark-roast coffee and croissants.

He'd never been to a ballet, but Pike could recognize a dance troupe in the first group holo, a corps de ballet of graceful young men and women, mostly human, with a duet poised downstage in front of them. The female, clad in white feathers to look like a swan, was Andorian; she bowed from the waist, her outstretched hand almost touching the floor. The partner who held her about that delicate waist was a human male of slightly less than average height, his fine-boned face turned toward the camera so that it was clear he was meant to be the focus of the photograph.

A second holo showed the same man, somewhat older, dressed in black, a stark white towel around his neck, instructing a young Vulcan male at the *barre* in a room surrounded by mirrors. Again, the camera's focus was on the human male, his posture even in repose graceful and assured. Whoever had taken the holo—the signature *Violette* was scrawled in glowing letters at the bottom—had clearly been very fond of him.

The third holo, centered between the other two, was again of the graceful man, on one knee on the floor of the same mirrored room, holding the waist of a tiny dancer facing away from him toward the camera, a little girl of no more than seven or eight years, in the traditional pink tutu and toe shoes, arms curved above her head, balanced perfectly en pointe. This time the focus was on her, and the brilliant smile she presented to the world. Behind her, her father had tried to look serious, but he could not help beaming with pride.

The three images, capturing moments of grace and joy long past, visited Pike with an almost physical pain. He turned away from them abruptly to thank the young woman, intending to say he did not wish to purchase anything today, thank you, and make his exit, but too late. The young woman had been replaced behind the counter (too preoccupied with the images, he hadn't heard the shuffle of slippered footsteps, the soft exchange of words in French) by a petite elderly woman in a flowered dress covered with a long white apron. Pike would have recognized those eyes and that smile anywhere.

This is what Vina would have looked like at this age, he thought, then realized he was thinking of her in the past tense, as if she were dead, as anyone on Earth who had known her—including this tiny woman studying him so intently—no doubt assumed she was.

He was about to blurt out "Your daughter is alive!" when the woman spoke.

"Monsieur is admiring my family. My daughter was lost to me some years ago—an accident in space."

She said it calmly, with only a little trace, not of sadness, but of regret, as if thinking of all the years her daughter might have lived, if only.

"My husband . . ." she went on even as Pike drew breath to speak. ". . . I have lost only recently. It is one year today. His heart was not strong. I think because to lose a child is the saddest thing a parent can bear, and for a father to lose a daughter . . ."

She checked herself, as if wondering why she was telling this to a stranger, however receptive. Or perhaps, Pike thought, seeing one of the locals at the tables look up grimly, she repeated this tale to everyone who entered the shop.

It was then that he asked himself what he would accomplish by telling Vina's mother what he knew. What would it serve? The truth? After more than two decades of accepting her grief, what truth would be served by his giving her a new one?

"Monsieur will forgive me," she said in her soft voice. "I am being a poor hostess. You come to buy sweets, not to listen to bitterness. How may I help you?"

He had ordered some pastries then, inventing some story about attending a Starfleet reception the night before at which this particular patisserie had been mentioned. This brought a wintery smile to her face, a pride in the work of a lifetime. Their hands touched briefly as she handed him the small cardboard box, tied up with string from a spool that hung above her head over the counter in a tradition centuries old. She cut the string with practiced ease, using a small blade attached to a ring on one finger, then presented the box to Pike. The hands that touched his were Vina's hands, warm and giving, seasoned by the passage of time.

Pike thanked her and hurried out of the shop, along the cobbled street, the pastry box clutched carelessly in one hand, his throat constricting. Impatiently he tossed the box into the first trash receptacle he could find, regretting it the instant he'd done so.

And for some reason he felt compelled to tell Spock about the encounter years later.

He had to do something to distract himself from the events of the day while he and Spock waited for the coldest part of the night, when it might be safe to move again. The predators pursuing them, they had discovered, were cold-blooded and could not move about once the temperature dropped below a certain point during the coldest part of the night. Until then, there was nothing for the two of them to do but wait.

Pike and his science officer were the only survivors of a landing party gone horribly wrong, trapped on a planetoid without a name swarming with reptilian beings intent on capturing them and eating them alive.

He'd seen it happen to the fourth member of the landing party. They'd been too late to do anything for the other three.

They were on routine patrol in the final year of a second five-year mission. They'd been mapping a previously uncharted system, one of a five-star cluster in the region, and had decided one of the inner worlds looked inviting enough to stop and investigate in person. Scanners had found indications of some trace ores that might be worth harvesting, and no life-forms larger than a prairie dog. A large temperate zone suggested research could be combined with a little shore leave.

"Indications of considerable vegetation, Captain," Mr. Spock reported, interpreting the scans. "Much of it in the form of pericarpal and indehiscent drupoid arborescent foliage."

"Mind giving me that in small words?" Pike quipped. Spock had mellowed a bit since the first mission—he was less often compelled to shout for what he assumed was inferior human hearing—but he was as literal-minded as ever. Either that, or he had a wit so dry no one on board had yet been able to fully appreciate it.

"Berry bushes and fruit trees," Number One remarked from the helm. "Might be nice to have some fresh produce for a change, if the stuff is safe for humanoid consumption."

"You may have a point there," Pike mused, signing yet one more diagnostic report. "The very least we can do is find out."

They'd been mapping uninhabited systems for weeks. Of the five stars in this cluster, one contained a single planet which suggested it might have been inhabited at one time. The rest were either gas giants or near-barren rocks populated by nothing more intelligent than lichens. In comparison, this world looked like paradise.

Pike found himself wanting very much to go hiking on real soil with a real sky over his head, maybe cool his face with the water from a real stream. "Nothing to indicate any habitation, even historically, Science Officer? Wouldn't want to go picnicking in somebody else's backyard."

"Negative, sir," Spock reported, looking as if he were tempted to ask what the captain meant by "picnicking" in this context. "No signs of habitation, no ruins, no orbital construction. Only normal background hydrocarbons in the atmosphere. And no indication of ship traffic of any kind anywhere in the system."

"Any inhabited worlds nearby that might claim this as part of their territory?" Pike asked.

"Just that one we scanned a ways back," Number One chimed in, bringing up a schematic. "And, from the looks of things, it may have been inhabited at one time, but it isn't now."

"Indeed," Spock concurred. "There is evidence of considerable activity on the second of two planets orbiting this star . . ." He indicated. "However, preliminary scans indicate no advanced life-forms."

Pike studied the readouts that meant ship's traffic, orbital satellites, numerous industrialized areas on the surface.

"A mechanized outpost of some kind?" he wondered.

"Very possibly, Captain," Spock concurred.

"Interesting," Pike mused. "And no indication any of those ships have ventured in this direction?"

"None at present."

"Well, in that case . . ." Pike handed the report back to the ensign from engineering who had brought it for his signature, and allowed himself the luxury of a yawn and a stretch. ". . . captain's discretion suggests I lead a landing party for a look around, and if nothing tries to eat us, we may be able to combine business and pleasure."

He had no way of knowing how soon his words would come back to haunt him.

The planet seemed idyllic at first. Slightly smaller than Earth, it had a concomitantly lighter gravity, which made it hard to resist bouncing on one's feet. The landing party—Pike, Spock, a biologist, a geologist, and a security team—had beamed down in a kind of sunny meadow surrounded by primeval forest. Trees that would have put coast redwoods to shame towered above smaller, more plentiful specimens heavy with blossoms and fruit in appealing scents and colors. Tricorder readings indicated the fruit was safe to eat. Chisholm, the team biologist, quickly confirmed this with some empirical testing.

"Delicious, Captain," she reported, offering Pike a section of what looked like a football-sized nectarine. "Kind of a cross between a custard apple and a kiwifruit."

"We should have brought baskets," Pike suggested, though he waved the fruit away for now, turning in place a full three hundred sixty degrees to look carefully around them. Something about this place made him uneasy. For one thing, it was entirely too quiet. The predominant local fauna, small gray-brown marsupials with batlike ears whose subterranean habitats dotted the open field with small molehills, had gathered in a mob to chatter angrily at them when they first beamed down but, seeing that the newcomers, who were much larger than they were, were unfazed by their threats, they'd quickly ducked back into their lairs. Once they were gone, the silence was uncanny.

"Science Officer? Any evidence of birds or insects?"

"Negative, Captain," Spock reported, frowning at the readings on his tricorder.

"Predators of any kind? Something must eat the marsupials to keep the population down."

"None in the vicinity, Captain," Spock replied. He might as well have still been on the ship for all the notice he was taking of the landscape around him, except as it could be reduced to scanner readings. At last he looked up, his frown deepening. "Curious. The plant life clearly reproduces by cross-pollination, but without avian or insect agents, I am at somewhat of a loss to explain how it is successful in doing so."

"Maybe the wind," Chisholm suggested. She nodded toward the edge of the meadow where the sunlight was particularly bright. There was a constant stirring in the air, and as they turned away from the sun they could see golden dustings of pollen carried on the breeze.

"I'd still be happier if there were birds," Pike said vaguely, not sure why he'd said that. Maybe the sunlight was getting to him; he felt like lying down in the long fragrant grass and taking a nap. Instead, he focused.

"All right, let's not get distracted, people. Fan out . . . D'zekeo, you and Chisholm that way, Brandt and Norgay in the opposite direction. Mr. Spock and I will take the remaining quadrants. Take samples and tricorder readings of whatever you find, report in at hundred-meter intervals. Keep those tricorders active, watch your footing, and stay in contact with the ship as well as each other . . ."

If there had been birds, he thought after they'd lost contact first with Brandt and Norgay, then Chisholm, and the sound of laser fire told them that D'zekeo was in trouble, and he and Spock ran toward D'zekeo's last position even as Pike tried to contact the ship to get a fix on them and beam them out, *they'd have warned us we weren't alone down here. They could have reminded us that every Eden has its snakes . . .*

Days later, alone in a holding pen on the alien ship, heading, he assumed, for their homeworld, Pike considered what he and his landing party had learned the hard way about this species.

For one thing, their interplanetary vessels were almost impossible to read on Starfleet scanners until they dropped out of hyperdrive. For another, they only visited this planet during hunting season. Which, unfortunately for his crew, coincided with the day his landing party chose to beam down to what they thought was an uninhabited world.

They were the predator that kept the "prairie dogs'" numbers down. And they were not averse to hunting larger prey.

Hindsight is always twenty-twenty, and Pike would regret his lack of information for a long time afterward. For now, all he knew was that he'd lost contact with three of his crew, a fourth was under apparent attack, and he couldn't get in touch with his ship.

He and Spock arrived almost simultaneously at the grove where they'd heard D'zekeo's weapons fire, just in time to see the security officer swung off his feet as if he were a rag doll, into the opening maw of—

Just because they look like snakes—two-meter-tall, standing-upright, able to unhinge their lower jaws to swallow prey, hairless and scaled and slit-eyed and forked-tongued snakes, some rational part of his brain that wasn't frozen in horror at what he was watching told him, *doesn't mean they really are snakes.*

Reptiles, at any rate. To judge from the streamlined shuttle half-obscured in the tall grass, highly evolved space-faring reptiles. Reptiles who had evolved articulated limbs and opposable digits and who were proportionately stronger than a humanoid, strong enough to grapple the security man, D'zekeo—either already dead or at least, mercifully, unconscious—toward the unhinged jaw and down the throat of the largest and most brilliantly colored of the creatures, who swallowed twice, its sides expanding to accommodate its prey and then, with the leisure of a sated beast unaware of any threat, lowered itself onto its forelimbs and strolled slowly toward a sunny rock, where it stretched itself out and basked in the sun.

The tricorders must not have picked them up, Pike thought. *The entire planet could be teeming with them. We'll need to figure out what's wrong with the tricorders, assuming we have the time.*

In the handful of seconds in which they'd watched their security man being ingested, Spock had instinctively raised his weapon to fire and Pike had stayed him, because they were too late for D'zekeo, and outnumbered four to one, at least here. No way of knowing how many more were in the shuttle, or if there were others.

Of the remaining seven creatures in the clearing, three more were as bloated as the leader. No mystery, then, what had become of Chisholm, Norgay, and Brandt. As these three joined the leader in stretching out on the rocks, the four who had not yet eaten continued hunting.

And, moving with deliberate speed, forked tongues long as a man's arm flicking out before them to smell and taste the air, the ground, the grasses and tree trunks their prey might have brushed against, they fanned out in ironic parody of what the humanoid landing party had been doing only moments before. One of them was headed directly toward Pike and Spock.

Pike found his voice at last, released it in a whisper. "Are there snakes on Vulcan, Science Officer?"

"Indeed there are, Captain," Spock said equally quietly. "Most of them quite deadly."

Snakes are also deaf, Pike remembered, and wondered if this species was as well. No time to test it now. Everything Charlie had ever taught him about snakes flashed through his mind. Fortunately Spock would know these things as well. It was time to act.

"Split up," Pike ordered, still whispering, gesturing with his phaser in the direction each would take. "Better odds against our both being captured. My guess is there's a larger ship up there, and it may have spotted *Enterprise,* maybe even engaged her."

He didn't finish the thought with *maybe unsuccessfully*.

"On the assumption these creatures are deaf, they'll rely on vibration as well as scent to track us. Tread lightly. Contact me at five-minute intervals. I'll try to raise the ship."

"Understood," was all Spock said. Even as he began to move off, light-footed as a cat, Pike moved as well, wincing at the squeak the communicator made as he activated it yet again. "Pike to *Enterprise*. *Enterprise,* come in . . ."

"I am unable to get a fix on them, Number One," Chief Engineer Moves-with-Burning-Grace reported solemnly. "Something is blocking the readings, and has been for the last several minutes. One minute I was tracking the entire landing party, the next—"

"Unacceptable, Mr. Grace," Number One cut him off. She had no patience with what she saw as incompetence. In an ideal universe, she thought, she'd have been able to run all ship's functions, including the transporters, from the conn. "They haven't just disappeared. Keep scanning until you find them. Comm?"

"Nothing, sir." Dabisch shrugged. "Captain Pike didn't check in at the quarter-hour mark, and there's no response to our hails. Either something's jamming them, or . . ." He left his thought unfinished.

"Number One?" José Tyler sounded nervous. "Unidentified vessel at seven o'clock. Scanners didn't pick her up until she was practically on top of us."

"Hailing frequencies," Number One instructed Dabisch without looking over her shoulder. "Standard greetings."

"Aye, sir."

The universal translator was not rigged for a species that could not hear and, as it turned out, had no provision

for communicating with a species that did. As soon as the
alien ship was within firing range, it did so.

The exchange was brief. Number One ordered evasive
maneuvers, and *Enterprise* managed to dodge the alien vessel's fire, which ceased as soon as *Enterprise* retreated
beyond the outer planets of the system. The message was
clear: *This world belongs to us, stay away!*

"What now, Number One?" Tyler asked, wiping his
sweating hands on his trouser legs. "We can't just leave the
landing party down there."

"Unless we can communicate with that ship, that's
exactly what we'll do for the time being!" Number One said
a little too sharply. "We're trespassing. And if Captain Pike
and his team have gone to ground, there's no point in alerting
the aliens to their presence until we have the means to
retrieve them. Mr. Grace . . ." She spun the command chair in
his direction. "Scan that ship and tell me how many are
aboard her."

"Already done, sir," Grace reported crisply. "But the sensors are unable to penetrate their hull."

"What about comm?" Number One demanded.

"It's the same code that Mr. Spock intercepted from that
mechanized system," Dabisch confirmed.

"So we don't know what we're dealing with," Number
One said angrily.

"I'm afraid not," Grace said. "However, whoever they are,
they are releasing shuttlecraft all over that planet's surface."

From where Pike and Spock had taken refuge in the tree
canopy, they could see the shuttles, perhaps a dozen more of
them, each containing a crew of ten. The creatures emerged
from their hatches and immediately began hunting the native
marsupials, which they captured live, except for the occa-

sional one swallowed as a snack, anesthetized with a quick bite to the neck, and bound up in nets they stowed in the holds of the shuttles.

The aliens were also setting up a handful of temporary structures and what looked like a comm transmitter, suggesting, Pike thought, that they intended this world to be some sort of outpost.

"Captain?" Spock's voice interrupted his thoughts. "With enough time, I believe I may be able to recalibrate my tricorder to penetrate whatever jamming these creatures are using to cloak their life-form readings. It may also be possible to gather enough of their . . . unusual form of communication . . . to feed into the universal translator . . ."

"All well and good if this were a laboratory experiment, Science Officer. But if we don't manage to get out of this alive—"

"Captain, if I may, I estimate sunset in this sector in approximately three point five-six hours."

Pike opened his mouth to ask what the hell that had to do with anything, but then he understood. "Meaning the temperature ought to drop, and these creatures will either have to retreat to their ships or at least slow down."

"Precisely. I believe I have already noticed a subtle reduction in the rate of their activity."

Pike could see it, too. The speed with which the aliens captured their small prey was beginning to slow and, if they'd ever figured out that there were still two members of the landing party on the loose, they were no longer actively looking for them.

"Good to know, Spock. If we haven't heard from *Enterprise* by nightfall, this is what we'll do . . ."

17

ONE YEAR LATER

The event was now nothing more than a memory, a bad dream, only one of many from a second five-year mission which had only recently come to an end. *Enterprise* was due for another refit and so, Christopher Pike thought, was he. Very soon he would have to decide which way he allowed his career to take him next. Did he want to go back out there again? He didn't know. For now, he sat in the officers' lounge on Starbase 11 with his old friend José Mendez, staring into his drink as he told the story of his captivity by the creatures who, he came to know, called themselves Kan'ess. As he raised the glass to his lips, he suppressed a shudder.

"Snakes, eh?" Mendez shook his head. "Helluva thing, Chris. But it's over. You're reliving it as if it were yesterday."

"Sometimes it seems as if it was," Pike said grimly. He put the glass down. He'd always been able to hold his liquor, but lately he seemed to be holding too much of it. He'd never been drunk in his life, but he hated to think he was becoming dependent.

"You ever talk to anyone about it?" Mendez asked, concerned.

"You mean a therapist?" Pike shook his head. "No."

"Maybe you should."

"No," Pike said again. *There are too many other things I'd have to keep to myself, even under client confidentiality. Whatever's inside my head will have to stay there.*

"Well, you survived it," Mendez pointed out, studying his old friend warily. "You're here."

"I wonder . . ." Pike began, then remembered himself barely in time. The more years between him and Talos IV, the more difficult it seemed for him to keep his silence about it. He and Mendez were old friends, but even he couldn't know about Vina, about the power of the Talosian mind.

Particularly if that mind, as he'd suggested to Spock as they watched the reptiles and waited for the sun to go down, was still connected to his.

IN THE KANES SYSTEM

As day faded to night and it was clear *Enterprise* was out of reach, at least temporarily, Pike and Spock managed to elude the hunters by staying off the ground and moving from tree to tree. Movement was slow and arduous, particularly in the half-light, but, agile as the aliens were, it apparently did not occur to them to climb trees when there was so much game available on the ground. And empirical evidence suggested that whatever the aliens used to mask their life signs also kept them from detecting the Starfleet officers.

"However, Captain, I would advise against underestimating their ability to track us via their senses alone," Spock cautioned. "If our supposition is correct, and these creatures evolved from reptilian ancestors, they will possess a vomeronasal organ making them capable of both smelling and tasting with their tongues. This highly developed sensory ability compensates for the absence of hearing, and their limited visual capabilities."

"Vomero—who?" Pike asked. Charlie had simply taught him that snakes could both taste and smell with their tongues. He hadn't needed any fancy words.

"In reptiles the vomeronasal organ is a highly developed passageway within the nasal cavity which connects olfactory impressions directly to receptors in the brain," Spock began, settling his long frame into a crook of the tree as if it were his natural environment, and settling his voice into lecture mode. "This makes the processing of tastes and odors instantaneous, whereas in the mammalian brain, lacking this connection, an extra process is required in order to associate smells and tastes with the memory of previous encounters. In fact, most mammals, including humans, retain a primitive vomeronasal organ, but it is no longer directly connected to the brain."

"Well, that's a big help!" Pike joked, wishing he had Spock's confidence that the aliens couldn't hear them, wishing he had a Vulcan's night vision as well, to help him see the creatures still moving, however slowly, below them on the forest floor. "Any luck getting the tricorder to penetrate the interference?"

"Negative, Captain," Spock replied. Did Pike only imagine a tinge of disappointment in his voice? "However, I have made a start on encoding some of their language into the universal translator."

Pike sat up straighter, then regretted it as a small branch poked him in the back.

"What language? If they're deaf—you mean some kind of code? How the hell did you manage to do that?"

"In their haste to devour Dr. Chisholm, the aliens did not notice that her tricorder had fallen into the tall grass," Spock reported evenly. Silently Pike cursed himself for not even noticing that Spock was carrying two tricorders. "It remained running in the clearing while they pursued and captured Lieutenant D'zekeo. The creatures communicate via head nods, hand gestures, and a kind of rhythmic drumming of their feet and tails on the ground. Dr. Chisholm's tricorder was able to capture much of this language. Insufficient to build a communication base as yet, but I shall endeavor to capture more. If I can interface with the *Enterprise*'s library computer . . ."

"If there still is an *Enterprise* library computer," Pike said grimly, then realized just how much work his science officer had accomplished in an afternoon. "Can you give me anything to work with now? Maybe a gesture that says 'Hello, beautiful morning, isn't it?' Because if we are stranded down here, our best hope is to communicate with these creatures."

"Not at present, Captain. However, given enough time . . ."

"Speaking of time," Pike interrupted, restless, peering through the branches at the ground below. Not seeing the creatures was almost as unsettling as seeing them, and the growing darkness made it difficult to see anything. "How much longer do you estimate before it's safe for us to move around down there?"

"Judging from the present ambient temperature and the rate at which it has been decreasing since sunset, I would estimate another sixty-seven point eight minutes."

"An hour, then," Pike said, folding his arms and repositioning himself for about the twentieth time.

He could dimly see Spock against the foliage, bent over the tricorder, shielding the visual display lest the light give their position away. Pike felt useless—at least Spock was doing something meaningful; all he could do was keep trying to contact *Enterprise,* getting nothing but static—and the darkness around them taunted him with the memory of watching D'zekeo being eaten alive by one of the creatures, and realizing what had happened to the others.

One minute they'd been talking, picking fruit, enjoying the sunshine, the next they were gone, forever. No matter how many times he lost people on a mission, he would never get used to it. To keep the horrors at bay, Pike found himself thinking aloud.

"Spock? You ever wonder if all of this is an illusion?"

"Sir?"

"What I mean is, what if the Talosians succeeded in luring us all down into those caverns and we never escaped, and everything that's happened to us since hasn't really happened at all?"

"Dubious," was Spock's opinion.

"How so?"

"Captain, for the Talosians to be able to sustain the illusion, for this much time, for every one of us who came in contact with them, without ever once making a detectable error, is something of which, even with their vast powers, I believe them incapable. The expenditure in mental energy alone, the ability to know so much about each of us that none of us ever detected the illusion, not to mention the question of *why* they would wish to do such a thing, would be incalculable."

That was when Pike told Spock about his encounter with Vina's mother in the pastry shop.

"What would you have done, Spock?"

"There is a saying on Vulcan, Captain," Spock said after a thoughtful silence. "'It is not a lie to keep the truth to oneself.'"

"So you'd have done what I did? Said nothing."

Spock considered. "I doubt I would have sought out the pastry shop to begin with."

"Not even out of curiosity?"

"No, sir."

Pike shifted over to a different fork of the tree. No position was comfortable, and he couldn't wait to be on the move again.

"That's my point, Spock. Neither would I. At least, not

the person I was before Talos IV. Ever since then, I don't know how much of what I do is of my own volition, and how much might be . . ."

He shook his head, couldn't finish.

"You don't know how tempted I am to jump down there and throw myself in the path of one of those aliens just to see if they'll actually kill me, or if, like the Kaylar, they're just an illusion, and a minute later I'll be right back here talking to you."

"Captain . . ." Spock said seriously. The human impulse to act first and think later was nothing new to him. ". . . I would strongly advise against it.

"In any event," he went on once it was clear Pike was not going to act on his words, "I believe it is now relatively safe for us to travel. The temperature has fallen below the range at which most cold-blooded creatures should be able to move with any alacrity, and I detect no hunters in the vicinity."

For the rest of the night, Spock with his superior night vision leading the way, they endeavored to find someplace the hunting parties hadn't reached yet. Without the ability to read them on tricorder it was a challenge, and several times they passed quite close to shuttles or temporary structures containing, they assumed, any number of the reptiles, sheltering until daybreak.

By the time daybreak came, they had traversed several kilometers, sometimes doubling back on themselves, crossing streams in an attempt to obscure their scent. Only when the sun began to peer above the horizon did they seek shelter in the tree canopy once more, halfway up one of the larger trees so that, with luck, they would neither be seen from the ground nor spotted from the air should any more of the alien shuttles pass by overhead.

They were also close enough to some of the fruit trees

to help themselves, since they'd only brought sufficient Starfleet rations for a single day. The presence of the native marsupials, creating a ruckus over the pillaging of their food supply before retreating to a wary distance, was reassuring. As long as the small furry ones were nearby, the reptiles wouldn't be.

They took turns keeping the watch. They continued to attempt, without success, to contact *Enterprise*. Until the sun went down again, there was nothing else to do but wait.

Unless, of course, you were Spock.

Pike awoke after a fitful nap, grateful after all that there were no insects on this planet, since the heat of the sun was distracting enough, to find Spock just as he had been when the human had drifted into sleep, studying something on his tricorder screen. It was unnaturally quiet; the marsupials were gone. Glancing cautiously below, Pike saw a party of perhaps a dozen reptiles in full hunting mode moving through the clearing.

"Captain," Spock began without preamble, handing Pike one of the tricorders. "I have backed up the data from Dr. Chisholm's tricorder on my own. In the event one of us is captured . . ."

"Good thinking," Pike said. Even if only one of them survived, the other could store the collected data aboard *Enterprise*. Pike forced himself to overcome his revulsion at the sight of the creatures and began to study the translator's attempts to create a language algorithm out of their gestures. He glanced up at Spock gratefully. "This is incredible, Spock—we can use this."

But Spock's attention was on the hunters passing beneath them. "It is still not enough," he mused. "Captain, request permission to follow the hunting party and attempt to capture more of their communication patterns."

"Negative, Spock. There are too many of them. If even one catches your scent, you'll end up like D'zekeo."

"We have discovered that they do not climb trees. If I remain above them in the canopy—"

"I think I've made myself clear, Science Officer."

Spock's face wore what on a human would be a stubborn look. "Captain, you have instructed me to capture enough of the aliens' language to communicate with them. If I am to succeed . . ."

And if you don't, I'll be alone down here. Stranded like Robinson Crusoe, every deep space traveler's unspoken nightmare, alone with these creatures and my memories. I don't know which is worse.

Pike shook himself, disguising it as an attempt to stretch his muscles after sleeping in an uncomfortable position.

"All right, Spock. But stay in the trees, and stay in communication. Meanwhile, I'm going to see if I can get a better look at that transmitter. Rendezvous back here in an hour."

"Affirmative."

The last of the hunting party moved off without noticing them. Spock peered through the foliage to ascertain their likely direction and soundlessly disappeared among the branches.

Pike climbed as high as he could in the swaying branches. From there he could look out over the entire valley and ascertain that this region too was now swarming with hunters, perhaps fifty or sixty in all on the ground, with more emerging from several shuttles. Peering in the other direction, he could see the skeleton of the structure the aliens had begun to construct yesterday. It was almost certainly a comm tower, possibly meant to interface with an orbital satellite.

The sound of engines overhead made him duck below the

canopy just in time, as yet another squadron of the sleek alien shuttles roared by.

Pike reached for his communicator, prepared to order Spock back, then stopped himself. Wherever Spock was, he was probably in no more nor less danger than he would be here. If the entire region, perhaps the entire planet, was soon to be filled with hunting reptiles, no place would be safe.

Spock returned as silently as he had departed, precisely within the hour. Pike, his nerves raw, had to stop himself from jumping out of his skin when Spock suddenly appeared.

"Captain, while I have not succeeded in establishing an algorithm for 'beautiful morning, isn't it,' I believe there may be enough data here to establish a basis for communication," Spock reported dryly.

As they transferred the data to the second tricorder, Pike felt himself grinning for the first time since Chisholm had offered him some of the native fruit yesterday. They might yet get out of this alive.

The next step was to wait until dark and have a closer look at the comm tower. What they saw confirmed Pike's fears.

"Considerable advanced weaponry," Spock observed, stating the obvious. "It is also shielded, quite primitively, but successfully."

Pike saw it, too, a high fence of some fine metal mesh surrounded the facility, apparently electrified, meant to keep the marsupials away. Several which hadn't been clever enough to recognize the danger clung to the wire, frozen in place by the current that had killed them.

"Guess they only eat live ones," Pike commented wryly. "What are the odds the current's strong enough to kill a humanoid?"

"I would not recommend experimentation to find out," Spock replied, frowning at his tricorder.

"What is it?"

"I believe I have an answer to why we have lost contact with *Enterprise*."

Pike read the tricorder screen over his shoulder. "And they with us. There is a ship up there transmitting on the same frequency. Since these creatures can't hear, it doesn't matter to them that their ships' shielding blocks audio feeds."

"Indeed," Spock said, switching screens and showing Pike something else. "Their visual comm is quite sophisticated. I shall endeavor to capture as much of it as possible."

"Later," Pike ordered. "Right now we find the source of the electricity powering that fence and shut it down, then get in there and disable that comm system, even if it's only for a few minutes."

They found the transformer for the electricity, a simple device housed in a makeshift guard hut whose guard had begun dozing as soon as the sun went down. When the dead marsupials fell free of the fence, it was easy enough to slip under the mesh and break into the comm center.

"Never knew Vulcans were such expert lock picks," Pike joked, scanning the perimeter, phaser at the ready. "Wouldn't imagine there was much need for that kind of skill on your world."

"There is not," Spock assured him, easing the outer door open. Even knowing the aliens were deaf and, most likely, in a somnolent state, they strove for stealth. "However, the acuity of Vulcan hearing . . ."

"Save it!" Pike said, clapping him on the back and going first down the darkened corridor. Trying to gauge where the main controls might be, he noticed something else. "It's warm in here. Some of the creatures may still be active."

"Indeed," Spock concurred.

They found the main controls. Spock contemplated them for a long moment, his familiarity with the technology of several worlds suggesting a certain logic to the configuration before him. With a surety Pike envied—he thought he knew which control was for what, but he couldn't be certain—Spock moved toward one of several panels busy with lights and toggles, and went to work.

They knew he'd succeeded when the power grid went down abruptly, plunging them into darkness. Moving toward where they remembered the door to be, Pike whipped out his communicator.

Number One considered her dilemma. More than thirty hours had passed since they'd lost contact with the landing party. Mr. Grace had determined that the alien vessel's shielding emitted some sort of dampening frequency that was blocking *Enterprise*'s comm. Not only was it impossible to contact or even locate the landing party, but attempts to reach Starfleet Command were blocked as well, as long as they remained in the vicinity of that ship.

There was only one thing to do. Deliberately, Number One opened the intercraft.

"All hands, this is the first officer. Prepare to leave the system."

She counted the space of a nanosecond before José Tyler spun around in his chair and said, "But—!" Ignoring him, she went on.

"As you know, we have lost contact with the landing party. All comm into and out of this system is blocked by that alien vessel, which has made it clear it will not allow us to approach any nearer to the planet. Given the presence of numerous shuttlecraft on the planet surface, it's obvious whoever built those ships considers this planet their territory, and one lone starship is not in a position to dispute that.

"We will reestablish communication with Starfleet Command and await advice. There will be no grumbling or speculation in the meantime. First Officer—"

"Number One!" It was Dabisch, nearly shouting. "Message from the surface. It's Captain Pike!"

". . . could be cut off any second . . ." Pike was saying, feeling his way down the corridor and through the outer door. He'd counted the number of paces to the fence. If they could get clear . . . "Can you get a lock on us?"

"Mr. Grace?" Number One barked.

"They're moving quite rapidly," the engineer reported. "I'm unable to get a fix on them unless they can get to a clear place and stand still."

"Captain—?"

"I heard that, Number One. Stand by . . ."

He and Spock cleared the fence just as the lights inside the complex fluttered back on. Someone activating backup power, he assumed. But they hadn't reset the comm controls—Spock had cross-circuited something that would keep them guessing for a few more minutes—so he could still talk to the ship.

Just a few more yards into the forest, and they could—

Pike skidded to a halt as one of the creatures loomed in front of him. It was moving slowly in the chill night air, but moving, blocking their path. A phaser blast stunned the creature, which fell heavily. But the flash of the phaser fire had no doubt given their position away.

An eerie thundering behind them made Pike turn in spite of himself. The aliens were stamping on the ground, communicating with each other in the absence of their commcoders. Several silhouettes against the bright light inside the compound told him they were headed this way, moving much more quickly than they should have been.

He didn't wait for them to get close enough to see that they were wearing heat suits. He would learn about those later.

For now he and Spock ran, dodging low-hanging branches and plowing through underbrush, disturbing nests of marsupials who chittered at them furiously. How much longer before the aliens blocked their comm again? When the chittering suddenly stopped, Pike did, too.

"They're close," he gasped, out of breath.

"Indeed," Spock concurred, scanning the darkness. "Seven of them . . ." He gestured toward where he could see them and Pike couldn't. "Possibly more."

"You can see in the dark . . . elude them better . . ." Pike said abruptly, shoving his phaser and the second tricorder into Spock's unwilling hands. "I'll distract them. Get to the ship . . . work on that translation . . . Go!"

"Captain—!"

"That's an order!" Pike yelled, literally shoving Spock toward the woods and starting off in the opposite direction, communicator open as he ran. "*Enterprise*, get a fix on Spock and beam him up now!"

"Sir, we're trying to get a fix on both of you—" Number One began. Pike cut her off.

"Negative! Beam Spock up and get my ship out of here! Do it!"

With that Pike clapped the communicator shut, flung it as far as he could into the darkness beneath the trees, and kept running.

STARBASE 11

"Were you out of your mind?" Caught up in the narrative in spite of himself, José Mendez was leaning forward in his chair, incredulous. "You actually let them capture you—!"

"And to this day, I don't think Spock's forgiven me for it," Pike mused.

"But why?"

"Spur of the moment decision," Pike said, gesturing to the bartender for another round, though he didn't remember finishing the last one. "If Spock could get to the ship and get a handle on their language . . ."

"Blah-blah-blah, of course!" Mendez said crossly. "That doesn't explain why you didn't stand still and let your first officer beam you both up. Or why you jettisoned your phaser and your communicator."

"Easy to explain. Didn't want them capturing our technology."

"But it was all right for them to capture you?" Mendez's voice was laced with skepticism. "That goes against half a dozen regs I could cite, and you can, too."

Pike ducked the question, went to the bar to retrieve their drinks. "Command was satisfied with my explanation after the fact," he said a little smugly, handing Mendez his cognac.

"Only because you lived to tell the tale!" Mendez snorted. "Why? Why let them capture you?"

Pike sipped his drink, determined it would be his last, even if he and Mendez talked all night.

"Sitting in that tree all day, I learned as much as I could from the translator. There were certain basic gestures . . . I thought I could communicate enough to convince them I was intelligent, at least too intelligent to be a between-meal snack. At best I was hoping for first contact, at least to learn enough about their technology to see if they posed a threat."

"And if they did have you for breakfast, how were you supposed to convey that information back to Starfleet?" Mendez wanted to know.

Pike shrugged. "I told you. Spock was going to learn their language. With what he'd learned on the planet, he could work with Number One and Mr. Grace to get around the Kan'ess ship's dampening field, ask for my release—"

"And you had that all worked out while you were running through the woods?" Mendez fixed Pike with his steely gaze. "I think there's more to it than that. I think you have some kind of death wish."

Pike started to argue, but Mendez knew him too well. Instead he tried to laugh it off. "Well, as you say, I'm here. If I was really trying to get myself killed, I wasn't very successful, was I?"

When they surrounded him, he didn't struggle. He'd heard the whine of the transporter and knew that Spock was safe. When he found his way blocked by half a dozen of the creatures, he assumed one of them would have him for a midnight snack. Thinking crazily of vampires, he saw rather than felt the largest of them sink its teeth into the side of his neck. The venom, if that was what it was, didn't cause him to lose consciousness, merely made it impossible for him to move. He found himself trying to remember something Charlie had told him about a poison the indigenous peoples of South America used, but couldn't get his thoughts to coalesce. As the aliens lifted him off his feet and carried him back to the compound (*curare,* he thought crazily), he soon had other things on his mind.

The paralytic didn't clear his system until after they'd loaded him into one of their shuttles and brought him up to the mothership, dumping him like so much cordwood in some kind of enclosure. By the time he was able to move his arms and legs again, pull himself up to a sitting position and, eventually and not without leaning against a bulkhead, climb stiffly to his feet and walk about, the vibration of the deck plates told him the ship was moving, probably leaving orbit, possibly headed for what he and his crew had thought was an uninhabited, mechanized world.

The holding cell was dimly lit by the bars of light across the doorway, which obviously comprised some sort of force field. The cell and, he assumed, the entire ship, was kept at a slightly higher temperature than a human ship might be. No warmer than a late-fall day in Mojave, Pike thought; he'd get used to it. A slightly musky smell and a vague chittering from somewhere down the corridor told him he was being held in the same part of the ship as the marsupials.

Just great! he thought. *Another cage. And this time they're saving me for dessert!*

"You were trapped on that world for a long time," Mendez observed soberly.

"Long enough . . ." Pike answered.

He'd always been a quick study and, unable to sleep after that first fitful nap in the tree, he'd used the time to memorize every bit of information Spock had gathered on the alien signing language. When the first one (a guard, he assumed) appeared at his cell door, Pike greeted it (it would be a few days before he learned to distinguish male from female by the patterns of their scales) with a gesture—a combination of a leftward tilt of the head and a right-handed motion—that he'd seen the aliens make whenever one group neared another, and which he hoped meant something like "Hello."

Startled, the guard recoiled before it could deactivate the force field, nearly dropping the container of food it was holding. It hissed, its nearly two-foot-long forked tongue darting in and out, but did not retreat further. Figuring he had nothing to lose, Pike made the gesture again.

The guard hissed again, and pulled out what looked like a weapon before deactivating the force field just long enough to thrust the food container inside before it moved off. Pike waited until he could no longer hear its heavy tread on the deck plates before picking up the food container and tentatively having a look inside. If whatever they'd decided to feed him was still alive—

It wasn't. It was some sort of food dispenser ration with a vaguely grain-like taste—probably the same thing they fed the marsupials, he thought. When the first mouthful went down without protest, he realized he was starving and started on the rest.

He had barely finished when he heard the heavy tread again. There were two of them this time.

The one just behind the guard was larger and more gaudily decorated, both in terms of its scales and in the trappings it wore. Someone in charge, Pike decided. Uneasily, he realized it looked familiar. Was it the same one that had devoured D'zekeo? Its sides still bulged slightly. Well, maybe it wouldn't be hungry again for a few more days.

The larger alien and the guard were deep in conversation, their gestures and head nods happening so quickly Pike couldn't follow. Something else was happening, too, a vague buzzing in his head that reminded him of the Talosians. Was there a telepathic component to the aliens' language as well? He forced himself to focus on looking for gestures he might remember from the translator, but the conversation was as brief as it had been rapid. He suddenly found himself under scrutiny.

The larger alien had large golden eyes, actually quite beautiful, with vertically slitted irises, and one of them—as with most snakes, its eyes were on either side of its head rather than forward—was studying him. Pike steadied himself and made the "hello" gesture once more.

The larger alien wasn't as startled as the guard had been. Only the depthless black pupil expanded, then narrowed, then returned to normal before the creature gestured to the guard to turn off the force field.

What happened next was so familiar Pike almost burst out laughing.

The guard balked. Pike could hear the conversation behind the gestures.

"Sir, are you sure it's safe? What if the creature tries something? What if—?"

"That's why you're here, isn't it, Ensign? That's why you've got a sidearm. Shut down the force field, Ensign. That's an order!"

Once the force field was down, the larger alien made an almost human gesture that said "Come with me."

Falling into step behind her (yes, *her,* something about the accoutrements said "female"), the guard falling into step behind him, Pike obeyed.

18

THE KANES HOMEWORLD

"Wot ahr yu?" the Director purred, flicking his face gently with one tip of her forked tongue.

"Human," Pike replied. He'd worked with one of her scientists to develop the voder. It had its flaws, but it was adequate for small talk. He'd reasoned that since the Kan'ess already had access to Starfleet technology, it was no violation of the Prime Directive.

Eggshells, was his first thought when the Director released him from the pen and brought him to her quarters. He was thinking of the number of times both in Mojave and on other worlds that he'd watched a snake disjoint its jaw, swallow a bird's egg whole, use its powerful muscles to crush it, extract its contents, and disgorge the compacted, empty shell.

Four Starfleet communicators, three tricorders, two phasers, and Ensign Norgay's universal translator lay spread out on a low table. Three of the communicators were crushed beyond salvage, and there were strange striations on the casings of the tricorders (powerful stomach acids?), but the other instruments were apparently still functional. They'd been ingested with the crewmen the Kan'ess had captured in those early moments on the wilderness world, and subsequently egested, cleaned up, and displayed for Pike's perusal.

As he approached the table, intending to pick up the last functioning communicator, the guard who had accompanied him from the pen instinctively reached for his weapon. A rapid gesture from the Director stayed him. Another motion instructed the guard to back off and take his position by the door. Pike memorized both gestures, then realized the Director was focused intently on him.

Time for the dog and pony show, he thought, sensing that she wanted an explanation for how a species her kind considered food could produce such advanced technology.

Feeling more than a little foolish—but first contact was first contact, regardless of whether it was acted out in mime—Pike picked up a tricorder and, mindful of the guard's whereabouts, slowly ran it over several objects in the room, including himself, to register the different readings. As he ran it over the guard (dicing with death, he thought, but at this point what did he have to lose?), he remembered that Spock had been unable to read these creatures, and was not surprised when the tricorder picked up only the molecular structure of the guard's uniform and weaponry. When he ran it over the Director, whose head was tilted in a gesture of frank curiosity, he was surprised. She gave off a faint reading, and he recorded it.

Interesting, he thought. *She's not in uniform. The creatures themselves can be read, but something in their military trappings must give off the same kind of sound waves as their ship's shields and the planet's. No wonder Spock couldn't penetrate the "interference"—it wasn't that they were trying to jam us, just a by-product of their clothing.*

He filed that thought for future reference. Something else

was tickling at the back of his mind, and he almost spoke aloud.

You can stop the illusion now! he thought, but nothing happened. If he'd expected to find himself back on the ship, or standing in front of a Parisian pastry shop, or even back in the Talosian cage (which, compared to his present situation, might almost be a relief) it was not to be.

Steadying his nerves, he showed the Director the results of the tricorder's scans, at the same time trying to memorize the difference between her bioscan and the guard's.

She studied the readouts and moved her head in the gesture Pike had learned meant "yes" or "I see." Then she motioned to the guard in a gesture that clearly meant "Wait outside" because, hand still on his weapon and, if Pike was any judge, an expression on his face of pure loathing for the human, he did so.

On the journey back to the Kanes homeworld, and for the next several days confined in a niche carved out of the native rock, Pike worked with the universal translator and whatever else he could cobble together from the devices given him, to create a voder that, when worn against the Director's throat, translated vibration into speech. A sensor placed against the aural spot on the side of her head, behind the slitted golden eyes and the venom pit, made it possible for her to hear the human when he spoke. Her expression of wonderment (at least Pike took it to be wonderment, watching her pupils dilate as she discovered the world of hearing for the first time) was almost as priceless as his ability to communicate with more than gestures.

If he'd had time, he'd have congratulated himself on his ingenuity, though he suspected a Vulcan or an engineer would have been able to knock something together in an afternoon.

In any event, he and the Director could now communicate, at least a little. And while his repeated attempts to use the same equipment to penetrate the dampening field that prevented human comm from getting in or out of the homeworld had so far been unsuccessful, he continued to try.

"U-mun," the Director said now. While, not unexpectedly for a species whose natural vocalizations consisted primarily of hissing, her standard fricatives were outstanding, she was apparently incapable of a number of other sounds, most notably voiceless glottal fricatives. In short, she had a Cockney "aitch," which was to say none at all. Nevertheless, Pike was becoming more adept at understanding her.

Now she was weaving her head in the gesture that meant *Come closer to me.* Pike almost wished he could pretend he didn't understand that. Hoping she couldn't read his squeamishness (he'd had ample opportunity to observe that the Kan'ess could not only stun their prey with the powerful curarelike venom in those six-inch fangs, but they could outdo the largest of Earth's boa constrictors in crushing the life out of anything smaller than themselves; if he displeased the Director, his life span would be measured in seconds), he rose from where she'd ordered him to sit on the floor at first, and sat on the edge of the long divan where she reclined. She reacted by wrapping her tongue around his wrist like a bullwhip and pulling him closer until he could no longer keep his feet on the floor without actively resisting, and had no choice but to stretch out on the divan and lie beside her. She, in turn, coiled her powerful lower body over his, effectively pinning him in place.

The patterns of her scales were actually quite beautiful, the contrasting reds and yellows reminding him of the shovel-nose snakes back home. Her skin was cool and dry, not unpleasant to the touch. In contrast, he could feel himself sweating, not only because the room was warmer than was strictly comfortable. *She killed D'zekeo,* he reminded himself. *Ordered the deaths of Norgay, Brandt, and Chisholm, but she personally executed D'zekeo!*

The Director tilted her head, her nearer eye studying him in a series of slow flickers that he'd learned meant *Unhappy?*

"Not unhappy, no," he said, speaking slowly so the aural patch would catch it all. "But not happy." The rest had to be explained in gestures. *Don't belong here . . . caged. Free?*

It had taken all his skills to get this far, to get her to understand that he was not just a larger version of the marsupials, not something to be treated like a pet (a step up from being considered lunch, he supposed, but still), but an equal. As she continued to flick his face with her tongue in what, if it wasn't affection, could certainly pass as a reasonable facsimile, he wondered if he'd gone too far. Or perhaps, he thought, as she pretended not to understand his bid for freedom, he hadn't gone far enough.

"It's obvious they've taken the captain to their homeworld," Spock insisted as *Enterprise,* having followed the alien ship at a discreet distance away from the wilderness world and toward their home planet, now hung at station-keeping just outside the system.

Number One sighed inwardly. The briefing was not going well. She'd expected a ruckus from Tyler, but not from Spock.

"It's not obvious at all, Mr. Spock. From your report on what happened to the landing party and the fact that there's no trace of Captain Pike on the wilderness world, what would be *obvious* is that they've made a meal of him and it's time for us to move on."

"If we could get close enough to scan their homeworld—" Spock began. Number One silenced him with a look.

"You've decoded their language?" she demanded.

"Not entirely. The translator was not designed for a solely gestural language."

"But you have enough to be able to communicate with these . . . creatures?"

"Face to face? Affirmative. But their comm code is another matter." Spock worked a toggle on one of the screens in the center of the conference table. "The creatures utilize a hieroglyphic alphabet which could take weeks to decode. However—"

"Never mind then," Number One decided, brushing it aside. "You and the computer can play with it at your leisure, but we need another alternative. Mr. Grace? What about the shielding on those ships?"

"They're unusual, Number One, but I think I've managed to ascertain the mechanism."

"Let's hear it."

"It's a phased ultrasound wave, too high for us to hear. Because the creatures *don't* hear, they're completely unaware of it. It would be like a human trying to see on an ultraviolet wavelength."

"All well and good. Can you penetrate it?"

"If the frequency were regulated. But it alternates among several subfrequencies, and I haven't as yet deciphered the pattern. I have worked out a preliminary algorithm. In a few more days—"

"I'll give you thirty-six hours," Number One said. "If you're successful, we'll get in as close as we can and scan that planet. If we don't find Captain Pike, we're leaving, getting out of range, and contacting Starfleet Command for further orders." She got up from the table. "Dismissed."

The guard didn't look well, Pike thought.

He'd had ample opportunity to study a number of the Kan'ess by now, even to learning their name for themselves.

If he had to be imprisoned here, he supposed, at least there were a number of ways he might manage to escape.

The Director was apparently some sort of regional governor. Her function offworld was to lead the hunting parties that supplemented the region's native food supply (as nearly as Pike could tell, they had no agriculture, but were entirely hunter-gatherers, a reminder to him that not every species developed all of its technologies in parallel). Her function here in her city—a complex of caves and tunnels augmented by some artificial construction, but following the contours of natural rock formations—was apparently to deal with endless bureaucratic decisions.

The daily parade of petitioners allowed into her presence with their wants and grievances was a treasure trove for Pike. As the Director's pet, he was eyed with some curiosity whenever a new visitor entered the room, but quickly forgotten once the petitioner began to address the Director. Pike was able to learn more and more of the language, and more and more about Kan'ess society, with each passing day.

He noted that the Director did not wear the voder except when he and she were alone, as if, while she couldn't seem to accept that Pike's species was as intelligent as her own, she nevertheless wanted to hide this clever toy from the eyes of the curious.

Pike hoped he could work with that, too.

To assuage his claustrophobia, his sense that he might be trapped here for the rest of his life, he told himself that this was a first-contact mission, that he was a diplomat sent to treat with the Kan'ess, a scientist sent to infiltrate their society and study them, and this was an adventure. Knowing that his life could be snuffed out at any moment only made it more challenging.

He would continue to impress the Director with his species' intelligence, and perhaps with the advantages of communicating with his people. He would also learn as much about Kan'ess social structure as he could, in order to find its weaknesses if the first course failed.

He noted that there were as many different "species" of Kan'ess—distinguishable by the markings on their scales, the shapes of their heads, the length of their fangs—as there were snakes in the Mojave. He wondered if these represented different castes that were forbidden to intermarry. All the guards, for example, had the same markings and came from the same "caste."

And this morning this one didn't look well. His skin seemed dull, and more than once Pike noticed him scratching.

A reptile's skin didn't grow. The guard and all his kind, if they were true reptiles, would have to molt, shed their old skin as they grew larger. That would take time, probably several days. This could work to Pike's advantage. He took the opportunity—the Director had not yet summoned him to her offices—to "talk" to the guard.

Well? he gestured. *Not-well?*

The guard neither liked nor trusted the human any more than he had the first day. Still, after he'd tilted his head and examined the question from all sides, he did reply. Rubbing his head irritably with one hand, he explained without having to explain. When he was finished, Pike noticed the skin covering his eye was dulled, ready to split away and reveal the new eye. After the midday meal, a new guard Pike had never seen before appeared to relieve the familiar one. And when the Director summoned Pike, he asked her about it.

"Sssskkinnn," she repeated the new word he had taught her. "Yesss." She followed this with a gesture which, accompanied by that buzzing in the back of his head, suggested to Pike a primitive telepathy (or maybe only his inability to hear it): *Not you?*

"No, not me," Pike answered aloud. "Humans stop growing when they reach adulthood. We don't need to shed our skin."

She watched him in wonderment, not entirely understanding, but ever more intrigued by her new pet. It was then that Pike noted a few rough patches on her usually glistening skin, a slight clouding at the corner of her nearer eye.

It would be her time soon, he realized, keeping his face and—he hoped—his more obvious thoughts neutral. Still, he suddenly had hope. And a working communicator.

The new guard clearly wasn't happy about the fact that Pike still had access to all that working Starfleet equipment scattered around the Director's office, and he told the Director as much. While they discussed it, Pike for once didn't watch their dialogue, concentrating instead on swapping out several pieces of the crushed communicators with the working one, secreting everything in his boot as the two Kan'ess hissed and gestured and flicked their tongues at each other heatedly.

The guard apparently managed to convince the Director, because he came to collect every piece of human equipment he saw lying about, including the empty communicator casing. Pike breathed a sigh of relief when the guard didn't notice it was empty, and another when the guard's reluctance to touch anything as ugly as a human spared him a search.

So he still had enough components to rebuild a working communicator. He might never have an opportunity to use them, but they were there if needed.

By late afternoon the Director was restless, irritable, off her feed. Pike didn't mind that last part. The Kan'ess ate a variety of small creatures, all of them live, and having to be in the same room with the Director while she ate was not one of his favorite things to do. But her increasing mood swings, as her old skin started to itch more and more, could either work to his advantage or get him killed.

She had taken to ignoring Pike. She wanted him in her presence, but paid no attention to him when he was there. She seemed to be catching up on her paperwork, waving off visitors, spending most of her time at a computer console that Pike had calculatedly not shown any overt interest in.

For one thing, the keys and toggles were designed for Kan'ess fingers; they were long and narrow and arranged too far apart for human hands, and he realized it would take him days to be able to use them efficiently even if he could decode what all of them meant. For another, if he pretended the tech was too advanced for him to understand, the Director would become overly confident and he could observe what she was doing.

On the several screens in front of her, he saw street plats, visuals of many cave dwellings, commsats connecting this region with others. He tried to memorize as much as he could. It was apparent he was being kept in a backwater, far away from any central control. Communications facilities would be less sophisticated than, say, something in a capital city. If he could only get to them . . .

His thoughts were broken by the Director's irritable hiss. She began rubbing her back against the back of the chair, then remembered she was not alone. Glaring at Pike, she snapped off one of the screens and turned away from the others, pulled herself up out of her chair as if with great effort and, swaying slightly, moved away from her desk on all fours rather than upright.

Not-well? Pike gestured. She glowered at him and moved toward the tangle of corridors that led to her sleeping chamber, where he was forbidden to go.

She doesn't want to be seen this way, Pike realized. *Some sort of cultural taboo or just pride?* For a moment he almost pitied her.

He was alone. He assumed the guard was just outside as usual, ordered there first thing this morning by the Director, who didn't want him to see her in the early stages of molting, either.

If he was to have a chance, this was it. He approached the computer, wondering if he could find a way in. But the toggles didn't respond; the Director must have locked it.

Cursing silently, working furtively, Pike reassembled the communicator parts he'd salvaged and, just on a whim, tried to contact the ship. Nothing. All comm still blocked. He had to get out of here and think of something else.

Moving lightly, he approached the door to the outer corridor; it was little more than a large, flat stone designed to slide flush against the wall when moved with enough strength. If he could somehow disable the guard, he might actually be able to find his way outside. After that . . .

Think! he told himself. *Think of everything you know about snakes. Where are they most vulnerable?*

With that, he wedged his fingers into the space between the door and the wall and began to pull. As the door slid slowly open, Pike hoped the guard wouldn't feel the vibration, and readied himself.

Every Starfleet officer takes a turn at guard duty early in his career. Pike remembered how deadly boring it could be to stand in a corridor staring at a wall or bulkhead for hours on end, trying not to daydream so deeply that you lost your concentration. He'd never succeeded. Fortunately he'd never been asked to stand guard over anyone or anything of importance, but he remembered that dreaminess, that lack of focus, the distraction of wanting to shift your feet to keep your calves from cramping, the slow drip of time as you waited for your shift to end.

The Kan'ess guard was no different. He also had the disadvantage of not being built to stand upright. His slumped posture said he was bored, uncomfortable, and only the sudden appearance of someone important in the dimly lit, winding stone corridor would get him to stand at attention. As Pike positioned himself flush with the open doorway and peered cautiously into the corridor, he could see the guard swaying on his back legs, his forelegs nowhere near his weapon, head tilted back, the usually active Kan'ess tongue lolling in one corner of his half-open mouth, for once not flicking out to test the air.

Pike launched himself at the creature, the sheer momentum of his weight toppling them both onto the floor as he fisted both hands and drove them, hard, against the aural patches on either side of the creature's head, where he knew the skin was thinnest. The blows were just powerful enough. When Pike got to his feet, the guard didn't stir.

Seizing the guard's weapon—the shape was wrong for human hands, and he'd never seen one fired, but he'd figure something out—he ran.

Luck was with him. Not only was this section of corridors deserted, but when he finally did find his way outside, it was night. He found himself standing at the mouth of a cave, its floor worn smooth by the passage of countless Kan'ess, perhaps some seven hundred feet above a desert floor.

Reconnoitering, he saw what he'd expected to see from studying the visuals on the Director's computer—an extensive cliff dwelling like that of the Pueblo back on Earth, augmented by structures of native stone stretching as far as the eye could see, to another range of cliffs that no doubt contained still more tunnel dwellings.

Of course. Where else would a species descended from snakes live? But where would they house their communications networks, and how could he get access to them?

First, though, he needed to take care of some basic needs, the most basic of which was to find his way down from the cave mouth, on trails designed for elongated reptile bodies, without so much as a piton or a length of rope, in the dark. He was helped a little by the planet's moon, an overly large orb skulking close to the horizon this time of year. Of course, in helping him see better, it also made him more visible.

Fortunately, there was no one around to see him. The pueblo, as he began to think of it, was deserted. The chill night air of the desert had driven all the Kan'ess indoors. He would be safe, or relatively safe, until morning.

Reaching the valley floor, though not without skinning his hands and tearing the knees out of his uniform trousers, Pike dusted himself off and considered the next order of business—food and water. He didn't expect to find much that he could eat among a species who ate live prey.

Except, of course, if he found where they kept that prey penned up until it was ready to be eaten.

It was easy to find the open-air markets by the noise generated by the many species of prey the Kan'ess fed on. Wherever there was live prey, there were bins full of grain and tanks of fresh water. Pike helped himself, stealing with impunity since no one was around to challenge him. Once he'd eaten, he roamed the winding passageways separating the buildings on the desert floor, no doubt worn into the bedrock by thousands of generations of Kan'ess traveling on four limbs, possibly even gliding along like snakes before they evolved those four limbs. As long as there was moonlight, and well into the predawn light, he searched the exteriors of the buildings where wall met roof for what he finally recognized as transmitter nodes, noted which way they were pointing, and followed their direction in an attempt to find the central locus where the power was transmitted.

By the end of the night he had reached what he took to be the center of the city. Reluctantly, as he watched the sun peer over the horizon, he thought of where he could conceal himself for the warm part of the day. He wondered what the guard had done once he came to, if he'd been forbidden to approach the Director because she was molting. While as yet no one seemed to be actively searching for the Director's lost pet, Pike wasn't about to take the chance that someone might stumble upon him and bring him back to her for a possible reward. He kept out of sight, not an easy thing to do in what became a teeming urban area once the sun was up.

He spent the day hiding in an empty grain bin, dozing fitfully, nearly suffocating from the heat. That night he found his way into what looked like the commercial center of the city, a small hill honeycombed with heavily traveled caves decorated with elaborate archways marked with official-looking sigils that, if he guessed right, designated the centers of control. One cave in particular attracted Pike's particular interest. He had found what he was looking for.

"I got complacent," he told José Mendez, suppressing a yawn. The primary would soon be coming up over Starbase 11, too; they really had talked all night. Fortunately Mendez was off duty tomorrow, and Pike was nominally on leave. "I didn't realize until too late that the voder I'd built for the Director was a two-edged sword. In my urgency to communicate, I hadn't figured on her scientists using our technology to try to lure my ship in for capture."

He suppressed a shudder. "Apparently ingesting four of my crew had given the Kan'ess a taste for human . . ."

Not only had he found the pueblo's main transmitter, but he was able to enter the cave where it was housed unchallenged. Apparently there was no such thing as vandalism on this world, because the facility was neither locked nor guarded. There wasn't even a proper gate or door, merely an open cave mouth. Suppressing a lifetime's conditioning against entering dark places where there might be snakes, Pike crept into the cave, leaving moonlight behind him, hoping to find banks of lighted instruments to see by.

After following several interminably long corridors largely by feel, he was not disappointed. What he was, was horrified.

Of the four banks of screens transmitting visual and/or coded communication, three were devoted to everyday comm—the Kan'ess version of television, Inter- and intranets, comm. The fourth bank of screens showed long-range views of *Enterprise,* at station-keeping well beyond the Kanes system, but clearly under observation and, it was safe to assume, not for peaceful purposes.

Using what he'd learned from watching the Director work at her personal computer, Pike studied as many readouts as he could decipher. It wasn't until it dawned on him that he could *hear* some of the comm as well as see it that he realized just how much trouble he and his ship were in.

Using the very technology he had provided them, the Kan'ess scientists had developed audio comm, based on the model of a Starfleet communicator. They'd recalibrated their high-frequency planetary and vessel shielding to let audio comm in and out, and were apparently working on a way to send an audio message to *Enterprise* inviting her in for a visit, a chance to retrieve her lost captain . . . and the opportunity to be captured and stripped of her technology, her crew imprisoned and fattened for Thanksgiving.

There were innumerable Starfleet regulations and scenarios against just such a contingency. By now Number One would have been trying to penetrate the planet's shields to punch a message through. Ironically, the Kan'ess scientists would have worked with that, too. Pike could hear Number One and Lieutenant Dabisch, as well as the *Enterprise*'s computer, droning out repeated messages of greeting. He realized that the Kan'ess would build a language base from this, enough to formulate a standard greeting and—

The hair on the back of Pike's neck stood on end as, this time, he heard his own voice.

". . . this is Captain Pike . . . want to welcome you to Kanes . . ."

19

ENTERPRISE

Number One wore a determined look as the bridge crew prepared to abandon the search and leave the Kanes system. She tapped her brilliantly colored fingernails on the armrest, anticipating resistance, a resistance she would not tolerate. Captain Pike might have treated this crew as a team, but when she was in charge, she was *in charge,* and the first person to raise an objection to her order was going to get their head bitten off.

The silence was palpable. No one spoke or even made eye contact with her or with each other, but she could feel the reluctance in all of them against leaving Pike behind. Even the ship seemed sluggish in her response.

But there were procedures, and they had to be followed. Mr. Grace had been unable to penetrate the planet's auditory shields. There was no way to scan for Pike on the Kanes homeworld, if he was even there. Every time *Enterprise* had ventured too close to what the Kan'ess considered the outer perimeter of their system, she'd earned a warning shot across her bow, and Mr. Spock had reported that the planet's weaponry, if fired consistently and with enough force, could penetrate their shields.

Which was not to mention that engaging that fire, without

knowing for absolute certain that their captain was being held prisoner on this world, would be a violation of the Prime Directive.

They were leaving. Starfleet Command would tell them what to do next, and that was that.

Cursing himself for a fool, Pike realized he'd given a powerful enemy the means to destroy his ship. He had to find a way to warn her away, or at least terminate that outgoing transmission. If his tampering with the main comm transmitter attracted attention, he was already dead. Maybe he could hold off a few armed Kan'ess for a while, if he could figure out how to fire this weapon, but—

First things first. There'd been a particular sequence the Director had keyed into her personal computer to send remote messages. Hoping the instrument panel before him was similar, Pike started pushing buttons.

"I hear it, Mr. Dabisch," Number One said before the comm officer could speak. "Relay it here. Captain?" she began immediately, automatically assuming Dabisch had done his job. "Captain Pike, this is *Enterprise*. We read you. Please respond . . ."

Something Pike touched had triggered an alarm. The three banks of screens not focused on *Enterprise* suddenly became hyperactive with scrolling messages and visuals. After a brief glance at them to see what was happening, Pike blocked them out. The automated recording of his voice was still being broadcast to the ship, and Number One was attempting to respond. He'd only made matters worse.

"Number One . . ." It was Mr. Grace's voice from engineering. "I think I've got something. They've had to alter the frequency to let that message through. If I can punch through and—"

"Moment, Engineer," Number One said irritably, permutations racing through her mind. Was the message from Pike genuine or a trap? Would the wrong move here ruin a possible first contact, or at least get the captain killed? "Recalibrate for that weak spot and see if you can scan for a human reading, then stand by. *Enterprise* to Captain Pike. Please respond."

The exact sequence of events was a little fuzzy after that. Did Pike hit the right button to shut off the faked transmission before or after Mr. Grace punched through the audio shield, or did they both happen simultaneously? Did three armed Kan'ess arrive in the transmitter room a split second before or after Mr. Grace got a transporter lock on Pike? Did he ever figure out how to work the Kan'ess weapon and return fire? Did the planet's defense system fire on *Enterprise* while Pike was still in transport, or a few seconds after, in either case allowing for a near hit on the starboard nacelle before the shields snapped on?

Eventually the engineering logs would sort it all out. For now, everything seemed to happen at once.

"Pike to *Enterprise*—disregard that first message! You can't save me—get that ship out of here!"

Number One bit her tongue. No time to argue. "Mr. Grace?" she barked.

"Have a tentative fix . . . Starfleet communicator frequency. Not stable . . . I'm not certain . . ."

"Do it!" Number One barked.

Kan'ess weapons apparently fired some sort of short burst plasma, Pike noted dreamily as, simultaneously, he felt the familiar and ever-so-welcome tingle of the transporter and watched as if from a distance as a series of bolts from three weapons fired past and through him. The transporter effect was slow through the auditory shields, slow enough for him to spend several seconds suspended between Here and There before the communications hub and the three disappointed Kan'ess guards finally disappeared and the transporter room of the *Enterprise* coalesced around him.

Moves-with-Burning-Grace and Spock were waiting at the transporter controls—Grace smiling quietly, Spock somber but, it seemed to Pike, considerably relieved. Boyce materialized out of nowhere, scanning him with a medical tricorder, hypo full of something-or-other at the ready.

Pike waved him off and managed a lopsided grin. He was stepping precariously down from the transporter pad—dusty, his uniform torn, a five-day growth of beard only partly hiding the haggard look of his face—when the ship was rocked by weapons fire from the planet surface.

With what seemed like the last of his strength, Pike lunged for the intercraft panel on the wall. "Number One?"

"Got the shields up as soon as we had you, Captain," she reported crisply, all but reading his mind. "We're out of here."

STARBASE 11

"I need to see daylight," Pike said after a long silence, pushing himself away from the table and onto his feet, stretching the stiffness out of his lower back.

He and Mendez left the lounge, found themselves outside under the pale red sky just as the distant sun was coming up. A soft breeze ruffled their hair and brought the smell of the native sage from the distant hills. This place, too, reminded Pike of home.

"Home." He always considered Mojave home, no matter how long he stayed away. He and Charlie had barely communicated in the past five years, but Hobelia always made him welcome, even though she gently needled both men about patching things up between them. Was he willing to be away for another five years? What alternatives did he have?

José Mendez eyed his old friend warily. He wanted to say something, but wasn't sure about the timing. He and Pike put the high-rise administration building dominating the plaza behind them and walked in silence until they came to the edge of the inhabited part of the base.

"Penny for your thoughts," Mendez said, watching Pike stare off into the foothills, scuffing at the red sandy soil where the pavement ended, as if contemplating a hike even after a night of no sleep and too much Saurian brandy, or perhaps because of a night of no sleep and too much Saurian brandy.

Pike scowled, massaged the back of his neck. "It was anticlimactic. My crew rescued me from Kanes and we beat it the hell out of there. There was no resolution. I kept thinking there was something else I could have done. Last I heard, there was some sort of directive in the works to cordon off that sector of space until it's determined how much of a danger the Kan'ess pose now that I've managed to teach them a whole new form of communication," he finished bitterly.

Maybe they'll need another General Order 7, he thought. *Seems like everything I touch is poisoned somehow . . .*

"I wouldn't get too exercised about it," Mendez suggested. "None of that was your fault. You did everything you were supposed to do."

"But it wasn't good enough!" Pike heard the lament in his voice, heard Charlie admonishing him ("It's not your fault she died, Chris"), wanted to hit something, or jog off into the hills for miles and miles until he was too exhausted to return, anything to get the voices out of his head. He took several long, deep breaths to slow the pounding in his temples and his heart.

"Not every mission has a clear-cut ending, Chris," Mendez pointed out. "You win some, you lose some, and some just fade off into nothing."

"I suppose so. I just wish it hadn't been the last place we visited before we returned home." Pike bent down to retrieve a smooth stone, brushing the sand away from it, studying it. "It made me wonder what exactly I've accomplished in ten years out there."

Mendez was wise enough to give him enough silence to finish his thought. Part of him was yearning for a cup of hot coffee and maybe a nice long nap, but he'd wait for it.

"It was so strange," Pike went on. "For the first few days after my capture, I had no idea if *Enterprise* would find me, or even if she was still out there. I figured there was a good chance I'd be trapped on an alien world for the rest of my life."

And not for the first time, either, he thought, suppressing it immediately.

"And yet, here I was, barely able to communicate, in constant fear for my life, but at the same time . . ." He seemed to have difficulty finding the right word for it. ". . . almost exhilarated. Relieved, anyway. I was completely on my own, with no responsibility for anyone else, for the first time since I took command. It made me realize what a terrible burden the captaincy of a starship really is."

Thoughtfully he replaced the small stone where he had found it. He and Mendez headed back along the pavement, found a bench to sit on where they had a full view of the rising sun.

"You've had more than your share, Chris," Mendez offered after another long silence. "Most of us don't see as much action in a lifetime as you have in only two missions. Maybe you ought to sit out the next dance."

"What do you mean?"

"Do what I did." Mendez leaned back on the bench, hands folded over the beginnings of a gut, the picture of complacency. "Let them kick you upstairs. Ride a desk for a few years until you decide what you want to do next."

Pike shook his head. "Who was it that said 'you can't go home again'? That's a one-way voyage, José. Once they get you behind that desk, they don't want to give you back the captain's chair."

"Would that be such a bad thing?" Mendez wondered.

"The damnable thing is, I don't know!"

Mendez thought for a moment. "You know, there is a way to combine the best of both worlds."

"I'm listening."

"There's been talk about promoting you to fleet captain."

Mendez always seemed to have a direct line on all the gossip, Pike recalled. If what he was saying was true . . .

"You don't have to do a damn thing, Chris. Just don't turn down the promotion when they offer it to you."

And so he would, when the time came. A good part of the decision would be his confidence in the young man who would be replacing him as captain of *Enterprise*. James T. Kirk was as different in personality and command style from Pike as another human could be, but Pike had to admit he liked the kid's style.

Besides, Kirk would have Spock as his first officer. If the human felt compelled to make any seat-of-the-pants impulsive decisions, he would have that voice of unassailable Vulcan reason in his ear to provide balance.

Once they reached the Sol system, *Enterprise* would be refitted yet again, this time to allow for a crew of four hundred thirty, more than double the complement Pike had commanded. He had never been attached to the ship *qua* ship, investing his vessel as some captains did with a personality, an almost spiritual connection, as if she were a living being. He admired her for her functionality, acknowledged her idiosyncrasies but, ultimately, she was simply a means to an end. And now that the people he'd served with would be scattering throughout the fleet like so many dandelion seeds—all of his command crew except Spock were transferring elsewhere—Pike knew he would have a chance to work with many of them again from his desk at Starfleet Command.

He'd never been close to any of his crew, except maybe Boyce. He'd never bothered examining it before. Only now that he was leaving did he begin to understand why.

He was afraid of losing them. Afraid of the decisions a starship captain had to make to send his crew into harm's way, and of how he would feel when some of them didn't come back. If he kept his distance, he'd kidded himself, he wouldn't feel.

It was safe to consider Boyce a friend. The cagey old ship's surgeon had managed a decades-long career in Starfleet without ever being shot at. And for all his peccadillos, Boyce was a good keeper of secrets. But Boyce was retired, holed up in a cabin somewhere on the rocky coast of New England—not out of comm reach, but talking to him from a distance would not be the same as sharing a drink in person.

Then there was Spock. Whether he was comfortable with the fact or not, Pike realized Spock considered him a kind of mentor. He had, after all, fostered the raw young talent—all intellect and social ineptitude, so aware of his mixed heritage and wanting so much to be accepted by humans that he sometimes out-humaned them—making maximum use of Spock's skills and intelligence, promoting him to science officer over older officers with more years in in spite of some grousing by those he passed over, tempering that eagerness with his own steadiness. Pike wasn't certain at what point he realized Spock considered him a role model, but by then it was too late to alter course. The best he could do was try to live up to the assignment.

Could he consider Spock a friend? They had served together, as Spock would have pointed out, for over eleven years. Spock, of course, would have known the exact number of months and days, perhaps even down to the minute. Was that how Vulcans measured friendship?

In any event, Pike decided, he would make a point of saying something to Spock before they reached Earth, if he could do so in as painless a way as possible.

They were on the final leg of their journey from Starbase 11 to Earth. The crew had somehow gotten wind of Pike's impending promotion, but he'd neither confirmed nor denied it. He was no more willing to accept his crew's congratulations than he was to say good-bye. Good-byes always reminded him of the one person who'd been taken from him before he'd had a chance to say good-bye.

It's not your fault she died, Chris.

Maybe not. It wasn't his fault Vina had chosen to remain on Talos IV, either. But he still felt no better about that.

Two days out from Earth. It was gamma shift; they were deep in secure Federation territory where it was safe to set most of the bridge stations on autopilot. Pike couldn't sleep. He'd been walking the near-deserted corridors and found himself headed for the bridge, thinking he'd have it to himself. As the turbolift doors opened, he noticed Spock at the science station, running some calculations.

"Couldn't that wait for morning, Science Officer?" Pike asked, a slight note of teasing in his voice. Was Spock ever off duty?

"Indeed, Captain," Spock acknowledged. "But it can also be done now."

Not knowing how to argue with that, Pike didn't try. He took his seat in the command chair with his back to Spock and his eyes on the star field, when he heard the creak of Spock's chair.

"Permission to speak candidly, sir?"

Pike rotated his chair toward the science station. "Granted."

"I remain curious about your reasons for allowing yourself to be captured by the Kan'ess."

It was not a subject Pike particularly wanted to talk about. He thought of offering the same explanations he'd entered in his logs—an attempt to infiltrate Kan'ess society, learn their technological capabilities, communicate with them, maybe even establish first contact. But he remembered the conversation he'd had with Spock about the pastry shop, and wondered if his motives would seem . . . unbalanced, maybe even suicidal.

"You read my official log entry," Pike said.

"Indeed."

"And?"

Spock hesitated.

"What was it you said about its not being a lie to keep the truth to oneself?" Pike reminded him. "You think there was more to it?"

"Perhaps. It did seem . . . an unusual level of personal sacrifice . . . for a human."

Pike found this amusing. "You mean it's the sort of thing a Vulcan would do. But you have to admit allowing myself to be captured was illogical."

"Not necessarily, sir. Your actions did possess an intrinsic logic, despite their seeming impulsiveness."

Pike found himself smiling. "So you're saying you approve of what I did?"

"In essence, yes."

"What if it had turned out differently? What if the Director had simply made a meal of me on the trip back to Kanes?"

Spock considered this although, Pike suspected, not for the first time. "I believe, Captain, that sacrifice in the acquisition of knowledge is commendable."

"Even if I didn't live long enough to impart that knowledge to anyone else." Pike made it a statement, not a question, and Spock did not reply. This conversation was straying into dangerous territory. Pike tried to make light of it.

"Why do I get the uncomfortable feeling, Mr. Spock, that this means I've earned your loyalty for life?"

"Captain, you would have my loyalty for life in any event."

It was more of a burden than Pike wanted. How many Earth cultures were there that believed if you saved someone's life you were responsible for that life? The thought was almost more troubling than the responsibility for all the lives that had been lost on his watch.

Pike eased himself out of the command chair. He'd have to sit here tomorrow and the next day as they brought *Enterprise* into spacedock, then never again. Wherever else his fortunes took him, he was certain of that much. As for the burden of a Vulcan's loyalty . . .

"I was afraid you'd say something like that," he told Spock. His tone was joking, the lopsided grin was there, but the dark brows were drawn down over the steel-blue eyes, and those eyes were sad.

2320: TALOS IV

Spock stepped the long-range shuttle's speed down out of warp as he made the final approach to the Talos star group. Before he could even open comm to send a standard greeting to Talos IV, he heard the Magistrate's voice in his mind.

You are punctual.

Indeed, was his response.

You are prepared?

Prepared for what? Spock wondered. *How can one be prepared for the unknown?* Nevertheless he replied, *Affirmative.*

Excellent! was the Magistrate's response, with still no hint of what Spock would find when he landed. *We will feed the proper coordinates into your ship's system. We eagerly await your arrival.*

20

2264-67

The transition to fleet captain was less harrowing than Pike expected. It was almost with gratitude that he accepted the promotion when it was offered, handing *Enterprise* off to Kirk with something like relief. The fleet's youngest captain was all but bouncing on his heels in his excitement. Pike felt like a parent handing over the car keys for the first time, and wondered if he had ever been that young and eager.

His new assignment suited him. As fleet captain he could deploy a dozen ships or more without leaving his desk, or lead an expedition into uncharted regions, cataloging gas giants without an enemy in sight. It was a pleasant change of pace. Yes, there was paper to be shuffled and seemingly endless staff meetings to attend, but there were also the perqs, like being closer to Earth, and having more leave time, and being invited to the right parties.

Over the course of the next few years, he began putting down roots, buying himself a tract of undeveloped land within the Mojave enclave, close enough but far enough from Charlie and Hobelia's place. He and Charlie had barely spoken since the revelation that Charlie was his biological father, and Hobelia had given up trying to patch things between them

("You two want to spend the rest of your lives out-stubborn-ing each other, it's no skin off mine!" was her decision).

Pike thought of moving Tango to the new spread once he'd gentled the land away from the wild in a careful pact with nature—taking only as much as he needed to build himself a house, leaving the scrubland around it alone—but the old devil had built lifelong friendships with Charlie's other horses, and it would have been cruel to uproot him. Besides, who would look after the big bay when he was off on assignment? He left Tango where he was happiest, using him as an excuse to visit with Hobelia.

"That and my cooking!" She snorted. "You don't fool me. Somebody's got to keep you fed, and if it's not a wife, it might as well be me. Left alone, you'd subsist on reconstituted stuff until your taste buds atrophied."

"That's not entirely true," Chris protested. Hobelia's favorite topics of conversation were as predictable as rain. "I've finally mastered the delicate art of boiling water."

"So when are you going to settle down?" Hobelia demanded, as if this were a natural segue from Chris's last statement. He tried to steal something from the salad she was making and she slapped at the back of his hand, just as she had done when he was a child. "You've been home for three years."

"I don't see what one thing has to do with the other," he joked, stealing a slice of jicama anyway.

Funny how Hobelia sometimes knew what was on his mind before he did. He'd been thinking about the women in his past lately. Hana Flowers had been too upset over the *Aldrin* trial to stay with him. He'd gone so far as to ask Janeese to marry him, but his need to be out in space for long periods of time had been too much for her, and she'd broken their engagement, preferring to be with someone who was around more often.

Then there had been Vina, and whatever other relationships he'd become involved in since had perforce been temporary, not only because so few of the women he met could countenance the idea of a husband who was gone more often than he was at home, but because he couldn't get Vina out of his mind.

He couldn't tell Hobelia about Vina. If there was anyone he wished he could tell, aside from Charlie . . .

Damn Charlie, anyway. The more time passed, the more difficult it was for Chris to see a way to reconcile his differences with Charlie. Why did he cling to this childish resentment about not knowing that Charlie was his father? Seeing the bond Charlie had with Hobelia, wishing for something like that for himself—was he actually jealous? Chris put that thought out of his head as well.

Hobelia had stopped chopping vegetables and was studying him. She wasn't a mind reader, but she came uncomfortably close sometimes. Chris treated her to his most brilliant smile.

"Truth is, Hobe, you've spoiled me. I want what you and Charlie have. If I ever find a woman who measures up to you, she'll be the one."

"The sun don't shine just 'cause you're crowing at it!" Hobelia muttered, trying unsuccessfully not to beam at him. Wisely, though, she let the subject drop then.

The United Federation of Planets continued to expand, adding ever new planets to its membership. One of the newest members was a fog-shrouded world known as Argelius II which, it was hoped, would one day serve as a remote spaceport at the then-boundary of Federation space. Delegates from this new world were being welcomed at a diplomatic reception on Earth, and all senior Starfleet officers in the vicinity were required to attend.

Pike read the official invitation and grimaced. Seemed half of his duties nowadays consisted of attending these fancy-dress balls.

Settling the medals and insignia on his dress uniform tunic with resignation, he decided he'd do what he usually did—put in an appearance, sample the buffet, make polite noises for a couple of hours, nod to the CinC so that he'd remember Pike had been there, then duck out. He was off duty for the next couple of days, and wanted to see about some fences at the back of his property before winter.

The reception was held at the Terran ambassador's main residence, a sprawling rococo mansion clinging improbably to a cliff on one of Northern California's wilder coasts. Pike lingered on the terrace with the wind in his face contemplating the pounding surf below, wishing he could go for a late-night hike among the coast redwoods that hid the residence from the nearest road some five miles east. The chatter and the moil of bodies juggling hors d'oeuvres and protocol in the glittering ballroom behind him was grating on his nerves. Did he hear a string quartet playing somewhere? Perhaps in one of the inner courtyards, where there would be fewer people and he could listen to the music and pretend he was alone.

He had to pass through the ballroom to get to the courtyard, and found himself waylaid by, of all people, a three-sheets-to-the-wind José Tyler. His former navigator had made commander, Pike had heard, and was now first officer on a frigate. Well, good for him. Pike would listen to Tyler's wild tales for a few minutes, hoping to catch the CinC's eye and fulfill the evening's obligation, if he could only shake loose of Tyler after the fact.

"Argelius, Chris—imagine," Tyler was saying, grinning like a schoolboy. "Are we ever lucky to have brought them in. Not only strategic importance as a spaceport, but—you ever been there?"

"No, can't say that I have," Pike said distractedly. Something—a splash of color, or was it light or sound?—drew his glance toward the far side of the room. It was as if the crowd had parted momentarily to provide him a glimpse of something incredibly enticing, then closed again, tantalizing him. He only half heard what Tyler was carrying on about. "Recently cleared for shore leave. Have I got that right?"

"You do," Tyler burbled, swaying slightly on his feet. Pike half considered taking the drink out of Tyler's hand and steering him toward some black coffee, but he remembered Tyler's temper and decided he was a big boy now and could take care of himself. "And while it ain't exactly Tahiti, the women are—shall we say—accommodating? Unless they're married, but sometimes even then. The advice from here, though, is always make sure you ask first."

Pike laughed tightly, but the sound didn't change the expression on his face, which was frowning. What was it he had just seen over there near the fountain—on the way toward the courtyard where he could still hear the string quartet, and where he would have been heading anyway—and why did he have an overwhelming desire to brush past Tyler and go there?

"I'll keep that in mind, José," he said, clapping Tyler absently on the shoulder, already moving past him. He held up his empty glass as an alibi. "Excuse me . . ."

"Sure thing!" Tyler managed, the brief impact of Pike's hand on his shoulder almost enough to tip him over. The last Pike saw of him, he was weaving toward the buffet, almost spilling what was left of his drink on the Tellarite attaché's wife. Pike winced and turned away. If there was going to be an incident, he wanted to be far away from it.

He set down his empty glass—he'd only wanted Tyler to think he was going for a refill—and homed in on whatever it was that had disturbed his concentration, drawing him like a siren song to the other side of the room. He found it. Her. A woman, of course.

As he watched her, her face mirrored the emotions of everyone who spoke to her. Not mockery or even mimicry, but a silent empathy, as if their emotions became hers merely by being listened to. And not just the emotions, but suggestions of the very shapes of the faces of those speaking, regardless of age, gender, species.

There were four of them, all male, two Starfleet officers and two civilians, forming a loose little circle. Her back was to Pike, and yet she seemed to sense him, turning as if she'd heard him approach, despite the thick carpet and the voices, the crescendo of the string quartet just beyond in the garden. She looked at him and smiled, though her eyebrows, despite their delicate shape, drew down in exact replica of his.

For a moment her face reminded him of Willa's, and Pike had to stop himself from recoiling. Something made him laugh instead, and for the first time that night the merriment encompassed his entire face. He stopped frowning, and that ready white-toothed smile which had dazzled many a woman was mirrored on this one's face. Then he looked puzzled, and so did she. Somehow the other four males faded into the crowd as if on cue, and the two of them, he and the woman, were a little island of quietude unto themselves in a sea of laughing, chattering strangers, and he realized he had to say something, anything, to assure himself he hadn't imagined her.

"I—I was admiring your hair," he said, stuttering like a schoolboy. "I've never seen anything like it."

It was extraordinary, a single curtain of blue-black silk flowing to her waist, shimmering when she moved. He thought at first that the blue highlights must be artifice, but he would come to find out that they were natural. A streak of pure white like a lightning bolt began at her high pale brow and zigzagged up over the crown of her head, blending into the darker hair at about shoulder length. The effect was so alluring he almost forgot to take in the rest of her.

Neither tall nor short, neither thin nor voluptuous, she had only to tilt her head slightly to meet his eyes. A high-cheekboned face, a sensual mouth and, from what the filmy, multi-layered garments and graceful movements suggested, a lithe and pleasing figure. He detected a slight fragrance of sandalwood that, like her hair, was natural, the innate scent of her skin. Whatever else he was thinking or feeling, this was lust at first sight.

She offered him a smile and one long-fingered hand and said only, "Christopher."

"H-how do you know my name?"

He was frowning again, though he didn't want to.

Her face stopped mirroring his then, and her eyes took on a cloudy cast so that he couldn't discern their color even though he was looking right into them.

"You're the only fleet captain in the room," she said lightly, but they both knew that wasn't it. Maybe someone had pointed him out to her. Maybe— "I am Siddhe. It's spelled as if it should be 'Sid,' but it's pronounced 'She.' As in She-who-must-be-obeyed, as another human once told me. If I were from Earth, I'd be an elf."

"Sh-shee," Pike tried, still stuttering. He had no idea what she was talking about. If he caught himself blushing, he was going to turn on his heel and walk out right now! To cover his embarrassment, he kissed the proffered hand, hoping the gesture was acceptable on her world, wherever that was. When he straightened up again, her eyes had lost their clouded look. Now they were the color of quicksilver, crystal clear but changeable.

Her voice was a smoky contralto, with an accent he couldn't place, though he assumed from the way she was dressed, all flowing bright garments in a variety of shades of blue and green, that she was Argelian. His gesture seemed to have pleased her, but she withdrew her hand gracefully and asked quite seriously, "Do you still dream of her?"

For a moment Pike was startled. Were Argelians telepaths? If so, he'd have to end this conversation now. He was heartily sick of telepaths and of secrets, and the vague sense of dread he had brought back with him from space still followed him like a cloud. He couldn't allow anyone ever again—not family, not friends, certainly not a stranger, however enticing—to see into his soul.

Now, wait a minute, he thought, collecting his wits. *That's an old fortune-teller's trick. Do I still dream of her? Which "her"? My mother, Vina, or some girl who smiled at me when I was in high school, even Silk or Maia? This—Shee— finds me as attractive as I do her, and if this is how people get to know each other on her world, that's all it is, a trick, and I'll play along.*

"I mean you no harm," her smoky voice was saying. Her hand was on his arm. "You may walk away if you wish and, unlike your Earth women, I will not be insulted. Or perhaps we can go somewhere where we can talk."

I need to make it an early night, he wanted to say. *I have to get up early to mend some fences . . .*

But the excuse sounded silly even in his mind, so he didn't speak. Instead, for once, he stopped looking for explanations and followed his heart.

"So what are you?" he asked her the next morning, propped up on one elbow, marveling at the silken fan of her hair spread out on the pillow like an aura.

"Why, an Argelian, of course."

He ran a strand of her hair through his fingers, holding the ends like a paintbrush with which he gently stroked her cheekbones, her brow, the tip of her nose. Her eyes danced, and her smile was sunshine.

"I know that!" he laughed. "I mean, what are you in the delegation? I didn't see you in the receiving line—I would have noticed—so I'm guessing you're not the ambassador . . ." He tried to look serious, but he couldn't stop smiling. ". . . or the ambassador's wife. So what are you? Cultural attaché, official observer, translator, security chief, sous-chef?"

Siddhe stretched her long arms above her head, arching her back and yawning. Not for the first time, Chris wondered if the Argelian spine was differently articulated than a human's, given its remarkable flexibility. Distracted by a particularly pleasant memory from the night before, he tried to concentrate on what Siddhe was saying.

"We Argelians don't put ourselves into boxes the way you humans do." With a lithe movement she was sitting on the edge of the bed, searching for her shoes. "I am a little of all of those things, except perhaps security chief . . . though I would know how to snap your neck with two fingers if I needed to . . ."

More than a little startled, Chris wondered if she was joking, but she had her back to him, retrieving her clothes from among his where they'd scattered them the night before, and he couldn't see her face. She disappeared into the shower, and he half sat, half lay in bed, wanting breakfast, but too lazy to get up just yet. He couldn't remember the last time he'd felt this relaxed.

Siddhe emerged from the bathroom, dressed and brushing her hair. "I can be cultural attaché in the morning, art historian in the afternoon, a linguist over dinner, and a courtesan at night," she said, taking up the conversation as if no time had passed.

"How do I know you're not a spy?" Chris asked when she was sitting on the bed beside him.

Her laugh was deep and rich. "You don't. Though I easily could be. I am, for weal or for woe, one of the Gifted Ones."

"One of the what?"

She ran her fingers lightly through the waves of dark hair above his left ear. He'd started to go gray at the temples in recent years, just as Willa had. "Do you know of the Argelian Empathic Contact?"

He shook his head. "Until a few days ago, I'd never even heard of Argelius."

She explained. "It is an ancient art, usually hereditary, passed down through the female line to the descendants of an ancient priestess caste, though in my case it emerged as a kind of mutation. Mine was a merchant family for generations, with no trace of the Gift until I came along."

Her face clouded with her own emotions for a moment, then cleared. "It isn't telepathy or clairvoyance in the strictest sense, but something somewhere in between."

Pike sat up now, tucking the sheet around his waist, leaning back against the headboard with his hands clasped behind his head, all attention. "So you can't predict the future?"

She shook her head. "No. My greatest gift is for the past. But sometimes I can feel the touch of the future."

"Feel it? What does that mean?"

She studied her hands in her lap, her silken hair falling about her face like a curtain, hiding it from him. "I'm still learning your language. Perhaps that's not the right word. But sometimes I can touch someone, or even something belonging to them—something important and personal— and get a sense of . . . something. If I spend enough time with you, I can tell you what forces went into making you the per-

son you are. From that I can—surmise—how you will face
your future.

"Someone at the reception last night said I'd make a good
psychiatrist—another of your human boxes. On Argelius,
almost everyone can sense another's past in their actions."

Now Chris was shaking his head. "I don't understand."

She caressed his face. Was her expression sad because she
was mirroring his? He couldn't tell.

"You will, in time. But speaking of time, you have work
to do, and I must leave you to it."

Had he told her his plans for the day? They'd talked about
so much last night—and not only talked—his mind was
awhirl with memories and he couldn't seem to grab hold of
any of them.

"Somehow that doesn't seem so important this morning.
There's always time to mend fences."

He reached for her hand, intending to pull her toward
him, but for once she resisted.

"No, there isn't," she said. "Not always."

Looking back, of course, Chris Pike would understand
exactly what she meant. For the moment, however long that
moment might be, he would simply follow wherever she led.

He asked her how long she would be on Earth. Her
answer was "as long as you need me to be." He told her he
was leaving on an inspection tour in a few weeks and would
be out in space for a month or more after that. She said, "I
can be here when you return, if you wish."

"Don't you have diplomatic duties?" he wondered, not
eager to get rid of her, but puzzled at her freedom to come
and go without a schedule, or some superior barking at her
on comm.

"Naturally," she said, and would not elaborate.

"Then you must have appointments, a schedule, someone

to answer to," he insisted. "As easygoing as your people seem to be, you must operate under some rule of law."

"The law of Argelius," she said, caressing him, "is love."

He scowled at that. "That's an oversimplification, I'm sure. The Federation has very strict entry criteria for new members. I don't think—"

Siddhe smiled. "The Federation wants Argelius for its strategic location, and as a shore leave planet. Nothing complicated about it at all. But enough about that. Tell me about your dreams."

That phrase of all phrases bore the onus of bad memory. "No, thanks. Too many others have tried that already. I'd rather show you my world instead."

For the rest of Pike's leave time, Siddhe dutifully accompanied him to the places he thought she needed to see. She peered down into the Grand Canyon, gazed up at three-thousand-year-old redwoods, went cross-country skiing across the snowfields of Kilimanjaro, sailed tranquil Tasman seas. They talked, ate luxuriously, stayed in the best hotels a fleet captain's salary could afford, talked some more. She didn't pry, she simply took him by the hand, and by the time he realized he had told her almost everything there was to know, except of course what lay behind him on Talos IV, it didn't seem so terrible.

"What about you?" he asked when, off in the Mutara Sector on that inspection tour he'd told her about, he had some time to send personal subspace messages back to Earth. "When do you get to tell me about your life?"

"When you pass this way again," was her answer.

For the greater part of the next year it was like that, though eventually he realized she only wanted to see his world through his eyes, and the travelogue wound down. She did accompany him to official functions, and they were both so striking and so well suited to each other that heads turned the moment they entered a room, but they spent most nights when he was home gazing into the flames in one of the several fireplaces in the ranch house, keeping each other's counsel.

What did she tell him about herself? Surprisingly little, yet when he pressed her he felt as if he was prying. What was the hurry, after all? If he chose, he could spend the rest of his life discovering the mystery of her.

That thought startled him. He hadn't thought about spending his life with a woman since Janeese. *No, that's not true,* he reminded himself sternly. *Since Vina.*

Vina. A now long-ago memory of a dream of a woman who was real and not real, and who was forever out of his reach. Was it only Siddhe's warm, immediate presence that made Vina seem suddenly nothing more than a pale vision?

"You'll tell me about her when you're ready," Siddhe spoke to his thoughts, startling him.

"I can't," he said adamantly.

"Starfleet secrets?" Siddhe murmured, her head on his shoulder, their hands clasped between them on the broad sofa facing the big stone fireplace in the main room. "You've told me about Willa. Are Starfleet secrets that much more sacrosanct?"

Pike studied the top of her head, the sleek blue-black hair with the sharp delineation of white down the center. Would all her hair turn white with age? A flash of Vina's spun-sugar blond intruded. He shook it away.

Yes, he'd told Siddhe about Willa. It had been less painful than he'd expected. She'd made some chance remark—or was it? Was anything about her by chance?—wondering why he'd built a house with so many fireplaces but never used them. He'd given her some uneasy explanation about having been burned once when he was a child, but the question got him thinking.

Why had he built the fireplaces? Some arcane notion about roughing it in the wild? That would have been non-sense. Traditional adobe houses in this part of the world had used wood, rare as it was, sparingly. The early builders hadn't put a fireplace in almost every room. And he'd taken the trouble to install special flues to be environmentally friendly and not clog the local atmosphere with woodsmoke, then never used the fireplaces until Siddhe asked.

So he told her about Willa, and a loss inside him that nothing could fill, and instead of palliative words about how someday he would meet a woman who would fill that loss and replace his mother (and perhaps, a less wise woman would have suggested, she was in fact sitting even now beside him), she'd said:

"No one can replace a mother, Christopher. That loss will always be there, be a part of you. But you have to decide whether you wish it to be only a scar, or an open wound."

"You think I have a choice?" he'd demanded angrily, and she hadn't soothed him, had waited while he stormed around the room with his fists clenched, perhaps tempted to drive one into the unforgiving adobe wall. When he said nothing further, she added quietly:

"We all have scars, Christopher. But a scar is stronger than the original tissue it replaces. A wound only saps you, makes you more vulnerable to further injury."

He was a man of action, not of metaphors, but he was smart enough to understand what she was saying. He opened his mouth to reject it, but before he could speak he felt some-thing release inside him, a knot of grief he'd carried away from Elysium until this moment. He would never forget Willa, but she would no longer haunt him now.

It's not your fault she died, Chris.

Charlie's words. What was he going to do about Charlie?

He was holding Siddhe's hand as they got out of the air-car in front of Charlie and Hobelia's ranch. Hobelia had heard the 'car and was waiting in the open doorway, shading her eyes against the sun.

"Hobe, I'd like you to meet someone . . ." Chris began, but his stepmother waved him to silence, her eyes meeting Siddhe's.

"You come into the kitchen with me, *chica*," she said, extending her hand to a guest she'd never met as if she'd known her all her life. And Siddhe, a head taller and half as wide, followed Hobelia as if from old familiarity.

"Charlie's in the living room," Hobelia said over her shoulder. Whatever easy time he thought he'd have of it with a stranger in the house was taken from him, and Chris had to face his father alone.

Charlie had his back to him, working at something on his computer, the screen set into a handmade table Chris remembered helping him build when he was in his teens. The first thing he noticed was that Charlie's hair had gone completely gray—near-white at the temples, iron-gray and still stiff as a brush on top. The ubiquitous slouch hat lay to one side of the computer screen, a glance at which told Chris Charlie was working on the month's accounts.

"How's it going, Hoss?" he began awkwardly, wondering where he should sit, if he should sit. The room had always been comfortable, with big soft chairs arranged every which way to accommodate one guest or a dozen. Uncertain, Chris decided to stand.

Charlie looked up at him under his eyebrows, sat back away from the screen and contemplated his son.

"Can't complain. You?"

Chris had rehearsed this a dozen ways, but none of them seemed to work right now. Not a demonstrative man, he found himself down on one knee so he'd be at Charlie's level.

"Is it too late to say I'm sorry?" he said before he could give himself time to think about it.

"Never too late to set things right," Charlie said with a twinkle. He looked thoughtful for a moment, as if he too had been rehearsing something for this moment, hoping it would come. "Guess I've been as much to blame. Could have ended this a long time ago if I hadn't been so stubborn."

Chris scowled. "No, it was me. I started it. Up to me to finish it."

"Still, I could have met you halfway . . ."

"No, I shut you out every chance I got. I—"

They could go on like this all afternoon, Chris realized. He shut his mouth and reached out a hand to Charlie. The twinkle in Charlie's eye told him Charlie had come to the same conclusion simultaneously. The older man clasped his son's hand, used the momentum to pull himself to his feet.

"If they see us watching 'em, we'll never hear the end of it," Hobelia whispered from the hallway, giving Siddhe a little squeeze as the two men embraced, decades of silence ended in a single gesture.

"Just a couple of weeks," Chris was saying, trying to decide if he could manage to eat just one more chile relleno and still have room for dessert. "Taking a group of cadets out on a training exercise. I'll be home for Christmas."

Content and stuffed with good food, in the company of the people he loved, he was at peace. The last thing he expected was what Siddhe told him later that afternoon.

They stood at the corral fence and she stroked Tango's nose, murmuring to him in a language Pike didn't understand.

"Every time I see him, he's got more gray in his coat," he remarked, fussing over the big bay, who was loving the attention. "This old devil is the last link to my childhood. I don't know what I'm going to do when he goes."

"You might start by not talking about his death while he's listening," Siddhe said a little sharply.

Pike snorted in disbelief. "Oh, come on, now! I know you're gifted, but you're not going to tell me you can read a horse's mind."

"He senses your sadness in your scent, hears it in your voice," Siddhe said, and began to walk away.

"You up for a hike?" he asked her. He'd noted when they set out that morning that she'd worn jeans and practical shoes. Her adaptation to Earth-style clothing only enhanced her Argelianness, if there was such a word. "There's a place I'd like to show you where the sunsets are really special."

"All right," she answered, and took his hand.

The trail he took her on had a gradual upslope, a footpath worn through natural gardens of every kind of cactus and yucca and creosote native to the region. The stark outlines of Joshua trees, like broken crucifixes, made long shadows in the waning autumn sun. This was the best time of year for sunsets in California. Up a gradual incline, they came to a small escarpment where Chris had gone to be alone sometimes when he was a boy, and sometimes not alone as boyhood flowed into manhood.

Even absent the Argelian Empathic Contact, Siddhe would have known what was on his mind.

"I want you to marry me," he said as the sun slipped over the horizon into a Pacific they could only imagine from there, splashing the surrounding sky with blues and oranges and pinks and purples and even a suggestion of the palest green. "If you say yes now, as soon as I come back from this training mission, we can—"

"No," she said quietly, her eyes on the changing light.
"What?!"

It was the last thing he'd expected. Ever since he and Charlie had ended their differences this morning, he'd felt as if he were floating. Sitting at the dinner table, surrounded by the people he loved most, he'd been almost drunk with the joy of it. He could see that Charlie and Hobelia were crazy about Siddhe and she about them, though he'd somehow expected no less. For the first time in his life, everything made sense. The ghosts were gone. The should-have, would-have, could-haves of his past were laid to rest. He'd finally found a woman who could accept him without trying to change him. He'd been imagining what their children would look like, and then—

She was on her feet, looking back in the direction of the ranch house, as if uncertain he could lead them both back there safely in the gathering dark. She'd never lacked confidence in him before. Pike was wounded.

"I'm sorry to be so blunt, Christopher, but I cannot marry you. Before you return, I will most likely return to Argelius."

The chill he felt was not about the sudden drop in temperature of the desert night. How could he have guessed so wrong? Was there some custom, some nuance of her culture he wasn't aware of? Why couldn't she—?

"You're married, aren't you?" he asked slowly, remembering José Tyler's warning, the words sticking in his throat. "Is that why?"

Siddhe shook her head. "No," she said again. "But please don't ask me for reasons I cannot give you."

He reached out for her hand and she gave it willingly. How could she be so warm and so rejecting at the same time?

"Then give me some reason, even if it's a lie."

She looked at him curiously. "Is that what you want? A lie? Shall I tell you I won't stay with you because I won't stay anywhere for more than a year? That I'm an urban creature, and while your desert is charming, I need seacoasts and fog? Will that satisfy you?"

"We can buy a house on the coast," Pike offered. "I don't care where we live. You don't even have to stay on Earth. I can—"

She put three fingers on his lips. "You can what? Remake your life for me? No one should have to do that for the one they love. It only makes them bitter afterward. What you and I have is unmixed sweetness. Don't let's make it bitter now."

Pike stood there dumbfounded, at a loss for words. Whatever reasons she gave him were not the real reason. Should he press it, or let it go for now? Maybe she would think it over, change her mind. Maybe when he returned from the training mission, he could ask her again.

They hiked back to the ranch house in silence, hand in hand, sure-footed even in the darkness. His perfect day was now less than perfect, but he told himself there would be other chances. He had plenty of time.

21

STARDATE 1709.2

Subspace chatter talked of nothing else.

"An old class-J starship," Commodore Mendez would characterize it later in the official log, in his personal log, and in person to James T. Kirk when he asked. "One of the baffle-plates ruptured . . . the delta rays . . . He went in, bringing out all those kids that were still alive . . ."

There were one hundred and one aboard, ninety-five cadets, five instructors, and Fleet Captain Christopher Pike. The initial explosion killed everyone in the engine room— thirteen cadets and two instructors—outright. The class-Js were antiquated and poorly designed, and the blast doors were too far down the corridors to stop the radiation from seeping through the Jefferies tubes and into the turbo-shafts—one of those "structural flaws" Mendez had talked to Pike about when he'd passed by less than a week ago. By the time those on the bridge realized what was happening, nearly everyone belowdecks was feeling some effect of radiation poisoning.

Pike ordered the blast doors lowered and the environmental controls set on high throughout the rest of the ship. Reverse flow began venting the excess radiation into space, and a remote diagnostic indicated the rupture hadn't damaged anything vital, so they could make it back to Starbase 11 once the crisis was contained.

Pike's quick thinking spared those on the bridge and in the barracks, but it left several dozen cadets and the transporter chief trapped behind the doors, most probably too sick to even drag themselves into the corridors to await rescue crews in rad suits. Intraship beaming was something only an expert would try, and the ship's only qualified expert was in the transporter room, which was inside the hot zone, and he wasn't answering hails.

Every minute of exposure to delta radiation meant tissue damage, first to the lungs, which meant oxygen deprivation, unconsciousness, eventually coma and brain death. Before the victim died, however, the radiation attacked nerve tissue, inducing first paralysis, eventually cessation of autonomic function—heart rate, respiration, all the processes that made it possible for a human being to live. After that the internal organs would begin to break down irreparably.

Immediate treatment could stop the damage, and the younger the patient, the quicker the recovery. If help could be gotten in time.

Trapped behind the blast doors, silent to hails from the bridge, those kids were dying by the moment. Pike could hear them in the silence.

Leaving the conn in the hands of the senior of the two remaining instructors, with standing orders that no one ("Do you hear me? *No one!*") was to leave the bridge, he stationed the other instructor, who had some paramedic training, in sickbay and, violating his own orders that no one was to open the blast doors without a rad suit, assembled those who'd been off shift and were still rubbing the sleep out of their eyes, gathered at the blast doors where they could see their fallen comrades through the clearsteel beyond, those who were trained scrambling into the regulation half-dozen rad suits aboard, then slid the doors open just far enough to roll himself under and, to the horror of those watching, went in and began bodily dragging his cadets to safety, handing them off to the suited-up cadets (who then handed them off to those who didn't have suits but at least had breather-masks), as they bypassed Pike and hurried down the curve of the corridor in search of more survivors.

No one took the time to say, "Sir, you're at risk here. Let us do this." The fire in Pike's eyes (*It's not your fault they died, Chris*) would have melted their words in their throats if they'd tried.

When he picked up and began to carry the last of the cadets fallen in the first stretch of corridor, a petite female Centaurian who weighed no more than a child, he felt his legs buckle. His eyes had sealed shut minutes earlier against the smoke from burning conduits coming from engineering in spite of the reverse venting, and he was aware of a slickness on the palms of his hands which he took to be sweat, but he paid neither any heed. What concerned him was that it was getting harder to breathe. *Has to be the smoke,* he told himself, though there was less smoke now, and screaming alarms and flashing lights told him more about the radiation levels than he wanted to know.

Just one more, he told himself, staggering toward the transporter room. He'd always had a soft spot for transporter personnel, because of Charlie. His chief on this tour, a heavyset human, was snoring weakly against the wall which was as far as he'd been able to crawl before the coma that made him look as if he was sleeping. Pike was crawling himself now, unable to move the deadweight of the man, the wall comm shouting at him.

"Captain, the rupture's still leaking. The rad levels are off the scale. You've got to come out now or we can't . . ."

His muscles began to scream at him then and he realized: *You've miscalculated. Not only can't you save your transporter chief, but you've just killed yourself. Always trying to be a hero! What was it Phil Boyce used to say about setting standards for yourself no human could . . . could . . .*

The pain ratcheted up then, a fire coursing along his nerves, shutting down his mind until there was nothing left but the fire . . .

Of those rescued from the radiation zone on the "flying death trap" as Commodore Mendez would characterize it, weeping openly when the worst of them were brought to the hospital section at Starbase 11, the transporter chief and two more cadets succumbed to their injuries within a day. The others—seventeen altogether in addition to the ones Pike had dragged or carried out—had at least some radiation exposure, as well as first- and second-degree burns, and one young engineering student had fallen from a catwalk during the initial explosion, breaking her leg in two places. They were young and strong and would eventually recover with only minor sequelae, except for Christopher Pike.

He had to be told how long he'd been lying unconscious in the medical wing at the starbase. Even when he heard the words "six weeks," they made no sense. He thought he knew enough about current medical treatment to understand how the docs would treat severe burns and radiation poisoning, and couldn't understand why they'd immobilized his entire body, even his eyelids and his vocal cords, in some sort of body cast or stasis field—

No, his eyes still worked, and what he could see by just lowering them to study the length of his supine body in the diagnostic bed (he couldn't move his neck to look up far enough to see the panel he knew was above the head of the bed with its jumble of readouts, but he could hear it bleep-ing) told him he was dressed in Starfleet-issue medical section pajamas and covered lightly with a sheet. There was no body cast.

What then? A stasis field? He looked for the familiar shimmer and couldn't see it. Besides, stasis fields required vacuum. Even if he'd had to be put in stasis from the neck down, he'd have had to be able to move his head and to breathe.

A glance to one side showed him respirators and feeding tubes leading in a maze over and into him. To the other side there were waste tubes leading away, and more machines humming and chattering with readouts he couldn't begin to fathom.

Why the hell couldn't he move?!

When José Mendez explained it to him, he found he couldn't even weep. Whatever part of his brain experienced emotions like rage, grief, despair, was still active, too active. But the synapses that would allow him to cry had been destroyed.

"It's just as well, Captain," the day nurse told him gently, watching his throat work after Mendez had had to leave to control his own grief at the sight of him, and knowing what Pike wanted to do. "Too many tears and your upper respiratory system would get clogged. You'd have trouble breathing, might even start to choke . . ."

I am choking! Pike wanted to shout at her. *Can't you see?*

At first his body played tricks on him.

Once the surgeons were able to fit him with the artificial heart—more a nexus of interconnected devices to control each of his autonomic functions, placed in the chest cavity surrounding his human heart with a neural net, supplanting its function without necessarily replacing it—and interface it with the controls of the chair that took instruction from the few undamaged neural pathways that allowed him to move it slightly and to respond to binary questions, he no longer needed to remain in bed. His view of the universe from the perpendicular rather than the horizontal was physically improved somewhat, but his sense of entrapment was only mitigated, not cured.

And there were the "phantom limb" effects, the sporadic return of sensation in his arms or legs which momentarily fooled him into thinking he could move, only to thwart him when he tried. At other times one or several of his limbs would twitch uncontrollably, sometimes only once, at other times for hours at a time. At still other times he would feel the fire, subsequently replaced by ice, an interior cold that made his teeth chatter no matter how warm the room.

His doctors offered him sedatives, sleeping potions to provide oblivion until these assaults passed. He refused them. As daunting as the feelings were, at least he was feeling *something*.

Gradually, as his damaged nerves accepted the fact that they could not be restored, the false sensations ceased, leaving Pike with a fine lamina of resignation separating him from his despair.

That was when his mind began to trick him, too.

Mostly it was voices, the siren song of every woman he had ever known but, unlike Odysseus, the danger to him lay not in responding to those voices, but in not being able to. He had already driven his ship onto the rocks. As he lay broken on the strand, dark waters washing over his unresponsive limbs, the susurration of the waves became the softness of voices.

There were three Sirens in the *Odyssey*, he recalled. One by one, he heard them.

Chris . . . Was that Willa, calling to him from beyond the grave?

Mom! he thought, and for a moment he was twelve years old again, but this time he could change the past and rescue her from the fire.

Chris-to-pher! That was Silk, calling from a life he'd long ago left behind. Where was she now, doing what? Probably the matriarch of some extended clan of little blond Neworlders, unless her spirit had somehow broken free. In his mind he could make her fly the way he had the first time she saw him on the ship on the way to Elysium.

Now there was a third voice. This one called him *Chris* and *Christopher* by turns. *Siddhe,* he thought at first, because she'd called him by both names. But Siddhe had not drawn him on; she had sent him away.

As if she knew, he realized at last. As if the Argelian Empathic Contact had foretold some doom, though she could not know exactly what it was or when it would befall him. If she had been able to tell him something, warn him somehow, would it have changed a thing?

Would you have failed to rescue those kids if you'd known what it would do to you?

The question wasn't even a question. He could have done nothing else and remain who he was.

Good-bye, Christopher, the third voice said.

Good-bye, Siddhe . . . and thank you . . . for bringing me this far.

There was a fourth voice, which was many voices, only some of which he knew. And sometimes, especially at night, when the lights in the medical wing were darkened out of courtesy for those patients who could sleep, Pike imagined he could see her, too, but only if he closed his eyes.

Long after all the phantom sensations had passed and he had reconciled himself to the fact that, while his spirit was rubbed raw, his body would be forever numb, he could have sworn he'd felt the touch of a woman's hand on his face. If he opened his eyes, she was gone.

Then Spock arrived, and everything changed.

"Why?" Commodore José Mendez demanded of no one in particular, and not for the first time. "Why Talos IV? Why would he take Pike there?"

"You saw the answer in the images the Talosians sent us," Captain James T. Kirk explained. He had to keep reminding himself that it hadn't really been Mendez in the shuttle with him or at Spock's court-martial, but that the real commodore had been here all along, on Starbase 11, watching the images at the same time those aboard *Enterprise* were, silently fuming as he wondered what it was all about.

The illusion of Mendez had been perfect, uncannily so. The Talosians had somehow duplicated the irascible commodore to a hair, with all of his tics and short-tempered outbursts, even down to the scent of his aftershave, as "he" co-piloted the shuttle with Kirk until it ran out of fuel. Jim Kirk was still trying to wrap his brain around it when *Enterprise,* no longer ferrying Christopher Pike to Talos IV in violation of General Order 7, returned to the starbase to find an irate Mendez waiting for them.

"You know damn well that's not all there was to it!" the real Mendez said now. He'd ordered a debriefing the minute Kirk's boots touched ground. Spock and McCoy, as the other witness/participants in this little escapade, were cooling their heels in the anteroom and would be called in later. For now, Mendez wanted to talk to Kirk alone—informally, friend to friend, and both of them friends to the late and revered Christopher Pike (Mendez, having visited the injured Pike daily since the accident on the cadet ship, couldn't shake the impression that the Pike he saw, trapped inside his own body, was more dead than alive). "I want to know how Spock could be so sure that was what Pike wanted.

"Oh, of course, you were the one who asked him that at the end of the 'trial,'" Mendez went on, cutting across anything Kirk might have wanted to interject. Kirk exercised the greater part of valor and closed his mouth on his half-formed thoughts. "But what if Spock had guessed wrong? Risked his life, *and* your career, not to mention the entire crew? When *Enterprise* first arrived here, I'll remind you, all Chris Pike kept telling us was 'no.'"

Kirk remembered only too well, the light on the chair blinking repeatedly, twice for "no." It had driven McCoy nuts. And whenever McCoy was disturbed about something, he felt he had to share.

"He keeps blinking 'no,'" he'd growled, glowering at the viewscreen that monitored Pike's activities around the clock. "'No' to what?"

Kirk hadn't had an answer then. He wasn't sure he had one now. He waited until he was sure Mendez had wound down. "José, I don't know what to tell you. Vulcans don't use words like 'intuition,' but if I had to guess, I'd say Spock knew something about Pike that even Pike himself didn't know . . .

". . . then again, maybe the only thing Pike was trying to tell us wasn't even addressed to us," he finished. "Maybe it was addressed to Spock alone. 'No, don't take me there. No, don't risk your life for me.' That would be in keeping with the Chris Pike we knew."

"'No, don't take me there'? Because he didn't want Spock to incur the death penalty, or because he wasn't sure what he'd find on Talos when he arrived?" Mendez wondered. He sighed. "Well, too late now. It's done. Jim, do you have any idea how they contacted Spock?"

"The Talosians?" Kirk thought about it for the first

time. He'd been so wedded to the notion that Spock had in fact gotten a comm message. "It never occurred to me to ask."

"Because if they can reach someone telepathically from that distance . . ." Mendez suppressed a shudder. "That's the part that worries me the most. Minds that powerful, able to reach across distances. Touch telepaths are one thing, but this . . . What have we done, Jim? In letting Pike go there, waiving General Order 7, have we satisfied them, or only made them lust for more?"

It was a question Spock had pondered as well.

"How did you know, Spock?" McCoy asked him as they waited for Mendez to summon after he was finished grilling Kirk. "How could you be sure he'd want to go with you?"

"I knew Captain Pike," Spock explained simply, as if it were that simple. "He was an active man—energetic, physical. For a man of that nature to be trapped in that way, when there was an alternative . . . the choice seemed logical."

"Logical, my Aunt Fanny!" McCoy said skeptically. "You're going to have to do better than that, Spock."

"I also had reason to believe he would be pleased to see the woman Vina again."

"Oh, well, now you're talking. Nothing like a good romance." McCoy grinned, then frowned. "Still, you took a helluva risk. And why do I get the feeling you're still not telling me the whole story? Another one of those 'it is not a lie to keep the truth to oneself' deals?"

Spock merely looked at him. McCoy's scowl deepened.

"That's what I figured. Dammit . . ."

Spock could not have told McCoy the entire truth, because Pike had been correct. Once the Talosians entered your mind, they could always find you again. And there was an aspect to that which even the Talosians hadn't reckoned on until it was too late.

No telepath has ever successfully explained telepathy to a non-telepath. One of the reasons why it is a skill beyond words is that it is, quite simply, beyond words.

Spock hadn't lied when he informed Kirk he had received a message from Starbase 11 requesting *Enterprise* divert there for reasons unexplained until they were informed of Pike's injury. The trace of the Talosian mind within his own was just powerful enough to make him believe he had actually seen such a message on his screen.

As for the rest, if he'd had to describe it to a human, he would have characterized it as a little voice in the back of his head, like a radio played at a subliminal level, informing him—as *Enterprise* headed toward Starbase 11 in answer to a summons that did not exist—of what the Talosians wanted him to do, and why. The conversation went something like this:

"In our initial arrogance," the Magistrate explained, *"we neglected to consider that so primitive a species as humans might possess a power of mind sufficient to penetrate ours. What the human mind lacks in telepathic power, it compensates for in, shall we say, strength of will. Christopher Pike is particularly strong of will. In short, he remained with us long after he had physically departed."*

"I am not certain I entirely understand."

"He suspected that once we had made an incursion into his mind we would never entirely depart. You and he even discussed it as you concealed yourselves in a tree and waited for nightfall so as to elude the Kan'ess."

"Indeed."

"Pike's suspicion was correct. The connection was tenu-

ous, but it remained. What we did not understand until too late was that it was not unilateral." The Magistrate waited for Spock to reply. When he did not, s/he completed the thought. "*Christopher Pike's mind remained within ours as well. The entire Talosian race has been . . . infected, if you will . . . with the virus of his consciousness. It has had some interesting ramifications.*

"*If you bring him to us, we can maintain him physically. We can nurture his thoughts and allow him to escape his physical reality within the power of dream. And perhaps he can also be of assistance to us.*"

It was in Spock's mind to ask, "Did Pike send the message from Starbase 11 or did you?" but he refrained. If the Magistrate confirmed what he suspected, he would have to lie to Kirk. He would not do that, not even to save Pike.

"Then you do not intend to imprison him as you attempted to do once before," Spock said.

The Magistrate's mind-voice was dry. "*I believe we are all aware of how little success we had with that the first time. We do not wish to imprison him. We wish to set him free.*"

Just as there had never been any question in Pike's mind whether or not he would have rescued the cadets from the delta rays, so there was no question in Spock's mind about what he was willing to do for Pike.

"Very well," he replied. "I will endeavor to effect an outcome that will be of benefit to all concerned."

The Magistrate's mind-voice then was quizzical. "*Excepting yourself? Is self-sacrifice a human characteristic or a Vulcan one?*"

Spock's meditation was broken then by a hail from the bridge. It was Lieutenant Hansen, letting him know that they were approaching Starbase 11, and Captain Kirk and Dr. McCoy were waiting for him in the transporter room.

* * *

Had Kirk questioned Spock about the summons instead of simply taking his word and setting a course for the starbase, Spock would have been able to state unequivocally that the message did exist, even though he would have been unable to produce it after the fact.

But Kirk hadn't questioned Spock's word. He'd never had any reason to, though the events of the next few days had stretched his trust in his first officer to the extreme.

Jim Kirk couldn't know that what drove Spock was contained in the words he said, against Pike's protests ("No, no, no!") when they were alone.

"I know," he said, kneeling so that he would be on a level with Pike. "I know it is treachery, and it's mutiny. But I must do this. I have no choice."

He had waited then for Pike to grasp the full import of his words. The ensuing silence told him that he had.

"They know," Spock said simply. "They are aware of everything that has occurred. They are aware of what your doctors will not tell you, which is that your condition is degenerative. While you may live out a certain number of years, your condition will only get worse. Unless you allow them to help."

Briefly, then, because the success of his mission hinged on precise timing, Spock had told Pike of his "conversation" with the Magistrate. When he had done, Pike was silent, his head bowed, the prematurely white hair—a result of the profound shock to his system—obscuring his scarred and all but expressionless face from his former first officer.

"Will you allow me to help you, sir?" Spock asked softly.

When Pike didn't answer, Spock realized he had slipped into what, in his condition, passed for sleep. This happened often, particularly when he was in a state of stress as he had been since Spock's arrival. Before Pike could change his mind, Spock cued his communicator to interface with *Enterprise*'s transporter, and beamed them both aboard.

Now that it was all over but the shouting, as McCoy might say, Spock answered every question Mendez put to him at the debriefing. Yes, he had been led to believe that he was in fact in receipt of a message from Starbase 11. Yes, the Talosians indicated they were offering Pike a home, a place to be as free as his ruined body would allow him, and not the cage they'd tried to imprison him in before.

"Their brief exposure to Captain Pike's dynamic personality, and the thirteen intervening years in which, having downloaded the contents of the *Enterprise*'s library computer, they embarked upon an in-depth study of the human species, gave the Talosians a greater understanding of why they had failed the first time," Spock explained. "They were aware of the captain's physical condition and that, if his mind was not stimulated, it would deteriorate over time, shortening his life span and condemning him to immobility for the years remaining to him. They offered an alternative."

"And you believed them?" Mendez said, a little impatiently. All the pretty images of Pike and Vina he had seen still didn't convince him there wasn't some sinister motive.

Spock weighed the question thoughtfully. "In my experience, Commodore, the telepathic mind cannot lie."

"The Talosians lied to get you here!" Mendez barked. "What was that spurious message from Starbase 11 if not a lie?"

"An obfuscation?" Spock suggested. Mendez glowered, and Spock tried to explain. "Sir, the kernel of truth was contained in the message. My presence was required on Starbase 11 in order to retrieve Captain Pike and bring him to Talos. That the message was not actually sent via comm from Starbase 11 was immaterial. The message was contained within Captain Pike's desire to be freed from his disabled condition."

"That's supposition on your part!" Mendez roared, then stopped himself.

What the hell was he shouting about? Mendez wondered. Pike was free, as free as he ever would be in this life. Spock's court-martial had been overturned, and Mendez no longer had to contemplate sending him to his death. The sight of Pike and Vina holding hands on Talos, walking toward the turbolift, was as close to a storybook ending as anyone could hope for, except for all the paperwork generated after the fact.

Mendez exhaled wearily. There was no question in his mind who would end up doing most of that paperwork. He passed a hand momentarily over his eyes and wondered aloud, "How am I supposed to explain this to his family?"

Even in the twenty-third century, rain in the California desert was a rare and welcome thing. The parkland surrounding the city of Mojave might benefit from the nightly shower provided by the orbital weather shields, but the desert beyond still relied on natural weather patterns. While it might rain anytime from November through March, the rains usually fell most heavily in January and February.

It was raining very hard when Siddhe stepped out of the 'car into the yard to see Hobelia once again waiting at the open ranch house door. Wind tore at the fan palms in the distance, and the surrounding hills were hidden by veils of sheeting water pouring unrelentingly out of a dark gray sky.

Charlie and Hobelia had been informed of Chris's condition immediately after the accident. They also knew he'd left instructions that if he was ever seriously injured far from home, they were not to disrupt their lives to travel halfway across the quadrant to be with him. Knowing him, they knew this was as much about his pride as about any inconvenience to themselves. They had honored his wishes and waited, receiving weekly updates from Mendez, making arrangements, if Chris could be moved from the starbase and cleared for space travel, to bring him back to Earth if that was what he wanted.

Something about Siddhe's arrival told Hobelia that Chris would not be coming home to them. The greatest gift Hobe could give to the motherless child she had raised as her own would be to let him go.

Hobelia watched the younger woman raise the hood of the practical slicker she wore against the downpour and start across the yard. But Siddhe was an Argelian and open to all sensual experience, including the pristine joy of nurturing rain. For a moment she stopped and lifted her face like a flower and the rain coursed down her cheeks like the tears she had not shed when her premonition about Chris's fate had come to pass.

Those who had the gift knew they could not change what they foresaw. There were Argelian empaths who had walked knowingly into their own deaths in order to caution others. Physicists might talk of parallel universes and alternate timelines, but an empath knew it was never quite that simple.

Mindful of her wet shoes and Hobelia's immaculate floors, Siddhe came up only to the porch. Hobelia hugged her in spite of the sodden rain slicker.

"Charlie's in the barn," she said. "Let me get my poncho and I'll walk with you. Tango . . ."

She didn't have to finish. The rain drumming on the barn roof when the women entered only partly masked the sound of labored breathing. Charlie sat in the straw of the box stall with Tango's head in his lap.

The big bay was only thirty-six, not at all old for a horse in these times, but he had decided it was his time. The vet had come and gone, confirming what Charlie suspected, that there was nothing physically wrong with him. But the old devil was grieving. He knew.

Later that evening, when Tango was at peace and the rain no more than a memory dripping from the eaves under a cool and distant moon, the three sat before the hearth in the big comfortable living room and Siddhe told Charlie and Hobelia what José Mendez couldn't find words for, that Chris was safe and whole and setting a course for the second half of his life, though none of them would ever see him more.

They didn't ask how she knew. It didn't seem strange to them that, while she didn't know where he was, she knew this much. Some knowledge transcends even Starfleet secrets.

The room contained a listening quiet, punctuated by the snap of piñon logs and the sift of ashes in the grate, quiet but little grief. When humans grieve for someone they have lost, more often than not they are grieving not for the loved one but for themselves, for the absence of that person from their lives. Christopher Pike was as present that night as he was absent, as contained in the hearts of those who loved him as he was free in the realms of dream.

"Vina . . ." someone said.

Was that his voice? Pike wondered. He no longer remembered what it sounded like. He watched as if from a distance as he stood and walked and moved toward Vina to take her hands in his. Her hands were cool, small, and delicate, just as he remembered them; when he held them, they fit neatly into his, as if they were meant to be there.

"Christopher . . ." she said in return, her voice as sweet as he remembered, her small, heart-shaped face tilted up toward his, those feline eyes always a little sad, even when she smiled. "Chris . . ."

EPILOGUE

2320

The first two times Spock had watched Talos IV loom on the forward screen, it had had a wounded look—huddled, gloomy, shrouded in the sickly yellow-gray pall of nuclear winter. But the planet he saw on his viewscreen now was welcoming, veiled in normal cloud cover, a pretty blue world of oceans and landmasses glimpsed coquettishly through wisps of clean white cloud.

Were he in any doubt about his navigational skills, he might wonder if he had gone off course and made orbit around a different planet entirely. But, being Spock, he was certain of his coordinates. Yet this would appear to be a planet much altered in the fifty-four years, two months, and sixteen days since he had last been here.

Nevertheless, not trusting mere visual observation, Spock scanned the planet's atmosphere, and one eyebrow quirked involuntarily. The greater part of the radiation seemed to have dissipated, at least in the region he scanned. This could not be a natural occurrence. Given their prolonged half-lives, the radioactive isotopes ought to have registered in the ionosphere for at least another millennium. Skeptical, Spock altered course to do a sweep of the entire planet.

"You will find approximately the same intensity of background radiation elsewhere as you have here," the Magistrate said equitably, appearing in the copilot's chair, unchanged as always, delicate hands clasped demurely in hir silver-clad lap, eyes clear, smile faint but not a little smug. "In fact, I would venture to guess that even factoring in normal solar radiation, concentrations on our world are less than the ambient radiation extant in the atmosphere of Earth. But feel free to conduct your scans to satisfy your curiosity. Now that you are here, there is no urgency."

Spock glanced in the Magistrate's direction, though he knew hir "presence" was an illusion. For that matter, the absence of radiation could as equally be illusion. Away from the Talos star group, his instruments might tell him something quite other than they did now.

No urgency. Pike was dead, then. Spock had risked his life merely in order to escort his former captain's remains back to Earth.

"Do not be so quick to judge," the Magistrate intruded into his thoughts. "If I give you my word that your instrument readings are accurate, will you continue to scan our world until your curiosity is satisfied?"

"Is that what you wish?" Spock asked.

"It will help explain things later," the Magistrate replied cryptically.

Spock reduced speed, angled the shuttle's nose downward, and began a glide through the cloud cover into the troposphere.

At the Magistrate's instruction, he made three low orbits in all, one at the equator and two at an inclination of sixty degrees either side of the equator. With considerable field of view overlap, he succeeded in scanning the entire planet in a very short time. What he saw intrigued him. The atmosphere was indeed virtually free of all but natural ambient radiation. Even the hydrocarbon ratio was lower than that of a combustion-engine free Earth. In fact, the atmosphere of Talos IV was almost as pristine as it might have been in a preindustrial era.

Flyover revealed the familiar broken mountain ranges, like jagged teeth, which seemed to dominate the planet, the scattered rock plains evidencing ancient volcanic activity, where the force of volcanic upthrust had hurled chunks of lava hundreds of miles in all directions. But where he expected to find what *Enterprise* had encountered the first two times—the ruins of cities destroyed in the war—Spock found a very different topography indeed.

Only one continent had ever been populated before the war which nearly destroyed the Talosian race. Contemplating it down the decades, Spock had always wondered why the opposing factions hadn't simply moved outward and settled somewhere else. With their minds so interconnected, he supposed, even distance wouldn't have assuaged the differences between them. Only near-annihilation, it seemed, had done so.

It was spring on that main continent now and, if Spock were to judge from what he saw below him, the dawn of a new era. The ravages of the long-ago nuclear holocaust which had almost annihilated all life on the planet were nearly invisible under an ongoing process of terraforming.

Flora and fauna of all descriptions, some from the ships the Talosians had lured into their space long before human arrival, others native to their world, their genetic codes preserved for thousands of years, flourished across the land and in the skies and seas. At one point a telltale warned Spock of the proximity of a flock of birds the size of geese off the shuttle's starboard nacelle. Oceans so clear he could see where the continental shelf dropped off into the depths sported schools of fish so numerous they seemed to move as a single kilometers-long entity. Herds of antlered herbivores, startled by the shadow as the shuttle passed above them, began to run at first but, after scattering a short distance, soon settled back to grazing.

Most of the long-destroyed cities had been leveled, the land reclaimed and sculpted into parkland, agricultural tracts, forests, open fields. Some very few had been rebuilt and, from the look of things, quite recently, for construction was still going on.

At the Magistrate's nod, Spock brought the shuttle in closer to the largest of these cities, skimming over the tops of skyscrapers as ornate as cathedrals, and extensive multi-storied housing complexes with terraces and flower boxes spilling an effusion of colors. Spidery bridges spanned gleaming rivers flowing between mossy banks, and connected some of the higher mountain peaks one to the other, incorporating them into the city plan.

Silver-clad figures could be seen traversing broad pedestrian walkways in the centers of the bridges, even as all-but-silent transit pods housed in transparent tunnels shot by at speeds so quick they were almost a blur. Elevators flowed effortlessly up and down the sides of buildings; automated multilevel pedestrian walkways passed through open plazas as well as streets like narrow, deeply shaded canyons between the taller buildings.

Much of what Spock saw was distinctly Talosian, in ways he was unable to quantify, yet the rest looked strangely familiar, as if it had been transplanted from Earth during the rebuilding after World War III, and he recognized an homage to the technology the Talosians had downloaded from *Enterprise*'s memory banks the first time. He did not know enough about Earth architecture to also recognize in some of these structures the signature style of the late Willa McKinnies.

Everywhere silver-robed Talosians, still as seemingly frail as ever, yet possessed of a new vitality, moved about purposefully under the open sky. No longer needing to live underground, they were as if reborn. There were so many of them! Spock extrapolated from the number he could see in a single plaza below him to the size of the city as a whole and calculated at least a million. And were those children? Yes, Talosian children, from infants carried in slings to spindly adolescents whose oversized crania looked disproportionately larger set upon their gangly frames, moved with the adults or gathered in small groups of their peers. Spock thought he saw one group playing a sort of elaborate game of tag in one narrow lane. Were they the first children born since the war? He would ask this later, and more.

He didn't realize he was smiling, at least inasmuch as Vulcans smile, mostly with their eyes. (Though in more recent years, Spock had occasionally allowed the smile to venture as far as the corners of his mouth.) For a fleeting moment he recalled his first visit to Talos IV, and how very callow he had been then, smiling broadly as he and Pike discovered the secret of the blue-leaved plants whose vibrating leaves had filled the air with singing. What he saw now was even more pleasing, if inexplicable, unless it was illusion.

"Not illusion. Quite real," the Magistrate answered his unspoken thought. "All this was made possible by Christopher Pike. Did you truly think such a dynamic man would so easily succumb to the lure of dream?

"When I asked you to bring him to us so many years ago, I said he had infected us with his . . . enthusiasm, his strength of will," the Magistrate went on, gesturing to Spock to bring the shuttle down in one of the plazas, which had been cleared of pedestrians, who stood around the perimeter craning up at the shuttle, anticipating its arrival.

"Intellectually, he reminded us of what we once had been, and could be again. But there was more. The interaction of his mind with ours had physiological effects as well."

The shuttle was designed to hover and descend vertically in tight spaces, and Spock guided it down slowly so that the thrusters kicked up minimal turbulence and did not disturb the gathering watchers. As the shuttle descended, he caught sight of several large animated murals displayed on the walls of the buildings surrounding the plaza. Each depicted what could only be described as a movie exploring some aspect of Christopher Pike's or Vina's life.

From ground level, as he stepped out of the shuttle, Spock became aware that nearly every building in the city hosted one of these living murals. The ones he could see in the distance featured what he took to be epic stories from Talosian history, and scenes from other worlds the Talosians had visited thousands of centuries ago. But all of the screens facing this particular plaza seemed to be devoted to Pike and Vina.

"We never abandoned dream," the Magistrate explained, emerging from the crowd. The illusory Magistrate who had accompanied Spock in the shuttle had, of course, vanished. "We simply brought it out of the tunnels into the light. Pike's consciousness affected our proprioception, our way of seeing and interacting with each other and the world around us. He became part of us, and we a part of him. A favorite game among our children is 'Pike Against the Kaylar.' Some of us are not entirely certain we approve. Nevertheless . . ."

The Magistrate's eloquent gesture encompassed the city around them, the alterations to the planet beyond.

"He gave us the energy, the impetus. He taught us how to speed the removal of the radiation from our atmosphere. His fascination with terraforming, his mother's skills as an architect, his leadership, have restored us. His love for Vina inspired us, and encouraged her to use her skills as well. We have with her assistance found and extensively catalogued rich veins of mineral ore with which to trade with other worlds. The synergy between Talosian intellect and human ingenuity has rebuilt our world."

S/he gestured for Spock to follow hir into one of the buildings surrounding the plaza; from the grandiosity of its facade, Spock assumed it was some governmental edifice. Inside, beyond a whimsically Art Deco foyer, he found himself walking beside the Magistrate along a series of high-ceilinged corridors and into a lift which brought them first down and then sideways, opening out into an archive whose computers issued a busy subliminal hum suggesting considerable activity. On free-form screens set into walls carved out of natural rock, familiar to Spock from the record tapes transmitted during his court-martial half a century earlier, thus suggesting they had been here for the millennia the Talosians remained underground, he saw verification that the whole of Talos IV was alive with reconstruction and renewal.

The Magistrate allowed Spock a moment to absorb all that he saw around him.

"Inspired by the hope of once again living on the surface of our world, we were able to throw off our addiction to dream, setting aside only certain times when we permit ourselves to live inside our minds," s/he explained. "Most of our time has been devoted to channeling our energies, under Pike's guidance, into the here and now. In effect, he has done more for us than we could ever have done for him."

Later Spock would take the time to view as many of the Pike stories as he could. He would find not only Pike's past as he knew it, but a detailed history of everything Pike and Vina had done in more than half a century on Talos IV. For now . . .

"Then . . . Christopher Pike is dead?"

"In the most obvious respect, yes," the Magistrate replied. "His body has ceased to function. Vina faded from us first, and he followed soon after. And yet . . ." Hir gesture encompassed the archives, the city above them, the planet beyond. "He is here."

When they emerged from the underground chamber, the watchers who had been waiting silently around the edges of the plaza drew closer, gathering around them. At the forefront, Spock recognized the other three Talosians who had been present from the beginning. He felt the collective warmth of all their minds touching upon his, not intruding, but communicating. One of the overhead screens, which had been busy with images but silent until now, suddenly began to speak. The face and voice, however much larger than life, were those of Christopher Pike.

Illusion, of course. Gone was the scarring and the paralysis, and the gray in his hair was not the shock-white of violent physical trauma, but the natural progression of a man of one hundred human years. The face was sculpted by years, but no less handsome. The steady voice, the lopsided grin, the intense blue eyes accented by the serious dark brows, were unchanged.

"If you're watching this, Mr. Spock, it means I've come and gone. You and I never talked about belief systems, so I won't bore you with mine now. What I know about you is that you'd be willing to risk your neck a second time to fetch me home as readily as you did the first time to bring me here."

The image of Pike hesitated, as if searching for just the right words.

"By now Talos has been my home longer than Earth, so I guess that means I belong to both worlds. So, yes, I did drag you halfway across the galaxy to bring some of my ashes back to Earth. But I also wanted Earth and the rest of the Federation to see Talos through your eyes and, instead of locking you up this time, maybe give you credit, Mr. Ambassador, for adding a new member to the Federation.

"Oh, I know, I know, it's not that easy. Regulations, red tape—I don't suppose those things have magically disappeared since I left Earth. But the Talosians and I have been watching your career from a distance, and we agreed you'd be the logical person to plead our case."

The lopsided grin widened. The man's natural charisma shone through the screen. Even a Talosian illusion couldn't have manufactured that.

"But I know you, Science Officer. You're going to want to look around, examine everything, draw your own conclusions. Just putting in my two cents. The final decision's up to you. Go well. Pike out."

The Talosians remained silent, their expressions expectant. Spock considered what he knew. The Federation incorporated many planets whose inhabitants possessed psionic gifts. Perhaps none were quite as adept as the Talosians at the power of illusion, and yet—

The Talosians had nurtured and safeguarded Vina and Christopher Pike for the greater part of their lives, and been repaid in the rebirth of their world. The two species had come to understand and trust each other profoundly. Surely any Talosian would respect the boundaries nontelepaths required and keep them sacrosanct. It was a good place from which to begin.

Applying for admission to the Federation was tedious and time consuming, and there was no guarantee that the request would be fulfilled. But Spock could at least be instrumental in establishing a rapprochement between Talos IV and the Federation Council once he returned to Earth.

At least this time, he thought wryly, he might be spared the ordeal of a court-martial.

Sulu and *Excelsior* would be waiting at the rendezvous point to retrieve him in a few days, sufficient time for Spock to see and learn more, though he had already made his decision. He would do what was logical to fulfill Christopher Pike's dream.

AFTERWORD

Christopher Pike, by the very paucity of information we have about him, invites our curiosity. Protagonist of a story deemed "too cerebral" by some long-forgotten studio heads, Pike haunts us down the generations, not only for the terrible thing that happens to him, but because Jeffrey Hunter, the actor who portrayed him, died tragically and too young.

We would wish for a better outcome for them both, and so we extrapolate from the little we know about either man and try to imagine great things, outcomes that are better in our minds than in reality. In that way, we are not unlike Christopher Pike ourselves. Dreams *are* important.

I have tried to pay homage, at least in passing, to others who have featured Pike in their work:

* Michael Jan Friedman who, in *Legacy,* offers Pike a beach to walk on.

* S. D. Perry, whose story "Sins of the Mother" in *The Lives of Dax,* shows us Pike at his most sensitive and intuitive.

* Peter David, who in *The Rift* shows us Pike the leader, not averse to making decisions that involve risk.

* Jerry Oltion, who proves in *Where Sea Meets Sky* that Pike can hold his liquor and tell tales as tall as any sailor's.

* D. C. Fontana, because *Vulcan's Glory* captures the desert vagabond in Christopher Pike's heart, straight out of Jeffrey Hunter's swashbuckling cinematic past.

I have not included the young adult novels or the comic books that feature Pike (beyond the use of Chief Engineer Moves-with-Burning-Grace from the *Star Trek: The Early Voyages* comic). Incorporating every plotline where the character appears was not possible, and I hope no one feels slighted. To me, *Star Trek* has always been akin to Arthurian legend—there are many voices, many dimensions, but it is essentially always the same tale.

ABOUT THE AUTHOR

MARGARET WANDER BONANNO sold her first novel in 1978, at a time when "serious women's fiction" was not an oxymoron. Characterized by one reviewer as "the new Mary Gordon," she followed this first mainstream novel with two more, before the Recession of '82 changed the face of U.S. publishing forever and she, along with several hundred other midlist writers, found herself needing to rethink her career.

A *Star Trek* fan "from the time of the beginning," Margaret recalibrated her style and wrote first one, then a second *Trek* novel entirely on spec. That second manuscript became *Dwellers in the Crucible,* which was followed by *Strangers from the Sky.*

Following a bit of strangeness which resulted in 93 percent of *Probe*'s being written by someone else, Margaret segued into straight s/f with two trilogies, *The Others* and *Preternatural* and, with Nichelle Nichols, co-authored *Saturn's Child.*

A bit of pseudonymous fiction here, another mainstream novel there, a bio, ghostwriting and book doctoring, oh my, and Margaret was welcomed back to Pocket Books when Marco Palmieri invited her to participate in the *Lost Era* series with *Catalyst of Sorrows.* Most recently there has been the challenge and delight exploring the character of Christopher Pike in *Burning Dreams,* and an opportunity to participate in the upcoming eBook series, *Mere Anarchy.*

A native New Yorker, Margaret currently lives on the Left Coast, where she dabbles in bonsai and has found a beach to walk on and a Romulan to walk with her. She has two adult children, and is the co-founder of Van Wander Press, www.vanwanderpress.com. Please visit her website at www.margaretwanderbonanno.com.